François Maspero was born in France in 1932. He has been a
bookseller and an editor, but it is as a journalist that he has earned
his formidable reputation in France, reporting over the past thirty
years on developments in the Third World, particularly Cuba,
Latin America and Africa. A passionate anti-colonialist, he has
published several books opposing French policies in Algeria
and elsewhere, and has translated the works of John Reed and
Che Guevara, among others. He founded two periodicals: in
1961, *Partisans*, a magazine of the radical Left, and in 1972,
*L'Alternative*, which gave a voice to dissidents of the Iron Curtain
countries. *Cat's Grin* is François Maspero's first novel and he is
now at work on a second.

# François Maspero

# CAT'S GRIN

*Translated from the French by*
*Nancy Amphoux*

PENGUIN BOOKS

PENGUIN BOOKS

Published by the Penguin Group
27 Wrights Lane, London w8 5tz, England
Viking Penguin Inc., 40 West 23rd Street, New York, New York 10010, USA
Penguin Books Australia Ltd, Ringwood, Victoria, Australia
Penguin Books Canada Ltd, 2801 John Street, Markham, Ontario, Canada l3r 1b4
Penguin Books (NZ) Ltd, 182–190 Wairau Road, Auckland 10, New Zealand

Penguin Books Ltd, Registered Offices: Harmondsworth, Middlesex, England

First published in France, under the title, *Le Sourire du chat*, by Editions du Seuil 1984
This English translation first published in the USA by Alfred A. Knopf, Inc. 1986
First published in Great Britain by Viking 1987
Published in Penguin Books 1988

Made and printed in Great Britain by
Hazell Watson & Viney Limited
Member of BPCC plc
Aylesbury Bucks
Set in Garamond

"All right," said the Cat; and this time it vanished quite slowly, beginning with the end of the tail, and ending with the grin, which remained some time after the rest of it had gone.

"Well! I've often seen a cat without a grin," thought Alice; "but a grin without a cat! It's the most curious thing I ever saw in my life!"

—*Lewis Carroll*

# CAT'S GRIN

*The world was never seen aright*
*Except the looker dreamed what he was seeing.*
—GASTON BACHELARD

What follows is subtitled "a novel" because although everything related in it is imaginary to some degree, nothing in it is entirely so, and yet it is not autobiography—definitely not.

Maybe imagination was the way—the only way—in which, after a lapse of forty years, the narrator was able to approach an experience that was his own. Nothing is more bewildering than memory. Fixing its fragile glints and shadows in the matrix of a tale that claimed to be authentic would mean freezing its thousands of possible facets in order to hold one of them prisoner forever, trapping it in words and pretending that it and it alone had been true. But in the game of truth, memory, even when aided and abetted by History, is always the loser.

So I want to make it clear now that every person and event in what follows is both completely false and completely true. Some of the things mentioned in these pages may actually have happened to the narrator; others not. Some characters resemble those he knew, loved, and sometimes (seldom, and not for long) hated; others not.

Be that as it may, the book was written because a child, those many years ago, asked himself some questions; and now, forty years later, a man is still trying to get those same questions straight, even if he knows full well that most of them seem timeworn and out-of-date today, so many people having answered them definitively in the meantime. Still, I hope this story won't be just another period piece.

The problem that I had to try to deal with is the problem of the simple meaning of words. I had a hard time remembering what the word "freedom" meant.

I would like to thank the people who have traveled this road

3

with me. I cannot name them all, but special mention should be made of Bahadur Shah, baggage elephant No. 174 on the Indian Register, who formerly assisted a more illustrious predecessor and whose tutelary shade accompanied and protected me, even though I came along too late to have the firsthand benefit of his courteous erudition. That is not the least of the shortcomings of this tale (it may be felt most acutely on pages 54 and 289), although the stature of Bahadur Shah far transcends the present context—but that is another story.

# The Alder Wood

In the family, they call him Cat. It was his brother Antoine who first gave him the name, maybe because he is scrawny as a cat. Ever since he was a baby, he liked it when his brother came into his room at night, after the light was turned out, to stroke his head as one would a cat's. In those days he would stretch his arms around his brother's neck and press his cheek against his. He often said "I love you" to him, in an impassioned tone that made them both laugh. His brother would stay there close to him and explain all the things the others didn't tell him, whether because they simply didn't think of it or because they didn't have the time. His brother is very good at explaining, you might say he knows everything: about stones and stars, trains and planes, why there is a war, what things were like before and how they will have to be afterward.

Cat, whom other people call Luc, is thirteen. They say he is big for his age. He has skinny legs with big knobby knees sticking out of his short accordion-wrinkled pants and a heavy hank of black hair falling over his eyes—his mother says they are lavender, it depends on the weather, blue eyes, gray eyes, almond-shaped eyes, Persian-cat eyes—and a mouth that stretches from ear to ear when he laughs, like a mouth on a cat piggy bank. In the summer freckles come out around his nose; he likes that.

Right now Cat is living in a kind of exile. It was his brother who told him how in Italy they exiled people who didn't agree with the government and sent them far away to some forsaken village in the south, sometimes to an island. Cat imagines himself walking alone through narrow, empty streets or along pebble beaches, and he thinks that wouldn't be so bad: there are worse forms of punishment. Because when he was little he lived so long on the seacoast that wherever he goes he still listens for the ceaseless whisper of waves. But this is a boring sort of exile, twelve miles from Paris. In the evenings when the wind is in the east you can hear the last métro train starting out from Saint-Rémy, terminus of the Sceaux line. He can walk along the paths through the woods, discover abandoned millstone quarries and tell himself that he has been sent by a powerful underground movement to lay plans for the installation of secret bases. But it's all flat and small, and there are no strong smells.

Right now is late May 1944. Cat's residence-in-exile is an odd-looking turreted cottage roofed in blue slate. One room on the second floor has collapsed into the living room below and there is a big hole where the fireplace used to be. Part of the house is uninhabitable and in other rooms the hangings and paper have been ripped off the walls. His father says it was the thirty German noncommissioned officers camping there in the winter of 1940–41 who wrecked the place. When the pump broke down during the cold spell in February 1941 they set aside a room to do their business in, just like that, on the floor. It is in the order of things that Germans should behave so grossly. That's the way they are.

⁜

Cat's family is in Paris. They sent him into exile here at the beginning of spring. It seems that things nowadays are so complicated, people no longer have much time to spare for Cat. Anyhow, he was finding life in town hard to bear. It did not take him long to decide that no fate could be worse than spending day after day after day in gray or yellow classrooms watching, and having to endure, puffed-up men who were vociferating or shouting all alone on a platform. The distribution of vitamin-enriched cookies was always over too soon: he was amused then for a few seconds by the German teacher, who would stuff his pockets full of them. His name was Coquin [Rogue, Rascal], almost too good to be true. Sometimes Cat got good grades—especially when there was nothing that had to be learned by heart—because he's clever. But otherwise, school was a sinking dread, waiting to be called on to give the answers to questions he didn't know; and on the report card that had to be signed at home, trying to change a series of *o*s into *10*s by sticking *1*s in front—a risky business. School was the wild hope of an air-raid alert, the sirens wailing just as a quiz was about to begin, that would send the whole school to the basement.

He had come up from the south coast a year before and most of the boys in his class still seemed to him to be welded into a solid block, with only him on the outside. They seemed to be following some code of rules that everybody had learned except him, because he got there too late and nobody had given him the key to it. He had managed to assemble a few fragments but at any moment he could be called upon to recite the whole thing and be unmasked as an impostor. It was like in algebra: inevitably, at some point he would reject the whole idea of the equation that had just been set out because he couldn't see any color or thickness at the end of it. It rushed out of his head like nausea and everything grew blurred, he tried to fasten himself to *x, y,* he felt like crying. His brother mouthed grand phrases at him about abstraction. What he liked at school was piggyback battles. There was a boy in the next row who was strong and placid as an ox; perched on his shoulders, Cat would flail about wildly with his arms and mow down anything that came near him. He was unbeatable at that, and admired for his prowess. The other boys learned their lessons on time; all they had to do before the end-of-term test was "run over" them, whereas he would fling himself like a madman at a whole century of history the night before the exam. The ones who got bad grades worked just as hard as the rest; they hadn't understood, that's all, even after sweating over their textbooks like slaves; or else they didn't know how to use words. And then they made him sick, with their fathers who were all prisoners in Germany; they even got a special Christmas tree. They put on virtuous, deserving airs, but there wasn't anything to be so proud about. All their fathers had to do was not get caught, or else escape. He had seen escapees, back on the coast in the south.

He had one friend with thick glasses who was at the top of the class. They would walk home together and talk for hours about everything that had ever happened to them, they could never come to the end of it all. His friend wore the yellow star. The two of them never discussed that. Nobody ever talked about it in class either. It might almost not have been there, except that the silence was not so simple as that, much too heavy. It was sewn carefully onto all his clothes. The star, the silence, made Cat furious. In the unoccupied zone, where he came from, all that didn't exist. If any kids ever started jeering and telling jokes about yids, he charged them. He was always the youngest of his class but he was quicker to hit out than the others and, like a true-to-life alley cat, he would turn himself into an uncatchable ball of fists and claws that scared them all to death. (His brother had told him when he was practically a baby: Once you've made up your mind to hit somebody, remember, you've got to hurt him, otherwise it's not worth it; hurt, and hit first. If you can't be best you'd better not try. Aim for the nose and guts. And he gave him lessons.) But in Paris, there was the silence. That was part of the code. He couldn't figure out how people could live with this thing right under their noses and keep acting as if there was nothing there. He had talked to his brother about it. But his brother kept saying that was just one of the things they'd be made to pay for after the liberation. Pay dearly. Once and for all. What we would build then would cleanse the world forever of all that injustice and all that stupidity. But what about now? Couldn't everybody just do like the King of Denmark, who went out on the streets wearing a yellow star?

Cat had learned that it was often simpler not to go to school at all. Starting at eight in the morning, he would set out on endless tours to the end of the Paris métro line, in the penetrating reek of citronella and urine and the protective warmth of winter filth; there were breakdowns, alerts, promising discoveries such as that moment he had spent in a jam-packed car with his stomach glued to the whispery soft rayon dress of a perfumed lady (was she really perfumed or was it his imagination, supplementing his memory with this postscript that was indispensable to the overall image. . . ?) who had smiled at him, smiled so hard and rubbed the back of her hand against the corduroy of his short pants: and, for the first time, another person, a woman, had given him that drowning pleasure he had previously experienced only alone and by mechanical means—

only to leave him at the next stop, red-faced, his heart thundering. Later in the day he could also sink into a hushed torpor, let himself be engulfed by the comforting twilight of the twenty-four-hour picture palaces where newsreel and propaganda films were shown, at Saint-Lazare or on the Champs-Elysées. That was how he happened to see the lamentable and highly improbable story of three young men who had shirked their duty as Frenchmen, their STO [*Service du Travail Obligatoire*—compulsory labor duty, in Germany], letting themselves be led astray by hideous shady creatures, unshaven and greasy-haired, with cigarettes sticking out of the sides of their mouths—quintessential hoodlums, sinister procurers for the resistance, terrorists, Jews, all three at once. The boys get involved in an attack on a train and are caught, while their yellow-livered accomplices run away. The film ends with the camera panning slowly along the smashed and gutted railroad cars lying on their sides, the graveled ballast heaped with the bodies of civilians, French women and children, while a true-blue police inspector delivers to the weeping lads, who have seen, too late, the error of their ways, an edifying sermon on true values: the fatherland, building a new Europe, faith in Field Marshal Pétain. He chortled at the idiocy of the story. He knows that the resistance means freedom and that the people in it survive only because other people trust them. He saw another movie, an out-and-out horror story this time. To the throbbing moan of a funeral march it showed German soldiers digging up mountains of cadavers, pieces of skeletons like scarecrows with shreds of rotting overcoats sticking to them, out of endless ravines in a thin grove of birch trees: Katyn Forest. The commentator said it was the Russians and Bolshevik barbarism that were to blame for the assassination of these thousands of captured Polish officers, and that the crime was brought to light by the German advances. Cat is convinced that this, like the first film, is sheer propaganda, and his brother says so too. The Germans, he explains, cynically filmed themselves digging up the bodies of the Poles they themselves had executed. The Red Army is the people's army, his brother adds: it liberates, it does not assassinate. (This was not the time for half-certainties.)

The only thing about these absences from school was that crosschecks could be made by parents and teachers, leading to horrendous scenes in which Cat, after being called a craven liar, sobbed his heart out, drowning in an ocean of despair and racked with hiccups by which nobody seemed to be moved, with the result that his despair finally turned to rage and he switched from sobs to screams of fury. It was at this point that he discovered the virtues of a particular form of acute stomachache. Sometimes he felt as though a needle-toothed animal were biting into the very core of his guts. His parents were much alarmed by these pains. Soon he was simulating them. Whereupon the benefits of country air and fresh farm milk occurred to his elders. In this respect, they were right. The early 1940s for Cat had meant not only southern sun but also an assortment of nutritional deficiencies which were not unrelated to his skinniness.

❖

So Cat has been sent into exile in this house, which is also inhabited by other exiles, genuine ones, refugees newly arrived from Boulogne-sur-Mer. Their part of town was leveled by English bombs, and the whole region, a prohibited zone since the beginning of the occupation, has now been evacuated. There is a grandmother and a daughter, each trying to outscream the other; a grandfather with a thick moustache and wooden leg, or rather pestle, that sticks out of the bottom of his trousers and has a black rubber tip. He's a veteran of Verdun. He spades the vegetable garden with his good leg. There is also a son who is a bit dim, the army didn't want him, or even the STO; he works in the fields. When he talks, his mouth always twists to one side; but they all talk a little like that, with their northern accent that repels and depresses him; he feels alien among them. The daughter has two little boys who scream even more than she does. Her husband is a prisoner. She invokes his authority a hundred times a day for everything and nothing: a man so unfortunate and so unhappy, so far from his loved ones, cannot be wrong. Cat is vastly irritated by the mute, omniscient presence of this martyr and when nobody's looking he pinches the kids to make them scream even louder. Then their mother slaps them, yelling about how miserable they are making their daddy, who must hear them screaming because he is always thinking about them so hard.

Cat tries to endure all this northern agitation without getting too mixed up in it. There's the water chore several times a day. Since the assassination of the pump motor by the barbarians, they have had to fetch all their water from the municipal pump. He piles six enameled water cans onto the wooden wheelbarrow and pushes it down the street. The pump is old, he has to lift his arm very high, and for most of the downstroke all he pumps is air; only at the last second, just before his arm hits the body of the pump, does he feel a resistance, then the spout gurgles and water comes out. The barrow is heavy and the cans all leak. It takes forever. Equally interminable is the chore that consists of grinding wheat or rye in a coffee mill. Then the flour has to be sieved and the dough cooked in damp cloths without any leavening; it makes something that looks like dough sausages streaked with bran, and they are cooked on the iron top of the woodburning stove, where a pot of blackish juice, a mixture of chicory and grilled barley, is permanently on the boil. The result is ghastly. There's only one task more monotonous: the one he performs alone in a hut he's started to build at the bottom of the garden. There, he spends hours filing away at a large aluminum container. It's a bullet-riddled reserve fuel tank that an American plane flying at treetop level dumped in a field on the plateau; he and the two boys from the neighboring farm dragged it back. He collects the filings in a newspaper spread on the ground and pours them into a big biscuit tin. The aluminum is hard, the little he manages to scrape away clogs the file, and the noise is horrible. His brother has asked him to make all the filings he can, he needs them to manufacture explosives.

Cat's own realm is, first of all, his animals. His livestock is a heterogeneous assortment. To begin with, there are three rabbits, they live under the lime trees in hutches made of loose boards. The oldest is called Patachou, he's gray and ordinary. A tough guy. At first Cat kept him under a sort of screen without any bottom, right on the grass—that saved him from having to pick dandelions. But Patachou always found a way under the screen, and then there would be a great chase through the tall weeds, with Cat finally catching the rabbit by the ears. Timoshenko is a Russian rabbit with one white ear and one black; the name was given him in homage to the chief of the Red Army. Cat was long in doubt as to his sex, because Patachou rushes at him with manly ardor whenever they are put together. His painstaking exploration of the space between Timoshenko's thighs had to be repeated many times before producing erect and irrefutable proof of his virility. Then there is a fat tricolor doe, allegedly pregnant; but nothing has happened for so long now that her real trouble would seem to be simply obesity. With the guinea pigs that makes six hutches in all, their screen doors hanging awry on hinges made of bits of old tires with nails driven through them. They are lined up alongside the refugees' hutches, which are crowded with rabbits totally lacking in personality. The guinea pigs are his great pride and worry. After fourteen, he has lost track of their names. Furthermore, there is a persistent rumor to the effect that people do not eat guinea pigs; or rather, some people admit to having heard that excellent pâtés can be made from them, only to protest vehemently and immediately that they personally could never condone such a thing. Which obviously removes any rational justification this breeding experiment may have had. It can hardly be denied that the idea of eating Patachou is also a purely academic hypothesis; the issue is avoided on the ground that Patachou has been chased so hard and often around the garden that he has become tough in the literal as well as the figurative sense. As for Timoshenko, who could eat the leader of the Red Army? Cat has a secret plan for an expedition to Paris to find out whether the shops on the Quai de la Mégisserie, where they sell guinea pigs far less prepossessing than his, might be prospective buyers and at what price. Meanwhile, he often carries one around in his pocket; but the animals lack intelligence and never show the smallest sign of complicity.

Lastly, he has a bantam hen and rooster. Maybe they weren't such a bargain; people say a bantam hen eats as much as a full-sized one. It all makes for a lot of work.

Three times a week, when he goes to do Latin and Greek with the priest at Magny, he has a half-hour walk through the forest before he reaches the plateau. Along the path through the Alder Wood, red-dish clay alternates with very fine white sand stained with red streaks.

If he is late, and he almost always is, he adopts a compound gait, one hundred strides at a run followed by one hundred strides at a walk: highly efficient. He knows every signpost on the way, the trees—groups of chestnuts, oaks, beeches, and a few birches—the rocks and rotting trunks, and at the top of the rise the muddy bog that used to be a millstone hole, where you can fish for frogs and carp. After a rain big puddles of yellow water lie in the ruts, with water beetles streaking across them like skaters. Along the side of the hill facing the sun there's a whole warren of wild rabbits in the heather. Ever since he once saw one scampering down the path he has carried a carefully chosen rock in his left hand on his way through the woods. He has met no more rabbits, however, so he practices launching hand grenades instead as he walks, the way his brother taught him: both arms outstretched, hands joined together in front to aim, whip the pin out, then a big backward swing of the arm holding the grenade, and finally he releases his stone just as his hand reaches the high point of the return swing. Then he measures the length of his throw by counting his strides and picks the stone up again.

Upon reaching the top of the rise he comes to the open ground at the end of the woods and heads for a solitary tree standing among the fields: the Shepherd's Elm. An eroded boundary stone marks a right-angle turn of the path. Magny is at the end of the plateau. Along the walls of the silent church stand the tombstones that once paved the floor of the abbey church of Port-Royal, and he has often come there with his father to puzzle out the archaic lettering worn away by the tread of feet.

The priest gives him his lesson in the library, a sort of little shop on the village's single street, which is just a dirt road under crushed rockfill, pitted with potholes: cool shadows, a gentle ray of sunlight sequined with dust motes on the leather of old books, the warmth of the honey-colored wild-cherry table they lean over. A former missionary with a square-cut gray beard, he gives Cat Caesar to translate and explains the origins of the names of local villages. Romainville or Villeneuve, those used to be *villas,* that is, Roman farms. The plateau has been cultivated for nearly two thousand years, often, maybe, by the same families. At Marles-l'Eglise, for instance, the name of the Laînés who live on the Saint-Rémy road appears on the very first parish register in 1680, where their trade is given as plowman. The dirt path he takes to get here, which was the postman's path not so long ago, probably follows the course of a Roman road, at least the part around the elm. Are there any traces of it? He remembers that down south his father once showed him the vestiges of a Roman road off to the side of a path through the garigue: a deep groove in the stone formed by centuries of passing chariots. He went back there many times, to run his hand along the smooth curves of the hollow in the gray limestone, gently, as though to caress it. He would have liked the stone to move and purr.

But here no traces of Roman chariots have survived in the soft earth that has been plowed two thousand times since Caesar passed. He wonders if the landscape has changed all that much. The priest quotes a passage from *The Gallic War* in which Caesar tells how his soldiers had to carry torches in broad daylight so as not to lose their way going through the woods in Brittany. The forests of Gaul, at any rate, are no more.

They eat walnuts and plums out of a big bowl on the table, cracking the walnuts between their palms. Sometimes Cat fools around, making a nutcracker noise with his teeth: a sharp blow on the back of the head and crack! The priest tells him he isn't so funny and says he should learn that he won't always be the toughest. Then Cat recites the great speech of the Queen of the Mice, the one who had seven heads and seven golden crowns, from the story of the *Nutcracker:*

> *Krakatuk, Krakatuk, hazelnut of stone,*
> *On your account I now anguish and moan!*
> *Farewell, life, source of strife!*
> *Farewell, sky, source of pie!*
> *Ah, I die, wee pee pee, scronk!*

The priest is proud of his walnuts. The presbytery tree is the descendant of an offshoot of the Port-Royal walnut that was planted by

Pascal. "These are Pascal's walnuts," says the priest. Cat likes him because he never talks rot about the Sacred Heart of the Infant Jesus. Nor does he pretend that France is being punished by God for her sins and that everybody has to pray very hard to the Virgin Mary so she will put an end to the country's misfortunes and bring the prisoners home again. (Cat can remember, as in a nightmare, the great collective prayer sessions in 1941. He was nine years old, they packed them in by the hundreds, Cubs and Brownies, kids from the church clubs and communion classes, into a big dark cold cement church dedicated to St. Bernadette where they had to recite Hail Marys on their knees for hours, asking God's pardon for the sins of France. He was absolutely certain that he had nothing to do with the whole business—and when he came to think about it, he couldn't see what sins France had committed.)

The priest comments passionately on the Russian advance in the Ukraine and the Allied advance in Italy. He calls Laval a "bloodthirsty coal man" and keeps saying all the time that Christ was a Jew. When he talks about the Gospels he mostly tells about the time he spent in Jerusalem, and then it all seems so plain, as though it were this very morning that Christ went by on his little donkey along the road to Bethany. "If you want to imagine Christ, start by thinking of the poorest of the fellaheen in a djellaba you meet by the fig trees on the path to the vineyard." The priest glows with all the sun of Palestine. "But above all, remember that he can be any man, on any piece of ground. At any hour of the day or night." He tells him the story of the pilgrims of Emmaus. "Lord, abide with us: for it is toward evening and the day is far spent." Cat sees the eucalyptus-lined path of his southland very clearly, glinting with quartz and mica, the path that leads up to his grandparents' house. Night falls fast there too and, in the lengthening shadows, the wind drops almost to nothing and the smell of myrtle and rosemary grows stronger. "You understand, they were wrong. They ought to have spoken those words *before*. Before he let their eyes be opened. Maybe, then, he would have stayed among us. . . . But how can you reach God if you don't take care of men?" His laugh shows all his yellow teeth and he shrugs. Cat likes things to be clear and to him all this biblical simplicity seems a little woolly: "Any man? Even Germans?"

The priest laughs again. "Yes. Well, almost any. . . . I think," the priest says, "that men go about things the wrong way. In the Holy Land things were done in the name of God that are enough to make your blood curdle. Even the basilica of the Holy Sepulcher, they say it is such a beautiful hymn in stone but it also looks like an armed fortress, and all those monks camped inside it hating each other. . . . I used to pray better in the thick of the crowds in the souks and the smell of fried doughnuts outside the church. I'm not certain that St. Francis' hut was not a much finer act of faith. I've seen one of the most beautiful spots on earth, and it is also one of the most terrible: the Krak, the Castle of the Knights built by the Crusaders. . . ."

"I know," Cat says. "My grandmother told me and I've seen pictures. One of our ancestors went on the Crusades with Godefroy de Bouillon. That was the third Ponte-Serra of the name."

"Of course," the priest answers. "My ancestors went on the Crusades too. Except that they went on foot. . . . The Krak may well be the dream of stone that Satan showed Christ to tempt him. A monument in stone, a soul of stone—everything there is petrified, you breathe evil there because you breathe war. Those men never understood anything about faith."

"I don't know how things are going to turn out for us," the priest also says, looking through the windowpanes at the washed-out colors of the empty street. "The people here are tired. You can't blame them too much. Every Sunday at mass I read out the list of those who died in the last war—yes, the one that was supposed to be the last of all. You know, it's the same here as at Marles, the family names come like bunches of grapes, often three, even four at a time: brothers who fell, sometimes the same day in the same attack, because it was always the peasant regiments that were sent to the front line. The people in them came from the same district, the same village. The reserve officers, even—sometimes they were the schoolmaster and the mayor's son—you felt closer to them than to the professional soldiers. This time it's not like that . . ."

Cat knows. At Marles too, on Sundays, the priest walks across the church to stand in front of the tablet bearing the names of those who died in the Great War, settles his spectacles, and reads out the names in alphabetical order, as though he were calling roll. And every Sunday, just before the three Simon brothers, Cat hears the sound of his own family name; that was his uncle, who was twenty-six years old then—a brilliant historian, author of a monumental *History of Egypt under the Ptolemies*—Uncle Antoine, who kicked his shoes off so he could run faster leading his men in the assault on Vauquois in the Argonne in September 1915, and died, his head shattered in the mud. Cat feels a small knot in his stomach then, a little as if it was his own name that was being called.

"It was so utterly useless, that war," says the priest.

Cat knows that too, but he stops interrupting. He has read *All Quiet on the Western Front,* a novel he found among his brother's books, and in it he learned, even though the book was written by a German, that in fact wars have nothing but victims and that heroes are something the survivors invent in order to excuse themselves for being alive. Uncle Antoine's gesture with his shoes was ridiculous, or maybe it was just that the shoes they had issued him didn't fit. But wouldn't he have done the same? His brother explained it all very clearly: war serves the interests of the wealthy alone. The French had colonies. The Germans wanted colonies too. The proof is that when the poor people in Russia rebelled everybody clubbed together to put them down. But then, for the first time in history, the poor people won. This time it will be the same. It's the poor who have to win. And forever.

"You need to know," the priest says. "So much rot, so much mud, so many dead. And now that senile old fool, just because he was the leader in the other mess, has stirred up all those stupid veterans in their berets, who never had the first idea about anything. . . .

"This country is still worn out from the last time. And yet I feel sure it's different today. We can't let scum like that lay down the law to us for the next hundred years. Rationing, nothing to eat, prisoners, and all these dead; yes, but that's not all. They're killing men, they're killing souls, they're killing the world: they're killing God. Forever. The ones who say 'Dogs and Jews not allowed' or 'Communists, not French' "—because the priest, a great reader of the underground pamphlets published by *Témoignage chrétien,* has read the story of the execution of the Châteaubriant hostages—"we can't let them get away with it, you understand; because otherwise we become like them. They turn everything to rot but they themselves are worse than rot. Stones. An empire of stones. A world of stone.

"The country around here is waiting, but I don't feel it moving yet. People are not really bad. The ones I know, anyway. They've been dealing in black-market goods with the Parisians. By now they're probably about ready to help the resistance. Everybody listens to London. When the English land, there ought to be thousands of rifles, tens of thousands of pitchforks, rising up behind them. But I'm not sure that's the way it will be. All those young men who died in '14, the Simon brothers and the rest of them, they'd have done it. They did do it, but it was too soon. For nothing. The ones who are left . . . And then there are all those prisoners, the Field Marshal, sheer cowardice being passed off as a national virtue . . ."

He shrugs again. "When your dad comes out from Paris, don't forget to remind him that he promised me a ration of tobacco."

"Sure," says Cat, who intends to keep a pinch of it for himself.

Twice a week, the daughter of the Montainville farmers comes for lessons too.

She's two years older than Cat and they are very careful always to call each other *vous*. She has been sick and isn't any farther along than Cat in Greek and Latin. Actually, she's a young lady. Her eyes and her long hair both are an amber mixture like autumn leaves. He walks back home with her, he doesn't know what to say and doesn't want to part from her. At Marles he swears to his buddies that he will soon do things to her that are as crude and definitive in the terms he uses to describe them as they are indistinct and indeterminate in his imagination. Apart from the little girls on beaches who were smooth all over and don't count, and the Venuses by Italian painters one sees in museums, the ones his grandfather pastes sepia-colored reproductions of into big albums, who seem to come from another world and who for that reason also don't count, Cat's only knowledge of the female body comes from his lengthy and repeated inspections of the cast of the Hottentot Venus in the Musée de l'Homme.

When they sit together at the priest's table unraveling Latin syntax he sometimes steals a glance at the young lady from behind his eyelashes, and then he ceases to hear anything distinctly, all he feels is a sweet pleasure that rises up in him from his belly and rolls through him to his fingertips. Once or twice, burning hot, he slipped his elbow down to press against his sex in the hollow of his stomach. The priest was talking and she was reeling off Caesar, the sound of her words reaching him like a far-off trickle of cool water. He felt fiery and sweaty, ashamed at the thought of being discovered, and he didn't have the courage to squeeze his thighs hard enough to relieve himself with an even greater shame. And when he is walking beside her on the path home and they are about to say goodbye, he wonders whether it was really the same boy who was capable of such a thing back there, or who told his buddies how he was going to skewer the broad, because what he would like, right now, is just to have her run her hand through his hair, or maybe to hold her hand and have her never go away. The long and short of it is that she is a totally untouchable young lady, like all other young ladies, Cat is just a kid with a filthy mind, and all there is left for him to do is let a sob slowly tie a knot at the bottom of his throat and feel very lonely.

❖

Cat is happiest of all when he's at the neighboring farm. He often joins in the daily round of work there, starting at dawn, and on several occasions the farmer's wife has had him to stay for weeks at a time. He slept in the same room as her two boys, who are a little older than he. The world of the farm is a kingdom, with far-flung frontiers reaching to the end of the plateau in the direction of Chevreuse, complex enclosures surrounded by other farms, and unsuspected outlying colonies squeezed into the edges of the wood in the folds of the valley. A true kingdom—the farmer's wife holds absolute sway over all its humans and animals, and every day the farmer confirms his dominion over his territory by marking it interminably with the imprint of his tools. It has its own law, beginning with the law governing time: the farm lives by the sun. In the big kitchen buzzing with flies that glue themselves in clumps to the brown sticky paper hanging in spirals from the ceiling over the table, the enameled clock bearing the name of a brand of apéritif marks one hour earlier than the official prewar time and two hours earlier than the official German time. German time, all-powerful on the radio and at the Saint-Rémy railroad station a mile and a half away, and in every house in the nearby hamlet, does not exist within the boundaries of the farm.

The farmer's wife has gray eyes; she is precise and calm, except for occasional well-aimed and furious outbursts against livestock and children. Cat likes to follow her on her long tour of the hutches, pushing the clover-laden wheelbarrow, or to carry the pails behind her when she milks. There are two hands: Cat's buddy René, who is fifteen or sixteen years old and looks after the livestock; and a town boy named Lucien, who is working as a farmhand now but whose real job is in a factory and who is only there in order to get out of going to Germany for the STO. But at least he's a real worker, not like the two students the Les Brosses farmer has hired for nothing, only too happy to have an excuse for not doing their STO.

To get to the fields they go up the slope to the plateau, following the oxen that pull the wagons that are always empty on the way up—except in spring, when they have to carry tons of liquid manure; the reek of it lingers for days in clothing and on bodies. At the beginning of the war, when his horses were requisitioned, the farmer had to buy two teams of oxen to make up for them. "They don't do the same work," he says regretfully. Cat loves the long days spent bending over the handle of his hoe and following the rows of beans to weed or potatoes to earth up. The immensity of the task is a challenge to him, and trying to keep level with his fellow workers is another. The snail-like progress to the far end of the field, then the relentless way back along the next row, with just time to straighten up once, stretching his whole body—it makes him dizzy, so certain is he that the excruciating crawl will never end; and, winded and drunk with fatigue, he lets sky and soil flood into him and empty him of everything that is not the smell of the earth.

One job he doesn't like, on the other hand, is catching Colorado beetles; only the boys do that. They pick the insects off the potato plants and drop them into a bottle, one by one. The only interesting moment comes when the bottle is three-quarters full: then there is the ritual of peeing carefully into it, standing astride the furrow. The fact that the Germans are commonly called Colorado beetles adds to the pleasure of the act, for then he is peeing on Germans, and as the condemned creatures scramble and swarm about, he sees whole armies being brutally destroyed.

The Parisians come out in flocks. They arrive by the métro on Sunday, or they ride out on their bikes; some even come in cars. The young ones sing as they go along the roads, but most of the others are interested only in food. The farmers can't sell to everybody, there has to be some rule, like restricting their dealings to people they know, because of the danger. The Germans come by car, and they go to the Les Brosses farm, where they are well known and the farmer makes his own butter. One outraged neighbor woman saw them there eating butter "by the spoonful and all in their boots and helmets." Using a spoon, of course, is vulgar, although Cat himself, if he happened to find himself in front of a big enough slab of it . . . But why should you have to take your boots off to eat butter? *His* farmer doesn't like Krauts and has no desire to talk to them or touch their money. Anyhow, they ought to have enough, what with all they requisition.

Twice a week his wife bakes a special white bread, like a brioche. Because the kingdom of the farm is an autarchy. The clock isn't the only thing that's different a mile and a half away. The only law that prevails a mile and a half away and even in some houses closer than that, like the one Cat lives in, and the law that prevails in all of non-farming France, is the law of rationing, shortages and sometimes real hunger. The bread ration is 8½ ounces a day for J2s and A's (older children and adults), 11 ounces for J3s (adolescents) and manual laborers, and only 7 ounces for V's (old people). A half-pint of milk for E's (children), J2s, and V's, provided they are on only one vendor's books and buy their milk at the same place every day. And there are coupons with letters printed on them, but you don't know when you get them whether they entitle you to artificial jam, "national" coffee, or wooden-soled shoes, or whether they simply won't be honored at all. That law does not exist on the kingdom of the farm, where production is supplemented by barter.

"I'd like to go on being a farmer," Cat says one time to René, sitting on an arm of the wheelbarrow during a break in the vegetable garden.

"Farming's okay if you're the boss," René says. "Being a hand is just hard work and you don't make any money. You get old and then who's going to look after you? I've got sheets here to sleep on and Lucien has too because he's from town, but look where he sleeps, in the stables, his home is like a cage with screen walls. On big farms, all the hands get is some straw in the loft over the horses. The wagon drivers are the only ones who get a place of their own. No farmhand ever gets to be boss. Land costs too much to buy, and who'll ever trust you enough to rent to you?"

"I'll ask my father," says Cat. "And I'll go back to the south."

He's thinking of orange trees and eucalyptus. But he knows perfectly well that he will not ask his father. He can't even begin to imagine how he would go about it. Anyway, his father would only start talking about schools of agriculture or forestry.

"I'm not going to be a farmhand forever," René says. "My father will come back from Germany and my uncle will give his land back to him."

So René is a fallen prince, a prince without a country, and his exile is also only temporary. But he has doubts about the future. In his father's absence his drunken mother reels through his village bawling. One night she narrowly missed drowning in the château pond, after trying to dance on the blanket of bright green duckweed that covered it.

The people on the farm are waiting for the liberation, asking no questions except how much longer it will be. Up on the plateau, they pick up the leaflets scattered by American and English planes. They listen to London more or less openly, over the radio in the bulky varnished wooden cabinet. On one of his visits, Cat's brother stretched almost invisible wires across the courtyard and out to the big trees in the garden next door, making an efficient aerial that gives them much better reception. "You can even hear Japan," the boys say admiringly. They giggle over the parade of "personal messages" and know some of the refrains by heart, like the óne broadcast most often: "They're the lads from the maquis / The lads in the resistance / They're the lads from the maquis / Boys from our own country." Cat finds it dreadfully flat.

But perhaps the sounds should have been the first thing to tell about, before the rest. The million sounds of the earth: at dawn cows mooing and the clank of pails in the barnyard; or the warble of the lark at midday climbing toward the sun above the fields; or, in the evening, the rattle of wagons, harrows, and rollers coming back down from the plateau and striking against the stones on the path. And on spring nights the murmur of frogs, tenuous as the chuckle of wavelets on the shore when the sea is calm. All everyday, reassuring sounds ... But now they are all relegated to supporting roles of counterpoint or muted accompaniment, when not actually obliterated, by the noises of armored cars and airplanes, hour after hour, in every register and every key, from the basso continuo of maneuvering tanks to the strident blare of fighter planes overhead and the sharp explosions of antiaircraft artillery. Here, at the end of this spring, the sounds of the country are not as usual; they are curtailed abruptly and without warning by the noise of war machines plowing up space.

Six miles away at the Satory camp, there's a tank school and proving ground. The training tanks go roaring up and down every road in the region. Big, heavy platforms, solid black, without cover or armor, on caterpillar treads; you can hear them coming from Saint-Lambert, the roar grows louder and more intense until it blots out everything else. Ground, walls, and windowpanes shudder as they go by, leaving just time enough to glimpse half-naked men moving about on top of them in helmets, their faces masked by thick goggles, before the enormous piles of metal disappear around the bend in a thick stinking cloud while the metal teeth gouge deep bites in the asphalt, except on some hillsides where they simply rip it off in strips.

Much nearer, only two miles north as the crow flies, just past the Montainville plateau and the Mérantaise valley, is the German fighter command airfield, between Voisins-le-Bretonneux and Guyancourt. It has been bombed several times and the villages at either end of it are in ruins. The Voisins church has collapsed, and the inhabitants have colonized the surrounding countryside, further swelling the population of Marles, among others. In the last few weeks the planes have been taking off as soon as the siren goes and then scattering and flying at low altitudes, to avoid being destroyed on the ground. People say that the runways have been extended into the woods nearby and that there must be more planes camouflaged there under the trees. In the daytime, at hourly intervals, there is a succession of screams of motors being revved up, one after the other, to keep them ready for takeoff. Between alerts there are training flights, fighter maneuvers, diving practice for Stukas that turn just over the valley. Cat often thinks they must have taken the turret on the old house as a landmark. The Messerschmitts fly very low over the plateau, people working in the fields see them shoot out from behind the treetops and rise just enough to clear the solitary apple tree in the middle of the field, like rolling thunder. They can see the pilot perfectly clearly above the two black crosses. The three-engine Junkers 52s also pass regularly, flying very slowly with a pounding wheeze like a basso continuo. They look as though they're moving sideways, like crabs, on their way to land at Toussus or Villacoublay.

American and English flights are announced by the far-off, distorted wail of a siren coming from Trappes or Saint-Rémy: it depends on the wind. In Paris, Cat had long since fallen into the rhythm of the great nightly waves flying up the Seine toward their German targets, moving over the city in an all-enveloping buzz punctuated by strident bursts of antiaircraft fire. He could recognize the sound of the nearest battery, the one at Passy bridge, a short metallic rip that made all the buildings on the street shudder to their foundations. It wasn't dangerous; the Allies were not bombing Paris. Out here, the spectacle is more grandiose. The road is the best observation point. At night he can see the beams of the searchlights coming from the north and the brief flashes of antiaircraft artillery around the airfields. And when the concert of airplane engines and cannon fire is over, there remains, hanging in the air and making it hum in every direction, the whine of fragments of falling shells, high, crystalline vibrations; they seem infinitely fragile. The best place then is under the roof of the big gate. Cat has picked up pieces of shrapnel of all sizes, grooved and notched. One that fell just next to him, hitting the paving stones with a dry crack, was still fiery hot. Sometimes, blown by the breeze, a litter of bits of black silvered paper, scattered by the planes to jam the radar screens, also drifts down. People string them into necklaces and hang them on the currant bushes to scare the birds away.

At the end of May the daytime flights become more frequent. Sometimes all the neighbors gather on the road and stand staring at the sky with one hand shielding their eyes from the sunlight, in which suddenly, for a fraction of a second, the wing of an airplane glints. The farmer and his wife, the hands, the three boys, and farther off, the refugees, or at least the two women and the idiot, and still farther away, other families strung along the road. They count off the formations passing by, wedge after wedge. Many years later, watching migrating geese fly north over the St. Lawrence, all Cat can think of is that other, far-off spring amidst thousands of white puffs of antiaircraft fire following the planes' advance. Then, when it seems as though the waves of planes will never end, Cat, his legs spread apart and his head drowned in sky, loses his senses, is overwhelmed by the unfurling of this immense force that fills the whole universe, and feels prodigiously free and happy. He can see that nothing will stop them. The others are shouting and he is certain of their joy too.

They can tell which are American Flying Fortresses and which are English Lancasters. Sometimes they count over a hundred. On the way out. Fewer coming back. These days, they are seeing more and more low-flying fighters, twin-fuselage Lightnings that pour past almost soundlessly, like racing gliders. They vanish behind the pla-

teau rise, then their passage over the Guyancourt field is punctuated
by heavy machine-gun fire. The German planes do not seek combat.

The targets are getting closer. Earlier in the year several hundred
people were killed in the bombing of Billancourt: an enormous red-
streaked black cloud rose up behind the plateau from the burning
storage tanks. Then came raids on the nearby airfields and now, at
the end of May, the pounding of the Trappes marshaling yard: they
had to dig the dead out from under the ruins of the houses, then
that town was evacuated too. The day after the bombing Cat rode
over on his bike to see it, but the gendarmes wouldn't let him into
the smoldering streets.

Very early one morning, a string of bombs hit the valley; they fell,
without doing any damage, on the marshy fields along the edge of
the stream where it comes out of the Les Brosses mill, a few hundred
yards from Cat's house. First, it was like a train plunging between
the hills, then the world nearly came to an end. Afterward, there was
just the ordinary roar of planes broken by antiaircraft fire, and the
smoke of explosions rising behind the river and mingling with the
morning mist. People said they had been trying to hit the airfield;
maybe they were aiming at those camouflaged runways in the
woods? It seems that somebody saw the first plane drop a red flare to
mark the target, but then the wind blew it off course to the south.

At nightfall a Flying Fortress came over, very low, out of the
east and visibly in difficulties, with one engine spewing thick smoke.
It unloaded its cargo of bombs between Marles and Saint-Lambert,
and even though that was much farther away the noise was almost as
loud and the impact as violent as before. "Six-ton bombs," Cat and
the boys said knowingly. They fell around the Favart mill, where nobody lives, and left a string of craters along the riverbank.

Bombings over France always take place by day and they say the
planes fly lower. Like Radio London, the masses of leaflets they
drop—*Courrier de l'air, Voice of America*—explain that the object is to
get as close as possible to the targets without hitting friendly popula-
tions.

·  ·  ·

One evening early in June they're all out on the road watching a formation of squadrons fly past at an altitude of seven or eight thousand feet. The clouds of antiaircraft fire crowd close to the Flying Fortresses and several start to smoke and drop out of position in their triangles. One that has fallen far behind seems to be shooting flames into a trail of white smoke. Then, in the wake of the formation, white specks appear, one after the other. Black dots sway under the open corollas: men parachuting out of the damaged planes. They count a dozen, drifting slowly down as the flight disappears in the west. The plane that was worst hit has already gone down behind the trees. But the men are safe. Will they manage not to get taken prisoner when they reach the ground? (One day the Germans locked a wounded parachutist in the town hall at Marles for a few hours and they say people brought him flowers.) Suddenly everything changes. Halfway down, the sky is peppered with smoke and flames. It takes Cat a minute, and the others too, to realize that some of those men are about to burn to death in midair. The last parachutes have caught fire. At first they still move slowly, then faster and faster, gaining on the others. They become more and more visible and Cat can see very clearly the sudden flashes of fire tearing the silk under twisting cables of smoke, and the thin black shapes, the flames licking them now, still dangling underneath. One after the other the human torches drop onto the plateau behind the treetops. How many minutes did it last? When did they realize they were going to die? Did the impact kill them or did they burn to death? There are cries along the road; screams from the women in the refugee family. Then everybody falls silent. The show is over for tonight. Besides, it's time for supper.

# *"Auf Wiedersehen"*

Apart from that, things are really pretty quiet. But Cat often wonders how much longer he can survive without a piano. Not that he actually plays. What he mostly does is spend hours banging out rough approximations of tunes and chords on the keyboard, from memory or out of his imagination. Even the most placid of the people who have to endure it are driven crazy eventually, their nerves shattered. His father's comment on his musical performances is that he would almost rather hear him playing a cat organ: a sophisticated instrument composed of a series of cats arranged behind a partition through which their tails are passed by means of suitable openings; seated facing these appendages, the virtuoso pulls or pinches them with speed and agility so as to produce a harmonious concert of meowings and chords. But is it his fault, after all, in this family in which making music seems to come as naturally as talking, singing, or knowing English, if everybody plays, sight-reads and improvises, except him? He ought to have started at seven or eight, the way his brother did, but what with the war being declared, somehow they never got around to it. So he alone does not share in this knowledge and it makes him feel inadequate.

Since the beginning of the war, whenever the family has been reunited for any length of time, the tangible expression of quietude restored has been the presence of a piano, as though time could stand still inside the space built by notes. His father plays Schubert and Schumann—*Carnaval,* Eusebius dialoguing with Florestan at acute angles, three pirouettes; during the march of the Philistines, Cat leans against the back of the upright with his ear to the partition, and it's as though he were *inside* the music, all the elephants in the

Amar circus about to enter the drawing room, each with its trunk wrapped around the tail of the one in front of it; then there is the dance of the bears, which one imitates by lurching heavily from one foot to the other with a stick pinning one's elbows behind one's back. He has to search through stacks of heavy albums for the music he wants, find the right piece and open it on the music stand above the keys; he knows his scales just well enough to be able to turn the pages. Sometimes his father accompanies his mother when she sings Schubert lieder. Cat's favorite song is the "Erlkönig": *"Wer Reitet so spät durch Nacht und Wind? Es ist der Vater mit seinem Kind."* "Who comes riding so late through wind and wild? It is the father bearing his child." He learned the poem in his first year of German at high school. His father makes his left hand thunder: the child is shivering with fever in the night and Cat doesn't understand why he has to die at the end of the song—didn't the father hold him tight enough? His mother sight-reads Strauss waltzes. The ritual gesture of fingers removing rings—one ruby, one dark blue sapphire—repeated generation after generation in every middle-class family, putting them down next to the sheet music on top of the piano; or else she plays tunes from an old red album with pictures in it that dates from her own childhood and has gone everywhere with them, called *Rondes et chansons populaires:* "Veillons au salut de l'Empire" or the Chouans' song, *"Prends ton fusil, Grégoire, prends ta Vièrge d'ivoi-oi-oi-re . . ."* or one he likes better, "La Parisienne": *"Peuple français, peuple de brâ-â-âves . . ."* His brother would like to emulate their grandfather, who can transcribe all the great opera classics from memory on the piano, from Wagner, whom he admires most of all, to Offenbach. So his brother replays all the themes they can remember from radio concerts. Also, the two of them sing enormous unaccompanied fugues and canons together, their voices dialoguing valiantly through numerous squawks, dissonances, and changes of key: "Le Veau d'or est toujours debout" by Gounod, or Offenbach's "Bacchus est roi, Bacchus est roi!" The best setting for these performances is a very large, echoing, and if possible multistoried house, the most pleasing effects being obtained when each person can station himself on a separate landing and their voices intertwine from floor to floor, the stairwell forming a resonance box. A few years ago they listened to a rebroadcast of Grieg's *Peer Gynt* over the radio. His brother told him the story: Solveig is faithfully awaiting the return of her sailor home from the seas after overcoming so many obstacles; but will the dread Button Molder encountered at the ends of the earth let him come back? He scoops up souls in a ladle and melts them down again in a great pot, so that the cycle of birth and death will never end. It was the theme of the Hall of the Mountain King that became their favorite tune, that sort of lurching and lumbering jig of death (like the half-obliterated red-shadowed fresco of "The Dance of the Dead" they saw when they visited the Chaise-Dieu). They have made up rather incoherent lyrics of their own to it, involving sea snails and elephants, and ordinarily follow them with a lugubrious recitative:

> *Old Ivan 'twas, who rang the bell*
> *For a sister-in-law whose name was Nell;*
> *'Twas a child of love, a child of play*
> *But he worked and worked both night and day.*

> *One evening when he'd been drinking wine*
> *He thought as a sailor he might shine*
> *So he climbed aboard his bicycle*
> *And went off to hunt the wild sea gull.*

The ending is a little confused but the general sense of it is clear: the old bell ringer (does a wheel of his bicycle come loose as he pedals toward the cliff?) goes, perforce, to join the Erlkönig's child and many others in the Button Molder's cauldron.

Once in his life Cat went to the opera; the Opéra-Comique it was, actually, in Paris, where they were performing *Tosca* that winter. He was rather overawed by the splendor of the sets and action; when the main hero, the valiant painter, appeared onstage, covered with blood from the torture to which he had just been subjected but loudly proclaiming his faith in the freedom of peoples and Italian unity, the dastardly Scarpia, chief of the Austrian police, had hardly begun to break into diabolical mockery when actors and audience alike were suddenly frozen by a bell: air-raid alert. Everybody assembled in the cafés on the street outside, the painter with stripes of red makeup on his face and a raincoat slung over his artfully torn bouffant shirt, the torturer, Tosca herself, stagehands, audience, Cat, his brother, the little girl cousin with the red nose of whom his brother was so fond, and a few German officers standing at the bar in their handsome uniforms.

"Well," said Cat, commenting on the action at the point at which they had left it, "I would never talk if I were tortured!"

"Don't be stupid," his brother retorted. "Nobody has the right to say that. Nobody knows what he'd do really. And nobody has the right to condemn people who do talk. Anyway, in real life things don't happen like that."

"But I wouldn't," Cat insisted.

The alert ended, everybody went back to their places, the singers sang, the painter fell, shot by bullets that were supposed to be blanks but were in fact real—the final treachery of the unspeakable Scarpia—and in a superb shriek of agony Tosca elegantly flung herself from the top of the parapet into a pit that was fortunately not as deep as the orchestra pit. In short, one lot died, the other lot applauded wildly, the German officers most of all, and everybody went home very happy.

Afterward, when he tries to remember those first days of June 1944 he will always be amazed by the amount of agitation and unrelated activity he managed to cram into them, and the number of events, great and small, in which he was involved (he who, as an adult, will spend whole days staring from the top of a cliff at waves crashing, always the same, beautiful and monotonous, over the same rock).

He sees himself, for instance, with the farm boys and other kids from the village, digging in the sand on the south side of the valley in bright sunlight, right at the edge of the woods, to build a little fort from which, once it has been roofed with branches and squares of grassy sod, they can overlook the road, watch the flight of airplanes, and sit in the cool shade of the soft sand smoking cigarettes made of viburnum and other revolting herbs—but sometimes also leaves of green tobacco surreptitiously torn off the plants at the far end of some vegetable garden and rolled in newspaper. One Sunday a German soldier comes there with a girl from Chevreuse; they stop right next to them under the trees, lie down in front of the green wheat, and make love. The boys don't really get to see much because the soldier's back hides everything; he didn't take off his uniform, and Cat, watching the verdigris mass writhing confusedly about, imagines he's aiming at him through the sights of a rifle. He keeps it trained on him a long time; but can you kill a man while he's making love? Right now, he thinks you definitely can. The question, and the doubt, come only afterward.

"That's what they call horizontal collaboration," says René. "The slut, she'll have her head shaved."

The next day they find a French letter close to the wheat field and comment upon this mysterious and rare product of modern technology which they are viewing for the first time.

These are the days of the Chevreuse village fair too. Lucien spends his whole month's wages in a few hours. The roundabout spins dizzily, pulling almost horizontal boats at the end of long chains: the boys' game is to try to catch hold of the seat of the girl in front; screams and fairground music ... On June 4 the Allies finally take Monte Cassino after six months of furious fighting, trench warfare, poundings with artillery and bombs, and enter Rome. In the leaflets that were dropped by reams in the fields they see a photo of French troops parading through Rome, wearing gandouras and English helmets. In a single night, eight hundred bombers drop two thousand tons of bombs on Berlin and kill thousands of people. The Russians are advancing in the Ukraine, they'll take a hundred thousand prisoners at Minsk and then head for Warsaw. He has to laugh at the stereotyped expressions in the news broadcasts on Radio Paris: "Following an enemy offensive which was contained after fierce fighting, in the course of which heavy losses were sustained, the Axis troops withdrew to positions prepared in advance. This readjustment of the front line will make possible a better concentration of forces." Jean-Hérold Pacquis, a ridiculous character who talks through his nose, then declaims, every evening at the same time like a cuckoo popping out of its Swiss chalet clock: "And you may be sure, my dear listeners, that England, like Carthage, will be destroyed." The sun shines a lot those days and the little fairground roundabout is one of the prettiest memories in Cat's life.

⊞

Also at the beginning of June, his mother comes to spend a few days at Marles. For Cat this is a time of rejoicing but also of great self-discipline. He has swept the courtyard, raked the pathways, changed the guinea pigs' litter, brushed the coats of Patachou and Timoshenko, patiently constructed a little brick of butter—rather lumpy and pallid, it is true—by removing the cream from his pint of milk every day for a week and combining it with the skin from the boiled milk, placed a bouquet of lupin by his mother's bed, and pulled up the carrots.

They are happy to be together, Cat is delighted to see her; there is no doubt about that. But parents are strange people. It seems to be their law never to recognize simple emotions, and they detect pitfalls on every side from which their children must be protected at all cost. At the same time they are incredibly naïve, because they seem not to realize that as a result of their behavior two parallel worlds develop, the one that is under their noses, the world of the proprieties, and another world somewhere else outside them, with multiple and unimaginable dimensions—the one, for example, in which it is perfectly natural to pick up the cast-off French letters of a sentimental German. . . . Three worlds, actually, because there is also their own carefully preserved realm composed of more or less ill-kept secrets (*not in front of the children*).* That makes too many. He can't keep them straight because he'd have to know the rules of all the different games and hold three threads of Ariadne all the time in order not to mix everything up and, inevitably, do something wrong in the end; only then would he have a chance of being considered "well brought up." Cat is not well brought up; maybe because people

---

*Italicized English words and phrases in this translation also appear in English in the French original.

haven't had time to bring him up at all. (For instance, in this family where for generations it has been customary for children to say *vous* when addressing their parents, Cat uses the familiar form, whereas his brother does not. One more tradition that has gone by the board with the war.)

Besides, they're absolutely obsessed with training. His mother hasn't been there five hours before they are already parted by mortifying questions of unwashed hands, unmade beds, and the abnormally low level of the reserve sugar supply.

The biggest thing that Cat would ever reproach his parents for, and the one thing that infuriates him about them, as about all adults, is their pretension that they are the masters of words. The absolute masters. They are the ones who decide what is to be talked about and how; and what it is forbidden to talk about and how it is forbidden to talk about it. They know how to ignore a question or to answer it in a way that is even worse than if they had ignored it. (His father has a whole range of all-purpose replies designed to squelch tedious or inopportune curiosity: "If anybody asks, tell them you have no idea" or "Who? The pope of bonzes!" or if Cat shows anxiety about some twinge or ache, "Death occurs after three days and the first one counts double." They claim to know what is the right thing to do and what would be ill advised; what is estimable and what is, by the same token, noxious; what is made for children's benefit and what is made to do them harm. And how, at the age of thirteen, is one to guess at the anxiety and doubts that may lie hidden behind all that assurance, all that firmly displayed sense of duty and enunciation of definitive truths? And yet he, Cat, considers himself big enough to be sole judge of what he can understand and not understand, know at once or put off till later.

In Paris he once found a rather old, shabby book called *La Médecine familiale* on his father's bedside table, well thumbed and with lots of dog-eared pages—the ones where it talked about mumps and false croup—and one page marked with a visibly new strip of white paper: the page about the "untruthful" child. Some of the words had been underlined with a pencil. He felt irrevocably exposed. That whole business of the *1* added in front of the *0* to make a *10* on his report card, and many other and more serious incidents, were collected together on that page, defined and stigmatized. The doctor who wrote the book didn't seem to favor dishonest children; he recommended great firmness, severe punishment, wrapping in cold wet sheets, and he linked this shortcoming to the abhorrent and redoubtable practice of "masturbation." And the masturbator, he explained, is a "hypochondriac." Cat consulted a dictionary: hypochondria is a condition which causes the subject to become strange and morbid. The author further explained that the lying masturbator, becoming habituated to deceit and dissimulation, loses all willpower and sense of duty. And Cat felt very sure that such vices would lead him to damnation.

But then, how is a person supposed to attract his parents' attention when he senses that it is always somewhere else, when he feels—do these hard times have something to do with it?—that they have so many other things to take care of, so many other fish to fry? A person is never able to satisfy them; is it really love that blinds them, or is it, more basely, self-love? What else can he do to capture their attention, except tell them stories which (incidentally, quite incidentally) may not be absolutely true (but which might just as well be, after all)?

At the same time, he knows he is partial. Other people's parents he mostly finds silly, unpleasant to look at, and vulgar; he would never allow them to be put on a level with his own. With other people there is almost never that feeling of shared trust that he has known in the finest hours of his family life.

⁑

On the subject of the preoccupations of Cat's parents during that period it should be explained that one winter evening at the beginning of 1944 his father had taken his mother on a strange visit to the heart of the market district. For some time, his brother had been a source of deep concern to them both. He was studying in one of the best schools in Paris, preparing to take the entrance examinations to the Ecole Normale Supérieure [the most prestigious of the *grandes écoles,* "Normale Sup." prepares students admitted on the basis of a very tough competitive exam for top positions in education and research]; but with the ever more sweeping conscriptions of young people for compulsory labor in Germany, the fate of a nineteen-year-old student was becoming increasingly precarious. Some of them took the initiative by finding jobs in France that would exempt them from service in Germany; many got themselves taken on as farmhands, one friend of his brother's had even been seen in a fireman's uniform. But his brother absolutely refused the easy way out and his parents shared his noble principles, for which they had only themselves to blame. At the same time, they couldn't help seeing that he was becoming more and more deeply involved in the militant underground movement. Also, his father did not like his son's systematic identification of patriotism with Communism, and that was a sore subject between them. Perhaps he was also willing to take risks for himself that he could not accept for his son. What is certain is that he saw his son's activities leading him inescapably toward violence and bloodshed, and he did not believe that men so young were ready for that (even if he understood that they might feel driven to it by the abdication of a majority of their elders); assuming, that is, that he himself subscribed to the logic of terrorism, which is by no means certain. In a word, between father and son there were two antagonistic conceptions of resistance at issue: on their faces, the foreign occupation produced the same expression, the same disgust, but in all other respects they were divided as only two such widely separated generations can be. Antoine, who swallowed hungrily and indiscriminately every word of the literature on the great Bolshevik revolution that was secretly making the rounds, and who was associating with veterans of the Spanish Civil War brigades, saw the struggle against Nazism as the prelude to a new society to be built; while his father viewed the Communists and de Gaulle with equal mistrust. A lifetime spent in the study of the history of societies since the dawn of mankind presumably inclined him to skepticism and misgivings in regard to any great scheme, religious or political, that set out to create universal happiness in one fell swoop; what it was more likely to create, in his opinion, was universal misery; and his faith in heaven-sent saviors was hardly greater.

In the end he decided that the best solution would be for his son to join one of the maquis units that the resistance movements were organizing in those days for defaulters—mainly in the mountainous terrain above Grenoble. He was particularly sensitive to the apprehensions of his wife—about their son's nocturnal absences after curfew that no affairs of the heart, even unknown and complicated ones, could explain; the heaps of leaflets and the stockpile of stencils, the evening visits of friends assuming airs of complicity which it was impossible to misunderstand, the overnight stays of other friends which were becoming more frequent, the waltz of bicycles of unknown origin; later, the discovery of a pistol; and finally, the eruption into the family circle of a jacket with large bloodstains on it—all these were violently at odds with her notions of the life of a son whom one still occasionally requested not to put his elbows on the table.

Madame Ponte-Serra had a very clear idea that these activities probably ran parallel to but were not the same as those of her husband. She had been badly frightened when *he* had spent two weeks in prison back in 1941, for something which to her mind had never been satisfactorily explained. Also, there was the ordeal of everyday life—her family, which had to be not only protected but also fed, the incessant and obsessive quest for provisions, in a grotesque, degrading, almost hysterical atmosphere in which the need to put food into their bellies seemed to have obnubilated every other sentiment in the French middle classes, and not only them. She had somehow to keep a balance, maintain a basic moral sense, the one in which she herself had been brought up and to which she was attached more strongly than to anything else, between the dogged struggle to protect her own family, household, parents, and the refusal to cave in utterly to the fierce temptation of the egotism of sheer survival, just getting enough to eat, hanging on to one's comforts at any price. In the vicious world of the Parisian middle classes in the 1940s she obstinately strove to follow a line of conduct that would reconcile dignity and love of family, silence her own fears, and also, while preserving the appearances of a family life as perfectly and naturally tranquil as in the palmiest days of peace and her own childhood near La Plaine-Monceau, enable her to hold her head high in the face of a worldly, indifferent, or even hostile society. Desperately, and on the whole successfully, she *coped*.

Through his own activities, his father had a contact; he used it to get in touch with somebody who was in charge of recruiting young candidates in Paris and starting them on their way to the maquis. And because he saw his wife beleaguered by a thousand unanswered questions about their son's doings, he insisted that she meet this person too, so that she could see for herself that the organization was a serious one. This was the significance of the trip they made together one evening to the premises of a transport agent in the central market, Les Halles.

In the gloom of a chilly warehouse, surrounded by mountains of crates, they saw a dozen boys about to depart, all of whom were conspicuous for their untidy appearance, sickly looks, and excellent manners. Each one introduced himself in turn, in the best etiquette-book fashion, adding with an offhand air certain details of his activities: So-and-so (the name was a false one), "terrorist," escaped from prison in Rouen. So-and-so, master's degree in philosophy, sentenced by default to thirty years in prison for armed robbery. So-and-so, three train derailings, two shootings. Even though the official they had come to see proved to be not only an honest tradesman but also a reserve officer visibly of "very good family," levelheaded, precise, and reassuring in the particulars he gave them of the organization of the maquis and the advantages of enlisting an adventure-loving young man into a fully staffed movement with organic ties to London, it is not certain that this visit allayed quite all of Madame Ponte-Serra's fears. In any event, it had no aftermath because the contact was broken off soon afterward.

"You see," the father said as they left, "now you understand why it's better that I tell you as little as possible."

Her nature was such that she agreed with him.

But her nature was also such that, very certainly, not for one second was her mind visited by the thought that was uppermost in the minds of most of her friends and the members of her huge family: the main thing is not to get mixed up in anything, to spin oneself a cocoon and wait until it's all over. . . . A few years from now they'd all be looking back and laughing about the hard times they'd had—provided they had been clever enough to keep their heads down and survive.

On June 6, when his mother leaves, Cat feels that he wants her to stay—a little more warmth. . . . At that moment he is no longer thinking with his head. But her mind is already filled with Parisian preoccupations, and there is food to take back to the rest of the family, the ones who are waiting for her and worrying. He launches a big offensive and goes into his leg-rubbing cat act: couldn't he go back to Paris with her, just for one day? He could come back on the métro, and it would mean an opportunity, at last, to visit the Quai de la Mégisserie and investigate the potential market for his guinea pigs. He walks to the Saint-Rémy station with her, carrying her bag that contains a rabbit killed the night before, eggs, butter, and twelve pounds of potatoes, and makes one last attempt to persuade her. The walk takes about three-quarters of an hour. They go past the local *Kommandantur,* a big villa behind a thick hedge where a helmeted sentry in full trappings is always on guard at the gate, his long green overcoat belted so tight at the waist that his behind juts out grotesquely like that of the Hottentot Venus, like those of all German soldiers (it always makes one long to sneak up and stick a pin in their rear, his brother says), his rifle slung across his chest, a grenade at his waist, its long wooden handle thrust through his belt; he always stares after the people who walk past him with a cow-like gaze which they hope is uneasy. Cat follows his mother onto the station platform and even gets into the carriage with her: he sits down across from her, the sun in his eyes. But this last attempt is also a failure. She is immovable, and, his spirits dashed, he kisses her and stands up. A lady who has just boarded the train takes his place and he doesn't dare make any further pleas with a witness looking on. He starts walking away before the train pulls out.

He has just passed the sentry when he hears the air-raid siren. Softly, he sings his own version of "Lily Marlene":

> *Outside the barracks, stands a big giraffe;*
> *Every night he's out there weeping like a calf.*

*I asks him, why the sorry mood,*
*He says to me, look how we're screwed:*
*We got the Russians up our ass,*
*The Russians up our ass.*

When he gets to the valley he watches the planes' movements absentmindedly. A few American Lightnings, not in formation, zoom gracefully past quite low. They're certainly throwing caution to the winds these days, he thinks. He hears a few bursts of machine-gun fire, isolated and unanswered, over toward the east. A skirmish with the German fighters that are buzzing all over the place? Pretty ballet in the sun and blue sky. Nothing worth noticing. He takes the long way around by the hillside to inspect the sand fortress.

When he comes within sight of the house an hour later, the old refugee woman is outside waiting for him, gesticulating and calling his name. As he gets nearer, he sees that her face is gray and she's sobbing heavily. She seizes him, clutches him to her dirt-stiffened apron, and says, "Oh, my boy, my poor little boy, be brave, your mother's had an accident." She keeps sniffing and hanging on to him. He wishes he could move, stop breathing that unpleasant smell of leeks; he thinks that he's read sentences like that in novels, they're meant for when you have to tell people gently that some loved one has died. They're idiotic enough to read but even worse, more unreal, when they're actually spoken. She's still sniffing, damp all over, her eyes and nose are dribbling; at last she lets go of him, repeats that he has to be brave, it isn't serious.

"They just came over from Canard's to tell us," she says. "They got a telephone call. Your mother has been taken to the doctor at Chevreuse. It was an accident, it's not serious, she's only hurt. The train was machine-gunned."

He gets out the huge old apple-green lady's bicycle named Mammoth and pedals crazily through the rocks and potholes over the plateau.

The sweat is running off him. His mother is lying on a sofa in the doctor's living room. The first thing he sees is that she's smiling at him. Her hair is undone, her masses of long, very long, chestnut-colored hair full of golden glints—her hair that always makes him think of the fairy tale she used to tell him about the woman who was kept prisoner in a tower in the middle of the forest and who let her hair down from the window at the top so it would fall at the feet of the Prince Charming and he could climb up to kiss her.

He does not kiss her. He looks at Pétain's portrait on the wall, framed in red, white, and blue and surmounted by the words: "I have made France the gift of myself." His mother follows his gaze and says nothing, but her very blue eyes signal him not to comment. He moves over and sits on the edge of the sofa, stiff and intimidated. He doesn't dare take her hand. Then she tells him there's a piece of shrapnel in her thigh, she can't move her leg but it doesn't hurt very much. They've put on an emergency dressing and she's waiting to be moved to Paris to be operated on. She also tells him that she doesn't know exactly how it happened. The train was hardly out of the station and the carriage was almost empty, the lady across from her had started to explain that she was going to join her children in Paris and was bringing them jam and a loin of pork, she said the sun was in her eyes, they discovered that the curtain was stuck. Then the train stopped short, there was a loud noise of metal and broken glass, and the lady had fallen forward face down on the seat. Then, in the confusion, some people helped her get out and she saw the wounded lying alongside the train. She cut up her raincoat to make a tourniquet for a man whose leg was almost torn off, the blood was squirting out. She knows how to do things like that because she was a hospital nurse in 1940. "It's a shame," she says, "because it was a beautiful raincoat that your father bought me in Montpellier. And I lost the rabbit. After that . . ."

"What about the lady across from you?"

"She was dead. There was a piece of shrapnel in her neck."

"But," says Cat, "that's where I was sitting . . ."

"I know, little cat." His mother is still smiling. "But it wasn't you. And you can't stand the sun in your eyes."

The doctor comes in and says that the ambulance has come. He also tells them that the English have landed in Normandy. The ambulance leaves and Cat gets back on his bicycle. Night is falling and on the shady downgrade to Marles, as he bumps and skids over the stones, the cool air raises goose pimples on his skin where the sweat still hasn't dried. That evening somebody else comes over from Canard's to say there was a phone call from Paris: the operation was a success. They also say a beachhead has been established.

Two weeks later Cat will go back to the doctor's to pick up his mother's shoes and the remnants of her raincoat. Pétain's portrait is no longer in the living room. The rabbit was not found.

⁂

That evening at the farm, he listens to the Field Marshal's speech on the radio. The tearful voice has adopted a piteous tone: "Citizens of France, I beseech you . . . This so-called liberation is the most deceitful of the mirages by which you could be tempted. . . . Do not listen to those who seek to take advantage of our unhappy situation and would lead the nation to disaster." The quavering bleat makes Cat squirm, as though it were something obscene, and he swears crudely. It's hardly necessary to beseech that pack of cowards, all those people who have shut their eyes and minds to everything except their food, their fuel, their tobacco, their gas generator; the people who are always sneaking into the back rooms of shops to butter up the grocer; the people who see a classmate whom their son has brought home for an hour as a threat, or worse, a sworn enemy, a Jew, a leper, who might reduce the family hoard by two ounces of bread (in some families each person's ration is weighed out every morning on a scale and carefully stored away in his own individual bag), whose parents might be Gaullists and therefore highly compromising; the people he has heard everywhere, in food lines, on trains, in identity checks during alerts when the German or French gendarmes would take away anybody they didn't like the looks of, saying how it was a terrible shame but what could they do about it, if only everybody else would follow their own example: just obey the rules. All people have to do is obey the rules. . . . The rules, the rules, the rules. . . . No, he doesn't really need to beseech those people not to budge, to stay indoors, not to get mixed up in it, not to do anything that might hinder the occupation forces —as though they had done anything else for the last four years, as though they weren't firmly intending to remain flat on their faces to the bitter end.

For the BBC, the thing was certain: the landing was a success, the liberation was beginning; all forces of resistance were called upon to mobilize. De Gaulle speaks: "For the sons of France, wherever they may be, their simple and sacred duty is to fight the enemy by every means at their disposal." London reminds listeners that from now on all lines of communication will be under constant pressure, railway junctions and moving trains may be attacked at any moment anywhere in the country and people are strongly advised not to travel. Cat thinks they might have said that a little sooner. In the ensuing days, the waves of bombers overhead become more and more frequent, and there is a hail of multicolored leaflets showing the first photos of the landing fleet. The Massy-Palaiseau railroad station is battered, métro service is suspended. Now, to get to Paris, you have to get off at Palaiseau and walk or take a bus to Massy-Verrières, where you board another train. It looks as though Cat will have a long wait before he can find out about the market for guinea pigs on the Quai de la Mégisserie. Power cuts are frequent, the lights are turned on only for a few short hours in the evening, and it is becoming increasingly difficult to call Paris from Canard's, the café that serves as a public telephone; sometimes you have to wait over an hour. On the farm, as in many other houses, a map of the western part of the country has suddenly materialized, with pins stuck in it. The English are held up outside Caen, while the town itself is being flattened by bombs. Curfew has been extended from ten in the evening to five a.m. Early one morning, when they go to the Champmercy meadow to fetch the cows that have been parked there overnight and bring them in to be milked, they find the remains of a sickening slaughter. A band of clandestine killers has raided the herd and quartered and cut up a cow on the spot. Nothing is left except the head and hooves and a slithering mass of pink and bluish intestines with green flies swarming all over them.

Then, a large contingent of German infantry on its way westward encamps in the valley.

Early in July, Cat's mother returns to Marles to convalesce and his father comes with her for a few days. Thirty men are quartered in the ruined left side of the house. They have put up straw partitions along the walls and on the floor and consolidated them with long wooden beams. The old place is groaning with the weight of all the people in it. The six refugees have crowded into two rooms on the top floor, and Cat and his parents are on the right side of the second floor; they all share the kitchen and dining room below. His father has managed to keep his study in the tower, although the bookcases have been torn out.

Under the lindens outside the front door there is a sentry on permanent duty, day and night, his everlasting wooden-handled grenade in his belt. At dawn, there are the voices of men going about their business below, the sounds of buckets and splashing water, the clatter of mugs and the big coffee urn brought over from a neighboring house. During the day they have firing practice, and the dry hack of Mausers is heard in the woods. In the evening, after the hour spent taking apart and cleaning their weapons in the fading daylight, they often stay outdoors, sprawling half dressed in the courtyard and garden, waiting, almost without speaking, for the mist to rise from the river and spread its moist coolness through the vale. They have built latrines behind the laurels: a long deep pit and six horizontal bars, side by side, fastened to stakes sunk in the ground. Six-hole latrines!

"They have always had a strong feeling for communal life. And for exaggeration," comments Cat's father.

"Besides," he adds, "it's natural; their intestines are a yard longer than those of all the other human races. It comes of eating sauerkraut."

"Is that really true?" asks Cat, who is hearing the story for the hundredth time.

"Why, certainly. Scientifically proven. And will remain so as long as they keep up their nonsense about inferior races."

What is true, anyway, is that they go to the latrines in groups and sit there chatting away, perched on the bars with their pants down.

These are not at all like the other soldiers Cat has had occasion to see in the last few years. The other ones talked in loud voices, wore impeccable uniforms, and had gleaming boots and highly polished arms. Their mere presence seemed to fill up all the space there was; the mass of their bodies, voices, noises, and weapons thrust the rest of mankind into a respectful, indistinct haze. In a group, they gave one the impression of living somehow on top of everything around them, in a separate and higher world, protected, as by impenetrable armor, by the solid affirmation of their potency, their cohesiveness; and affirming it further by the bursts of their laughter, their songs, their shouts, their orders, the resonant ring of their footsteps, the cymbal crash of all their warlike paraphernalia, the oversize helmets, swollen backpacks, grenades thick as kitchen pestles, the cumbersome, clicking Mausers, the bayonet-swords swinging on their right hips. And that was just the ordinary soldiers, hulking in their uniforms with the rigid folds, heavy jackets buttoned to the throat and thick woolen green or gray overcoats; because there were the officers too, in unbelievably magnificent array, with their dress caps that could compete in height with a Breton coif, their short or long close-fitting green jackets with white facings and gilt buttons; some of the especially elegant ones wore little gilded daggers on the end of a chain that one always longed to cut off surreptitiously; and there were the "dog collars" of the military police, always in pairs, always in helmets, with their black submachine guns across their bellies, porcine bulldogs who were called that because they had a sort of heavy chain embroidered across their chests; and the SS with the skulls on their ugly black caps and their pistols in their belts, who seemed to be in a world even further apart than the rest, even more noisy and arrogant; and there were the more middle-class, fat-bellied ones in the Todt organization [a paramilitary organization of civil engineers and technicians], comfortable breadwinners with shaven heads, the backs of their necks falling into folds and their rear ends jutting out under jackets reaching barely to their buttocks, wearing khaki-colored uniforms and red armbands with swastikas on them. . . . A whole self-contained world of men, men who were sure that they were men, real men, the only men who recognized each other as men, always together, to whom the rest of the human race, looked at from behind the ramparts of their certainties, their arrogance, even their momentary magnanimity and kindness, was as invisible as if they had been blind in one eye and couldn't see out of the other. And also, they were so isolated when they were among other people—on a train, in the métro—by a circle of silence that was hardly even hostile, only, in appearance, indifferent. A world of men which Cat cannot enter and does not want to enter. But he's got no choice in the matter. He's affected by them whether he likes it or not. Some indefinite threat radiates from these men. The threat of death? They carry death with them, even if they themselves, when they smile, don't know it or have forgotten. They hold the power of life and death. It is they who make the laws, set the rules: it depends on them whether or not one is "obeying the rules," and at any moment they can invent some new rule, as demented and absurd, for example, as the rule that some people have to wear a yellow star.

The soldiers living in the house now are not very much like that. Sometimes, if Cat stretches his imagination, they even remind him of the poor Italian soldiers he saw in the south, who were so sad to be away from home.

These are new recruits, not healthy-looking; their uniforms are too big for them and don't button up right. Except for a few noncommissioned officers with the red and black ribbon of the Russian campaign on their jacket lapels, they're all young. The "Aili! Ailo!" they sing as they go off in the morning is hardly inspiriting, and they look as though, if they weren't being bullied all the time and made to perform such futile tasks as digging trenches in particularly stony soil, all they would really like to do is lie around and stare up at the soft clouds floating past between air-raid alerts. Cat hears them talking among themselves. At first they had been glad to be sent to France, it took them away from the Russians; now that they're headed for the front, they're just scared.

After two and a half years of German at school, Cat has acquired a few rudiments. In his first year of secondary school his father had decreed that the fact that France was being subjected to Nazi oppression was no reason why Cat should not be introduced to German culture, as he himself had been, early in the century, hiking along the banks of the Rhine and Neckar. Cat was supposed to speak English at home, and he actually could, with a fair amount of stammering, reel off whole passages from *Alice in Wonderland*. He speaks the language fluently enough to carry on an everyday conversation, although he is teased by the family because of his accent and accordingly prefers to keep still. But German, by virtue of its rich grammar and syntax, was supposed to give him the real key to an understanding of foreign languages. He was touched by the first poems of Goethe he learned, the one about the heath rose that the little boy wants to pick—*"Röslein, Röslein, Röslein rot, Röslein auf der Heiden"*—and the "Erlkönig" of course, and the comrade's song in which he could already hear, but so mournfully, the tramp of boots: *"Ich hatte einen Kameraden / Einen bessern find'st du nitt'!"*—"I had a comrade / A better will you never find!"—and the stray bullet that strikes him down at his side, *"als wär's ein Stück von mir"*—"like a piece of my very self." By the end of the first year he had begun to learn the "Lorelei" that was printed in his school textbook (*"Ich weiss nicht was soll es bedeuten . . ."*); but the next year all the German textbooks were peppered with rectangles of paper which the publisher had carefully pasted, on page after page, over certain passages: over all Heine's poems, for instance, because Heine was a Jewish writer. (This happened in the "unoccupied zone," under the Vichy government.) Heine was excised from History. He had never existed. So Cat never learned, or rather he forgot, the ending of the "Lorelei," because even by holding the page against his lamp he was unable to see through the paper to decipher the censured Gothic characters and find out what was the cause of all that sorrow in the opening lines, the only ones he could still remember. But that is no help to him for conversational purposes. He doesn't know the name for sausage. He knows a few common words, like butter (that's obvious, you don't need to go to school to learn that, because the word *Butter* is apparently the rallying cry of all Teutonic troops on campaign and the quest for butter seems to have replaced the quest for the Holy Grail, for these knights-errant of modern times), and he has also learned, of course, that in German a French letter [known in French as an English cap] becomes a *Parisienne*.

One evening just at nightfall there is an explosion very close by, followed by a cascade of shouting and exclamations in German. Everybody starts to run, leaping down the stairs in a great clatter of hobnailed boots. He gathers that a cyclist came riding past, fired at the soldier on guard, and disappeared around the bend; the sentry threw his grenade at him but was too late, all he could see was a fleeting shadow in the gloom. Late that night the men are still up all over the village, motorcycles backfiring, trucks from Chevreuse speeding past filled with armed, helmeted men who leap out and rush to surround the woods. The officers tramp from house to house, voices bellow louder and louder, the night is filled with the thumping of boots and rifle butts. All of a sudden they're like beasts at bay, their voices hoarse or screeching, their eyes glazed, seeming to see nothing around them—automatons out of control. Cat almost likes them better that way. He tells himself that it was his brother, who had just come to town and couldn't resist taking a shot at the sentry. Cat's been waiting a long time for that. Anyway, he's sorry the sentry wasn't hit. It was the same soldier who had offered him a piece of sausage the day before. But of course it wasn't his brother. Besides, both cyclist and shot were probably figments of the fright of a young soldier alone in the dark.

He and his father go for a walk through the woods and fields. First they stop at the mayor's house, to settle the question of the allotment of seed potatoes for the garden. Then they go over to Magny to call on the Hellenist priest, who's busy pouring off his cider, and then back down to Port-Royal at the far end of the valley. It's raining, the trees drip slowly down on them through the mist; there is icy water running down his neck and his old shoes are like sponges. He's happy to be walking with his father, as he has done often before, here and in other settings. His father never tires of walking, maybe it's left over from the ten years he spent trekking back and forth across the highlands of Annam and Tonkin, and his expedition to the heart of Yunnan. Cat likes to walk the same way, taking the same strides at the same pace. This is not just walking: everything around them is noticed and commented upon as they go. Nobody knows better than his father how to explain the sense of each thing they see, from the simplest to the most obscure, the trees and stones, the lines of a building, the contours of the path and profile of a landscape. He has been teaching Cat ever since he was tiny. From one absolutely ordinary object, a leaf or pebble, he can unfold a many-faceted, infinite tale, go back in time, re-create the passing parade of vanished generations and civilizations, or, even further back, of geo-logical eras. He takes in everything his eyes encounter with deep re-spect, a little like the priest at Magny; but he goes much further and, best of all, he never, never adds a moral at the end.

A long time ago his father showed him that if he wants to get be-hind the surface of what he sees, the ideal way to do it is by making a drawing of it. One guides the pencil over the paper, moving one's eye back and forth from the horizon to the slowly darkening sheet, one patiently reconstructs what one is looking at, at the same time as one is constructing the drawing of it; one hesitates, makes mistakes, rubs out and redraws, performing a slow exercise in the reading and interpretation of lines and textures, a panoramic representation of the landscape in which, with one line tracing the outline of the hills, then filling in with lighter or darker grays, depending on the dis-tance, one discovers the logic of the lie of the countryside, the un-suspected connections, cutouts, things that fit around other things: here an invisible stream must pass because it has dug out this hollow, while that naked cliff face there could only be a quarry, a piece of mountain torn open by human hands, and the rounded hump over there must surely be all that is left of the worn-down peak of an old primary mountain range, and that line along the hillside above the treetops marks the path of a road or railway, and those bare patches are firebreaks or vestiges of ancient fallows, or, suddenly, an old threshing ground; and how else can one explain the fact that the tower of that ruined castle is intact, unless it was still in use not long ago for visual signaling, or as a fire warden's station? And those darker masses, those enormous trees, cedars or sequoias thrusting out above a pale stand of beech: they're a sure sign that the master of some manor house, now invisible or gone, lived there back in the eighteenth century, some man of enlightenment, a disciple of Buffon or a traveler home from the New World, maybe one of Lafayette's companions; especially if, not far away, there is also a clump of three acacias sticking up in a triangle, which could only have been planted there by a Freemason, that being a secret rallying sign among them.

And so the passage of human generations scratches the surfaces of things. Here on the plateau subside the last ripples of adventures far more ancient and violent than those of the gentlemen who brought new species of trees from over the ocean. The homecoming Crusaders, for instance, have left traces all over the countryside: names borrowed from the Holy Land, like the château of Damiette six miles away; lazar houses to segregate the lepers that became legion after their travels to the Levant; or the village of Lévy-Saint-Nom, so called in honor of the Virgin, because the Crusaders knew that for believers there was no name more holy or closer to God than that of Lévy. (But in 1941, after a debate in the town council, the village's name was Aryanized, and is now written Lévis-Saint-Nom.) His father is also clever with his hands. A few years ago, during a ramble through the Massif Central, Cat and his mother bought him a little knife from Thiers with innumerable blades on it—it even has a minute saw and scissors—and he always carries it on hikes and uses it to carve pieces of chestnut into objects that are suggested to him by some knot or vein in the wood: a dagger-shaped paper cutter, for instance, that balances perfectly in the hand, or a walking stick with a pommel sculpted into a vaguely Grecian head (because, of course, one has to resist the temptation just to peel the bark along the stem into a coiling snake).

Here, walking with him in the rain, dawdling by the bramble thickets to pick the first water-gorged berries, he feels much closer to his father than anywhere else, and especially Paris and the big apartment where his father used to sit by him until he finished translating some Latin text he didn't understand, absolutely could not understand, his nerve ends raw, his eyes brimming with tears.

"I don't understand. It doesn't mean anything."

"You're a nitwit."

But his father refused to help him, and it was like a trial of strength between torturer and victim. However hard he tortured the text himself, meanwhile, clinging like a shipwrecked man to the one comprehensible word that swam to the surface of the sentence and trying to deduce the rest from it, all he could produce, through his tears, was a shapeless pottage that drove his father to paroxysms of icy exasperation.

The only thing left for him then was to admit to himself that it was true: he was a stupid, lazy nitwit. But that did absolutely nothing to help him out of his predicament. Latin was far, far harder to construe than landscapes, woods, hills, and stones.

Once when he was still little, he was playing with another boy in the Bois de Boulogne. Walking over the wide lawns, they came upon two couples lying in the sun, who gave them candy and asked them questions.

"What does your daddy do?"

His friend had prudently answered that his father did like all daddies, which meant that he went to work every day, leaving his mommy at home. He could have been a soldier or a fireman or an aviator.

But Cat was specific. He was very certain of his answer.

"My daddy is a professor of Chinese."

They made him say it at least three times, rolling on the grass and hooting with laughter. They couldn't stop giggling over it. He felt himself turning crimson as it came over him that there was something bizarre and mysterious in the words and they were not to be released to the public at large without taking due precautions.

When he told them about it back at home his parents had laughed too. His father told him, "If you really want to give a proper answer you must say professor of Chinese and Tartar-Manchu languages and literatures."

"But," his mother added, "it's better just to say professor."

Yes, but that wasn't enough for everybody. When he got older and started going to the homes of his classmates there was always somebody who would ask, "Professor of what?" or "Professor where?" and he had to say, "Professor at the Collège de France" [the "highest" of French scientific and literary university institutions, whose members engage in research, give (few) free lectures open to the public, and publish]. Then people would look suspicious and ask if that were a religious institution of some sort and he suddenly felt like a complete idiot as he tried to stammer out a convincing reply.

Everything in the big apartment in Paris was both absolutely familiar and at the same time strange to him. His parents had moved there after their last trip to the Far East, the year he was born. It was a little as if they had temporarily berthed a ship full of the things that had made up the largest part of his father's life and nobody had bothered to unload the whole cargo because it was awaiting orders to set sail again. But then there had been no more voyages. The family silver gleamed in the shadows next to blue-tinted Chinese vases, pale celadon, kakemonos. The entrance hall was huge and dark because the light that came in through a skylight was blocked by two Chinese umbrellas hanging upside down; when his brother was younger, it had been an ideal place for showing Kodak silent films to their friends at birthday parties; to make a screen, all they had to do was hang a sheet over the Piranesi on the back wall. The closets were crammed with fantastic draperies for fancy dress, terra-cotta objects wrapped in faded tissue paper, and startlingly new-looking Japanese dolls that lay forgotten in their boxes.

His father worked at night, perpetuating the peculiar routine he had adopted in the heat of Tonkin and Annam. Sometimes when Cat was getting up for school he would meet his father on his way to bed after sitting up all night. He worked in a library, its walls lined with bookshelves overflowing with European, Chinese, and Japanese writings, the oriental ones consisting of separate sheets of paper tied with silk cords or held together by wooden boards. To the children, the library was an unfathomable space, its boundaries as invisible as those of an underground cavern, because they had to move very carefully, picking their way along a precarious path that wound among stacks of books, papers, scrolls, small pedestal tables, open crates of camphorwood stuffed with documents, until they reached the desk, similarly littered with papers but also jars full of extremely fine calligraphy brushes with slender bamboo handles, inkwells with crackled dry black bottoms, ivory figurines. When he was about five, Cat had organized quite a comfortable lair for himself beneath the enormous desk with its countless drawers, and there he would crouch, silent, listening to the faint rustlings of his father working, completely oblivious to his son's presence; Cat was happy then.

He has understood that what his father is studying, with endless patience, is the history of ancient civilizations. But how can one capture those far-off times and the men who fashioned them without meticulously following the traces they left? And before one can understand the working of some ancient swing plow or astronomical telescope one also needs, of course, to know all about modern European techniques of crop rotation and plowing and about the methods of celestial observation and calculation employed by different societies in the past and also in the present. Just as, in order to follow the slow mutations of language and expression in ideograms, the twists and turns and metamorphoses of words, one must go behind the surface decoys and disguises to find, still alive in the dialects of mountaineers living in oblivion high above the deep forests, a language that is three thousand years old. And so he edges forward, holding all the threads he has so carefully tied, accumulating signposts, one by one, to consign to books that are still far from finished, with never a thought for the passing years.

Cat can remember one winter when his mother spent her days in the linen room, ironing a great pile of precious papers, crumpled, torn, and spotted, sometimes only microscopic fragments. They were archives which a wealthy Englishman on an expedition to the heart of central Asia had unearthed by some miracle in a Tibetan monastery-caravanserai. They were a priceless find, more than ten centuries old; once they had been pieced together, like a jigsaw puzzle, they would enable people to reconstruct a chronicle of the entire material and spiritual life of a Buddhist convent over a vast period of time. It would seem, however, that a few hundred years back there had been a definite falling off in the monks' spirituality, for the noble Englishman' had discovered the papers, much soiled, in a "facility" that bore no relationship to a library, although, fortunately, it had not been in use for some time. After ironing and many years of effort, the decoding of the faded ideograms had led to the publication of huge tomes bound in red, with titles inscribed in gold letters.

Cat never doubted that the ship was only temporarily in port here in this rather dreary Paris street, or that it would one day put out to sea again; any more than he doubted that he would be on board it when it left. If he had not yet traveled the banyan-shaded road from Siem Reap to Angkor, past the tame elephants that carry whole trees in their trunks, it was only because the story had taken a wrong turning, a momentary breakdown. But soon it would resume its natural course. Cat would sail away as his father had done. He would find the elephants and maybe climb on the back of one of them, and it would be none other than the scholarly and accomplished Bahadur Shah, baggage elephant No. 174 on the Indian Register, the very elephant from which Kipling claimed to have heard his finest tales. Anyhow, Cambodia would wait until he got there: it was the quietest country in the world, its people the mildest and most peaceable; nothing ever happened there, or ever would, other than the slow passing of days spent laboring in the fields beneath the drowsy gaze of domestic divinities.

One mustn't judge by the apparent inertia of this place and the things in it, the air of resigned tranquillity of the apartment half slumbering in the gloom. He knew that once a ship has raised anchor, once it has steamed a few miles out to sea, its space is transformed and bursts apart, light pours in everywhere, hallways become promenade decks, everything that was cramped and shriveled expands, opens up to infinity between sea and sky. He knew every stage of the way by heart, from stories and family photographs: Port Said, Djibouti, Bombay, Colombo, Singapore, and, at last, Saigon, on the yellow waters of the Mekong between corridors of mangroves.

It was also when he was about five or six that his brother had come in one time to kiss him good night—he was waiting in bed with his eyes open, watching obscure shapes bathed in the dim glow of the streetlight filtering through slatted shutters—and told him that he had just returned from a flight in an airplane. There was a landing strip on the roof, on top of the eighth floor, and he had climbed in and sat beside the pilot and flown over Paris, after strapping on a small parachute in case of emergency. Cat asked if the plane was still there and begged his brother to take him too. His brother had hidden him in a blanket and carried him on his shoulders, gliding stealthily down the corridors; just as he was opening the door to the outside world, the lighted landing, they were intercepted by their mother, who, as they said in the family, screamed herself "horse" and categorically forbade them to go playing Peter Pan. The end of the journey his brother had in mind was actually not so remote. Their grandmother lived on the floor above. All one had to do was climb a flight of stairs and one was on a different continent, inhabited by a very tiny, very formidable, and very old lady who ruled over the even more labyrinthine world of her Egyptian memories with all the aplomb of a person who has never forgotten that her maiden name had no fewer than three particles in it and that the work of her deceased husband—who was "in the encyclopedia"—had earned her the title of Lady, and of Sir for himself, although it was probably the children who got the most enjoyment out of the fact. They often called her Lady Ponte-Serra, with at least as much respect as mockery. She herself seldom used the title, her fierce Germanophobia extending even to perfidious Albion, about which she entertained definite reservations dating from the days when, in Cairo, she had offered hospitality and commiseration to Captain Marchand after his retreat from Fashoda and put Lord Kitchener (*of Khartoum*) in his place, in her salon, with one of those crushing historical utterances she was so proud to repeat, especially as she had had fifty years in which to polish it. . . .

❧

They reach Port-Royal, still in the rain. This is a visit they have often made before. It is not necessary to repeat what Cat tries to get his father to explain to him about that complicated business of the Jansenists and the wrath of Louis XIV. The fact is that he is more intrigued by the personal collection of the custodian of the ruins, who shows them around his home while his wife makes them a cup of black tea. Out of what? Certainly not real tea, in these days of rationing and shortages: carrot tops are said to make an excellent substitute. The custodian collects uniforms and weapons, sabers, cuirasses, and plumed helmets. His specialty is the Siege of Paris. He has some posters from the Commune of 1871 listing the prices of cat and rat meat. This is where Cat first hears of the Commune, which is not mentioned in his history textbook, the textbook used in every high school in France, the *Mallet*. (Because the Vichy government decreed in 1940 that the *Mallet et Isaac* in which three generations of French youth had learned their history would henceforth be called simply *Mallet*, for the same reason that Heine has ceased to be a German poet. Who cares if Mallet died in 1915 and never had time to write anything, and it was only out of loyalty to the memory of his dead friend that for twenty years Jules Isaac, who wrote every volume in the series single-handed, always signed both names to them?) He reads a poster dated May 22, 1871, but can't see what it was doing nailed up on the walls of Paris:

COMMUNE OF PARIS:
*All good citizens, arise! Man the barricades!*
*The enemy is within our walls!*
*Forward, for Republic, for Commune and for Liberty!*
THE COMMITTEE OF PUBLIC SAFETY

"Was that at the end of the Siege of Paris?"

"No. Later."

"When the Germans entered Paris?"

"No. The Versaillais."

"Versaillais? French? Then were they the enemy?"

"Yes."

His father spends a long time in conversation with the custodian, who is talking about how hard the winters are because the climate is so damp at this end of the valley. His father always listens so patiently. There is no point in knowing how to look at *things* if one does not pay attention to people too. Ever since he started coming on walks Cat has known that his father would always spend a long time talking, never raising his voice—and often speaking so quietly that he had to listen hard to follow him—that he would ask people questions about particular things that interested them both, and never tire of listening to their answers. And every time they come back to a place the people greet them like old friends as soon as they recognize him; up here they give him bitter tea, in the south it's mulled wine. What does a person have to do to be so naturally at ease with other people?

The tarnished arms and uniforms add a few glints of brightness to the dark, damp house. They start home again, still in the icy rain and dying light. Cat proclaims his admiration for the caretaker's collection. His father tells him, kindly but firmly, that he's a nitwit.

❖

The German soldiers are leaving. The sun is shining and they are being moved on to the west. They have painstakingly filled in the latrines and removed the straw and planks and swept the floor indoors. Cat picks up the one remaining trace of their passage in a corner of the ruined drawing room, three pictures, in color, of amazing naked ladies, blond-haired and pink-skinned, with breasts that stick straight out and carefully blurred crotches, by which he is keenly disappointed—not a single new detail.

Lolling in the courtyard with their jackets open in the hot summer morning, the soldiers wait for their trucks. The little lieutenant, the one who has the iron cross and ribbon from the Russian front, asks to see Cat's father.

He bows very politely and explains to *Herr Professor* in German that he and his men want to thank him at the end of their stay and that he doesn't want to leave without saying *au revoir.*

*"Und ich möchte Ihnen auf Wiedersehen sagen."*

*"Nein,"* his father says, smiling. *"Nein. Nicht auf Wiedersehen, bitte."*

The lieutenant says he doesn't understand.

"How do you say *adieu* in German?" his father asks. *"Zu Gott?* No. I think it's *Lebewohl."*

Not *au revoir. Adieu:* goodbye forever. Cat watches the lieutenant, who just stands there; once more, in a lower voice, he says he doesn't understand, no, he doesn't understand, and then suddenly he looks much less young than before, very tired and very sad.

His father looks tired and sad too, in spite of the smile that is still frozen on his face.

That evening his parents also leave, for Paris. Cat doesn't tell his father either *au revoir* or *adieu.* He's out in the woods picking up used Mauser cartridges. He puts five of them together in a clip, piles up several clips, and blows on them as though they were panpipes; it produces a very pretty music, for a more exotic type of tune. He thinks of the end of the little girl's dream in the *Nutcracker,* when the wicked stepfather Drosselmayer, sitting astride the clock, squeaks out:

> *Perpendicula*
> *Has purred, has roared;*
> *Face out and about,*
> *O shining horde!*

Whereupon all the lead soldiers and gingerbread hussars who were fighting the troops of the Queen of the Mice hop smartly into their boxes and quiet descends.

# "Fábrica Española de Armas Automáticas"

Cat receives a letter from his cousin Gabriel, who is a prisoner in Germany. It is written in indelible blue pencil on small pieces of squared paper. It reached Paris by some obscure route—Switzerland? In Paris, his mother gave it to somebody who was coming to Marles.

*Lieutenant Gabriel Delage*
*Oflag 48 X 13, April 2, 1944*

Dear old Cat,
    I suppose it's eons since they stopped calling you that. But as I myself am immobilized I pretend that time has been immobilized with me. It's hard for me to imagine the solemn young man you must have become by now.

Gabriel says he's bored. This opportunity to write without being censored is unique and won't come again, so he's taking advantage of it to send letters to the whole family. He says everything a person can say in a letter like that, about how he hopes Cat is getting good grades and that food supplies in Paris have improved, what he has to eat where he is, and the cold, and the time that won't pass; and his three failed escape attempts, adding details to make Cat laugh. He says he dreams a lot and has two great longings: the moment he is liberated he will go sit on the terrace of a café on the boulevards and order *café au lait* and croissants; and then he will take the first train to Toulon, run all the way to his grandparents' place at La Valerane, and sit down at the old Steinway piano and play and play, facing the sea. It's a long letter.

A long letter, ending with a passage that Cat finds somewhat cryptic.

> I have written to Antoine. I tried to tell him a couple of things. But I know him, he'll follow his head, his blasted headstrong head. He is so intelligent, he understands so quickly, he thinks he's so strong. I worry. I've got plenty of time to worry here, and imagine all kinds of things. And convince myself that they're true.
>
> Tell Antoine this: you have to take your time if you want get the best of Aunt Nina. Aunt Nina and her friends are a trial to the whole family, but you have to be patient. Wait until the family is together again, and then we can shut her up for good. Yes, for good. Alone, he won't be able to make things happen any faster.
>
> He won't listen to me. You'll ask him questions and he'll have to answer whether he likes it or not. Maybe that will make him think a little. I know you both, you can't have changed. You and your eternal "why, why," and him always wanting to explain everything to you.
>
> It was very cold this morning. There was ice in the water jug again. It snowed until the end of March. I have been reading an old book by Kipling I found, in German, *Just So Stories*. The story of the Cat-That-Walks-by-Itself. It made me think of you.

Aunt Nina is an old acquaintance. Legend has it that an aunt of that name, and indisputably Teutonic, actually existed in the family once. But her rebirth occurred spontaneously in the summer of 1940, in letters written by various members of the family, without anybody ever needing to explain. Those were the days when the so-called family cards were introduced, the only and hence compulsory means of communication between occupied and unoccupied zones. A series of model statements were printed on the cards, to be crossed out or completed in the tiny spaces left blank. Aunt Nina automatically found her place here. At first she was simply a little liverish, then she became unbearable, then downright sick, and sometimes, in moments of elation, she was almost at death's door. By that time the character had put on flesh and blood. Cat could see her; she was straight out of some illustration by Hansi, with her greenish suit hanging down to her big square-toed sensible shoes, her crabby weasel face and her chignon stuck like a turd on the top of her skull.

The letter from Gabriel makes Cat happy. The last time he saw him was in the spring of 1940. Gabriel was a lieutenant in the Moroccan infantry. Quartered on the Luxembourg border, he crossed the whole of France to spend a two-day furlough at La Valerane. The memory of those two days was like the memory of a hurricane. Gabriel was an excellent pianist and he sat down at the Steinway concert grand to make up for a wasted winter. Like a madman on a rampage, he sight-read nearly twenty Beethoven sonatas at one go. Nobody had been able to stand it. Cat's mother had gone up and shut herself into her bedroom—they thought she put a pillow over her head in order not to hear any more. His father fled to the farthest corner of the vast edifice, but even there, he said later, he was unable to put two thoughts together. The grandparents emigrated to the greenhouse to tend their cactuses. Nobody had been able to stand it, except Cat and his brother: at the end of every sonata Antoine demanded another one, and between the movements he talked and talked. Cat said nothing; he turned the pages.

Before Gabriel left, Antoine challenged him to swim across the bay to Battery Point and back. Gabriel didn't take up the challenge, so Antoine went alone. The sea is coldest in spring. That day the mistral was blowing, which means that the sun is shining fiercely in a crystal-clear sky, but there is no warmth; the sea was Prussian blue and the waves short, choppy, and hostile. Antoine waded out onto the beach almost two hours later, exulting and frozen. They had a very hard time following him in the heavy flat-bottomed rowboat they called a "beast." There were blue blotches all over Antoine's skin, he was shivering so hard that it took two of them to rub him down. They gave him rum to drink. Gabriel admired Antoine.

Later, Cat learned that Gabriel had been wounded in the fighting around Lille. He was leaving the town after ten days of house-to-house grenade fighting, and found himself in open country facing a tank that stared at him with a malevolent eye. He threw himself into a ditch, but his behind stuck up and got deeply furrowed; he was captured, helpless and drunk with rage (and whiskey—his company had never abandoned the barrel they had picked up in the cellars of some English staff officers' quarters). Once he had recovered and was sitting in his German prisoner-of-war camp, he received a copy of a flattering citation awarding him the Military Cross. Later, because of his three escape attempts, he was sent to a special *Oflag* in East Prussia. An *Oflag* for "recalcitrants."

As for the philosophy, the ideas he asks Cat to discuss with Antoine, Cat can't really see himself discoursing on them, talking clearly about things that aren't clear to himself. Ordinarily, it's his brother who helps him find out the meaning of things. Antoine himself never seems to doubt that everything has a meaning, if you just take the trouble to look for it.

⊞

What can one do on a filthy gray afternoon, when a curtain of rain keeps one from going out to cut grass and the guinea pigs are squeaking miserably in their hutches? What can one do when one is sitting in front of a deck of cards that has been broken up and scattered all over the house by those lousy brats, except build card houses that topple with the first false move? Cat is left-handed; at home and at school they have badgered and bullied him into using his right hand for the things that count in life: writing and holding a knife. But all the gestures that come naturally to him start from his left hand. He often hesitates, his hands stutter. The scaffolding of his card houses cannot stand up long against his stammering fingers.

So that afternoon, after many tries, he has finally reached a fourth, steeply inclined level, when the door bangs open. His brother bursts into the dining room shouting, "Stick 'em up!"

The cards collapse. Antoine is holding a gun.

"Is it real?" asks Cat.

"Look." He holds it out.

"Not here," says Cat. "Can't you hear them in the kitchen?"

Up in their room, his brother shows him the gun—dull, black. He removes the magazine and gives it to him. Cat reads the engraving on the side: *"Fábrica española de armas automáticas. Calibre 9 mm."*

"It's no more complicated than your popgun. Take hold of it properly. No, the right hand, not the left. You remove the safety catch with your thumb. You cock it by pulling back the hammer there, the whole top, see, it slides. Then you hold your arm out and aim, moving down slowly and squeezing the trigger very, very gently. Because when the shot is fired your gun kicks and the recoil sends the bullet upward. You must always squeeze gently, gently . . ."

(That's a lesson one doesn't forget. Cat will remember. Years and years later, in the Caribbean, it will be his brother's voice he hears behind that of the instructor in olive-drab fatigues: *"Suave! Suave! Hay que apretar el gatillo hasta que el golpe te sorprenda.* Gently, gently! You must hold the trigger until the shot takes you by surprise.")

His brother slides the bullets out of the magazine, the rounded cylinders roll on the bed like big shiny marbles.

"Nine millimeters is a good size because it stops your adversary in his tracks. Even if he's only hit in the hand or arm the impact is enough to knock him down. With a smaller caliber you've got to shoot closer and be sure you kill with the first round. A Kraut with a 6.35 in him can keep coming . . ."

Cat follows his instructions. He performs the gesture of aiming, carefully, through the window, aligning the sights along the little door under the lindens as though an enemy silhouette were about to be framed in it. With his left hand.

"After dinner I have to go on a little expedition."

"Can I come?" Cat asks.

"Yes. If your bike's working."

In June it was announced that there would be no competitive entrance examination for the Ecole Normale Supérieure that year. In May, as in 1943, the Ministry of Labor had decided, allegedly for the purposes of the "rural civilian service," to take a census of all young people eighteen and over, so that anyone not employed in an occupation that was vital to the country's economy could be requisitioned, which meant they would be sent to the work camps in Germany. University students were becoming as scarce as hen's teeth. They were all looking for safe jobs or hiding places. A few opted for the maquis or got false identity papers and went underground.

After a near-miss the year before, Cat's brother had crammed hard for the exam and this time he was almost sure to get in; so suddenly he found himself at loose ends and completely free for the work he considered more urgent anyway. Since coming to Paris at the beginning of 1943 he had been up to his neck in the militant underground, of which he had already had a taste in the south. He had been involved in the organization of the student National Front and the formation of groups of Communist guerrillas and partisans from among its members. They started with impromptu demonstrations in secondary schools and universities, then in the streets during the rush hour; they set up protection groups for demonstrations; they sent out commando units against the duty officers of the LVF [Légion des Volontaires Français—volunteer troops for the Russian front], militia, or *Propagandastaffel;* and finally, they divided the groups into "triangles" and armed them. The watchword had gone out even before the Allied landing: "Unite, arm, and fight in cities and villages, factory hand and boss, farm laborer and estate owner, priest and schoolteacher, against looting and killing, and for the freedom of France." "Unite"—that meant difficult and dangerous contacts, meetings of officials from different organizations that were sometimes asphyxiated by the verbosity of their newest members and often rang with exasperation at the prevailing indecisiveness. And "arm"—that meant odd bits and pieces of fifth-hand sabotage equipment, explosive gelatin, detonators, parachute drops abandoned by the tide. A few symbolic, virtually mythical guns lie hidden in the homes of unsuspecting great-aunts, inherited from former groups that have been decimated by clampdowns in previous years. The only way to get arms is to take them from the enemy. The first attacks on German officers are not intended to kill; working in pairs, the assailants simply knock out the weapon bearer when he's far enough from help and remove his gun. Only afterward, when they're armed themselves, will they actually be able to kill anybody. Antoine makes no attempt to control his gnawing impatience; history is vacillating, he wants to tip it in the right direction—because there has to be a right direction. Now is the time, in any event, to make oneself believe there is.

✠

This night's expedition should not entail any real danger. The object is to break into two town halls in villages fairly close by, Senlisse and Choisel, and make off with all the food stamps for the last six months of 1944, which were delivered at the beginning of July but have not yet been issued to the population. The several hundred rations amassed by this means will then be distributed to underground militants in the towns and "recalcitrants" who have joined the maquis. As the villages are only two and a half miles apart, they may have the same town clerk, and he himself may have given them the tip.

Antoine, on all fours on the bedroom floor, is making his calculations using a map of the Paris region. He is meticulous and attentive. His eyes are very dark brown and nearsighted but always alert, his body is as square and close-knit as Cat's is lanky, but he is just as nervous as Cat, maybe more so, and, like Cat, he has a thick shock of black hair sticking out in uncontrollable spikes—donkey manes, their barber says. And he has that inexhaustible energy, curiosity, enthusiasm that have so often worn out Cat and many others.

"Counting the detours, it must be sixteen or eighteen miles. That's a lot for you."

"You and your detours; you always have to have everything better than perfect. This isn't some game we're playing."

"You can call it whatever you want. But we're not going through places where there are a lot of people and that's that; we have to keep away from Chevreuse and Dampierre. We'll start around nine-thirty, before curfew. On the way out, there's nothing much to worry about. We'll take our time. If everything works I'll finish Senlisse before midnight and we'll be back here by half past one in the morning."

"If everything works. And if it doesn't rain. And how are you going to get into the offices?"

"Look, we're fully equipped."

He pulls an assortment of objects out of his knapsack. First, a pair of long nickel-plated pliers, spotted with rust and curved at the end; they make Cat think of some weirdly shaped insect like a praying mantis, but also of a surgical instrument.

"That's a burglar's jimmy."

Cat has seen the word, in the adventures of Arsène Lupin. Next comes a wooden handle with a sort of immovable wheel on the end.

"A diamond."

"A real one?"

"No, you dope. It's for cutting glass."

"The glass will make a noise when it falls."

His brother shows him two small brownish sticks.

"No, it won't. Everything's been taken care of. Look at this."

Cat leans over, touches, sniffs. The substance is not rigid and has a sweetish smell.

"Explosive gel?"

"No, silly. That comes in cakes of a becoming shade of green and smells like almonds. This is chewing gum. It's American."

Like everybody else, Luc knows what chewing gum is, of course, and he knows that Americans are crazy about it and chew it nonstop from cradle to grave. But also like everybody else, he's never actually seen any before.

"Can I taste?"

"No. Not for greedy children. When you chew it, it sticks to anything. I stick it to the glass before I cut and detach the cut glass without a sound."

Last comes a heavy hammer, flat on both ends.

"Is that for braining Krauts?"

"Not necessarily. But it might come in handy."

"Yeah, but," says Cat. "You *could* kill a Kraut with that."

"Yes," says his brother.

They leave quietly after dinner, their stomachs full of chard and boiled turnips. The refugees have gone up to their rooms, the whole house is still and dark because the electricity has been cut; and the fire is going out in the kitchen. It's a warm night. Cat has pumped up the tires on his Mammoth, the aptly named bicycle with the pre- historic gait. Mammoth's greatest weakness is her brakes. Her front brake is unreliable and the cork blocks on the rear one have a regret- table tendency to jump out of their lugs when any real pressure is applied—whenever one really needs to slow down, in fact. In that case, one can always brake with one's feet, but that's where the gym- nastics begin, because Mammoth is such a huge bicycle that even with her seat lowered as far as it will go Cat's toes barely touch the ground. Needless to say, he is possessively, passionately, attached to her.

They each have a knapsack. Cat's is a shapeless lump with a grease spot in one corner that must date from the far-off days when they used to go on picnics around Ramatuelle and the Paillasse mills, carrying ham sandwiches on buttered bread. He has fastened it to his carrier with hemp cords, rejects from the reaper-binder. His brother has a flat flashlight with a dying battery in his pocket. They pedal in pitch-darkness: they don't use their bike lamps, the moon gives off very little light and there is none at all coming from the houses they pass. But until they get beyond Saint-Lambert, Cat knows the way almost by heart, even the potholes and places where the tank treads have torn up the asphalt. Now and then a shushing sound tells him he is going through a trail of fresh cow pies. He has to concen- trate all his attention on keeping out of the way of his brother's wheels, which turn with a regular creak; his bike is almost new and is named Bucephalus. They've often hiked and biked on darker nights than this. They ride through a variety of smells, made sharper by the rain, but the main one, carried up by the fog, is of freshly mown meadows and fermenting hay that wasn't brought in before the rain. This is his chance to prove that cats can see as well by night.

After Saint-Lambert they turn left onto the main road that leads up a long rise onto the plateau. Cat huffs and puffs and manages to keep up, standing on his pedals. They go down the "seventeen turns" and then, lost among the trees in total darkness, they can no longer see the edge of the road and have to finish the downgrade on foot. They turn onto the main Cernay road that runs along the wall of the château grounds, then down a narrow side road that takes them into Choisel. They can sense the outlines of dead houses, a narrow street, then open space: a square, the church, and, off to the side behind a low wall, the town hall, a shabby two-story block. They ease their bikes behind the church, groping along the cemetery wall.

"You wait here. If anybody comes, throw a pebble at the left-hand window, that's the secretary's office. Then hide, you and the bikes, and don't move."

His brother slips away with his knapsack, over the wall and around to the back. Darkness and silence. The village is sound asleep. A submarine village. Wait; just wait, trying to breathe naturally.

Five minutes later he's back.

"Got them. Let's go."

It's two and a half miles from Choisel to Senlisse. They have to go back up on the plateau and then glide down a long winding slope toward another valley. The road is full of holes, stones spurt away under their wheels, and Mammoth is making a horrible clanking noise. They stop short when they first sense the outlines of houses, suddenly very close in the night. Brakes squeal against the rims of Bucephalus' tires. More stones clatter. Now we've done it, thinks Cat, dozens of people must have heard us. Any second now a light will flash out and unmask them, something will happen.

At the entrance to the village a path gapes between high walls, houses or garden walls. His brother straddles the ground on either side of his bike and Cat edges closer to his shadow.

"I'm not sure. I thought the town hall was here."

Cat swallows his pride. "Maybe we've done enough?"

"Be quiet. It's got to be down at the end."

They continue along the slope, pushing their bikes as quietly as they can. The sky clears and the moon gives a little more light. Cat sees a projection on the right, at the end of a wall.

"The letter box."

The town hall is behind it. They go through the same gestures as before. They hide their bikes behind the hedge opposite, below the road. His brother takes Cat's empty knapsack and gives him his own, stuffed with the first consignment, which Cat gropingly ties onto Mammoth's carrier, using an assortment of unorthodox knots. Alone again, waiting again. He shivers in his old jacket and short pants. A familiar complaint, an old acquaintance, grips his guts and bends him double.

His brother comes back. They get on their bikes for the ride home, along a road that has become a little easier to make out in the moonlight. They start up the long rise. Is the whole country dead tonight? When they get back on the Chevreuse highway they try to speed up but the night darkens again—rain. Soon it's running off his hair, down his nose, eyes, neck, under his jacket. It mixes with his sweat. He tries to lick it off his upper lip; it's salty.

They coast down a hill toward the bottom of a ravine in what looks like a straight line. Cat has lost sight of his brother and pedals to catch up. His wheel collides with the wheel of Bucephalus and they fall off, on opposite sides of the road, legs and bikes tangled together; they swear and burst out laughing. Getting up, Cat feels something like a mattress of paper beneath his feet.

"My knapsack's come open."

His brother crawls over and snaps the flashlight on for a second.

"The stamps."

They begin picking up the sheets of stamps, already wet, in handfuls, and stuffing them into the knapsack.

"Look out," says Cat, who has just put his hand on something cold and sticky. "It's full of shit."

The stamps have fallen into a cow pie.

He looks up and sees lights moving at the top of the hill they have just come down.

"Germans," says his brother. "Grab your bike. Into the trees. Never mind the stamps."

They drag their way across the ditch toward the nearby bushes, pushing and shoving frantically to force their bikes through the snagging branches and brambles, and collapse onto the soaking ground. Cat catches his breath and tries to wipe the mess off his hand in the wet grass.

Five lights, coming closer, the swish of tires on the road surface, the faint hum of generators rubbing against the tires, voices in conversation. They pass, a few yards away. In the beams of the Germans' bike lamps, Cat sees helmeted shadows, voluminous coats, guns slung across chests. The last one stops and flashes his light over the splotch of paper on the ground.

"He's seen them," his brother whispers. Cat hears him grope inside his knapsack—a soft metallic clinking.

"*Hep: Moment!*" the soldier shouts to the others, who are riding on. They come back. They pick up the sheets of stamps. They peer at them and argue. The brothers can't catch what they're saying.

One speaks louder. They hear him, very plainly: "*Lassen Sie das. Was wollen Sie tun?*"

And they understand that he is expressing everything a man can feel when he finds himself alone in the middle of the night in a cold rain in a foreign country and is sick to death of the whole thing. "*Gehen wir! Gehen wir!*"

They ride away, still talking, with animation, anger, and weariness . . .

Cat is frozen. Bemused, he recites a nursery rhyme from his not very far-off childhood, one they still sing in the streets of Hyères:

> *Once there was a parakeet*
> *Had a colic in his seat.*
> *Every time he let a fart*
> *Gave off a smell of camel meat.*
> *Oh yes, Mama, she had a coronet-a.*
> *Oh yes, Papa, he had a pistol neat.*

Right now, the one with the colic is Cat. He gives his brother a dig with his elbow. To show he's not scared.

"Did you use up all the chewing gum?"

His brother feels around in the knapsack and holds out a stick. "Careful, you're not supposed to swallow it."

"Listen, what would we have done if they'd seen us?"

"Don't drivel. Now we get moving again, but in the opposite direction."

Chewing his gum, he thinks bitterly that in about one more minute his brother is going to start calling him a nitwit. He stays where he is, lying on his stomach with his arms and legs spread wide apart and one cheek on the soggy ground; he would like to let himself soak into the dripping night forever. He lies absolutely still.

He feels a hand gently stroking his sopping hair, and he whimpers, "I want to stay here. I can't go any farther. You still love me, though, don't you?"

His brother laughs. "We've got to get going right away. At the top of the hill we'll turn left toward Dampierre."

The hill is steep and slippery. The new road is full of puddles he can't see; it goes along the boundary walls of farms, then between tall trees along the château grounds, even blacker than the open countryside. The wind is icy. Cat's stomach hurts, he hurts all over. They're just coming out of the woods when the noise of Cat's bike becomes really terrifying; it lurches and skids, and every jerk goes straight through him.

"That's done it; I've got a flat."

His brother turns back. "Hush. There are houses."

They creep under a wall with an overhang. A gutter gurgles, they're out of the rain. Cat unties his knapsack and tries to pump up Mammoth's tire, heaving at the pump he has screwed on wrong in the dark; then he gives up and turns the bike over, wheels up. He feels his way around the tire. His brother flashes the light on for a second or two. He takes out the tool kit behind the seat and tries to unscrew the two wing nuts on the front tire. He forces his numb fingers but can't loosen the nuts; then, losing his temper, he aims a fierce kick at the huge bike and sends it crashing against the wall with a dying wheeze.

"Go to hell, you dumb thing!"

"Calm down. I'll do it."

They hear the sound of a key turning in a lock; a weak beam of light shines out in the wall a yard away from them.

"Who's there?" a man asks in a low voice. A lantern moves into the open doorway.

"Who's there?" the voice says again.

The lantern advances toward them.

"What are you doing there?"

"You can see, sir," says his brother very politely, standing up. "You can see, it's a flat tire."

The lantern swings back and forth in front of their faces.

"But curfew was long ago. It's after one o'clock. And in this weather."

"We're on our way back from our uncle's. In Cernay."

The lantern keeps swinging.

"Oh, yes. Well, you'd better come in. You're wet as a bowl of soup."

"We have to fix my little brother's bike. They're waiting for us."

"Oh, yes," the man says again, in an odd tone of voice. "Well, then, bring your bikes along this way. You'll be better off out of the rain. Follow me."

They are indoors, their feet squelching on the tile floor. An oil lamp is lit. They're in a sort of workshop, with a bench, tools hanging on the wall, and potted plants in front of a long row of glass panes covered by a thick curtain. The man blows out his lantern. He's small and seems old to them. He is bald and his feet shuffle in oversize slippers.

"Come and take a look at this!"

She is no bigger than he; she comes in tying the sash of a bathrobe.

"You certainly can pick up some strange articles along our road these days."

"You poor boys," says the woman, "if your parents could see you . . ."

"Ma'am," his brother begins, with all the dignity he can muster, "please forgive us for disturbing you. We've had a flat tire . . ."

"Oh, yes," the man says. "And they're on their way back from Cernay. From their uncle's."

He watches them as they put down their knapsacks. When his brother's hits the tile floor it sounds like the inside of a hardware store.

"Well, you're not carrying potatoes in there, anyway . . . Only thing," he goes on, "only thing is, this little fellow is shivering with the cold. And the German patrol went by not twenty minutes ago."

"We saw them," Cat says. "We saw them and we hid . . ."

His brother gives him a fierce kick in the shins.

"You poor boys. You poor boys," the woman keeps saying. "With this war going on. And on a night like this. You're too young."

"Around this time of night," the man says, "I don't sleep much. So I come out here and putter around fixing things. You were making enough noise for a herd of elephants. The whole countryside must have heard you. But that doesn't matter, they're all scared. Around here it's every man for himself. And the gendarmes haven't been out after nightfall in a long while. You're going to dry yourselves off. And we're going to fix that tire."

His wife comes back with a towel. "Rub yourselves hard. I've put some coffee on to boil. You'll wait here till day."

Just then, in the flickering light, he realizes that his brother, also shivering, is blue, as blue as the time he swam across the bay and back. Seated on old garden chairs, they drink bowlfuls of scorching-hot "national" coffee, with a peculiar sweet taste. The woman drinks with them, out of a smaller cup.

"I put honey in it," she says. "It's better than saccharin."

The man has removed the inner tube and found the hole; it's already clamped in the vise that is holding the patch in place until the glue dries.

"We think about our boy," the woman also says.

"We're not afraid to say it. He left for the Spanish frontier, two years ago."

"Have you heard anything from him?"

"We know he got there. One letter, from Switzerland. He was in Algeria. Since then . . ."

"Maybe he's in France by now."

"That's what we tell ourselves. But I don't know if we're right to hope it. A lot of damage being done around here. It doesn't look like they're getting much of anywhere. The Krauts are stuck in."

"Yes," his brother says, warming to the subject. "But the Russians are still advancing. And here in France things are starting to move. And after . . ."

"Never mind about that. I don't want to get mixed up in your affairs."

Cat, who was feeling the approach of the crucial moment, the flaming declaration in three periods with exordium and conclusion, is not unhappy to see his brother pulled up short with his mouth open. It's his turn to deliver a terrific kick under the table.

"You're safe here. Oh, we had plenty of trouble with them. Summonses and visits. Gendarmes in the house almost every week. But that's been over a long time now. The gendarmes came around again three days ago, but oh, they were so polite! All palsy-walsy. . . . But I've got nothing to do with all that." He shrugs and goes, slippers flapping, to feed the inner tube back into the tire.

"Take your bikes. I'll show you the shed. There's hay there, you'll be able to sleep. If you leave early, don't bother to wake us."

They find themselves alone in the darkness and up to their necks in scratchy dry hay.

"Whatever happens," Antoine says, "we'll have to come back and thank them after the liberation."

"What now?"

"Now we try to sleep until the sun comes up."

"My feet are cold."

Then, just before he slides into sleep, a thought comes to him. "Listen, you didn't tell me before. If they'd seen us, would you have clobbered them?"

"I don't know. You ask stupid questions."

"Yeah, but," Cat resumes, musing. "Yeah, but. Five is a lot."

("My brother," Antoine wrote in his notebook a few days later, "was clamorous and lyrical by turns.")

❖

By German time the sun rises late. It is after five when a rooster starts crowing just behind them.

"Back to your perch, garlic puss," growls Cat, who is shivering and trying to curl himself around his stomach. The bite in the hollow of his belly is gone.

"Make tracks," his brother says.

Out on the road, the curses of the night have melted away. The sky is swept clean, it's a beautiful summer morning. They pedal wildly to warm themselves up, and all the way down the long, winding descent to Saint-Lambert they sing nonstop, "Take care, / take care, / The white lady's caught you with her stare, / The white lady's heard your step." Outside the house, they pass René bringing the cows back from Champmercy.

"The Parisians are getting up early these days."

They slip silently up to their room and dump the contents of their knapsacks onto the floor. The sheets of stamps pile into a pyramid. They shove them under the dresser, his brother hides his gun under his mattress, and they sleep until noon.

Was Cat afraid?

Where does fear begin? The horrible void of the answer he didn't know at school, the absolute blank, alone in front of a class full of quizzical cynics, twisted his guts just as much, prickled in his veins the same way, paralyzed him even more totally than what he felt last night when that German soldier shined his light on the stamps lying on the ground and all he needed to do was raise the beam and point it into the bushes a few feet away. But then, he hadn't been alone. He can't ever be really afraid when he's with his brother. Maybe that dates back to the time when they spent several weeks alone together in Toulon while their mother was away. That was in 1941. Their father had just been let out of prison. Their mother had managed to get an *Ausweis,* a permit to cross the line of demarcation between occupied and unoccupied zones; she had applied for it months before, on a plea of ill health necessitating medical consultations in Paris. She had stayed there until the last minute, trying for an extension from the German authorities. Of course, there were friends who kept an eye on them. But when Cat fell ill and had those terrible bouts of fever—he would sit bolt upright in bed in the middle of the night, screaming with his eyes wide open, staring at shapeless nightmares that rose up out of the darkness, out of suddenly distended space—it was his brother who was there soothing him, holding a glass for him to drink, talking very softly, or just sitting with him, silent, reassuring, his mere presence driving away the dread and panic.

But what welds him to his brother even more than those weeks in Toulon is everything they experienced, did, built together at La Valerane on the coast, where their maternal grandparents live—Cat's true realm.

＊

A cataract of boulder and pine, red-earth terraces and stone stairs, orange trees, cactus, and palms, tumbling from the last summits of the Maures down to the sea.

Cat's grandparents met there just before 1900. One can imagine some peaceful afternoon, already hot in the late spring, the young lady seated among her family—a young lady with long chestnut-colored hair brocaded with golden glints and very blue eyes—the one whose parents asked Renoir to paint the portrait Cat likes so much because it also looks like his mother. In comes a tall young man, immensely tall and lanky, with short hair, wearing a badly cut blue uniform; he's not even twenty-five and he has just completed his internship and military service at the naval hospital at Hyères. He is gauche, timid, clumsy, and has great trouble making conversation, but when he sits down at the grand piano and places his huge hands on the keys the music pours out flawlessly, delicately, and everybody stops to listen. So they make a marriage of love, which, in those circles, is a sufficiently singular occurrence for Cat's grandmother still to be proclaiming it forty-five years later, as a defiance of every principle of her family, most of whose members continue to maintain that the practice of medicine may constitute a profession, albeit a highly unrewarding one, but could hardly be described as a "situation" in the world.

With the passing years the lanky young man has turned into a massive giant whom the Lilliputian Cat has looked upon since infancy as a benevolent mountain, shaken by rare but awesome tremors, that lets itself be climbed, all the way to its summit, where reign two extremely bright, extremely childlike eyes and two formidably prickly cheeks. He is a "chief," a professor, a renowned specialist, but throughout his career he has chosen to devote more of his time to hospital work in Paris than to the cultivation of a private clientele. No nook or cranny of what in his youth were still called the "natural" sciences is foreign to him, and in the early years of his marriage he liked to take his family on great month-long walking tours through the Alps, hiring a guide at Chamonix or Courmayeur and perching the girls, who were still almost babies, on the back of a mule. Then they would follow a zigag route through passes seven thousand feet high, rope themselves across glaciers, descend through the Italian valleys, and end with a visit to the primitives and Quattrocento painters in the little churches and great museums of northern Italy. His most conspicuous passions, however, were botany and entomology. This colossus never went anywhere without an assortment of fishing rods, butterfly nets, and flower presses slung over his shoulder, which, combined with the stacks of his wife's hatboxes, used to leave the passengers in railway waiting rooms gaping. Cat, standing on the station platform at Toulon, has been known to turn chicken and pretend his grandfather was a stranger he had never seen before.

"I'm going to show you how to set an insect trap," he would say to his grandson as they set off for a walk. And, like a trapper in the great American North, he would spread out the bits of a shredded mushroom in some magical way, returning the next day and extracting from his vast pockets the little tube containing a wad of cotton soaked in ether in which his catch would end its days. Everybody knew he was incapable of going through Nîmes—luckily this did not happen often—without making a special trip to the amphitheater to poke among the scorched slabs of the tiers for specimens of some very rare coleoptera, rather unprepossessing if the truth be told, that is found nowhere else.

Having settled permanently at La Valerane at the beginning of the war, he divided his energies among a profusion of seemingly haphazard activities. These included, firstly, the writing or revision of his medical textbooks. He was always late, and was happy to be at a distance—now augmented by the difficulty of communication between occupied and unoccupied zones—from his publisher, a mythical being endowed by him with every irrational and indeed ridiculous trait imaginable, whose alleged rapacity and business lust he stigmatized severely. "First cousin to a publisher," he growled when he caught one of his grandchildren committing some sin of avarice, dubious pilfering, or narrow-mindedness; or "I'm just going to call my publisher," he would sing out as he headed for the toilet. Cat's grandmother specialized in stories of publishers' receptions in Paris before the war, where a glance was enough to tell the publishers from their authors, by the florid countenances of the former and the undernourished pallor of the latter. The rest of his time was employed mainly in inspecting his domain, every corner of which he had filled with an endless variety of plantings: there was a special garden for aloes and agaves, an enormous rock garden climbing up the hillside, with slopes reserved for myriad different forms of cactus—nopals, tall hairy cereus, prickly pear; there was a large tract sloping gently to the south for big tropical trees; there were terraces for mimosas, several hundred species of which exist, and which can be crossed with eucalyptus to produce an infinite variety of hybrids; and other terraces for his vines and orange groves. His great disappointment was his inability to bring his grapefruit to maturity, a feat which Dr. Fournier, master of the Island of Porquerolles, had accomplished quite successfully only a few miles out to sea.

Down by the shore, above the pier eroded by the waves that rhythmically invaded the otherwise eternally empty beach, stood a little building which was used as a boathouse and place to store fishing tackle, surmounted by a red brick terrace baking in the sun; onto it gave a little chamber known as the "laboratory." Its door was never locked, because strangers seldom ventured into this out-of-the-way place. From the window one could see all the way to the Hyères Islands, on the line between sea and sky. Inside were innumerable jars, in which the more curious of the specimens regularly presented to the professor by fishermen floated in cloudy solutions of formaldehyde: weird creatures from tropical seas that had strayed into the Formiguette deeps, flying fish, moonfish, sawfish, and catfish, oversized sea horses or simple spotted dogfish and moray eels. And on a table lay the carcass of a giant turtle that may have come all the way from the Galápagos to wash ashore here on the beach. Neatly arranged around the monumental shell were its four clawed legs and the head with the dry, hard, smooth scales that Cat liked to hold in his hand.

Cat had stayed there for long periods ever since he was a baby and, after the autumn of 1940, when his mother took him and his brother to live in Toulon, spent all his vacations there and even part of the winter of 1941, when pleurisy put an end to school for him that year. This countryside had become his own, everywhere else he only passed through; this was his home base, the rest was exile. He spent the three summer months of 1941 barefoot there—out of necessity, not choice, because his one and only pair of cardboard sandals had split for good and he had to wait for the autumn ration to get a pair of wooden-soled shoes—and running over the burning earth and rocks from dawn to dusk had turned the skin on his feet to horn.

There was little to eat in those days, almost no meat at all, or milk, or fats, and no potatoes except the few pounds picked by the boys. In season, on the other hand, there were tomatoes and Swiss chard, both stalks and leaves of which can be cooked, and fennel, celery, cardoons, artichokes and their bitter stems; but they all become tedious when they are eternally served boiled. Just as the yellow-centered red arbutus berries and the pink and purple Barbary figs, picked at great risk to life and limb, are sweet but insipid. In the winter the huge house was unheatable and they had to huddle around the fireplace in the shelter of its vast canopy adorned with pewter jars and old Flemish mugs. In the winter of 1941 snow fell on the saddles between the hills; then, one day, it came right down to the shore, to the fringe of waves, where it lay and piled up for a few hours before melting. That was a winter of calamity and famine. In a single night many of the eucalyptus and orange trees froze, in one great dry blaze.

It was wild country, and sparsely populated; everybody knew everybody for five miles around and the names of many of the places were those of people who had lived there. The little patch of red-earth lowland open to the sea and surrounded by the dark peaks of the Maures was held almost entirely by a single owner, a domain of vines, fields of flowers, sheepfolds, and olive trees. The narrow road and the tracks of the little train swerved along the seafront, and over the years people had come down from the mountains to settle alongside them, but in those days that meant no more than a dozen houses in all, plus a hotel kept by a Swiss, a combined café–grocery shop that had been opened by a man from Normandy, the railway station, the school, and five or six more or less eccentric villas, one of which, built to look like a mosque, was marked on all naval maps. At the end of the autumn the little train brought transhumant flocks of sheep and sealed beehives back down from Digne and Forcalquier.

But it was also a country of paths that led nowhere, tracks that set out confidently and clambered up the mountainside only to disappear into an inextricable scrub, all tooth and claw against bare legs, or lose themselves on bald rocks strewn with empty tortoise shells and raveled snakeskins. At junctions one came across secret signs that could not be interpreted, the dried, golden pellets of rabbits that were sometimes hard to tell from garnets in their matrix, or a solitary print of a wild boar in the sparkling clay, or long chains of fat, busy ants crossing the path on their way from one anthill to another, one metropolis to another. To go up to the hidden dwellings in the mountains one had to know the way, among paths that were traveled only on foot or by donkey. The poor farms up there were kept by kindly, unsophisticated people whose names were more Italian than Provençal. When the railroad came at the turn of the century much of the land—terraced patches of raw rock—had been abandoned by the families that had farmed it for centuries, who moved down closer to the coast in search of less thankless soil to cultivate. Their places were soon taken by the first waves of peasants from the Piedmont, where poverty was even more acute, leading to a great and terrible exodus from 1900 to 1910. Then, in 1915, came another wave of Italians, those who refused to join the army and were opposed to the war. Later, there were the anti-Fascists. They lived by hard labor, working on the estates along the coastal plains or hiring themselves out in families to pick grapes or strip the cork oaks in the scrub, leaving their smooth ocher-colored trunks exposed and raw, or to pull up heather and sell the stumps and roots to pipe manufacturers. They kept one or two animals, half-wild pigs, meager coops of fowls composed mainly of the breed of chicken known as "bare-neck," their scrawny silhouettes adding a final note of destitution.

So as one walked up from sea to mountain, one passed through a series of belts, from wealth to comfort, comfort to poverty, poverty to bare subsistence.

Whatever the time of year Cat could guess what the weather was like as soon as he opened his eyes in the early morning, just by listening to the sound of the sea against the shore a few hundred yards below; also, the sound of winter was the echo of the bell-wether's jangle, the sound of spring was teeming birdsong, of summer the shrilling of cicadas.

He affected to understand Provençal. When he and his brother went up to the mountain farms, they were welcomed warmly (maybe because they were preceded by the professor's reputation) in tiny, cramped rooms. In the winter, when every opening had been stopped up with spongy gunnysacking, all other odors were drowned out by the bitter reek, thick and aggressive, of goats and cornmeal mingled with smoke; in summer the air was saturated with the buzzing of flies, punctuated by the click of the wooden bead curtains protecting the entrance. His brother would talk about the war and the people up there loved to listen to him.

They were always against the war, against every war; some of them had already lost their own war, having fought every day of their lives against the hardship and want that were their lot without ever winning a single battle, and anything beyond that war was too remote to be real. (And yet, in 1944, it is the men of the Maures maquis who come down from their mountains to play a decisive role in the Allied victory over the Nazis after the landing in Provence.) Antoine used to tell them how it was that life had become even harder than before, how the Germans were requisitioning everything and Laval and the Vichy traitors were giving them even more than they asked for. Why, after one offensive the Russians had found hundreds of thousands of hectoliters of wine behind the German lines— wine from the Var too (that's a bit thick, thought Cat, who listened to London like his brother; sure, there was wine, but it was from the Hérault), while here in the Var itself wine was rationed! The Germans were advancing deeper and deeper into the Russian vastnesses, they would lose themselves, would be trapped, just like Napoleon in the old days; the Russians were defending the country they had built themselves and it was beautiful, and in the end they would win. This war wasn't like other wars. This time the generals would not be allowed to make a peace that served only their own interests and those of the people like them, the people of their class (once he even talked about the "two hundred families" of France, who had monopolized all the profits from the people's work); wealth would be distributed fairly among the people who produced it, and then, and only then, no more wars would be possible. They listened closely to the precise, detailed information Antoine gave them about the course of the war in the world and its ineluctable consequences and were glad to hear it, especially as so few people came to see them in their huts and they had no radios and hardly any newspapers.

One day, as they were going back down to the sea, Cat asked Antoine what would become of their own land in this great universal sharing. His brother told him that it would of course be open to all, it would become a magnificent public park; but that would not prevent them from enjoying it as much as before, on the same footing as everyone else. Cat was unconvinced. What if the vacation-with-pay types came back, following the fashion they had started before the war, littering the rocks with wax paper and doing their business in the "witches' claw" plants and breaking branches off the rare mimosas to make pretty bouquets for themselves and stealing every last finger from the cacti and succulents to take home for cuttings? And what if they started putting up hotels all over the place, like the Latitude in Saint-Tropez? His brother reassured him. Once the people became the owners and were collectively responsible for all the earth's blessings they would conduct themselves, in this as in every other respect, with maturity and wisdom. It was the bourgeois who destroyed nature with their grotesque constructions, heedlessly wasting things for which they had never paid the fair price, the price of labor. If they didn't understand then, they would have to be treated without mercy. But afterward, people would learn to respect rare plants like all other beautiful things. In fact, funds would be allocated for new plantings and grafts, men like their grandfather would be commissioned to devise a way of acclimatizing the grapefruit, and the "laboratory" would become a proper museum with collections augmented by the discoveries of one and all. In short, the whole coast would be one big garden where everyone would look after everyone's property as though it were his own. Anyway, that was not what mattered most. Things could not go on the way they were, the way he saw them there: it was a perfect illustration of what he meant, a handful of big landowners rolling in luxury on the lowlands—and at Courdoulières there was only one, it was positively feudal!—while families all around were living on crumbs. That had to be changed. With this self-evident truth staring him in the face, Cat could hardly quarrel.

They were at La Valerane in November 1942 when the unoccupied zone was invaded. The All Saints' vacation was prolonged because the lines of communication around Toulon had not been repaired. A fanatical knowledge of the French fleet was one of Cat's specialties. He had a collection of gray lead models, each in a yellow box with a cellophane lid, of the major warships then in service. It was more than a collection, it was a treasure, to which each member of his family made a point of contributing periodically.

The Toulon fleet was scuttled on November 27. Three days later an uncle of Luc's, a ship's captain and commander of a cruiser which he had just sent gaily to the bottom, turned up at La Valerane. His ship had been built in 1937; it was a five-thousand-ton vessel, one of the most modern and fastest light cruisers in the world. Cat had paid an ecstatic visit to it one time in Toulon.

He was amazed to see his uncle. There was an east wind blowing that night, with rain and a raging sea, and the palm trees were thrashing and heaving and they were all gathered around the fire. The uncle seemed pleased with himself. He was still wearing his beautiful five-stripe captain's uniform, only slightly rumpled. He said that when Admiral Laborde transmitted the order from Vichy to scuttle the fleet, he hadn't known, not one naval officer in Toulon had known, whether the action was directed against the English or the Germans.

"Couldn't you put out to sea?"

"To go where? With what fuel? And anyway, the harbor channel was mined, we were blocked in the roads."

"Mined by whom?"

"By us, of course. Anyway," he added, "we obeyed orders. That's what counts. Blindly. It was a most beautiful example of military honor and discipline."

On shore his sailors had sung the "Marseillaise," holding the ship's pennant outstretched one last time and thereby compelling the German soldiers who had encircled the harbor to stand at attention, furious, from start to finish of three long verses. He appeared to consider this a victory; what more could one hope for after the fall of France, after Mers-el-Kebir?

Cat couldn't get over it. His parents had always laughed at him when he said he wanted to be a sailor and command a ship; didn't he know, they would say, that when a ship sinks the captain stays behind after everybody else has left and stands alone on the poop to go down with it? This, it had been drummed into him, was the code of honor and discipline, the two words that are inscribed on either side of all warships. So it's just a fairy tale . . .

The grandparents were talking about recent developments, now that the Americans had landed in North Africa. The uncle spoke of his compulsory demobilization and his worries about the future; perhaps he ought to look for some civilian occupation?

"Well, well," muttered Antoine in a low voice—Cat had noticed that he was being unusually quiet—"well, really, if the military don't even do *their* jobs . . ." And he went up to bed, bringing all his weight to bear on every tread of the long creaking wooden staircase.

Cat followed him into his bedroom and found him standing in front of the window that had been thrown open to the night and the thousand noises of the storm.

"A career officer, paid to make war, and he chickens out before the fight even starts."

"Yes," said Cat. "He scuttled his cruiser."

He took the model out of the closet, set it on his knees, and stared at it, sitting motionless on the bed and shivering. His whole collection—all those ships, gray metal oblongs with pointed or squared-off ends and mobile turrets in their yellow boxes—was to him a cemetery of wrecks, trivial, grotesque. Scuttled, sunk: the battleship *Strasbourg,* the *Suffren,* the *Marseillaise,* and the *Galissonière.* And even the old *Jean-Bart,* rechristened the *Océan,* so worm-eaten and rotten that they had to break up her hull by firing at her from the other ships, like at drill, like at a fair, because she wouldn't go down.

His brother finally shut the window; the rain lashed against the pane.

"Another weakling. There certainly are a lot of them around. When this war is over we're going to have to be tough with them."

During the following days, the Italian army arrived. At Christmas, the rain brings out all the scents of the mountain plants in the undergrowth that has turned bright green again. It's the season of the great squalls from the east, cavalcades of black clouds lower than the peaks of the Maures, sometimes running right down level with the sea, catching in the tall trees filled with raging sound and heaving up great waves that leave unaccountable bits of wreckage on the devastated shores. Water pours off every slope of the sodden mountain and down the rutted paths; the drunken soil lies diluted in big yellow puddles speckled with silver. Twenty years later, far away in the tropics when the cyclones come, Cat will think back to those tornado seasons, the wind shaking up a whole magnificent chaos of sky, earth, trees, and sea. He will be one of the people who watch for warning signs days in advance. The sky turns to lead, silence falls, the blood thuds against eardrums plugged by the sudden drop in atmospheric pressure. "You're a *ciclonero,*" his comrades in the mountains tell him. "In our families there's often a nut like you who's got storms in his blood and just has to go out and sniff the air whenever he feels one coming."

Some evenings, the sweet smells of scrub plants and flowers drenched with moisture filled every inch of La Valerane, drifted over the shore and climbed right into the house, floating across the big smoke-filled drawing room. It was on one of those wild nights that the Italians appeared, without any fanfare or parades. They edged discreetly along the coast and took up their positions in the occupation zone allotted to the Duce. The infantry had to come on foot, after dark and in the rain; the family saw big bright fires being lit here and there on the property, on Battery Point and near the beaches, among the eucalyptus trees and the rocks. They were setting up their bivouacs. Their officers turned up the next morning. They descended from the little train and requisitioned a few of the more luxurious villas. These officers wore splendid uniforms, especially the hats, which were decorated with amazing feathers, aigrettes, and plumes. They had nothing to do with their men and spent their time partying among themselves. Their infantry was composed of Piedmontese peasants, doleful *alpini:* they were a greenish hue from head to foot and they looked worn out, used up in some indefinable way, with their tired, peaked felt hats garnished with one sad moth-eaten feather. Unshaven and unwashed, they shivered in their big patched capes. Everything about them, including the wooden butts of the guns from which they were never parted—not even on Sundays when they came up the aisle one by one to take communion at mass in the family chapel, each kneeling in turn and getting tangled up in his gear—seemed coated with the mildew of that wet season. They reminded one, not of some victorious grand opera army, but of operetta brigands out of a tale by Alexandre Dumas with illustrations by Gustave Doré, and if one squinted a little, their guns made quite credible blunderbusses.

Having no tents, they spent their nights shivering in their blankets around their bivouacs, and their days performing some trivial task or other with chattering teeth. People heard them singing, and the story went around that their favorite song started: *"Mama, voglio tornare a casa."* They were starving, and they fed on unidentifiable substances which they boiled in their stewpots. One evening when they had been out marauding, however, some of them were seen coming back with a scrawny, underfed feline which they had baptized "Wildcat" and carried slung up by its paws, like explorers bearing a tiger back from a hunt in the jungle. Nobody was hard-hearted enough to treat them as enemies. Oh, there were loud altercations when people went out in the morning to find their potato patches and cauliflowers plundered or their orange trees laid to waste, but even then the tone was that of a southern squabble or the irate scolding of some pilfering youngster in the family. It was then that Cat, like everybody else in the country, first realized that these Italians spoke perfectly fluent Provençal. Or rather, more accurately, that the Provençal of which he was so proud had, after being spoken by two generations of Italian immigrants, been broadly transformed into a very close cousin of Piedmontese.

Many families, thus, welcomed the *alpini* readily, treating them with a slightly condescending friendliness, or even a mild contempt. One came across them at the Martinellis', the Andreis', and the Mascarellos', warming themselves by the corner of the cookstove or playing cards with the *padrun* all day long and speculating wistfully about the imminence of an American landing. "Once they're here the war'll be over." They were alarmed and worried by the thought of what they were headed for, so they mostly talked about their families, their land, their village. People teased them good-naturedly and treated them as harmless idiots; why, it was said they never had but one cannon, which was trundled up and down the coast from Saint-Raphaël to Toulon wherever they needed it to train their troops. When it came to Courdoulières they set it up on Battery Point and from there, for one whole day, they bombarded the Formiguette reef, a little black speck surmounted by a pole two miles out at sea, because, people explained, their high command had mistaken it for an American submarine.

The end of November, when the sea grew calm again, was the time for the *bargin.* A fisherman from Lavandou named Ravello and his crew drew in on their heavy oared boat in the middle of the night and set out a long weighted net a few hundred yards offshore, opposite the long beach at Courdoulières. In the morning, the whole village was at the shore to help the crew bring in the net. It took hours. Cat was up before dawn and went down alone to take his place in a gang hauling on the ropes, but it was almost noon before the fish appeared, in a living mass, sparkling and gleaming: the miraculous draft of fishes. All the treasures of the sea.

That was an especially bright, sunny morning, the kind when the air is so clear that every detail is knife-sharp and the islands seem to have drifted up and anchored a few crawl strokes away: a sign that the mistral is about to blow.

.  .  .

Soon after the day of the *bargin,* he left his kingdom. They all went back to Paris. There being no more unoccupied zone, his father saw no reason to keep the family separated any longer. One icy February night, in the darkness of the train compartment into which they had all crowded, he heard a loudspeaker announce in German, then in French—*Achtung! Achtung!*—that they had reached Châlons, which was the demarcation line, and had to show their papers: *Ausweis.*

When they wake up, they count the stamps on the pine floor of the room scorched by the sun coming through the open window; over one thousand unmarked stamps, an untidy pile of bits of paper.

"When the war's over," his brother says, "I think I shall be absolutely honest. I'll have done so many illegal things that I'll be sick of it. I won't want to steal anymore, I'd feel silly."

"Are you going to leave any for me?" asks Cat.

"I'm leaving you two bread supplements, for J3 and T. You detach the stamps for the baker ahead of time, there's no problem."

"But what about the rest? How do you get the writing on them?"

"By writing backwards in black ink, on cooked egg white or a raw potato, you can make a stamp that says *"Etat français. Mairie de . . ."* just as blurred as the real ones. I'll show you."

"I got a letter from Gabriel," Cat begins, still lying on his stomach under the window in a netting of golden dust motes dancing in the sun.

"I know. We all got one. Full of advice and blessings and considerations on the past and the future. Screeds and screeds of it. He's bored, he's depressed, I think he's even a little bit off his nut."

"He says you've got to be careful. That this is going to go on a long time."

"He said that to you? No doubt about it, he's off his nut."

Cat takes a deep breath. He can half hear the voice of the priest at Magny rumbling in his head and he catches hold of that familiar refrain. He plunges in: "I don't know how things are going to turn out for us, but . . ."

"But you don't know anything at all. I know."

"Then you tell me."

"It's simple. The English and Americans are getting nowhere. The Germans have got them stopped outside Caen and that can go on for a long time. Like in Italy. You remember last year, the German propaganda, the snail crawling up the Italian peninsula—'It's a long way to Rome.' But today we're there, in Rome. And meanwhile the Russians are advancing; the Krauts aren't going to be able to keep it up forever, fighting on all sides at once. The only way to weaken the front more quickly is to make the rest of France too hot for the German army. It's got to be so that no German soldier feels safe anywhere."

"Well, that's not the way it is now," Cat interrupts, unable to resist the temptation to show off his new knowledge. "I saw one last Sunday who was screwing a girl behind Champmercy and I can tell you he felt very safe."

"First of all, no obscenity," Antoine says a little sourly. "Anyway, we've started sabotaging their liaisons with the front. You know what they've done? To stop us from derailing the trains, they've requisitioned the old men and are stationing them every hundred yards along the tracks, with armbands. If there's an attack, the Germans take them as hostages. But that isn't stopping the attacks. And the old men are joining the maquis. And trucks are being blown up every day; it's easy to stick a load of explosive on them."

"What about weapons? Your pistol?"

"The only way to get more is to take them off the Germans, one by one. And kill them. I will if I have to. Officers. Only officers. Nazis . . . There ought to be a way of telling them apart. And we won't stop there. There are places, mostly in the mountains, where the maquis have such a strong hold that they can liberate a whole region overnight. The maquis can organize autonomous regions without the Allies ever having to set foot in them. In those places the resistance has already got an administration and a police force."

"But in that case," Cat exclaims enthusiastically, "de Gaulle will soon be able to move into the Alps or the Massif Central?"

"We won't need any de Gaulles. The people are capable of organizing themselves by themselves. There's no point in getting rid of Pétain if you're just going to put a de Gaulle in his place, or replace the Vichy police with some new police that will be almost the same as the old one. If the people have started using guns and fighting to drive out the Krauts and collabos, it's not so they can go back to obeying leaders—and their police—who have been shoved down their throats afterward as though nothing had happened."

"It's funny," Cat says, "how you're so sure people are going to start using guns and fighting, all of them, just like that. Like last night. We were lucky, weren't we? What if the people we bumped into weren't like that old couple; then what?"

"The old man told you himself. The others are scared. They won't budge. There wasn't any danger."

"Three houses away from here, there's a member of the militia. Everybody knows he's in the militia, he gave his uniform to Madame Chevrier to iron. We could have run into him."

"What France is mostly full of is middle-of-the-roaders."

"What's that?"

"That's what they used to call people who wait until the scales come down on one side or the other before they move. Why, our own family is a perfect hotbed of middle-of-the-roaders."

"But after all," Cat dreams, "maybe it's not so bad to be in the middle of the road."

"You're just a bourgeois."

"Me, a bourgeois?" Cat chokes. "What about you, then, what do you think you are? And besides, besides . . ." He pulls himself up with dignity. "I'll tell you what I am, so there. I'm not a bourgeois. No. I'm a peasant!"

His brother laughs. They're still swimming in a sea of golden dust motes.

"And anyway," Cat goes on, determined not to let himself be driven off course, "and anyway, right now the easiest thing would be to kill them all. Like, drop one enormous bomb on Germany and, bang, the whole problem would be settled."

"Nothing would be settled. You've got everything mixed up. You can't confuse Hitler and his henchmen with the whole German people, I've told you that twenty times. And the Vichyites and the militiamen and the Fascists and the black-market traffickers and the informers and the LVF and the French cops that arrest Jews and torture them—are you going to drop one big bomb on France to kill all of them too? And even if we could shoot them all, cleanly, without a mess, do you think that would be the end of it and there wouldn't be others coming after them, new ones, just as awful? No. On the contrary, ideally, we shouldn't have to kill anybody. We should be so strong that we could afford not to. . . . Anyhow," Antoine goes on, "anyhow, there'll be so much to do. It will take time. But in twenty or thirty years, maybe . . ."

"Yeah. But before then, will there be men selling french fries on the street corners? I can't believe that. What was it like, before?"

He loves to get his brother started on the subject of the fantastic things they had to eat before the war. Those are really fascinating conversations. His brother tells him extraordinary things, about zabaglione and eggnog, *crèmes renversées,* capons wrapped in bacon, veal olives, and smoked salmon. But best of all, there is that most excellent of the ten ways of cooking a potato, mythical, fantastic, sublime in its glorious remoteness: french fries. Golden, crisp, firm but melting inside; how was it possible to imagine that this exquisite, extinct foodstuff could ever have been offered for sale in paper cones on the sidewalk?

A tank goes down the road, making the windowpanes rattle and leaving a thick black cloud behind it that momentarily muddies the play of light and shadow in the leaves of the lindens.

"So," Cat resumes when the racket subsides, "so Gabriel was right. There will still be a lot to do. You have to watch out."

"I do watch out. Of course I'm careful. For other people. For you. For our parents. But not too careful for myself. Because otherwise . . . You know what Uncle François said to me? 'I absolutely approve of what you're doing, my boy. At bottom, I'm for de Gaulle. And I promise you that if I could, I would be in the resistance. Like yourself, absolutely. The only thing is, I have a wife and children. I have responsibilities. I have to be careful. Ah, if only I were free as you are!' It's true, I am free. And yet, if you only knew how badly I wanted to pass that exam this year. But if I were careful, if I were like that dumb jerk, I'm sure I would never, ever in my whole life feel free again."

"Why don't you join the maquis?"

"I'm going to. Soon."

❖

In the woods behind King of Rome crossroads there is an abandoned sand and millstone quarry, with the old rails and rusty carriers still there. Cat's been wanting to show it to his brother for a long time. They spend the afternoon there. The best game is to drag a carrier up to the top of the slope and then, giving it a slight push, vault into it and let oneself roll at top speed down to the level space before the turntable in the middle. But his brother tells him they can make it better than that. What they must do is use the extra rails to carry the line back into the woods, and in one hour they manage to add another ten yards and send a carrier shooting along it. What would be great, Cat dreams, is a secret train, known to himself alone, running right through the forest . . .

"We'll do some more when I get back," his brother says.

They get home about five and Cat loads his empty water cans onto the wheelbarrow to go to the pump. His brother walks alongside, pushing his bike. The farmer's wife has given him one of her loaves of special white bread for his mother.

"You'll be back for harvesttime. Hurry up."

"I'm not sure. I've got other plans."

"You've got to come back. They need you."

They walk another hundred yards down the road and Cat says, "You've forgotten something."

"Yes, my gun, under the bed."

They turn back and laugh at their forgetfulness.

"Yeah, but," Cat says again. "Yeah, but, you should be more careful."

They start out again. Cat parks his wheelbarrow by the pump and walks down the road with his brother. They say a polite good evening to three women kneeling at the washhouse below the road-

side. They start up the hill rising along the side of the valley toward
Montainville. The sun is riding the tops of the tall trees around the
château, stroking the newly mown fields. The smell of moist hay
that has been warmed all day floats up to the road. It's calm; no
planes, no tanks. The stillness of a golden summer evening, lovely
and soft the way all summer evenings ought to be. The loveliest, the
softest, perhaps, in Cat's whole life.

"See you," his brother says. "Mother will be out on Monday."

He climbs onto his bike and stands on the pedals, pumping
hard, until he vanishes into the woods at the top of the rise. Cat goes
slowly back down the slope, chewing on stalks of sweet weeds.

On Monday, his mother comes. And the next day the Gestapo
knock at the little gate under the lindens.

# Surprise Party on the Rue de l'Abbaye

A beautiful summer: the sun still heating the paving stones in the courtyard and a basket of nasturtiums, playing in the branches and the creeper. Three o'clock: the bell of the little gate under the lindens rings and it's Cat who goes to open it. There are two of them at the top of the steps and a third behind, sitting nonchalantly on the fender of the black front-wheel-drive parked along the wall.

Dark suits and artificial silk ties. *Korrect.* The tall dark one with the bluish cheeks walks in and across the courtyard to the house without a word. The fat one stays behind with Cat.

"Are you Luc Ponte-Serra?"

The knot in his gut, a tidal wave radiating like an octopus to the tips of his hands and feet.

"Is your mother here? We are from the German police."

He steps closer and strokes Cat's bare arm, smiling.

"And what about your brother, my boy, do you know where your brother is?"

That caress along his arm is horror. It marks him forever. He can do nothing about it. That caress along his arm is a nightmare. It doesn't last long, but the trace it leaves lasts an eternity. Cat shrinks himself into a very hard ball. That's what one has to do: curl up at the bottom of one's body, the very bottom, into a knot that nobody and nothing must ever be able to reach or undo again—tight, tight. If he can just manage that, then, maybe, by some miracle, he will stop feeling.

And at the same time as he hears the fat man repeat his question, patiently and kindly as though he were holding out a piece of candy, at the same time as he feels the white hand moving up his arm, at the same time as he becomes acutely aware of the nauseating smell of the brilliantine flattening the man's hair, he is thinking very clearly: That one's too polite to be honest. Anyway, they haven't caught Antoine.

Afterward, inside the house, there is some confusion, especially when the gawky silhouette of the simpleton in the refugee family appears at the top of the stairs. They swarm after him, thinking for a moment they have found Cat's brother. The women come out of the kitchen, with the children; and the grandfather with his peg leg stands in front of them, his moustache bristling, ready to charge. They make everybody show their papers and shove the refugees back into the kitchen.

Then they search. Not very exhaustively. They pull open closets and drawers. They express polite surprise at the sight of the gutted drawing room and touch the lacerated bindings of the books in the library with their fingertips.

"The house was occupied by German noncommissioned officers for a year," his mother says.

They make no reply. They say little. They look bored.

In the drawer of the bedside table in Cat's room, they find his whole collection of leaflets and flip through them without really looking: *Le Courrier de l'air, Voice of America, Témoignage chrétien.* They don't even see the bread stamps. Another drawer is pulled open and the empty cartridges clink together like bells, and there is the envelope full of aluminum filings.

"Pretty collection this boy has," the fat man says without smiling.

"Oh, you know," his mother says, "oh, you know, children pick up anything."

"When did you see your son Antoine for the last time?"

"The Sunday before last, I think it was." She hesitates, tries to remember.

"Here?"

"Here, at Marles."

"But you only got here yesterday."

"That's true. I have no sense of time."

"You see," says the tall one, with the stern and disgusted air of a schoolteacher reprimanding an incurable dunce. "You see, you're already starting to tell lies."

The fat one chimes in: "Do you know what your son has done, madame?"

"No."

"I'll tell you," he announces portentously. "He has murdered a German father."

And he looks as pleased with his effect as with the mint he is contentedly sucking.

Cat hears his brother: "There ought to be a way of telling them apart. Only officers. Nazis." Well, the Nazis must be fathers too, after all. And then, that one should have stayed home. And then . . .

"You will have to come to Paris with us, madame. You can bring some things with you. You will be questioned there, with your husband."

"What about this child?"

A short silence.

"How old are you, son? Fourteen?"

"No, thirteen and a half."

"Barely a half," his mother dryly corrects him. "He'll be fourteen in six months. You can't . . ."

"He will come to Paris with you. We shall decide there. These are mere formalities, madame."

They leave her in her room. Cat stays behind a minute.

"When they let you go," she tells him, her features taut, "and if you get back here before I do, I'm leaving five hundred francs in this drawer."

"Take the extra sugar," Cat says. He goes to the food cupboard and fetches its treasure, a one-pound package of lump sugar. He puts it in her suitcase without asking; at last he has done something useful. Effective.

The fat man is waiting on the kitchen stoop facing the garden, scrutinizing the bushes and trees with a nonchalance which Cat finds affected. He must be still looking, Cat thinks. He hasn't given up hope of finding Antoine. In fact, he's scared. He doesn't dare go down and look behind the trees himself. Cat imagines his brother, gun in hand, darting out from behind the blue spruce that was planted at his birth and shooting the fat man, who falls, bleeding like a stuck pig. But maybe the man from the Gestapo is just enjoying the syringas—"There I am, quivering, moved to tears by flowers and meadows"—maybe he's vaguely recalling the lines by Goethe that he used to recite at school when he was Cat's age.

"Come here, my boy."

Cat keeps his distance, because he doesn't want to endure another caress.

"Has it been a long time since you saw your brother?"

"Very long. Very."

"You really don't know where he is?"

His mother comes out with her suitcase. The fat man regretfully tears his gaze from the spectacle of bountiful nature. Noisy farewells to the battalion of tearful refugees. They walk past the hutches where the guinea pigs, hungrier than ever, are squealing loudly, desperately. The driver is still waiting, chewing buttercup stems. The fat one pushes Cat into the back seat, then his mother; then he locks the door and comes around to get in on the other side. Cat is crushed up against him, because the man has to spread his knees apart to make room for his fat stomach, and his thigh is rammed against Cat's bare leg. He smells the brilliantine again. A group of youngsters, boys in short pants and girls in bright-colored skirts, off to Port-Royal for a lark, come into view at the turning. They have branches of yellow broom stuck through their knapsacks. And they're singing:

> *A caballero*
> *Is not a po-et,*
> *A caballero*
> *Is not a female.*

They pronounce it "may-ay-ayle," dragging it out. A Junkers 52 drones heavily over their heads. The door slams. The song is muffled by other noises. They start.

"Rue des Saussaies," the fat man says.

He leans back against the seat with a sigh.

"Beautiful day. *Schöner Sommer. Als ob es keinen Krieg gäbe* . . .

*Ach! Frankreich!"* crows his mate from the front seat next to the driver. As though there weren't a war.

"You have a very fine restaurant at Marles."

That is how Cat and his mother learn that they've been in Marles since noon. Passing in front of Canard's, they stopped for information: "Which is Madame Ponte-Serra's house? Is she there now?"

Reassured, they decided to lunch peacefully in the open air and sat there until three o'clock savoring the rustic charm of Madame Canard's cooking, which she concocted from her secret supplies and patriotically served at astronomical prices. That's what has given them their air of mansuetude: they're still floating in the upper spheres of French gastronomy.

&#10059;

They get lost twice around Palaiseau, in a maze of streets disfigured by bombings. They ask pedestrians for directions; but the moment they hear, and see, who is calling to them the pedestrians immediately turn away, hunching their shoulders. One obliging young man with a Frankish battle-ax insignia [worn by those enrolled in or favorable to the organizations created by the Vichy (Pétain) government] on his beret finally gives them detailed instructions which lead them, after many bumps and jolts over loose paving stones and between peeling suburban cottages, into a dirt track that disappears in a field of peas somewhere near Arpajon. Is there nobody they can trust? Later, in a narrow side street in Bourg-la-Reine, one old woman, ordered to direct them to the Porte d'Orléans, dignifiedly declares, "I cannot answer you. There is an air-raid alert." And trots away at top speed in the opposite direction.

*"Scheisse. Nicht als Lügner!"* the driver mutters. "Shit—all liars."

At last they reach the Place de la Concorde. Beyond, the staggered barbed-wire chevaux-de-frise, concrete sentry boxes, an empty, narrow street, then French police in peaked caps, helmeted, dog-collared green gendarmes; the car drives under a long, dark tunnel of a vault and stops beneath the glass roof of a gloomy courtyard, deep as a bear pit, sunk between the walls of a tall black building. Rue des Saussaies. *Geheimstaatspolizei:* Gestapo.

The two men leave them in the care of the police on duty—
*French* police, *in uniform?* From this point on, his memory is shaky. A
gray sticky fog floats over his images, gray like all the corridors he is
going to walk down now, gray and sticky like the stairs, the offices,
the wooden benches. Later, he will ask survivors, people who are
more confident, more responsible than himself, and who also visited
the inside of that place: Were there French police wearing uniforms
in the courtyard of the Rue des Saussaies, headquarters of the Gestapo, in July 1944? Some say such a thing is unthinkable; others says
yes, there were, but not in uniform, or maybe ... There should be
some way to find out.

A fog in which the sequence of events is confused and he cannot set them in order with any certainty. A series of unclear images
and sounds, as on a screen when there is heavy static. In fact, maybe
he dreamed it all; maybe he really stayed behind alone, alone with his
pain and anguish, standing at the little gate under the lindens,
watching as the automobile drove out of sight around the bend with
his mother inside.

A dream? The time spent sitting in offices with slamming doors,
entrances and exits of persons speaking German, echoing footsteps,
sounds of boots on loose floorboards; or the opposite, silent
secretaries, diffident gray mice gliding over carpets. The presence,
all around him, of an indefinite, constantly changing number of
persons, a blurred mass that he can't bring into focus, swelling
and deflating, now hostile, now indifferent; how can he know
exactly?

*First,* certainly, the identification. He is pushed into a small office in front of a sort of bald-headed teacher in uniform who asks him
how old he is, in French, asks the same question three times over as
though he hadn't heard the answer the first two times, peering over
his glasses at his school identity card (the one with the photo that
dates from Toulon, he was going on ten; in that picture he looks like
a friendly frog with a mouth like a slit in a piggy bank and enormous
eyes; he loathes that photo).

"So you're fourteen years old?" And he counts on his fingers.

"No. Thirteen and a half. Next month."

He's still counting on his fingers.

"*So.* Thirteen years and five months, *nicht wahr?*"

"But you can see"—his mother is losing patience—"you can see, he was born on February 25, 1931."

"I see. I see." He counts on his fingers once more and dictates in German to a gray mouse who types things Cat doesn't follow. And then, his eyes vague, as though he doesn't really believe what he's saying, he asks, "Now, what about your brother, my boy?"

"No," murmurs Cat before he even hears the end of the sentence. "No. I don't know."

*Then,* it is probable that he waited alone for hours, sitting on a gray bench in a gray corridor with a worn linoleum floor over which busy feet are now clattering again, facing a padded gray door that has shut behind his mother. Night falls and widely spaced, naked, sad light bulbs are turned on. Time stops. From behind partitions and opening doors come bursts of typing. A young man in a jacket sits down and smokes a cigarette next to him.

"You're pretty young, my lad."

He's French.

"I'd like to go to the bathroom."

"You'll have to ask *them.* I'm not the one who decides."

There is a time when he is shoved into an office again, this one very big, with soft lighting. He sees his father, sitting down, he doesn't dare go up to kiss him, he doesn't dare speak to him, he stands by the door as though he had been forgotten. Behind the desk is a man in civilian dress with beautifully cut gray hair brushed back. One gray mouse, an interpreter, is reading a paper in a very loud voice with a hideous accent. A soldier is typing.

". . . the laws of the German Reich . . . Suspected of terrorist activities."

"Please read over and sign, Professor," says the man with the gray hair.

His father stands and Cat sees very plainly that his hand is shaking, which surprises and worries him. It makes him sick, horribly, to see that shaking hand. He looks at Cat and smiles faintly.

"You will release that child."

The man smiles too and makes a vague gesture in Cat's direction.

*Later still,* Cat is in the same office, his father isn't there anymore, and the man with the gray hair is leaning over his desk, still smiling. Cat is sitting, and behind him, around him, he feels the presence of a group of silent men, all standing, looking down at him and observing him. They form an unclear, compact, hostile wall, a latent nastiness, heavy as metal, waiting for what? A sign? Like the opening kick in a football game in which he is the ball? Like a pack of dogs on the point?

No, he must be dreaming again, because the men are no longer there. Were they ever? And he isn't alone, his mother is beside him and the man with the gray hair is asking him, as though for the first time, as though he were the first to ask the question, "Now, what about your brother, my boy?"

But he doesn't have to answer, because his mother is speaking, speaking in a loud, clarion voice, almost her society voice, as though she were in the drawing room of some old aunt who was a little hard of hearing. "No really this child can know nothing he was in the country and he has been in the country for weeks and he has been sick he has had bronchitis with a touch of pleurisy . . ."

She makes Cat feel terribly nervous and irritated.

*"Herr Doktor . . ."*

A big cardboard box is being placed on the desk. Papers. Another photograph, years old. One of his brother that he remembers very well, that one dates from 1939, it was taken when he came back from a period of residence in an English school, he is wearing a tartan tie with a big crooked knot and a perfect part in his hair, he's still a kid.

The man in uniform who brought the box is standing there. A handsome man, with light eyes and an open, frank face. He picks up a sheaf of papers.

"Your husband receives *these things*."

He reads. He trips over words. They come out in bursts.

*"L'Université libre.* 1942. 'The active patriots, the francs-tireurs, the living symbols of a France that is finding her feet again, vigorous and eternally young, will make the oppressors of the people of France and their French flunkies pay for their crimes at every street corner and every crossroad . . . On your feet, one and all! The time for passive resistance is over. We must attack their positions now.' "

He pauses.

"There is a mistake here," he resumes. "They wrote 'there,' 'there positions.' Absolutely, 'e-r-e-'. The *Université libre*—poor language. Poor France!"

He reels off other tracts, from the *Front national, Libération, Défense de la France, Bir-Hakeim, Les Etoiles, Les Cahiers du Témoignage chrétien.*

" 'Prepare for vengeance a bed in which I shall be born . . .' And look at this writing in the margin: 'Copy and pass on.' "

He sighs.

"Oh, you know," Cat's mother obligingly trumpets. "Oh, you know, my husband mostly reads the *Pariser Zeitung.*" (That's true. "No point in reading translated newspapers," his father would say. "Lie for lie, one might as well go to the source.") "We receive absolutely everything. *La Gerbe, Je suis partout.* Even a subscription for *L'Emancipation nationale.* One has no control over what comes to one's mailbox, you understand, when one's name is in the *Tout-Paris* and the *Bottin mondain.*"

*Herr Doktor* with the gray hair is polishing his nails with an air of mild distaste. Then there is something about a bicycle license that belonged to Antoine. It is there, heavy and yellow, on the desk. Then another photograph is shown to his mother. She looks at it absently. Cat manages to see it out of the corner of his eye and recognizes, as she certainly does too, the features of a light-eyed giant with curly fair hair, a friend of Antoine's whom she took in, with another boy, one winter night when they thought they had been denounced. (They looked worried and harassed. He was the one—how she reproached herself for that later—to whom she stubbornly refused to lend a pair of clean pajamas. "But, Mother, really," Antoine had tried. "No; now, that's enough"—she had cut him off—"I don't mind the risks, it's your business, they're your friends, but I don't want more laundry as well.")

"I don't know," his mother says in a lower voice. "My son has many friends. I don't know them all."

*Herr Doktor* comes out of his daydream and interrupts without raising his voice. "It is of no importance, madame. *We* know. A terrorist. Like your son. It is he who gave us your son's name. He is here."

And *later,* was that motionless body really brought in on a stretcher and placed on the floor between the chairs, like a table? Out of a brownish blanket emerges a swollen face, blond hair plastered to a forehead, and pale eyes, staring, very vaguely, scarcely alive. Nothing else.

"He recognizes you, doesn't he?"

Silence. The pale eyes are lost, very far away. No word comes from the stretcher. No sign. Nothing.

Is it in the same room, *afterward,* that something like a general confrontation takes place? There is a great deal of agitation, men arguing very loudly in German, and they keep talking all the time about the *alte Professor* and pointing at Cat's father, and they are all standing near the inert, abandoned body on the stretcher. His father; their cleaning woman, who was picked up early in the morning with a shopping bag and the day's half-loaf of bread, in a short, brightly colored dress; a boy who lives in the same building and had the misfortune to be on the stairs when the agents of the Gestapo came; and the concierge for good measure. The typewriter clatters, the gray mouse translates their statements.

The handsome man in uniform leans toward the *Herr Doktor.* "Herr Doktor. Der alte Professor ... Wir können nicht ..." He sighs. "Der alte Professor. Alle Lügner."

He says they are all liars. Even the old professor. He looks deeply aggrieved.

For Cat there is no statement. No signature.

And then, *later still.* They are sitting on the sticky gray bench, all three of them, Cat between his father and mother. They have released the cleaning woman, the concierge, the young boy on the stairs. Does he hear his father talking?

"They're going to let you go too. You and Cat. I'm sure."

"And you."

"Oh, me, that's different. Anyway."

He speaks softly. "Antoine is safe. That's the main thing."

And still more softly. Hardly audible. "That boy on the stretcher is going to die."

He looks at Cat.

"They were bluffing. He didn't talk. Nobody talked."

"No," says Cat. "Nobody."

He sees his father's hand on top of his mother's; it is not shaking. *At that moment,* everything becomes calm; and then people come to get them.

"*Adieu,* Luc," his father says.

He corrects himself and smiles, remembering. "No, not *adieu. Au revoir.*"

"Of course," says Cat.

Is it *then* that he is pushed, alone, through a door that shuts behind him? Where is he? In the gloom of an abandoned toilet lit by a faint yellowish gleam through a pane of frosted glass, very high up? He crouches on the tiles against a wall, under the lavatory basin. He spends the whole night waiting. He thinks about Antoine.

*At dawn,* a Frenchman in civilian dress takes him back into the corridor, where it is daylight again. He brings him a glass of coffee sweetened with saccharin. The old song: "You're very young, my boy."

More fog and waiting. *At last,* it must be that he is shoved toward the bald teacher, who gives him back his identity card.

"You're free. You will be taken home."

The men who come to get him are the same two from the Gestapo who arrested him yesterday. The fat man holds out a hand and Cat tries to avoid him.

"So, my boy, you see . . ."

The car again, and the streets, the sky, it's late morning. Has the fog of that night moved into his head forever, familiar and terrifying, drowning all his thoughts and movements?

In the old house at Marles the full chorus of refugees is assembled, still weeping. The police make another vague semblance of a search, but they're looking at their watches and seem in a hurry.

"You're free," the fat man says. "You'll soon see your mother again. As soon as we have found your brother. A terrorist can't get far. Everything is being watched. His description is everywhere. We'll find him. Very quickly. We have everything we need. He's as good as caught already. Then maybe we'll meet again, my boy."

The car doors slam. They head for Canard's. That's probably the only thing they came back for.

.   .   .

No. He will never meet that man again. For years he will go on feel-ing the trace of that viscous caress on his arm, he can recall his sil-houette and features with perfect clarity, the sprinkling of freckles on his chalky face, his babyish mouth, his black wavy hair combed back, the reddish glints in it, the reek of brilliantine, he will dream of meeting him again and killing him, there on the spot. The most blinding, most total hatred he will feel in his whole life. And then one day, much later, one day, he will realize to his stupefaction that the features have blurred, that he would no longer be sure of know-ing that man again, that he would not know what to do if he did see him, that he no longer really wants to kill him, that his hatred has gone, little by little, leaving a large empty space that nothing has filled, and the empty space will startle him and leave him perma-nently bewildered, as though he had lost his one remaining certainty. And from then on he will not be able really to hate anybody or even merely dislike them, *really,* because if he has no more hatred for that man, then who on earth could he hate? And he will feel both re-lieved and a little diminished.

Cat finds himself alone by the road, down which more singing youngsters are passing. The same sun. The same sweetness. He must have been dreaming. Maybe the truth is that the front-wheel-drive car with his mother inside has just this moment gone around the curve in the road. He is alone. Alone.

The refugees tell him that they have notified his aunt in Paris, and she said that if he came back alone he was to go directly to her home. He would like to telephone her too but he doesn't want to go to Canard's. He won't stay at Marles. Antoine will never come back to Marles. Maybe to Paris. His friends from the farm, René and the two brothers, are waiting silently for him by the roadside.

"Antoine has gone into the maquis," he tells them with convic-tion.

Yes. Antoine has gone into the maquis. It's certain. Absolutely certain. And there's nothing more for Cat to do here. He packs a few things in his old knapsack, his precious collection of leaflets and the two almost-complete sheets of food stamps; they'll make a nice pres-ent for his aunt, he won't be coming empty-handed to Paris. The five hundred francs in his mother's drawer.

"You poor child, you poor child," moans the refugee grandmother. And he has to endure the embrace of her sticky apron once again.

"Your parents, how dreadful!"

A little later she tells him, with a vaguely reproachful air, "One of the guinea pigs died last night. A male."

❖

He rings the doorbell of his aunt's apartment at the top of a dark staircase in a solid middle-class building in the seventh *arrondissement*. He took the train at Saint-Rémy, walking between the ruined houses and torn streets of the Palaiseau-Massy-Verrières section, where the line is cut and the station out of service; there were hundreds of people walking, hurrying, in both directions; he picked up a few new leaflets for his collection.

"Oh, my poor little Luc."

He ought to tell his story to the aunt, the uncle, and the two cousins, who are older than he is, but the story won't come, there's only one question that interests him: "Has anybody heard from Antoine?"

"No. Anyway, your brother, your brother, he'll be all right. He's not the one who matters right now."

He remembers his present. He hunts through his knapsack, pulling out his collection of leaflets in order to get to the bottom, and holds out the food stamps.

"Here. They're food stamps. I thought you could use them. I thought you'd like them."

The aunt reaches out a hesitant hand, not quite understanding. "What?"

"Bread stamps. J3 supplements. They're real. It was Antoine . . . I've already used them. They work perfectly."

Silence. A complete flop.

"My poor little Luc," the aunt says.

Here he's not called Cat anymore. Nobody outside his own home calls him Cat. Cat is finished.

"My poor little Luc, you're tired, you're absolutely filthy. You're going to have a bath. There isn't any gas but I've kept the artichoke water, it's still warm, at least it will cover the bottom of the tub. Afterward you'll have something to eat."

He goes to splash around in some greenish water poured out of a cauldron. It's true, his shirt is sticky and stiff. He puts on some clothes that belong to his cousins. He wets his hair, combs back his forelock and parts it, looking in the mirror.

"We're waiting for you in the library, Luc."

The uncle is a psychiatrist. He is head of a big hospital near Paris, the Chevigny asylum, and divides his time between there and here. His spacious library with the beautiful wood-paneled walls covered with books in monogrammed bindings, all neatly arranged, is used for consultations. In his absence, when Luc used to come to visit his cousins, they often played there, examining each other with the stethoscope, inflating the sphygmomanometer around one arm, shooting great gusts of air through the rubber bulb—the wonderful little hiss when one decompresses it, the pad deflates and the needle leaps crazily around—hunting for their knee reflexes with the little round rubber-tipped hammer, and poring through the enormous medical books in search of titillating color pictures of venereal diseases, the only pictures of genitals they ever get a chance to see. But today the atmosphere is not playful. The uncle is sitting at his desk, the aunt on one side. He is fiddling nervously with the little hammer and making it bounce off the food stamps spread in front of him. Luc has to try to tell the story again. But what else is there to say?

"Those leaflets, we must burn them. We shall do that at once, in the fireplace. It's madness."

The uncle is a war hero. The one before, the First, the Great, the one they also call "the last war." He *fought in the last war;* maybe he thinks he fought enough.

"It's madness," he repeats, appalled. "Why on earth have you kept all that?"

They set fire to the leaflets. The chimney smokes. Silly to make a fire in this heat.

Luc doesn't have to look far for an answer. He assumes an innocent air. "Oh, you know, children pick up anything."

This court is not disposed to leniency.

"But do you realize, if the Germans had found that?"

Yes, he does realize. He realizes so much that he doesn't see how to tell them that the Germans *did* find *that*, his leaflets, and *did* not get all steamed up about them the way his uncle is, they certainly had other things to do, all they said was that it was a pretty collection, what they are looking for is much more important, like people in the resistance who have guns and shoot the fathers of German children, preferably Nazis but not necessarily, it depends, and in any event it all has absolutely nothing to do with a few old leaflets. But maybe they're not talking about the same Germans?

"And these stamps, these stamps."

They have picked them up gingerly and are examining them as though they are afraid that by touching them they might set off some hidden trap, a spring that would suddenly snap down on their fingers as if they were overcurious mice.

"Where did you get these stamps?"

"It was Antoine who got them for the resistance in a village town hall and I helped him, so he left me some as a present."

"But these are stolen. They're very dangerous."

"No. I bought some bread with them in Chevreuse. They can't be dangerous."

Does he really have to explain everything? They're "special J3 stamps," that means extra sheets that one doesn't stick onto one's ration card, one detaches the stamps along the dotted lines, like stamps for letters, and at the baker's one gives them in separately, with the money. So? What could be simpler?

"It's dangerous," the aunt repeats. She sighs regretfully. The uncle is peering at the sheet. Will the temptation be too much for him?

"And what about this rubber stamp? The writing is illegible."

Luc draws himself up proudly.

"Antoine made it with a potato."

Now they are separating them carefully, with a look of disgust on their faces, removing all the extra margins around the stamps and tearing them into tiny shreds.

All right, he thinks with relief. At least they're going to use them. But what a fuss!

"Your brother, really, your brother . . . But what got into him? What has your brother really done?"

One sure thing, thinks Luc, I'm sick to death of being questioned.

He doesn't answer. His aunt smiles at him. Her smile makes her look like his mother. For one moment he feels something extremely soft and tender move through him. Her hair is red and she wears it pulled back, she has gray-green eyes and a pointed nose—really a little too pointed, Luc thinks. But her expressions are often like those of his mother.

"Now," she says, "you must forget about all that. That is no life for a child. It is not a world for you. You're too young."

"Thirteen and a half," Luc tells her. "Almost."

"Your parents will soon be released. This is just a bad moment you have to get through. It won't be long, people are taking steps."

"What about Antoine?"

"Don't you worry about Antoine. He . . . You are not going to stay here. It would be dangerous. They have searched your grandmother's place too. Tomorrow you will go to stay with friends. You'll have some peace and quiet there."

"What is dangerous?"

"Everything. You can't understand."

No. He can't understand. Is he supposed to be dangerous? That would be extraordinary. Who are they afraid for? For him? For themselves? He's going to be hidden. Who are they hiding him from? He knows the Germans won't come back because they will never find Antoine. Antoine's the strongest.

Alone with his cousins he tries again to tell them, but it still won't come. His cousins are nice to him, they show him their rooms: the older one makes pastel drawings of imaginary landscapes and pins them on the walls, the other one keeps a white mouse that smells bad. And then, when he suddenly feels that something in his body is about to untie, is rising up in his throat and getting stuck there and paralyzing him, when he feels that maybe he is finally going to start crying, to open up and burst, that the tears are there, that he is on the verge of tears . . .

"What's the matter with you?"

"You can't understand."

He doesn't like the sound of his voice, the words have a false ring to them. Is he overacting, hamming it up?

"Look," sneers his cousin, the short round one. "Look at Luc acting tragic."

Then everything falls back into place. At the very bottom of himself the knots tie themselves tight again, the compact ball of heavy steel solidifies. He will not cry. He cannot cry. Besides, it's true, he was acting tragic, he didn't really want to cry at all, he only wanted to make himself interesting, to be pitied; it didn't work, that's all. In the bathroom he finds a big enema bulb and squirts long jets of water at his cousins, running up and down the hall. They chase him. It's an exciting game. His aunt comes out and slaps him; he asked for it. But he flies into a rage anyway and hurls himself at the older cousin, legs and arms flying. With great difficulty they shut him up in a room at the back of the apartment and, over the loud beating of his heart that hammers in his head, he hears his cousin sententiously commenting behind the door, "I'm afraid of Luc's tantrums. I'm stronger than he is but when he has one of his fits it scares me. I think there are times when he is a little crazy."

Crouching at the head of the bed, he feels ashamed. But in the center of that shame there is also a kind of pleased satisfaction: they're afraid of him. So much the better. He goes to sleep.

⌗

A few hours earlier his brother had telephoned to find out if he was there.

"He's just arrived," his aunt had answered.

"I'll be right there."

"I don't want you to come up. I'll wait for you downstairs." She had hung up at once.

So she had waited for him in front of the main door on the street, which was almost empty. He had been limping.

"I want to see Luc."

"No. I'm not having you inside my home. It's too dangerous. You ought never to have telephoned. It's madness."

"It certainly is. I can't stand here in the doorway."

They had moved back into the passageway. At the elevator door she had repeated, "You're not coming up. I forbid you. Luc is a child. I don't want him to see you. He has to forget all this. What he needs now is a *family life.*"

He had shrugged. "I must say, everybody I see today . . ."

He hadn't finished. He had turned away. He had gone off down the sun-drenched street, still limping painfully, sick with weariness and misery, to see other people who weren't there. Had he even taken the money she brought down for him? Luc doesn't learn any of this until much later, and then not in so many words, only by piecing bits together.

In Paris, July 14, 1944, marked the beginning of a period that might be called a national insurrection. On that day demonstrations broke out all over town, there may have been a hundred thousand people, at Belleville, Maubert, Rue Saint-Antoine. "This should be a day of open war against the Huns," the Communist Party had proclaimed. It was a great day for the Party. From then on, they must take the offensive: "Let the unclean barbarians' blood soak the paving stones of Paris." The Party thought that the occupying army, faced with the prospect of a struggle that was likely to go on for a long time, with bitter, deadly, and drawn-out fighting—for nobody knew if or when the Allies would manage to break through—would begin to bear down more and more heavily upon the population. If the resistance did not act promptly, it might be wiped out. Its only chance was to impose a different balance of power, to make the occupier feel the weight of its presence and organization. To make itself respected. But the Paris resistance had almost no weapons and, unlike the units in other parts of France, was never given any. After organizing groups to protect the demonstrators, Antoine had been involved in many attacks against the *Soldatenheim,* sabotaging trucks, removing weapons from isolated noncommissioned officers. At last he had acquired what he called his "tool kit"—the gun he had shown Cat. That changed everything. He abandoned the endless discussions on the principles of unity of action and proportional representation in politics. "I'm finally going to be able to get down to work," he had said. And he had. Is it possible to imagine that he was, at least for one brief moment, relieved, released, almost happy? One can't be sure. He had no illusions about what he was doing. He wrote somewhere that action could be a drug. Or a bromide.

Within a single week, accompanied on each occasion by a different person, he shot and killed three officers point-blank, on the street, in broad daylight. The third time things went wrong. It was late in the afternoon. They were on their bikes. They saw an officer come out of a *Soldatenheim* on the Rue de la Faisanderie. They rode past him. They got off their bikes at the corner. They cocked their guns and separated. Antoine walked toward the man. He didn't have time to look him in the face, barely time to see the black uniform and the head that was his target. Maybe, as on the other occasions, there was a final instant of hesitation, that total *blank,* lasting a fraction of a second, when you have an indescribable feeling of surprise that everything is still unresolved, you have the impression that it isn't true, isn't possible, that you'll never make it, are not going to do it—another two, three steps and nothing will be changed, life will flow on without any obstacle. *Nothing* will have happened. He pulled out his gun and fired two shots from less than three feet away at head height. The man collapsed. He emptied the magazine into the body. He also forced himself not to race away, but bent over and removed the officer's gun. Only then did he head for his bike, his ears ringing, almost deaf from the shots. A group of Wehrmacht soldiers came around the corner at a run, not clear what had happened. He threw his bike at their legs. He turned the corner and ran at top speed until he came to an alleyway, climbed the spiked wrought-iron fence of a private drive, jumped, and landed in a boxwood hedge with a sharp pain in his leg; he had sprained an ankle coming down. He was sure it was a dead end, and it was. The only way out was the main gate, standing wide open, to the street. It is hard to know exactly how he got out of there. It is possible to imagine him catching his breath, then trying a trick which he and other friends of his had often used before. Perhaps he donned a Basque beret and pinned on the Frankish battle-ax insignia he carried with him, buttoned his blue jacket—like one of the Field Marshal's good little boys—and walked out the main entrance a quarter of an hour later without limping in spite of the pain. There was nobody in sight. At the end of the Rue de la Faisanderie he saw a compact, agitated knot of soldiers. Uniformed men on motorcycles were quartering the nearby streets. On the corner, a group of people from the neighborhood and agents of the French police were watching, at a respectful distance. He asked somebody what was going on. A policeman answered: Two terrorists had just shot a German officer. One had already been caught. They were on the trail of the other, who had escaped in the direction of the Bois de Boulogne. The whole district was cordoned off. He stayed as long as he could, mingling closely with the group of onlookers and police. Time seemed to stand still. Little by little, the group dispersed. An ambulance took away the body, several German cars drew up and raced away again. Night fell. He had to leave too, at curfew, when the police went back to their station. He followed, as though it were the natural thing for him to be walking along with them, talking about how hard times were and how absurd terrorism was and how judicious and necessary it was not to get mixed up in anything. On the way, they passed a German barrier on the Avenue Henri-Martin. He stuck to them all the way to the Rue de Passy and they parted with friendly farewells. He was out of the area of immediate danger. Were they completely taken in? Times were troubled and uncertain, the future already on the horizon.

From there, dragging his swollen leg, he went along dark, narrow streets to the center of Paris without encountering any further barriers. Shortly before midnight he reached the home of a friend who would give him a bed and help him to warn the members of the organization who might be endangered by his companion's arrest and the possible discovery of his own identity. And from there he set out again, still on foot, for his parents' residence, propelled by willpower, despair, and pride. He got there around two in the morning. As always, at that hour, his father was working. He told him. His father made no reproach. Perhaps he thought he had seen this moment coming for a long time and not known how to prevent it, how to give his son enough help, teach him to be more careful and less extreme.

He told his father that the Germans were likely to turn up any moment. That his father should go. His father must have looked around at the mass of papers, file cards, unfinished manuscripts piled on top of the enormous desk under the soft light of the green lampshade. He said he would not run away. He would not flee from the Huns. They would find him where he was. It wouldn't be the first time. They had already arrested him three years before. Anyway, they had long had other charges against him. He went to warn friends in the building who, early the next morning, would telephone the Canards at Marles and send a secret message to their mother; that way she and Luc would almost certainly be safe; and even if the message didn't reach them, once he was arrested the Gestapo would surely not bother with them. But Antoine had to go. He was not to let himself be caught on any account. His father asked that of him. He was not to give them that victory, that joy. And on no account was he to let himself lose heart. He was not to feel any regret. It was only if he let himself be caught that he would have anything to reproach himself for. He was still responsible, to his comrades and his organization. He had to fight the battle he had chosen to the end. That was an order, the last order he could ever give his son. Each of them had fought on his own side, in his own way, and they were going to go on, each his own route, the best they could.

But maybe he hadn't actually said any of that. Maybe they only talked about practical matters, because words were so useless.

Antoine hastily cleared out his room. He burned papers, with his father's help. Then, surrounded by his interrupted writings, his father let him wait there until daybreak, while he put his own affairs in order. At dawn, Antoine returned to his friend's home and collapsed, exhausted. Did he sleep? Late that morning he telephoned his parents' apartment. An unfamiliar voice answered that this was the residence of Professor Ponte-Serra and would he please state his name. He hung up and started running all over Paris. He tried to warn important colleagues of his father. "Young man," was the gist of what they all told him, more or less, "stop worrying. You're overwrought. This may well be a misunderstanding. We shall get in touch with the German authorities. Some of us are quite well connected. But why don't you approach them yourself? In any event, it would be preferable if you did not call on us again." Taking elaborate and difficult precautions, he managed to establish fleeting contact with two or three persons and learned that his instructions had been followed by his own group. He felt trapped in Paris, at the mercy of any chance raid or check in the street which there would be no way of avoiding, and even his false identification papers no longer seemed to offer sufficient protection, because a description of him must have been broadcast by now. There was nothing more for him to do in town. He could try to join a friend who had gone west, back to his hometown to build support for an insurrection in the near future. That was the direction of the front, too. And now, at the end of July, it looked for the first time as though the German lines might not be able to withstand the thrust of the U.S. First and Third armies toward Coutances and Avranches.

But he didn't want to leave without news of his mother and Luc and without knowing what had happened to the friend who had been arrested. On the evening of that first day spent scouring the city, he managed to see the red-nosed cousin, who had already heard the news and told him that his whole family had been arrested. She was nervous and cut the meeting short. He realized that except for a few friends like the one who had given him a bed, everybody from now on would be afraid, and he told her so, harshly.

Before going to meet his aunt, he prepared a note for Luc in case he didn't see him. "Now is the time to be the Cat-That-Walks-by-Itself. Silence and patience." Thrown off balance by his aunt's hurry to get him out of her sight, he couldn't even give it to her.

He was dogged by the thought that if he surrendered to the Gestapo his parents would be released. But he also realized that that was extremely unlikely. What his father had said was right. And his father had told him to go on fighting, and said he had confidence in him.

He also learned that the boy who had been with him and been arrested was brought back to the Rue de la Faisanderie on a stretcher, tortured and inert, and was shot on the exact spot where the killing had taken place. The body had been left there, with a sign saying: "I killed an *Offizier* of the German Army."

No. He had to get out. There was nothing more he could do in Paris.

❖

Luc spends the night in his uncle's library. He sleeps on the sofa used for consultations. The room has a pleasant smell, a mixture of tobacco, leather, and the indescribable odor of the Berger alcohol lamp that his uncle burns after each patient's departure.

The next morning he moves in with some friends of the family on the Rue de l'Abbaye. They live in a tall, old house at the back of a paved courtyard at the end of a long austere street lined with dark façades. There, from the moment one first enters the coolness of the monumental stone staircase with the wrought-iron railing, a soothing quiet prevails. In this part of town there are a number of such old dwellings hidden away, formerly part of the abbey of Saint-Germain-des-Prés; peaceful gardens shelter beside them. At the back of this one, the tall windows open onto a lawn where people play croquet under a chestnut tree. He'll stay there through the end of July and the beginning of August. The apartment is huge and complicated, a string of sun-filled rooms opening one into the other and corridors twisting between cupboards. His mother's friend is a gentle woman, her children are older; the son listens to swing records on a bulky electric phonograph—a marvel of technical progress called a "pickup"—when the electricity hasn't been cut off.

The husband is a senior official in the Ministry of Finance. He speaks of events with great detachment, and is patiently awaiting the arrival of the English and Americans. They will restore order, they'll take things in hand, people will calm down again. He is short and stout, with a few strips of white hair plastered over his pink scalp and extremely pale, almost albino eyes behind thick glasses. His moment of glory came on November 11, 1918. He had been serving in the balloon corps, and that day, in his balloon decorated with huge red-white-and-blue flags, he ascended and floated over the Champs-Elysées to the acclamation of an ecstatic and endless throng. Having *fought in the last war*, he was too old to be drafted in this one, and that's fine with him. He is good at assuming the all-knowing air of people who have ascended to the pinnacle of honor and come back with their heads unturned, those who have nothing further to learn from life, who are intimately acquainted with all its secrets and will divulge one or two on occasion. On all his clothes, even his smoking jacket, he unostentatiously sports the narrow red grosgrain strip of the Legion of Honor. He comes home every day at half past twelve and lunch is served at one, on a massive table set by a maid, with crystal, solid silver, and white china monogrammed in gold. The fare is good here. No chard or cardoons or boiled artichokes or carrot cake. It would seem that for the last four years the energies of this entire family have been concentrated on food and the means of ac-quiring it. "One more the Jerries won't get," the head of the family sighs victoriously as he polishes off an unctuous dish of sweetbreads or an exotic guinea fowl which cost its weight in gold and was pro-cured through the combined efforts of a priceless network of connec-tions. And victory is exactly what is reflected in his triumphant gaze. This is a daily battle, it's war, real war, the only one worth fighting, with its tight spots and moments of heroism. He conducts his resis-tance activities on the black market in perfect good faith. Luc con-fusedly feels a little ashamed when he thinks of his mother's daily ordeal, the exploits that now seem so trivial, the long pursuit of a packet of margarine or green coffee bought without stamps, the anx-ious wait for a rabbit begged from the farm a month before, the line she stood in at Toulon at four o'clock in the morning to "draw" some pig's ears—oh, opulent reminiscence—her scrimping with the skin on the milk, her mashed turnips and celeriac. He begins to feel doubts. Everything seems so natural here.

The wife never raises her voice. The very first day she stated her view of the situation calmly, peremptorily, sitting at the big dinner table behind the Chinese artichokes in white sauce.

"Well, if I were your mother and if my son had done to me what Antoine did to her I wouldn't forgive him."

And the son, who is two or three years older than Luc and doesn't know where to look, stares at his plate and says nothing. There is nothing spiteful about it. Simply the serene affirmation of elementary common sense. That's it. She is serene in her unshakable convictions. That evening she comes and tenderly tucks Luc into bed. He is a good little boy.

The evenings here are wonderfully tranquil. With every day that passes, this part of Paris becomes more and more amazingly calm. After dinner the whole family emerges to take a slow stroll through the streets that go down to the Seine. There are no automobiles, no traffic at all, only one or two people on bicycles and large numbers out for a quiet walk. Acquaintances are greeted, the latest news of the Allied advances exchanged. Every evening near the Quai Voltaire, they encounter old Raymond Duncan and his disciples, who are trying to recapture the simplicity of the ancient Greeks by dressing in peplumed tunics they have woven themselves and high laced sandals over bare legs, all out for a restful promenade and a breath of cool air. There are no more Germans to be seen in these parts of town. People say the troops are being moved through Paris by night, on the métro. The increasingly frequent electricity cuts have brought ordinary life almost to a standstill. The regular métro trains hardly ever run. It's the summer vacation.

Sometimes, with the sons of the house, he goes to the swimming pools by the Seine, Deligny or the Bain Royal, under the Tuileries. They paddle around in the tepid water, but there are so many people they can't find space to dry themselves off in the sun on the boardwalk around the edge of the pool. Idling along the banks, they stop to watch the corks of the numerous anglers with their tackle, their folding stools, their pouches, their cans of worms and wire baskets, hooked to a string, floating in the water, in which they can see, in flashes, the wriggles of the fish they have already caught. A whole little world removed from time, calm and closed, composed of slow, measured conversation in which no room is left for anything outside it: exchanges of recipes for bait, commentary on the cunning of fish, recollections of other days spent fishing in other years and other waters.

Boys his age play along the shallow slopes of the banks, in water up to their knees, creeping forward one step at a time and skillfully shifting the uncemented stones. He sees that they are hunting translucent gray crayfish, which they toss, rasping, into a bag. So, several afternoons running, he returns to the place between the Pont des Arts and the Pont-Neuf and he too takes off his shoes and heaves away, trying to turn the stones. But he hasn't got the knack of it. Every time he moves a rock he releases a cloud of fine silt that muddies the river's clear water. Sometimes he catches the merest glimpse of a quick gray shadow darting between his legs: too late. His new friends show off their catch, and tease him: "The best thing for you to do is just stick your big toe in front of the stones and wait until they bite it."

He catches nothing. He goes back to the Rue de l'Abbaye wet and happy.

❖

He feels comfortable there. Like in a cloud. Fluffy; he feels present and at the same time a little bit somewhere else, he doesn't quite know where. Like everybody else, he follows the action at the front on a series of overlapping Michelin maps pinned up in the entrance hall. Then, on the long afternoons when he has nothing to do, his impatience growing as he looks at the pins that mark the front and aren't moving quickly enough, he begins to draw imaginary maps for himself, in India ink and bright colors, on large sheets of paper. This will be a land known to himself alone, an island of course, with its capital, ports, villages, rivers, and railways. When he finishes, he has his armies land on it to conquer it, and there the front moves with satisfying alacrity, in response to his strategic impulses and the invincible force of his crack troops. Bending over his island, he lets whole days drift away. In the evening, when he has some stronghold firmly under siege, he comes down to earth, puts himself at the head of his troops, storms the bedroom next door, and flattens the unsuspecting boy on his bed with pillow bombs. The older one, lying on his back, parries the blows with hefty kicks, whereupon Luc beats a retreat, unable to sustain his assault against such heavy artillery.

"Your parents are being taken care of," the master of the house tells him daily. "Your mother is at Romainville, in the women's prison. Your father is at Fresnes."

"Can't we visit them?"

"No. For the moment, they are in solitary confinement. Soon it will be possible to send them packages. But that may not be necessary. Someone has taken steps. They will definitely be released."

Luc would like to know who this "someone" is. But the authority and conviction in the voice—the voice of the man-who-knows—discourage him from trying to find out. He even starts to worry that if his mother gets back too soon she may want an account of those five hundred francs, into which he has already dipped heavily. Among other things, he bought an *élytroplan*, a weird sort of glider that has a kind of feathered arrow stuck vertically through the middle of it and is launched with a rubber band. He sent it into the top branches of the chestnut tree, where the wind has been rocking it for several days without dislodging it.

In solitary confinement. When he thinks about it, he doesn't like the sound of that expression. He tries to imagine the prison. He doesn't have too much trouble as far as his father is concerned. He remembers his account of his detention in 1941 and he can see him alone in his cell at Fresnes, with the peephole and the grille in the door, the slop bucket, the clatter of tubs of food being dragged along the corridors at set times of day, the sounds of steps and calls, the prisoners' voices echoing in the courtyard, trying to send messages from one floor or wing to another, coming through the opening high in the wall, the bellows of the German guards—*Ruhe!*—as they try to silence the prisoners, and the banging on the pipes representing other attempts at communication. He knows that his father has certainly had his shoelaces and belt taken away. (In 1941 they didn't give them back when they let him go and he had to come all the way home from Fresnes holding his pants up at the waist.) He knows that he must be obstinately marking each day on the wall as he did on the previous occasion, when he also forced himself to write out a different verse of the *Odyssey* in Greek every morning. But for his mother it's different. He has been told that Romainville is a fort. He imagines cavernous dungeons with clammy stone walls. Did they at least let her keep the pound of sugar?

Early in August his hosts give a "surprise party." A very animated affair. It begins in the afternoon so that it can end early, because of curfew. Forty people stand talking in the big rooms, with the windows all wide open to the sunlight and hot breeze. Chic young men and women dance to swing music played on the "pickup." (The electricity is always turned on for a while at dinnertime.) The boys are in shirt sleeves, their collars unbuttoned. The record they play most often is the one with this song on it:

> With the devil I've made a pact,
> Now my power is a fact,
> All I have to do is ask for it
> And everything I want, I get.

Drinks are passed around, everybody looks relaxed and carefree, everybody is particularly nice to Luc, who stares diffidently at the dancers. People he doesn't know come up and make friendly little speeches to him. One or two shake their heads with vaguely sympathetic looks and almost everybody tells him in candid and reassuring voices that his parents will certainly be released very soon.

Near a window, far from the phonograph, the older men discuss events authoritatively and in measured tones.

"I'm glad to see my boy in a safe place. I got him an untouchable job as an accountant. Otherwise, it was either the STO or be classed as a defaulter, which is about the same as choosing between cholera and the plague."

"There are some decent resistance groups."

"You're joking. The Communists are all over the place. And the Gaullists. And a swarm of riffraff, just taking advantage of the situation."

"What is really a crying shame is to see how badly led those youngsters are. Those maquis who were wiped out in the Alps, why, they were too lightweight. They're all too lightweight. It's a question of personnel. There are no officers worth a damn in the whole resistance. You can't just improvise an officer, and I know what I'm talking about, I'm a captain in the reserves myself. In '40 . . ."

"Let's wait for the English."

"This man de Gaulle . . ."

A young man with reddish hair and an open shirt collar sits down next to Luc and tells him they are cousins.

"Don't you recognize me? I know you."

He talks as though they were bosom buddies. He has the self-assured voice and the attentive, dynamic, and engaging air of an overgrown boy scout or leader of a church boys' club; pale eyes with hardly any eyelashes and a damp smile.

"Your dad's at Fresnes? Don't worry about him, I know what it's like at Fresnes. It's bearable. I spent a month there."

He tells Luc what Luc knows already: the day's schedule, the colorless coffee, the German guards.

"But your brother, really. He must have done something very serious to have caused such a terrific crackdown . . ."

"What were you in Fresnes for?"

The boy shrugs vaguely. "Oh . . . nothing," he mutters.

"But what?" Luc insists. "Why?"

He hesitates, then pastes a smile on his face, the commercial smile of a prewar shoe salesman.

"Nothing. Misdemeanor on duty."

He squirms a little, gets up, and goes away.

Misdemeanor on duty? What on earth does that mean? Luc goes to consult the mistress of the house.

"You mean you don't know? Why, that's your cousin Bernard Maury. He was in the Ecole des Mines, studying to be an engineer. Then he signed up for the Todt organization, the ones who're building the Atlantic wall. Oh, yes, in German uniforms. Of course. Oh, he's not so proud of it now! Misdemeanor on duty? Why, that means he must have committed some petty offense, they're the same in every army. Or maybe he had his hand in the cashbox. But after all, when it's the Jerries' cash . . ."

Luc leaves the room where the dancing is going on. He's feeling a little sick to his stomach. It must be the saccharin-sweetened lemonade. He goes back and loses himself in the contours of his island map.

In the first days of August the American armies advance beyond Avranches and finally break through the German front, sealing it off from behind, while the English are still holding the enemy forces outside Caen. The American Third Army, Patton's army, drives toward Alençon; the German Seventh Army is cut off in an enormous pocket. The pins on the map change place several times a day. People say that curious contraptions are beginning to appear in Paris, retreating soldiers in horse-drawn automobiles or trucks. And sometime around August 10, when the whole family is sitting down to lunch, the master of the house, jovial and expansive, says to Luc:

"This time it's definite. Your parents will be sleeping in their own bed again within the week. All the political prisoners are to be released for the August 15 holiday. The Swedish consul conducted the negotiations and an agreement has just been signed."

He smiles, swallows some Burgundy out of his crystal glass, and blots his lips with his white napkin. He looks so sure of himself, so tranquilly satisfied, everything seems so simple. Luc is giddy with joy.

"And it won't be long now until the English are here. Paris will be an open city. All we have to do is wait."

All we have to do is wait. And listen to Radio London. On August 10, the railroad employees give the order for a strike, which spreads in the following days: "Strike, to drive back the Krauts!" And on August 15 the Paris police force also strikes, after learning that the Germans are planning to disarm them. Even the ones on the Rue des Saussaies, presumably.

Luc does not go back to poke around the wobbly stones beneath the Pont des Arts. He may now, he is told, return to his aunt's to await the imminent arrival of his parents. He may also visit Lady Ponte-Serra. They hadn't wanted him to go before—their eternal precautions. Apparently it would not be prudent for him to be seen on the family property. But the old lady was not at all pleased to be deprived of her grandson, the only member of her family she had left, and she said so, in very strong terms, to the aunt, over the telephone. It seems that sharp and definitive words must have been exchanged, because now they're in a state of armed truce, not speaking at all except in a few brief sentences referring to him.

Luc walks to his grandmother's. He goes down quiet streets along
the Seine toward the Trocadéro. Outside the Palais Bourbon and the
Invalides the rolls of barbed wire are in place and big barred iron
beams stand welded together side by side—heavy antitank barriers to
prevent access to the strategic points of the German defense system.
But there are no soldiers to be seen elsewhere, in the whole of Paris.
On the Place du Trocadéro he sees an open car with four officers in
it. Dry cracks are heard, the car veers, skids, and resumes its course
without slowing down, weaving from side to side on burst tires—
the four helmeted heads, stiff and dignified, jolting back and forth
like puppets—then disappears, still at top speed, into the green tunnel of chestnuts on the Avenue Jean-Chiappe, sending sprays of
sparks into the air from the rims of the wheels as they scream over
the paving stones. But farther on, between the trees and the bridle
path, off-duty German soldiers, leaning against their bicycles, are fur-
tively distributing butter commandeered in the countryside, cutting
it into slabs with their bayonets and doling them out to the servants
of the rich inhabitants of the neighborhood, drawn by this sudden
windfall.

In the streets he has seen people stopping to look at printed
sheets posted on the walls—resistance newspapers telling about the
uprising and massacres in Vercors, the atrocities at Ascq, Tulle, Oradour. In Tulle, on June 10, the SS hanged every able-bodied man
from the streetlamps on the main street while the rest of the population looked on. There are tales of torture by the Gestapo, eyes
gouged out, testicles charred, skulls crushed. But France is rising.
France is freeing herself. The people gather, read in silence, and move
away again almost on tiptoe, without speaking.

He climbs the stairs inside the building, passing the door to his
parents' apartment on the fifth floor. A strip of brown paper has been
stuck across it, held in place by two red wax seals stamped with a big
swastika beneath a spread-winged eagle. His aunt warned him, told
him sternly that it must not be removed. He stares at it, paralyzed.
He feels that it is wrong not to tear off this grotesque strip of paper.
How could it be dangerous? People certainly are strange . . .

His grandmother's apartment is on the floor above. In the semi-
darkness, behind shutters drawn, as in Cairo years before, to ward off

the heat of the day, the little old lady stuffs him with a heavy pump-kin cake mixed at home and then cooked by the baker after her maid had stood in line with it for hours, and tells him how she received the Gestapo.

"They did not stay long. Their chief asked me where Antoine was. I looked him straight in the eye. He must have understood, be-cause he recoiled. Oh, yes, they saw whom they had to deal with all right. There were telephone calls, several. Unknown voices asking for your brother. In the end I left the receiver off the hook for a week. Now, it seems that your parents are going to be released, thanks to this Swedish consul. But Antoine. Where is little Antoine? Your aunt doesn't tell me anything. Nobody tells me anything. They don't trust me. Perhaps they think I am old, that I might say some-thing. I, talk?"

"Antoine is in the maquis," Luc says firmly. "I'm sure he is. He told me. He'll come back for the liberation."

"I've been sewing flags for liberation day. You'll hang them from the windows of your rooms. I was able to buy some material. The English one is dreadfully difficult, with all those crisscrossed stripes. But what gave me most trouble were the stars on the Ameri-can flag. I didn't know how to cut them out. It was your friend Phi-lippe, the one who lives on the third floor, who showed me. Look."

She braces her frail frame to shift the corner of a dresser, pulls out a hatbox, and unfolds the rectangles of multicolored material with stitching all over them. He sees that the American stars all have six points and were formed by two isosceles triangles, one upside down on top of the other. Philippe has been wearing a yellow star for three years.

"But what about the Russian flag?"

"Really, that's going too far!"

"Antoine would certainly want a Russian flag. It's easy to make."

Luc stops to greet an old acquaintance—the blue cat from the Valley of the Kings that keeps watch in a glass case among statuettes and iridescent glassware, very tall and straight with its long front paws and drawn, stern face.

As in all buildings of this prosperous class, the apartments have two entrances: the way to the service entrance that opens onto the kitchen is down a back staircase, as shabby and peeling as the front one is imposing. Luc tells his grandmother that he's going down to the garage in the cellar to see if his brother's bike is there. He goes out through the kitchen and, without asking, takes the keys to the apartment below from the hook where they always hang. He goes down the back stairs. Just as he hoped, the service entrance on the floor below is unsealed: what bunglers . . . He goes in. He walks on tiptoe. Through the kitchen. Now he is in the great dark antechamber. A shut-up smell, the smell of home when one comes back at the end of summer after a long absence. No electricity. He pushes the door to his father's study and stops, frozen, among the scattered stacks of books; he will go no farther. In his brother's bedroom the traces of the search are even more evident: the bed overturned, the bookcase shelves spilled out onto the floor, Plato, Bergson, Aristophanes, Spinoza, Trotsky's *History of the Russian Revolution* hidden in two volumes of the *Vicomte de Bragelonne,* all jumbled together. On the desk, and on the floor around it, a pile of notes and folders: the Egyptian campaign and the beginnings of French expansionism in the early nineteenth century, material on the quantum theory, the American Civil War, the beginnings of modern capitalism in the U.S.A., all written in his brother's cramped hand. On one sheet of paper, the opening paragraphs of a review of a play produced last winter in Paris, called *Les Mouches,* by somebody named Sartre. A whole notebook on *La Chartreuse de Parme,* complete with a shaded sketch, drawn with an extremely fine point, of the massive tower in which Fabrice was kept prisoner and a cross section showing his location in the tower; then, in blue ink, the escape route he followed, down the sheer wall and over the moat, the gardens, trees, fields. And on another sheet, lines of poetry, also in his hand. Who wrote them? Did he?

*From the tree whose captive is not Merlin . . .*

The Norman cupboard in pale wild cherry stands gaping. A fresh gash, left by a brutal wrenching, scores the door panels around the lock, as though the visitors were in such a hurry that they didn't even notice that the key was there and all they had to do was turn it, but instead had savagely broken open the door. Everything inside is in disorder, but a knowing eye can still recompose, in the chaos, the strata corresponding to the stages of a rapidly outgrown adolescence. On the lower level, now heaved to the surface, there used to be the leaves of a flower press made of blotting paper, its dried flowers crumbling away, and cardboard boxes full of rocks classified by era and type. Primary: granites and micas . . . tertiary: metamorphic fossil limestone. His brother has often said to him, "You can carry the whole of La Valerane away with you in a little box: you put in one eucalyptus berry, three garnets, a seashell, a branch of coral with a piece of dried seaweed stuck to it, one false-lavender flower—the one that smells like sheep tallow—a few juniper berries . . ." La Valerane is there in his box, with a dried sea horse for good measure. Behind the big Meccano set with drawers that he has always been envious of, under the Japanese fish made of paper or pieces of multicolored cloth, with fake mother-of-pearl scales hanging from them like little bells, part banner, part kite, waiting to be spread out and hung from wires stretched across their bedroom ceilings the way his brother and he used to do on certain holidays, he finds a lump of something that looks like modeling clay, the true nature of which it doesn't take him long to guess. It is shaped like a green loaf, hardened, grainy, almost crystallized from having been left in the air too long, and it gives off a powerful smell of almonds. *Plastic.* There must be half a pound of it. Enough to blow up . . . What is he supposed to do with it now? He shuts the cupboard. He stands there, not moving. It doesn't even occur to him to go into his own bedroom. He left it too long ago. He's waiting. What for? Before, when his brother came home, he used to ring three very short rings to identify himself and Luc would run to be first to open the door. Nobody rings.

He spends the next few days with his aunt, who keeps the boys shut indoors. The uncle is in Chevigny and can't get out. All communications have been cut around Paris. They go out once a day, for some hurried shopping. The streets are full of posters calling for a "general mobilization." From around the Invalides and the Palais Bourbon, where the Germans have dug themselves in, shots begin to be heard, growing more frequent. On one of its quick daily forays the family is caught, on the Rue de Bourgogne, in the cross fire of invisible adversaries at opposite ends of the street, shooting down the length of it. The family hastily retreats. From the apartment they can hear giant Tigers and Panthers patrolling the nearby streets and, several times, the dull snore of a shell shearing along the rooftops and exploding beyond. The radio exhorts people to keep their shutters tightly closed and, whenever tanks go past, to stay at the back of their apartments as far as possible from the windows. When Luc grows weary of peering through the slits in the shutters as the tanks toil up and down, alternating with automobiles full of men in civilian clothes, with tricolor brassards on their arms and pistols or hunting rifles in their hands, the only thing left for him to do, there being no electricity most of the time and therefore no radio, is to return to the map of his imaginary country.

The Allies are still a long way off. The German pocket in Normandy has not been reduced, the fighting around Alençon is fierce. The English are moving up toward the Seine around Rouen. All the bridges across the river have been destroyed except in Paris. However swift and forceful the Allied advance, it is hard to estimate how long it will take: Two weeks? A month? Longer? Is it on August 17 that the radio is captured by the insurrectionists? "This is the broadcasting network of the French nation," young-voiced announcers proclaim between newscasts and communiqués, each taking over from the last and occasionally stammering with fatigue. Luc likes the sound of their amateurish voices speaking into the microphone, often breathless, happy, overexcited, sometimes contradicting themselves in the heat of the moment, firing off the news items in bursts. They seem close to him, almost familiar, he would like to be their friend; he keeps checking to see if the current has been turned on so he can run to the radio and listen to them. At any rate, it is on August 17 that he learns that the political prisoners in Fresnes have all been released. The Swedish consul's efforts have been successful. So why doesn't he hear from his father? The telephone is working. And what about the women in Romainville? What has happened to them? The radio says nothing more. Calls to arms come thick and fast, warnings to the Germans, who are said still to be shooting captured insurgents and refusing to treat them as regular soldiers, hymns to the heroism of the FFI [Forces Françaises de l'Intérieur, militant resistance fighters linked to de Gaulle in London], the fighters manning the barricades, the Garde Républicain which has rejoined the battle. The radio talks about the crimes of the SS, people shot in the Bois de Boulogne, tortured in the Luxembourg. It interviews the man on the Boulevard Saint-Germain who had already pulled the pin out of his grenade to throw it at an enemy truck but realized at the last moment that he had made a mistake and there was a Cross of Lorraine painted on the truck's side, so he let his hand be blown off rather than throw it.

On August 20 the radio announces a truce. Out the window Luc can see, at the end of the street, cars going past with a member of the Garde Républicain and a soldier of the Wehrmacht sitting back to back on the roof and looking equally uncomfortable, while a loudspeaker announces the cease-fire at every crossing. The family can emerge.

Everybody is out. The ordinarily staid streets of that part of town are filled with animation. On the Rue du Bac, the Rue de Bellechasse, the Rue de Babylone, outside the barracks of the Gardes Républicains, people are building barricades with the loose wooden paving stones and sandbags of the passive defense system. Boys Luc's age are helping, forming a human chain, and he wants to join them. The aunt snaps out a refusal. "Don't be ridiculous," she says. "We've only come out to see what's going on, that's enough." Luc insists.

"Don't be stupid," his cousins tell him. "Where would that get you?"

Excitement. Effervescence. There are men of every age, women too, wearing tricolor brassards and carrying a motley assortment of weapons, revolvers, lots of doubled-barreled shotguns. Some of them have on the battered old navy-blue helmets of the passive defense, and one or two are even wearing unmatched pieces of French uniforms. Luc stares intently at every person he sees around the barricades, everyone going past on the fender of a car or hanging from its doors, gun in hand. He does not see Antoine. If he dared, he would ask them, try to find out. Maybe some of them know him. But he doesn't dare. Most of all, what he would like to do if he dared is abandon the family to their sightseeing and go to the Latin Quarter, the prefecture, the town hall, where they say there are much bigger barricades and where there has already been a lot of fighting. But no, he definitely does not dare.

The fighting resumes the next day. People say it's the SS, who haven't accepted the truce signed by the Wehrmacht. On the morning of August 24 it is announced that an American column of thirty thousand men and three hundred tanks is marching on Paris and has already got as far as Arpajon. At dusk, the family, crowded around the radio, hears that three tanks have reached the Porte d'Orléans; then somebody shouts out that they're French. By nine that evening the tanks are outside the Hôtel de Ville. The radio calls for all the bells of Paris to be rung.

"If you don't hear bells, telephone the priest of your nearest church. And don't forget that you do not have to be a priest to ring church bells."

Luc makes his aunt telephone the priest of Sainte-Clotilde. How odd, she agrees without a fuss, she is all aflutter. The priest is rather short with her; he's already heard. The bells of Paris begin to ring and, booming under all the rest, the great tenor of Notre-Dame. The next day the fighting continues all over Paris, then it's the capitulation. De Gaulle has arrived. Paris is free.

In the evening of August 25 Luc's grandmother telephones.

"She wants you to come over tomorrow," says the aunt. "It's madness to send a child across Paris in these conditions. But she insists. In my opinion, it's irresponsible. It's insane."

"Has she heard anything?" Luc asks.

"I didn't ask. I suppose if she had she'd have said so. But coming from her, nothing would surprise me."

So early the next morning he sets out once more to walk to the Trocadéro. In front of the Invalides railway station, opposite the entrance to the Ministry of Foreign Affairs, he sees his first Sherman tank. It is a charred heap, its turret ripped open, its treads burst. Somebody has chalked some words on the carcass: "Three French soldiers died here for freedom." People stare, in silence. At a corner of the parapet on the Pont Alexandre III a huge puddle of blood is drying into a thick, almost black crust on the asphalt. A man must have been killed there, bled to death. Is it possible that so much blood can come out of a single body? He walks around it. The Invalides esplanade is devastated. Then, on the far side of the Seine, along the Cours-la-Reine and outside the Grand Palais—blackened, half ruined, its glass roof destroyed by fire—he sees them. He runs across the empty bridge toward the motionless line of khaki-colored tanks, much smaller than German ones, the armored cars and little high-riding vehicles with tall aerials. A wide band of pinkish-lavender oil-cloth, easy to see from the air, is fastened across the front of each one. He joins a crowd of excited people around the tanks. Over their heads he can see, on the tanks or in front of them, or by the rows of little tents that have already been pitched along the long grassy strip, soldiers in shirts or windbreaker jackets, most of them without helmets but wearing red forage caps or sailor's berets with pompons. He tries to work his way through to the front row, where everybody is pushing and shoving.

"They really are French, they really are!" people keep saying, amazed and incredulous. And commenting admiringly on the abundance, diversity, and opulence of their equipment, the simplicity of their uniforms, the quality of their shoes. Armed FFIs wearing brassards move back and forth between the tanks, talking to the soldiers with a knowing, busy, competent air. The soldiers invite girls to climb up on the tanks and be shown around the insides; the girls kiss the men, leaving large smudges of red on their faces, which the men do not bother to wipe off. One man in a red forage cap is throwing things to the crowd from the top of a turret, and Luc realizes that this is the cause of all the agitation in the front row. People are scrambling for every object, pushing and trampling each other to get hold of it. And he sees that all along the line the soldiers are doing the same thing, distributing a seemingly inexhaustible supply of rations, packs of cigarettes, chewing gum, cans of food; thousands and thousands of hands stretch out to them. He too is caught up in the press, suddenly he finds himself in the middle of hands reaching up to a tall man who is pouring something out of a big bag with Gothic lettering on the outside. It's German tobacco, the people are saying, and half of it spills on the ground. Automatically, he does what the rest of them are doing; he braces himself on widespread legs and, firmly resisting the pokes and shoves that keep throwing him off balance, he cups his hands together and stretches out his arms; feeling somehow that he has to justify himself, he tries to outshout the others: "It's for my dad!"

He stuffs his jacket pocket full of the black tobacco that trickles through his fingers and tells himself he's ridiculous, his father doesn't even smoke, and anyway . . .

He wriggles out of the crush, walks back up the column and angles off in the direction of the Alma and Trocadéro. Those little cars, whose name—jeep—he has already learned in the crowd, are speeding along the avenues. People on the sidewalks shout, sing, clap their hands, and wave flags as they go by. At the Place d'Iéna, a jostling herd of German prisoners trot past, all bareheaded and with their hands clasped behind their necks, preceded and followed by a muddle of FFIs and flanked by a line of regular soldiers, submachine guns in hand. From the sidewalks, men and women boo and yell at them, but without moving. There's something unbelievable in the spectacle of this sudden collapse, the overnight volatilization of their order, their imposing presence, in the unbuttoned uniforms, the absence of guns, the dirty bandages, the frightened faces; in their reduction to a pitiful flock of running men with unfocused eyes. Outside the entrance to the Musée Guimet the concierge, a beribboned cap on his head and medals and campaign ribbons dangling from his jacket, stands in the middle of a cheering group and shouts, "We're too good to them!"

"Yes," his wife says. "At the Gare d'Orsay the SS tortured twelve FFIs to death and kept the thirteenth one alive and made him drink his comrades' blood out of a bowl before they killed him too. They are monsters. They should all be killed. And not just shot with a gun. They've got to pay. They've got to feel themselves dying. No prisoners."

"No prisoners!" repeats the concierge. "Turn 'em over to the real resistance fighters. Turn 'em over to us. You'll see what we'll do to them."

At the Trocadéro, more tanks, more crowds. People selling newspapers, new names, *Défense de la France, Combat, L'Humanité, Le*

*Figaro.* Further on, outside the family residence, he sees the concierge there also haranguing the loiterers. He has no desire to hear another version of the tale of the bowl of blood and even less to be asked to applaud it, so he slips inside unnoticed. He goes up to his grandmother's apartment and, on the way, sees that the seals are still on the door.

The old lady is dressed all in black, her tiny body straight as an arrow, her eyes sparkling.

"I'm going to hang the flags in my windows. This afternoon we'll watch the victory parade. That's why I asked you to come."

One of her nieces works in an ambulance unit with offices overlooking the Champs-Elysées. She will come to fetch them in a car.

"We must keep our eyes peeled. Perhaps we shall see Antoine."

"But what about my parents?"

"I don't know. I've lost touch. They ought to have been released with the other prisoners at Fresnes. Now I hear that the Germans managed to get a convoy of prisoners off to Germany on August 14. I don't know. Your aunt should know. She doesn't tell me anything. Maybe your parents were in that convoy. No, it's not possible."

Her face twists.

"No," says Luc. "It's not possible."

❖

Because everybody has been telling him over and over again for the last two weeks: it's not possible. He mustn't worry. There were those negotiations. That Swedish consul, so dedicated. And then the whole of France up in arms, the railway workers out on full strike since August 10, the junctions attacked, destroyed, the bridges down, all traffic paralyzed. And anyway, now that the front has given way the Germans have more important things to worry about—reinforcements to bring up, retreats to cover—than sending out convoys of prisoners. The last time Luc saw his host on the Rue de l'Abbaye was August 15, and that day he had been more certain, better informed, more in the know than ever: "It's only a question of hours now. We shall all drink champagne together to celebrate the liberation. I've got the bottles. The consul has fixed everything. Besides, the Germans can't do anything else now. With the atmosphere in Paris the way it's been the last few days, it would be unthinkable for them to send out another convoy of prisoners. They know it."

❖

Not possible. Unthinkable. A little before midnight on August 15, the convoy of political prisoners set out from the Gare de Pantin. In the preceding days there had been an exhausting sequence of orders and counterorders inside the prison of Fresnes. Finally, on the afternoon of August 15, the prisoners were mustered for departure in the prison courtyard. Men on one side, women on the other. Contrary to the absolutely certain information Luc had been given, his mother was at Fresnes too, and his parents saw each other from afar, lost in the mass of prisoners singing, "Yes, we shall meet again, brothers. This is only an *au revoir.*" They were shouted at and warned that at the slightest breach of discipline they would be deprived of water and the men would be shot.

"And you know what it means to go without water on the fifteenth of August?"

They were packed into green-and-white Paris buses, ordinary decent buses, old familiar objects from a bygone age, and that must have given more than one of them a funny feeling. Each bus was driven by a French driver, an employee of the Paris public transport system wearing his cap, with a machine-gun-bearing SS riding shotgun. The rumor ran among the prisoners that the drivers had been told they would be sent with the convoy if they refused to drive, and some of them had even been beaten. They crossed Paris. The city was not exactly lively, but they had forgotten that there could be such a thing as men and women who were free to walk where they pleased; they could hardly believe it. The people in the streets looked at them in surprise and consternation. Several men took off their hats as the buses passed. At Pantin they were piled into cattle cars, without any water or toilet facilities. (Somebody in his father's car made the remark that it was probably lucky for them that there were no toilets; that way the Germans would have to let them out now and then and they could get some fresh air, whereas if there were slop pails in the cars they would soon be full and would stink and overflow; he knew about things like that, he had already been in one convoy. He was full of expertise. Later, one deportee would write: "Everybody in those convoys was so reasonable, so rational.") The Germans distributed bread. Then people from the Red Cross, looking panic-stricken, gave them food packages, the main component of which was canned sausages. The doors were bolted. The waiting began. Most of them were unable to follow what was happening at the rear of the convoy. Is it true that fleeing militiamen and their families, loaded down with paraphernalia—gray mice, as they were called—tried to force their way into the cars and take the deportees' places? For them, this train was the last chance. They were fear-crazed. The prisoners inside their cattle cars never knew about it anyway. They heard railwaymen moving along outside the convoy, shouting to them through the slats and telling them not to lose heart, they would never leave, and even if they did the train couldn't get through, there were no rails beyond Châlons. They sang "The Farewell Song" again. The train left before midnight. It moved slowly, jolting over gaps between rails and stopping often. Their guards made the prisoners get out at regular intervals, four at a time, to relieve themselves in rows along the convoy. But as the intervals were too long, the people in the cars were soon forced to use the Red Cross boxes and jam jars. Nobody could lie down. There were interminable stops beneath a sun that made the inside of the cattle cars a red-hot furnace, long halts in the middle of the night, air-raid alerts. At one point the whole train was stuck in total darkness inside a tunnel for several hours, the people were choking from the smoke. In the end it backed out. Everybody had to get out. They were lined up in a column, the women in front, and marched a mile and a half to Nanteuil-Saâcy. The women had heard that the men had not been given any food packages. Many dropped theirs so the men behind could have them. Local people who saw them pass picked up written messages. They were packed into another train. These were freight cars, old, filthy with horse dung and coal soot. They were given some straw—bales of unthreshed oats. Hope still ran high, they clung to the certainty: they would not go beyond Châlons. They went beyond

Châlons. Outside Strasbourg, the jolting of the wheels over rails that had been bombed and hurriedly patched together became unbearable, and they still could not lie down. That was the third night, August 17–18. In Germany, civilians flocked to watch, gleeful, while the women relieved themselves squatting in rows beneath the cars. One woman in the wagon Cat's mother was in went mad. She started raving and spreading excrement all around herself. At one stop the other women asked to have her removed. "Let all French females die," answered the stationmaster. On August 20 the train reached Weimar and the men were unloaded. The women went on toward Ravensbrück. The convoy stood a long time in the station in Berlin. As they finally approached the camp they thought the nightmare was coming to an end. Some of them put on clean shirts.

When the ambulance-driving niece comes to get Luc and his grandmother, she tells the grandmother that her son and daughter-in-law left in that convoy.

"They'll never reach the border," she says. "It's impossible."

❖

Luc and his grandmother are on the balcony of the third floor of a building at the top of the Champs-Elysées, a hundred yards from the Arc de Triomphe; both stand on tiptoe so they can see over the heavy stone balustrade, squeezed in by people on all sides. They see de Gaulle, surrounded by a joyfully screaming throng. He paces along in front of a shifting phalanx of mixed civilians and military. He waves his forearms like an orchestra conductor, making the sweeping gesture that later becomes historic and habitual. Behind them, the 2nd Armored Division, the parade of tanks, half-tracks, tank destroyers, self-propelled guns, jeeps, command cars, GMC trucks, even amphibious cars, carrying spahis, legionnaires, marines; sometimes one of them climbs down from his moving vehicle and starts running toward the crowd with arms outstretched, and they can see him, among the eddies, embracing somebody. To top it all off, when the deafening roar of the tanks is at its most thunderous, a huge German Tiger with a white Cross of Lorraine painted on it roars past, overwhelming the rest with its fifty-ton mass, while, behind, the disorderly flood of armed FFIs is swallowed up by the surging crowd. How can you pick out one face in that multitude? He tries.

"I didn't see Antoine," he tells his grandmother.

"What a chaos!" she says in mildly disapproving tones.

They're already back down in the courtyard when the shooting starts. Single shots and bursts of machine-gun fire, coming from everywhere and nowhere—the ground? the windows? the rooftops?—and echoing back and forth between the courtyard walls that act as an echo chamber. Voices shout, "Get down, get down, it's the militia, the sons of bitches are on the roofs." Everybody runs for cover under the entrance gates. FFIs, guns in hand, stand behind the pillars staring up. Luc's grandmother, who has just sat down on the front seat of the ambulance that is to drive them home again, is left alone and abandoned in the middle of the courtyard. In all the racket of thunder and firing he can't hear her but he sees that she is shouting too, her mouth twisted in fear, and he is surprised to think that a person can still be afraid of death at the age of eighty-six. Is everybody always afraid of death? Hemmed in by the crowds of panic-stricken people running for shelter, he can't move; but the truth is, he doesn't dare move; he's scared too. He yells at the person next to him, a tall, calm young man smoking a pipe: "My grandmother's out there. In the car."

The young man says something he can't hear through the din and shrugs. Then he steps out, and walks unhurriedly across the courtyard that is still ringing with gunfire, the sounds amplified and sent bounding back and forth by the walls; he reaches the door of the ambulance and holds out an arm to assist the old lady, who steps carefully behind him. Only then does Luc feel ashamed, he goes out to meet them, people are still shouting, "Get down, get down!" but the shooting tails off and seems to trail away like a storm driven by the wind, other people emerge.

Later, when they are home again, the maid, who also went to watch the parade but who was in the thick of the crowd in the streets, tells how she got down and crawled like everybody else, there were tens of thousands of people lying flat on the pavement and crawling hundreds of yards on their stomachs while the guns were firing on all sides. Why crawl? Why lie down? Luc wonders. From the rooftops people lying flat make even easier targets than those standing up, no? But he wasn't there. He would probably have crawled like the rest of them. If only not to be different. As skinny as he is, he'd have been protected by the backsides of the people next to him.

"I didn't see Monsieur Antoine," says Gilberte, the old maid. "Little Antoine. Oh, they were all very fine, all those lads, but there were so many of them."

❖

Luc has an idea. First, he telephones his aunt. He tells her that his grandmother wants him to spend the night with her. The aunt thinks this is an excellent plan. She herself has just been crawling for an hour. Then he tells his grandmother that his aunt absolutely insists that he come home that evening after dinner.

At nightfall, in the gloom of the unlighted building, he leaves, again taking the key to the servants' entrance to the apartment below. He sets out in the direction of the Cours-la-Reine. He wants to talk to the soldiers there. And, if he can, go farther, see other soldiers, as many as possible. Find Antoine. Hear about Antoine. But every time he draws near a group of motionless tanks, soldiers, or bivouacking FFIs, his courage fails him, he can't speak to them, he stands there mute and paralyzed among the milling groups of people who are still cheering and applauding. He sees more packs of cigarettes being handed out, he is given some Camels and Lucky Strikes, they smell of honey. At midnight he's back on the Cours-la-Reine, worn out. The crowd has thinned, soldiers and FFIs stand around talking, drinking wine, and smoking, some of them slip into tents with girls. It's very warm. He sinks onto the tread of a tank and just sits there, not speaking, in the dark. A voice comes down from the turret: "Hey, kid, what are you doing there?"

"Looking for my brother," says Cat.

"Is he in the 2nd Armored? We're the porpoises [marines] here." (Pretty word, porpoise, thinks Cat. He used to see them playing in schools out at sea, in the sun, when the mistral was blowing.

He and his brother would watch them through the big copper spy-glass. One stormy day, one was driven onto the cape rocks. They found it in the morning when the sea was calm again, it was still alive; they managed to push it back into the water, it dived, sending up a great splash that sprayed all over them, and sped away without a backward look.) A shadow climbs down the side of the tank; he can make out a moustache, glasses, a sailor's beret.

"No," says Cat, "I don't know. He left Paris more than a month ago, the Gestapo were looking for him. I know he went to fight. So he must have come back for the liberation. I'm looking for him."

"You'd be better off at home with your parents."

"My parents aren't there anymore."

He has trouble getting the words out. They quiver a little coming through his throat. He feels both pitiful and ridiculous. No family (Capi, the faithful dog). It's a role he's not used to yet. He can't really believe it himself.

"Where are your parents?"

"They were arrested by the Germans. I think they deported them."

"Are you a Jew?"

"No."

"Too bad . . . *Nobody's perfect.*"

Cat senses a smile under the moustache.

"It's because they were in the resistance."

"I'm a Jew myself."

"Where are you from?"

"I left Paris with my parents in 1941. I was fifteen. I was studying music. Preparing for the municipal conservatory. You can imagine what my fingers are like today . . . We crossed the line, my whole family, around Autun. We walked a long way, at night. There was a whole bunch of us. My father was carrying two heavy suitcases, he was having a hard time and it hurt me to see him. I was carrying my sister on my shoulders. She was so tired she started to cry, she couldn't walk any further. I remember the guide saying to her, 'Don't cry, miss, you mustn't cry, somebody might hear you.' He left us at the edge of a big field; he said, 'There it is, I'm off now, all you have to do is walk straight ahead until you get to the road and then cross it, the patrol comes by once every hour.' My father offered him double the money but he wouldn't go on, he kept saying that he had carried out his part of the bargain, we were headed in the right direction. The other families decided to turn back. We went on and we got through. I was never so scared in my life. Then we lived with some peasants in the Massif Central, Protestants."

"Why didn't you stay there?" asks Cat.

"You're right, we were pretty well off there. I could have stayed. But I left in '42, I spent six months in prison with those Spanish sons of bitches. I'm glad to come back to Paris like this. I went to the place where we used to live today, Rue Vieille-du-Temple. I saw the new tenants. I saw the concierge. At first they didn't recognize me. When they saw my uniform, people came out with champagne. When I said who I was the concierge looked like he didn't believe me. He was pretty embarrassed. I tried to find our neighbors, there wasn't a single one left that I knew before, I asked about them and I understood."

He doesn't speak for a while.

"I hope your brother has come back to Paris, like me. It's something worth seeing, the liberation."

Another voice speaks, close by. "What did your brother do?"

In the flame of a lighter he sees a gleam of submachine gun, brassards, the unshaven faces of two civilians, FFIs.

"Here, kid, want a cigarette?"

With great aplomb he lights his first American cigarette, which seems very mild to him.

"He was a student. He took part in some killings. Officers."

He doesn't know what else to say. It's a story he has never tried to tell before. He hadn't imagined that he would be able to talk about it openly one day, just like that. And until now it wasn't even a story, his story. He adds, at random, "He had a gun."

"He had a lot of nerve, your brother," says the boy with the submachine gun. "And he was lucky too. Guns . . . at Vanves, until last week, all we had was one old piece of tin for fifteen of us. A Manhurin. We passed it around. We had to keep changing the hiding place all the time. We never got anything from parachutes. We had to take it all off the Germans. The only time I tried, with my pals, it was like the Berezina. To begin with, the first one we cornered, in the street, was on the lookout; he got his gun out first and we barely made it out of there. And then when we finally did catch an SS coming out of a *Soldatenheim* my buddies were too excited, they started hitting him with the iron rods they had up their sleeves, he was screaming like a stuck pig and his girlfriend was squealing as hard as he was, he kept trying to protect his head with his hands, the iron bars were smashing his hands, there was blood all over the place; it was real butchery. Then in the end, the damn fool didn't even have a gun, his holster was empty. What a letdown, you can imagine. Luckily, the other Germans who were watching from a distance were even more scared than we were. But that poor guy . . . By now, though, he may be glad he's sitting pretty in a hospital."

"It's true," says the other one, "we were never given any guns. Maybe we weren't too popular, higher up. In June we did get some explosives, though. And sets of detonating sticks, in different colors, according to the length of time they took. The only problem was that there were no instructions, there was no way to tell which color meant how long. They could go off in ten seconds or an hour. When we laid the stuff under the fuel tank of a truck you can bet it was a race. One time I was laying one and all of a sudden I saw that somebody else had already stuck a piece of *plastic* there, some friend had been there ahead of me. Boy, did I move."

"We tried to enlist in the 2nd Armored this afternoon. We're from the FTP [Francs-Tireurs et Partisans, resistance fighters like the FFI, but more left-wing], we want to stay together. But no group enlistments, they told us, only individuals. One by one. As if they didn't trust us. What's the matter with us? Haven't we got the right style or something? Maybe we've got VD?"

"They're classy here," says the porpoise. "The elite. Back in the beginning, in Morocco, it wasn't like that."

"In Paris, some people are already saying the war's over. The students I know are all agonizing about whether they're going to hold second-chance exams in October. But what we really want is to see how it's all going to end. I don't want to quit. I want to be there. And then afterward, when the real peace has come . . ."

"Will you go back to school?"

"I don't know if I can. I hope there'll be something else to do except go back to school. That we won't have fought a war just to hear the same old song again. That we'll be able to change things. Otherwise, I'll go somewhere else. Change of scene. Breathe some clean air. Some friends of mine and I have got a plan. A great plan: a high-powered radio that will transmit to the whole world. Every people will tell the others its history and its treasures. That way, there can't be any more wars. We'll call it Radio Sucre. Because we're going to set it up in the highest capital in the world and that is Sucre in Bolivia, right in the middle of the redskins."

"Are you sure that's the highest capital in the world?" asks Cat.

"No. But it doesn't matter. Radio Sucre sounds good, that's the main thing."

"Me too," says the porpoise, "I'd like to stick it out to the end. After, I don't know. Maybe it'll be time to take a look and see what's happening in Palestine. Explain to those English creeps that the reason why we fought the Nazis was so the Jews could be left in peace, once and for all. A real country of our own. A new freedom. After that, back to music—but not before."

A sudden noise of radio static; inside the tank, a distorted voice calls. The marine climbs back up. Sounds of movement spread along the column.

"We're leaving at five a.m., heading for Saint-Denis," he says as he climbs down again. "We're going to have to straighten up the tents a little. Evacuate the young ladies."

"I hope we get to follow," says one of the FFIs.

"Kid," adds the porpoise, "tell us your brother's name, and your address. Here, hold my lighter."

A thick reek of gasoline. The flame lights up a small, torn notebook. Between the pages, snapshots, mostly of girls. Pages covered with scribbles. Cat recites his name.

"Like the historian," says the FTP student. "Is he any relation of yours?"

"He's my father," answers Cat. "And my grandfather too."

"What's your first name?"

"Luc. But my brother calls me Cat."

"Nice name. You're lucky. Here, Cat, keep my lighter. Take care of it. I hope we'll meet again. You can introduce me to your brother. We'll have plenty to say to each other. Here's my name, I've written it for you on this piece of paper. Julius Kleinberg. Now, go home."

He says goodbye to the FFIs. He gives them his packs of cigarettes. He'd like not to have to leave them. He felt good with them. Like one of the family. He'd have liked to go with them. All the way to Germany. All the way to America; all the way to Sucre, where the redskins are, at the top of the Andes. All the way to Palestine.

He walks back toward the Trocadéro in almost total darkness. Now and then, a gust of phonograph music, singing, laughter. Mostly women's laughter, peal after peal. Another convoy is stationed in the Avenue Kléber. From the empty sidewalk, very close, comes the voice of a drunkard, vociferating loudly to himself: "So I says to him, you don't scare me, I've seen plenty of bastards like you, the Krauts gave me a hard enough time, I'll show you. And you know what I did to my Kraut? Put his head in a vise and took a hacksaw. Oh, he hollered, all right. Right to the end. Then he had to be quiet, the son of a bitch. I wasn't scared. I'm not scared. I showed him."

Cat is scared and crosses to the other sidewalk.

╍

He is back in the big empty apartment again. Utter darkness. There is no electricity anywhere in Paris. He came in through the garage and felt his way up the back staircase. He's still feeling his way, from room to room. The ship has been abandoned by crew and passengers. Maybe it's adrift. He tells himself that it will never set out to sea again. It will never again see the far-off familiar ports, warmth, light, movement.

There never was a little airplane on the roof: illusions, fairy tales. He wants to go to his own room but once again he enters his brother's, makes his way to the bed, stumbling over the litter on the floor, and curls up in it without taking off his shoes, his senses alert, straining to catch the smallest sound, any sign of life, sniffing after a familiar odor, the odor of all the years of his childhood, finding it for a moment when he buries his face in the sheets and pillow. He opens his eyes as wide as they will go in the dark. He feels no presence, none at all. He can imagine the Button Molder prowling silently through the rooms, picking up the last lingering shreds of life and pouring them into his cauldron.

It must be past two in the morning. Sirens, all the sirens in the district sound the alert. Then silence again, and into it seeps the growl of low-flying planes. Cat clearly distinguishes the very special roar, a sort of throaty, muffled hammering, of the Junkers 52s. For an instant, the window is lit up by searchlights. Bursts of machine-gun fire break out in the distance, followed by the sharp, quick stutter of a rapid-fire gun, nothing like the ear-smashing din of the German antiaircraft batteries he has been used to. Then, still farther away in the east, as though at the opposite end of the city, the noise of a thunderstorm; that must be the bombs. One plane passes overhead, alone. Silence again. The Germans have bombed Paris.

When he goes out the next morning, the Avenue Henri-Martin is filled with a convoy of American tanks and trucks driving full speed ahead. People have formed a dense hedge along the sidewalk and are clapping and stretching out their hands. A khaki-colored tin can tossed from a tank lands right at his feet. Startled, he picks it up before anyone else can get to it: cheese.

At his aunt's, his cousins show him their loot: an impressive array of packs of cigarettes, mint- and banana-flavored chewing gum, even chewing gum that cleans your teeth. It annoys him that he can't compete, he makes a pitiful showing. The German tobacco has all leaked out of his pocket because the seam was split, all that's left is some blackish powder. Only the can of cheese, the interior of which reveals a creamy pink substance flavored with smoked ham, gains him any consideration from his aunt. The lighter is in a different category. He can feel it against his thigh, through his pants pocket. He does not show it.

The German bombs hit the Halle-aux-Vins district. Like all the other people in the building, the family went down to the air-raid shelter. His aunt asks if his grandmother sent him down to the cellar and he glibly affirms that she did not—he knows, in fact, that he heard no sounds of movement in the building. She twitches with irritation, says it is irresponsible.

"But all through the war we never went down to the shelters."

"That's not the same thing. This time it was the Germans."

In the following days he and his cousins go out onto the sloping roof; they crouch behind the chimney stacks and watch the round of American aircraft in the Paris sky, heavy Dakota transports, little Piper Cub observation planes. They wander the streets, and one time, near their home, they see a woman with a shaved head walking down the street clinging to the housefronts, wrapped in a raincoat clutched together at the top by one strained hand, her face gray and disfigured by trickling tears and snot, followed at a distance by men who are calmly but insistently calling her a slut and a whore.

"Come along," the irritated aunt orders the three boys, who are standing there gaping. "Don't look. That is no sight for you."

It occurs to him that there are moments when his aunt is decidedly odd.

***

A week later she joyfully informs them that Chevigny has been liberated, she has heard from her husband, they're all going there. The trains aren't running yet, they're going to go in a truck that leaves in the morning from the Porte de la Chapelle and takes passengers.

All these days, he has still been looking for his brother in Paris. Now he knows he's not there; he must have gone somewhere else, farther away, to one of the maquis units in the center of France or the Alps, to the mountains, the liberated zones which he was told were taken over by the resistance even before Vichy fell. They have heard about the landing in Provence and he tells himself that maybe Antoine will come up from the south with those liberating forces. He also knows that his parents are in camps in Germany, and his aunt keeps telling him that political prisoners there are well treated.

Very early one morning, they and a dozen other shivering shadows climb into a squat canvas-covered producer-gas-burning van and park themselves as best they can on crates and packs. He sits at the open back end, staring at the road that runs away beneath him; he shuts his eyes and tells himself he's in an armored car and he and his troops are driving eastward and he is going to join his brother. And after that ... Well, after that, they are both on the road from Battambang to Siem Reap, they're advancing toward Angkor between rows of banyan trees, maybe even on the swaying back of Bahadur Shah the baggage elephant. And after that ... The fat candy-shop owner from Chevigny who's traveling with them jabs an elbow into his ribs. They're at Creil, they stop in a moonscape of deep funnels filled with stagnant yellow water under the ruins of the V-1 launching ramps aimed at London. Near the rubble of houses that have collapsed but not been cleared away, blackberry bushes are already growing; they pick berries while they wait for the driver to finish reaming out his exhausted gas generator.

# The Asylum and the Hand Grenade

One doesn't say hospital, one says asylum. And one never says lunatics, one always says patients—however much one thinks the other
thing. And one is supposed to say nurse, not keeper; one often forgets.

Chevigny is an overgrown village, with a medieval town hall restored by Viollet-le-Duc on the roughly paved main street which is
lined with shops and rises to a chunky, rustic late Gothic collegiate
church. Everything that happens in Chevigny revolves around the
asylum. Even if they aren't actually employed by it, the town's six
thousand inhabitants are all directly concerned in one way or another
with the compound that houses nine thousand inmates, divided
among the central buildings and residences spreading like tentacles
on the outskirts of town.

Luc feels half at home in the place, having spent several short
periods there with his brother during vacations. He knows his way
around his uncle's house, a big three-story dwelling with its own
garden in front. It faces the narrow roadway leading to the main entrance—two broad, heavy, solid-metal gates flanked by a narrow
doorway for people on foot and a gatekeeper's lodge. The asylum is
surrounded by an extremely high wall. On the other side of the narrow roadway is another blind wall, dividing the prison from the sub-
prefecture; from his bedroom window he can look over this wall and
see faces framed in the low barred windows of the prison, a square,
peeling building erected a century ago. He can also see, beyond the
asylum entrance, the gray tarred and gravel walks, the strips of bare
earth planted with severely pruned trees, and the long decrepit
buildings behind them. Just past the entrance, on the left side,

stretches a row of low dilapidated constructions like big kennels, built side by side with gaping doorways opening onto crumbling walls: these are the remains of the cells where raving lunatics used to be chained to the wall, but they have now been abandoned, on humanitarian grounds. The walks all cross at right angles and are wide and empty. A few small blue spots, uniformed patients, creep lethargically about or stand, immobile, in the doorways of the buildings. In the road beneath his window the day's hours are marked by familiar sounds: employees changing shifts, hurrying groups of asylum workers calling out to one another as they cross and go in and out through the little gate. The big double gates open only to admit a few delivery trucks or sometimes an ambulance or gendarmerie van, but more often it's the hearse, horse-drawn, with a single driver; at this point he's the figure who comes through the gates most, sometimes several times a day. One doesn't even have to look out the window to identify the clanking of his wheels, the horse's hooves, the grating of the gates as they swing open.

Because in 1944 there are a lot of people dying in the Chevigny asylum, as in many other psychiatric hospitals and asylums in France. As the only home for the insane from all the *départements* north and west of Paris, it is overcrowded even in ordinary times, and its population has been substantially increased by the evacuation of asylums farther away, in particular Rouen. For the authorities trying to deal with an entire country in a state of acute penury and want, lunatics do not form part of the useful population. But that is something Luc won't understand until much later. For the moment, the hearse trundling in and out is just one item in the daily decor. The place is very quiet. All he knows of the asylum universe is the tranquil life of this brick dwelling shaded by chestnut trees. There are a large number of servants, obliging, peaceable, unhurriedly going about their business. The cultivation, at the asylum's expense, of a huge vegetable garden, the management of well-stocked coops and hutches, the daily provision, by the administration, of long loaves of fresh bread marked with the doctor's initial in a raised swirl of dough on the flat surface of the crust, all help to create an untroubled sense of well-being. All the servants are trustworthy inmates. Dressed according to the season in heavy blue cotton or thick blue wool, the women in very long skirts, the men with shaven heads and big hobnailed boots or wooden clogs on their feet, they go back inside the asylum at the end of their day's work. Edouard, the gardener who lovingly tends the rabbits and dexterously bleeds and flays them, is noted for his great gentleness with children. The boys adore him. It seems that sometime around 1932 he cut the throats of his wife and children in a fit of jealousy and delirium tremens; but even that wouldn't have been known had it not been for Luc's father, who, quite by chance and rather unfortunately, recognized him once when he was visiting Chevigny; because at the time of the incident Edouard had been working in a château near Marles. Otherwise, his past is lost in the mists of time and the doctor himself has only a dim recollection of it. Rosine, the cook, is a wrinkled and aged Norman peasant woman, half witch and half character in an old fairy-tale illustration, who has taken a fancy to Luc. Nobody else can remember why she's there and she herself seems to have lost all notion of the reason. It must have been forty years ago or more when she first arrived; maybe in those days she was a comely, robust young woman. She comes from Caen and her file didn't follow her, so even if the doctor wanted to find out the original cause for her presence in the asylum, he couldn't. What she very definitely does know, however, and Luc's uncle has confirmed that fact, is that she will never leave it. Her life has become inextricably bound up with the place. She will die there. The law states that in order for her to leave, some member of her family must claim her. But after all these years, what can she know about her family? And who remembers her? The people who saw her when she came, who may have signed the papers committing her, have been dead for years. What does it matter that she is, as the doctor says, "quite remarkably normal" or, even more, that she is an old woman who may be a little tired of life but the warmth of whose heart would make her, in some other place and circumstances, an ideal grandmother? After all, as he adds, her life here is no different from what it would be in an old people's home. In fact, she's better off here, she's used to the place. It's the only world she knows now, it would be cruel to uproot her. And she has grown attached to this family she works for.

The cleaning woman is the only one who shows some signs of

eccentricity. A tall, bony, brusque woman whose beak-like nose is always looking for trouble, she is named Madame Bataille and she wears the appellation like a title. Her hats are pugnacious concoctions which perch on her head at an angle of conquest, conglomerations of lacquered straw, artificial flowers, and exotic lavender ribbons. She has eclipses. She disappears for a week or two. Luc learns that these disappearances correspond to periods of "agitation" during which she takes herself for Napoleon more persistently than usual. To him, this is ridiculous and hardly credible. Crazy people who take themselves for Napoleon are, as he knows, mandatory components of a host of "funny stories"; but to admit that such people actually exist and, what is more, can be women, as in this case, is something he cannot do. However often his uncle tells him it's true, Luc has a feeling that he's being made fun of, things can't be as simple as that. Also, the word "agitation" doesn't convey anything real to him. What does she do, and what is done to her, during these periods of absence? All that comes from the other side of the asylum walls is silence, broken by perfectly innocuous sounds. He has little opportunity to go through the gate, although he has been sent on errands to his uncle's office once or twice, or to pick up the bread in the bakery. On those occasions, the characters dressed in blue whom he encounters along the walks don't make him feel too creepy; they move awkwardly, as though they live at a different speed, with different gestures, in a different time and space, and are occasionally ordered around by robust round-cheeked keepers in caps (who are entitled to T rations, for manual laborers). He walks across huge, empty, moldy rooms containing lines of greenish bathtubs connected by a complex system of tubes and pipes. He is told that they were once used for hydrotherapy. Are they still in use? No, judging by the dirt, peeling paint, pipes dangling in midair, broken windowpanes, and general air of decrepitude.

It was his uncle, Dr. Pierrard, who was the first, in 1936, to urge, on the strength of his diagnosis, the incarceration of the notorious Dr. Petiot, who in those days had not yet become the Jew-killer and arch-Landru of the Rue Lauriston. At that point, he had simply been caught stealing books in the Librairie Gibert on the Boulevard Saint-Michel. Dr. Pierrard was categorical: abulia, listlessness, a depressive condition with manifestations of anxiety, a psychological disorder apparently of long date, instability and bizarre behavior, non-delirious but constitutionally unbalanced, an unscrupulous and amoral personality. Petiot, thus defined, was a sufficient menace to society for Dr. Pierrard to recommend without reservation his internment in a psychiatric ward. His advice was not taken. Other experts considered the man to be as normal as Luc's uncle considered him abnormal. In any event, Dr. Pierrard was a skeptic and a sincere pessimist. He would agree readily and cheerfully that it was no easy matter to locate the precise dividing line between sanity and insanity—if, he would add, any such line exists. (A good many of his close friends and associates freely affirmed, moreover, as is customary among psychiatrists' acquaintances, that he himself had more than one screw loose.)

On previous visits Luc had heard his uncle talking about his work to Antoine. Usually this meant the long, disenchanted soliloquy of the overburdened professional.

"We should be treating people. There is one senior physician here for six hundred patients. I am essentially an administrator."

Antoine had spoken of recent discoveries in psychology. The uncle had shrugged and laughed wryly.

"Oh, indeed, extraordinary things are being discovered. But we don't have the manual that tells us how to use them. The electroshock is an admirable instrument. I often have recourse to it. But all we know for certain is that the discharge of an electric current into the brain produces a terrific upheaval which is capable of rupturing the logic of insanity. It is a purely mechanical intervention. Everything else is guesswork. We cannot vary the intensity of the shock or predict its effects. We are groping. Surrounded by fog. I'll take you to watch an electroshock treatment if you like. It will interest you."

For Luc, the thought of electroshock treatments conjures up nightmare visions. He identifies them with the electric chair they have in America; some of his schoolmates eagerly collected electric-chair lore. He imagines the monstrous metal seat, the condemned man's arms and legs imprisoned in heavy handcuffs, the iron cap and electrodes on the shaven skull, the screams as of a violated animal.

"If we could only find out where we are going . . . We ought to try everything. I'd like to adopt the positive aspects of every new technique. Insulin. And Freud. But all the administration wants me to do is keep the lunatics quiet. And frankly, what more can I do?"

Around him, the family would wait politely for the soliloquy to end. He was thought to be a man of great modesty; his patients worshipped him; he was a renowned expert.

It was all a little over Luc's head. He tried to talk about it to Antoine, who said, sadly, "He's given up."

Nothing has changed.

Sometimes when the uncle gets back from the asylum late in the afternoon, he goes to the piano in the empty living room, and Luc, in the garden, hears an avalanche of notes spewing forth like sprays of fireworks. He tells his cousins it's beautiful, his uncle plays really well. They laugh at him and tell him it's always the same passage from Wagner, it's his piece, the only one he knows by heart.

※

The toilet on the second floor contains treasures that set Luc's imagination aflame. On either side of the bowl and chain are shelves heaped with unsteady piles of old files filled with torn folders out of which leak sheaves of yellowed typewritten sheets. Some of them, in fact—the thin carbon copies, duly cut into small squares—are used as toilet paper. These are the psychiatric assessments of closed cases that have been thrust there for want of any better place to store them. Pulling out any sheet at random, one can catch glimpses of absolutely fascinating worlds, through the ornate although somewhat repetitive prose in which they are couched. By this means Luc learns, for example, that X, aged eighteen, began masturbating regularly at the age of ten (is this an aggravating or extenuating circumstance, he wonders, but can find no answer, and has a terrified presentiment that it must be a symptom which predisposes a person to crime and insanity), had sexual relations as early as the age of sixteen but, when no more than twelve years old, had already had a few experiences "of distinctly homosexual character" with friends, and can achieve a full erection only when fantasizing that his member is being chopped into slices (this is one of the favorite cases of Luc and his cousins, who often refer to it with prolonged giggles). That Z is subject to fits of profound melancholia which impel him to frequent prostitutes assiduously (Luc doesn't spend much time on the details, of course, so it may be the fits that are profound and not the melancholia and it may be the frequenting of prostitutes that brings them on and not the other way around, but it's the general atmosphere that counts, right?); and that Y, aged twenty-one, who has *confessed* to being subject to premature ejaculations, is afflicted with a failure complex because of which he is in a prolonged state of instability and that this may account for his penchant for delinquency but does not mean that he is not "liable to criminal punishment," an expression which keeps recurring at the end of these reports like an *amen* at the end of mass. A, a twenty-two-year-old prostitute of "great weakness of character," has never experienced orgasm; her defloration was painful, she exhibits an abnormally small clitoris and is prey to an obsessive desire for revenge upon the whole masculine sex. This is expressed in psychotic tendencies which make her unfit to live in society and create a latent risk of dangerousness justifying, in her case, treatment in a psychiatric hospital. And so on and so forth, by the hundreds . . . Luc now discovers the secrets of these unknown realms and he advances, uncertain, bewildered, and jubilant, on the razor's edge between sanity and perversity, the contours of both growing increasingly blurred as he strays further and further afield in his haphazard readings.

▪

The liberation rolled through Chevigny like a tidal wave. The American troops came and went, into the east. Just as the withdrawing sea leaves a scatter of miscellaneous objects in its wake, so a few gutted tanks have been abandoned by the surf at intersections of the country roads around the town, along with traces of bullets and gaping crevices on the ugly façade of the secondary school, while a body of bantering FFIs camps in the citadel; they can be seen now and then, with one submachine gun for every ten men, driving a flock of tattered, mournful, sodden German prisoners before them with mighty kicks in the behind, toward some supposedly "useful" task or other.

They follow the Allied offensive on the radio—the Moselle has been reached, Nancy is liberated on September 10—the rapid advances of the armies that landed in Provence on August 15, the Warsaw uprising; but when are the Russians going to help the resistance there? They're marking time, hanging back outside the city. At Chevigny, the most obvious sign that the war is still on is the continuous passage, along the main highway at the foot of town, of American trucks driving hell-for-leather to the east with their headlights on and never stopping; that's the Red Ball road, one of the vital arteries conveying supplies to the front. Sometimes, on their way back from fishing for sticklebacks, the boys try to thumb rides; they make hitchhiking motions and the drivers wave back, grinning, but never slow down. "They're stupid," the cousins decide. "Why don't they stop? They must not understand what we want." And they try again, with no more success than before. "It wouldn't cost them anything, just to stop."

A change of subprefect and the transfer of the deputy public prosecutor ("of the Republic" once again) cause the uncle some concern in regard to proceedings at the local chess club, where habitués meet weekly to replay famous matches of the past. A few genuine members of the resistance have emerged into the light of day and gotten themselves "substantiated." The town now has its hero—a posthumous hero, which is all the better: the electrician on the main street, who was working for London. He had a transmitter, and when the Germans came to arrest him late in July, he tried to escape over the roof. They shot him down with one burst. His wife was arrested, imprisoned at Fresnes, and deported. (And so one day, at the end of her period of solitary confinement, Cat's mother found herself in the same cell as his widow and was able to learn that only a few days earlier her brother-in-law the doctor had been in the shop to have his radio repaired; she was startled, almost shocked to realize that her family's everyday lives were pursuing their ordinary courses beyond the prison walls, and then she was amazed by her own amazement; was she expecting their lives to come to an end because she was in prison?)

When Luc and his cousins are on good terms, they call each other by the names of the characters in the *Pieds Nickelés* comics, of which they have masses: Filochard, Ribouldingue, and Croquignolle. Luc is Croquignolle, because he's the thinnest and has a big nose. They often go to visit the bailiff's son. He fascinates Luc because he tells, in the drawling voice—grossly exaggerated—of the Parisian who's seen it all before, an endless stream of tales of balls, bordellos, cat-houses, and cocks, dicks, pricks, and peters.

The bailiff's attics are also full of abandoned treasures, the un-claimed remnants of a long history of property distraints: billiard tables from the back rooms of cafés, covered in moth-eaten baize, along with their cracked ivory balls and blackened cues; varnished china stoves, stuffed animals, and above all, weird music machines, the ancestors of the phonograph, that play metal cylinders or disks bristling with pinpoints which cause thin blades to vibrate when they turn; and elaborate music boxes that play all the great operatic arias. Luc never tires of them. He brings them back to his room and tries to change the notes by bending and cutting the blades, or to combine several into one. He dreams up other instruments he could create with his own hands, to produce panoramic symphonies of which he would be sole master: water organs, more melodious than his father's cat organs, in which the water would emit high and crys-talline or low and throbbing tones as it flowed; crystal harps, like the goblets one can make vibrate indefinitely by rubbing a moistened fin-ger rapidly around their rims at the end of a meal; or Jew's harps made of rubber bands stretched in air currents that would hum at the whim of the breezes. He would include the whistling blackbird that gargles when one blows into the little rubber tube connected to its belly filled with water, and maybe the prayer wheels of the Ti-betan monks his father used to tell him about. But what are prayer wheels exactly? He has already forgotten. And nobody at Chevigny can help him. Are they those multicolored strips of cloth that snap in the wind, at the crossroads out on the high plateaus at the world's end, unfurling the written characters which repeat the same words in the sky with every gust, *Aum mani padme hum;* or are they those little metal rattles, like children's windmills, that one has only to spin in order to reproduce, interminably, the same treble notes? Of all these, and many other devices, he will concoct a "symphony of things," possibly incorporating phonograph records which play real birdsongs and various other sounds of nature, all flowing together like the scales on some great panpipes. Or else, in beautiful landscapes and mountain passes, along waterfalls and on the tips of headlands looking out to sea, he will position instruments that will play themselves at the whim of weather and events—his wind and water organs, yes, but also jingle bells and sleigh bells, cow bells and gongs, to give rhythm and order to the unending, ever-shifting background of the songs of waves and rustling leaves. And yes, percussion . . .

"I can't hear myself think!" cries the aunt, coming upstairs in exasperation. "This is not a lunatic asylum here. You'd better go outside and play with your cousins."

⊞

They soon discover the best game of all, one that is very popular that year all over the French countryside. A discreet investigation of the ruined schoolhouse puts them on the trail. Wandering through the corridors with their smashed glass roofs, they come upon a classroom, and in it, piled on the floor amidst the rubble, is a large supply of Lebel rifle shells. They're wrapped in thick paper, green, red, or gray, and tied in heavy packages, each of which contains twenty smaller packets wrapped in the same paper of the same color, with ten cartridges in each. In another pile are empty black metal three- or five-round carbine magazines and rigid twenty-five-round bands for repeating rifles. All that's missing is the guns. The floor is littered with German helmets. The green packets contain shells of a white, gleaming metal like nickel—they are the most beautiful, there's something rich about them; the shells in the red packets are black and dull, almost sandpapery; and in the gray packets there are copper-colored shells which they designate as "plain." The copper cases are all identical; unlike those of the straight-sided German Mausers, these widen at the base, which forms a broad disk with projecting edges around the capsule containing the percussion cap.

They make numerous trips, hiding from the school caretakers, to remove a portion of their find. Each boy installs his personal hoard in the attic of the doctor's house. Extracting the powder from the cartridges is easy but soon becomes boring. The cartridge is placed in the keyhole of a door and fixed there; then, holding the cartridge case with the whole hand, one twists and turns it repeatedly, forcing it both laterally and vertically; finally, the bullet works loose and all one has to do then is let the black powder run out into a container. Whatever the type and color of the shells, the powder is always the same, minute shiny grains. When one's box or bag is filled to the brim one can obtain a pleasurable sensation by running one's hand through the dark, cool, pouring mass.

Once the cartridge cases are empty there's not much one can do with them. The butcher's son, who has a reputation for being a wild devil and is anxious to maintain it, has become a past master at the art of striking a single well-placed blow, with a small hammer, on the base of the case, which is held vertically in one fist. The hammer strikes the percussion cap and the powder explodes; the case leaps out of the closed palm and springs high into the air. He has no competitors. The actual gunpowder, on the other hand, lends itself to numerous scenarios. They go out into the country, to a sandpit on the edge of the forest, and there they build small mounds, and sometimes proper castles, which they stuff full of powder. They dribble trails of it to a point some distance away, where they light it, and then watch the streak of the hissing blue-and-yellow flame (sometimes they have races, each boy with his own trail) until the ultimate muffled explosion which sends the sand flying in a great surge.

The boys in Chevigny have various carefully guarded sources of supply. This adds a felicitous element of emulation. The butcher's son, for instance, exploits a cache of 78 shells known only to himself. His method of extracting the contents—long, twisted strips of macaroni—is to saw through the neck of the big copper case with a hacksaw. The saw heats the copper, which must be cooled, as a safety precaution, while the operation is in progress. To do this, each boy urinates in turn on the cut in the metal, so the butcher's son can go on sawing without interruption.

In a pit among the hawthorn and nettles Luc and his cousins

find a pile of heavy machine-gun belts equipped with small .20-caliber shells, probably abandoned by some tank in distress. The belts are formed of alternating pointed black shells ringed in blue and yellow shells with snub silver noses. They discard the latter, having decided that they are explosive or incendiary or in any event dangerous, and take the others home with them. The simplest means of separating shell from case, since they have no vise with which they could hammer at it crosswise, is to grasp the case and pound the body of the shell against a limb of a big cedar; eventually a small degree of play is produced and it becomes possible to knock the shell off and empty out the powder, which in this case is composed of tiny black bars. By pouring these into an aspirin tube one can manufacture a rocket which, when placed on a launching ramp of sand and ignited by a train of powder, will zoom up to the treetops. This operation requires careful measuring and skillful setting, however, because if the tube is not properly filled or the slope of the launching ramp is wrong, the rocket may explode without taking off and that spoils the fun. Luc holds the record for failures and the others are very insulting to him on that account, telling him what a clumsy oaf he is.

The trouble starts when the cousins decide to play a trick on their father by putting some powder in the bowl of his pipe. They know he is so absentminded and preoccupied that he will fill it without even looking at it, and will conscientiously tamp the tobacco down on top of the powder. Which is exactly what happens, in front of a rapt audience clutching the seats of their chairs. He lights his pipe, sucks at it, and a tall yellow flame leaps up. The uncle goes, "Oh!" For a moment he is flabbergasted and stares at the pipe in amazement; then, seeing nothing further emerge from the bowl, he returns to his melancholy musings and refills it without further comment. A flop. The next day the cousins repeat the trick, increasing the dose. This time the objective is achieved. The flame shoots up to the ceiling, the uncle, momentarily blinded, drops his pipe and then, his attention startled into focus, flies into a rage and demands an explanation. Gunpowder is confessed to, perforce, but just a pinch, the merest pinch; they promise, they swear on their honor that nobody has any more. The uncle waves his arms and utters dire imprecations.

Then comes the real smash. The butcher's son tries to deal a little too summarily with a recalcitrant 105 shell, under the admiring gaze of his little sister; he fixes it in a vise on his father's workbench and bashes away at it with a sledgehammer. The charge explodes, the butcher's son has both hands torn off and is taken to the hospital at Creil. He dies the next day.

"He was crazy," the cousins say. "It had to happen. He was always like that."

Maybe it's a coincidence and maybe not, but that evening, while the whole of Chevigny is still buzzing over the folly of the butcher's son and the punishment visited upon him, the uncle goes up to the attic and finds the first cache of bullets and loose powder, half hidden near the door. Luc's hoard. The cousins' caches are farther away and better secreted, and the uncle, reeling from the shock of his discovery, doesn't even look for them. Hence, the entire wrath of the family is concentrated on Luc's head. The cousins assume angelic airs. He is ordered to remove his arsenal from the house within the hour. He loads it into a big gunnysack at nightfall. Not far away, behind the asylum wall, he knows of the site of an abandoned house; all that is left of it is a few stones and the maw of a very deep well gaping open at ground level, over which he has leaned and dreamed of subterranean secrets dating from the Middle Ages. He crouches by the rim of the well and drops the packets over, one by one; he hears the muffled impact very far away. Then he pours out the powder—two, four pounds? And finally, he chucks in a heap of macaroni from the 78 shells. He is still holding the last handful when he is suddenly visited by a vague desire to light up the bottom of the well in order to see how deep it is or what it looks like with all the stuff he has thrown down it. He stretches out on his stomach, lights one stick of macaroni, tosses the bright flame over the edge, and sticks out his head to watch it fall. What instinct causes him to hurl himself backwards before it reaches the bottom? Almost before he has done that, or maybe a fraction of a second later, a terrific effulgence leaps out of the hole and climbs high into the sky, and a searing gust flattens him to the ground. He lies there a long time in the darkness and silence, paralyzed by surprise and fear, his face pressed against the sharp stones and thorns and bright zigzags darting back and forth in front of his eyes. He calls himself an imbecile. He waits for people to come. But nobody does.

Later, when he is on the stairs going silently up to his room, he overhears a conversation between his uncle and aunt:

"I'm worried about Luc. He is so unpredictable. He is quite oblivious. He never talks about his parents. It's as though he never even thinks of them. Everything seems to be the same to him. Nothing really reaches him."

"Luc has always been a withdrawn child. Solitary."

"Perhaps he's only pretending."

"That ridiculous nickname, Cat, his brother gave him."

⁜

The holidays are over. The aunt is getting ready to take the boys back to Paris. On the morning before their departure, a letter comes from Antoine, which somebody has brought from Paris after long delays. It is dated August 19. Almost a month already. It's a short note addressed to his aunt, from Orléans.

"At present I am a soldier and interpreter in the American army. The unit in which I am serving is not going to Paris. I am giving this note to a person who is to go there as soon as possible and will pass it on to you. My address is: Hq. Co., 3rd Bn., 14 Infantry, AP 05 US Army. Tell me about my parents."

"If he was in Orléans," Luc says, "that means he's in Patton's army."

"You always have to know more than everybody else," says his aunt.

It's a beautiful morning; around nine o'clock, his uncle is shaving in the bathroom to the sound of Handel's *Water Music*, it fills the whole house and spills out the open doors and windows: the daily signature tune of the BBC "French Culture Hour." Upstairs, in his room, Luc is conducting the orchestra, holding the baton in his left hand, with *Sturm und Drang* fire and intensity. A roar of airplanes is heard, mingling with and then drowning the radio broadcast fan-fares. He scrambles down the stairs and races into the garden, staring up. Very low overhead, above the chestnuts, planes are flying past in formation, hundreds of them, each towing a huge dark glider, slowly, almost painfully. They are heading north. It's the beginning of the English offensive against Arnhem, which will be a bloody de-feat. Most of the men packed inside those gliders will be dead a few hours from now.

It occurs to him that there's not much left for him to do here; maybe it's the planes overhead. The time has come to migrate. Now he has an address and a direction, the direction being followed by the American army: east. He knows that a few trains are running again; he has heard there's one for Paris every evening. That night he pockets a thousand-franc bill from his uncle's desk—he has long known which drawer to look in—and goes down to the station. He leaves a note: "I have gone to join Antoine."

He is wearing his old navy-blue wool jacket with the tabs, his too short shorts, also blue wool, with the threadbare hem that rubs raw sores on the insides of his thighs if he has to walk very far, his espadrilles, and the grease-stained knapsack from which he is never parted. The railroad station is bedlam. Everybody in the crush is waving papers and trading insults with the two overwhelmed em-ployees who keep calling out, "Travel orders, travel orders!" In the throng, he slips through without a ticket and, at nightfall, boards a packed train that jerks its way toward Paris, screeching over the dam-aged rails and making lengthy stops. The cars are old, with yellow wooden benches and shuddering doors and windows, many with ply-wood where the glass used to be, dimly lit by one peeling blue-painted bulb in each compartment. He manages to wriggle his way to a bench. He is surrounded by men, all young, all from the north; they shout, sing, gesticulate, and drink cans of beer. They offer some to Cat; it's warm and tasteless.

The distance from Chevigny to Paris is forty-eight miles. It takes the train all night. Sometimes it stops in the open countryside. The noise subsides, those nearest the windows peer into the dark. They try to decipher the sounds and voices coming up from the tracks; snatches of information ricochet through the mass jammed into the corridor and inside the compartments. People try to work out the train's itinerary. Some get off at the stops and attempt to find out where they are. Around midnight, after a stop lasting even longer than the previous ones, they creep very slowly, more slowly than a man walking, across a creaking, moaning, echoing, heaving bridge that seems alive beneath the wheels. That's Persan-Beaumont, a temporary bridge over the Oise. Later, somebody leaning out into the deep night informs the silence within: "We're at Chaponval."

But nobody knows where Chaponval is.

Cat's companions are FFIs returning to Paris. They say they're going to the Romainville fort. It seems to give them a great sense of freedom to compare their repertoires of obscenities, as though by this means they are affirming their independence to themselves and the whole world. They all know "Les Filles de Camaret," and Cat himself has no trouble bawling out the first verse with them, the one about pricks and tapers. That earns him a certain degree of esteem. He earns even more when he recites the whole of the "Cadaver so pink, / Whose feet they do stink," because all his fellow passengers know by heart is the refrain. He teaches them the verses. He is then made acquainted with the adventures of the Convent Sister and the lament of the crafty Blind Man, which he finds pretty disgusting with its eggs, stick, and cream: "No, thank you, ma'am, I make my own," the Blind Man says. Whereupon the rest bellow, in chorus:

> *Give him a good time,*
> *Good good good good good time,*
> *The poor old Blind Man who can't see a thing!*

That's the top song, the slogan, the song that rules the night. Its only competition, very feeble, comes from the lament of the Motorcycle Crab ("It took my ass for a turnpike road"—a modernization which the author, Théophile Gautier, could not have foreseen but which is not incompatible with the poet's original intentions) and the "Grand Bal des cons et des culs": "For strings on my fiddle, I had three black, sticky asshole hairs." And of course, the spoken chorus, to the martial rhythm of snare drums:

> *Mess tins*
> *Mugs of canteens of mess tins*
> *Mugs of canteens of canteens of mugs of mess tins*
> *Bang your prick against my cunt*
> *Bang your prick against my cunt.*

In a few short hours that night, Cat acquires a royal repertoire, a truly dazzling repertoire, one that would enable him to shine for a lifetime in any masculine gathering. The high point is reached sometime after midnight; then the agitation dies down, the singers lose impetus, heads start to nod.

"When we get to Germany," bawls the boy on Cat's right, a tall farm lad who mashes him every time he moves, "we'll bugger all the broads, the old ones and the young. We'll run them through with our rods, one and all. We'll fill the sluts with little French babies, and that'll settle the German question forever."

The boy on his left is the only one in uniform, windbreaker jacket, high yellow leather shoes wrapped tight around his pant cuffs; the shoes are greatly admired by all.

"Gee, what if they give us shoes like that!"

"Don't make me laugh, they're going to dump their leftover puttees on us."

"On the black market you could get two thousand for those."

The wearer of the shoes is not talkative. He answers their questions briefly. Yes, he's in the 2nd Armored Division, on furlough. No, he wasn't at the liberation of Paris. Wounded just before. Maybe his taciturnity is not unrelated to the exhibitionism of the others. Initially, he hands out chewing gum and cigarettes all around; he empties his pockets, then huddles back into his corner.

"You can sleep on my shoulder," he says to Cat.

During a stop Cat sees him ferreting around in his bag, sorting things, one of which is a sailor's beret with a red pompon. He takes a chance: "Are you a porpoise?"

"Clever boy."

"Do you know Julius Kleinberg?"

"Sure. Top Sergeant Julius, alias the Astronomer, tank crew leader. We're in the same company."

"He's a friend," Luc asserts, trying to put some conviction into his voice.

"You choose the right friends. How do you know him?"

"Oh," Cat mumbles, "in Paris before the war . . ."

"Don't try to kid me; how old were you before the war?"

"Yeah, but I saw him again in August. On the Cours-la-Reine. He gave me his lighter."

He takes out the lighter and lights it; it smokes and stinks.

"Well, the last time I saw him was on the road to Saclay. I got a piece of shrapnel from a twenty-eight in the buttock, but close to the femoral artery, so I woke up in the hospital. What a waste of time. I'm glad you saw him. What about his family?"

"No," says Cat. "He went to the Rue Vieille-du-Temple. He didn't find anybody there. Except the concierge. He didn't look too cheerful."

"That guy is never cheerful. Except when he's playing the piano. Then he really lets go. Or when he's looking at the stars. He knows them all by name. You can never let him out alone at night. He forgets everything. He wouldn't even hear a bombardment. One night, in Morocco, he was on guard duty, they found him at the bottom of a hole. He was walking along with his head in the sky and fell in without ever knowing what happened. But he had spent six months in a Spanish prison with the lieutenant, so the lieutenant stuck by him. Even so, it's a good thing he was in on the liberation of Paris."

"About the piano," says Cat, "he says his fingers . . ."

"Yeah, that's what happens. In 1939 I was getting ready to go to engineering school. Do you think I still know anything? Do you imagine that at the age of twenty-four, when this war is over, I'm going to go back to high school with a lot of pimply-faced crammers? I've seen my old pals. They've already got their degrees. They're just what we're waiting for to rebuild France. We're going to be a funny-looking bunch of monkeys, we soldiers, when peace comes.

"I'm glad to have seen my family and friends again," he goes on. "I was at Val-de-Grâce Hospital and I went over the wall before my time was up. I had one afternoon off, so I took two days to go home to Amiens. But I'm glad to be leaving there too. There's nothing wrong with bouquets and champagne. And girls too. But I felt like a jerk. It's hard to go on being a hero after two or three days. Especially when I had used up almost my whole supply of rations.

"But what about you?" he continues, in the lunar stillness of another stop, after the locomotive, very far away, seems to have whimpered its last and given up the ghost, and a shudder of squeaking metal has run down the whole train from coupling to coupling. "Where are you going all alone like this?"

"I'm alone," begins Cat, "because . . ."

It doesn't bother him so much, now, to tell his tale. Sometimes it even seems interesting and believable to him. His parents deported to Germany. His brother in the American army. The killings. The Gestapo. The gun.

"Are you sure it was Spanish?" asks the porpoise. "From what I've seen of Spanish guns, I wouldn't trust it."

"No, but I really saw it."

"Anyway, I can see why you're a friend of Julius's. Exactly his type. Where are you headed?"

"I'd like to try to get to Nancy. I've got family there."

Because he knows that Nancy has been liberated by the American army for at least ten days—that's the right direction.

"Listen, there aren't any trains. If you can't find any other way to go, come and see me at Val-de-Grâce. Corporal Bérard. Bob Bérard. Room 75. I was supposed to have left this morning. By tonight at the latest I'll know where I join up again. If I'm not there, I'll leave a message for you. Maybe I can take you with me on a truck. That'll get you closer. And if I don't see you again, I'll tell Julius about you."

"Tell him the Cat's still got his lighter."

"He'll like that."

Cat sinks into a half slumber, his head against the porpoise's shoulder and his legs mixed up with those of the big farm lad, who has finally collapsed, his head in his arms and his arms folded over his knees. The poor Blind Man's song has long since ended.

At dawn, Gare du Nord, in a fine mist falling from the smashed glass of the roof, the porpoise buys him a cup of saccharin-sweetened black liquid.

"I only have one thing left," he says. And pulls out of his pack a can of sausages and beans. Cat thanks him politely and sets off on foot through the gleaming, empty streets.

■■

He walks in the rain among overflowing garbage cans. The too familiar beast that lives in his entrails starts to nibble. Then it gnaws; he bends over, one fist pressed against the hollow of his stomach. At the Gare de l'Est he sees a lot of people standing in lines or waiting on empty platforms for trains with uncertain destinations. "They say it's going as far as Meaux," he is told in one group of families. "But maybe farther, we're going to try, anyhow. We'll see when we get to the end." Mountains of bags and packages. People sleeping on the ground. Red Cross uniforms around a steaming cauldron. No, he's crazy. There is no train for Nancy. The track is not open beyond the Marne. Chalicourt bridge is down. Maybe in a few days . . . He buys himself another blackish cup of liquid to cauterize the bites of the beast, finds an empty bench near the reek of a urinal, curls up on it with his head on his knapsack, his whole body tied in knots, he's cold, he's miserable, he'd rather be anywhere else, even in his bed at Chevigny; it's the time of day when his uncle's clever little dog would be waking him up, scrabbling with his paws on the bare floorboards and licking his face. He falls asleep, exhausted, and the noise of the station lopes through his sleep alongside compact nightmare shapes.

Later, around noon, he pries the can of beans open with his knife and eats them cold, they stick to his palate and his guts. He stands in a line to drink some water out of the faucet. What next? An old habit sends him into the métro, toward Saint-Lazare, and he shelters in the damp warmth of the Cinéac. No more *Propaganda-staffel* films. Now they're showing a Soviet film, *The Rainbow*—"a masterpiece," is all the poster outside has to say about it—and he watches the sufferings of the Russian people file past, the atrocious story of the indomitable peasant woman who is condemned by the

Nazis to crawl around the concentration camp on Christmas Eve, moaning and sobbing in the snow, and who, in her final agony, gives birth at midnight in the cold and wind while the SS stand indoors in the warmth and piously sing *"O stille Nacht, heilige Nacht"* around a lighted Christmas tree; then the partisans come skiing up all dressed in spotless white with machine guns hanging around their necks, avengers arriving to save their people and punish the brutes.

He emerges back into gray light and a hastening throng of unfriendly faces. In the Cour de Rome, a bunch of people are gathered around a singing accordion player. His assistant is selling the lyrics, printed in bluish ink. "At last they are gone . . ." reads Cat, "to the tune of the 'Fête au Rancho' ":

> *At last they're gone, those sour Krauts,*
> *Resistance and Allies have chased them out;*
> *For four years here they made mayhem,*
> *But now we're truly rid of them.*

> REFRAIN
> *We'll never see them anymore,*
> *It's over now, they're out the door.* (bis)

> *Bulgaria and Rumania have understood,*
> *The little lands can see they're no good,*
> *No good at all, the lousy Huns,*
> *So leave them alone to play with their guns.*

The high point of the lyrics is the end of the final couplet:

> *Go on, you lanky German beans,*
> *Get eaten up by Scottish greens.*

The printed text laboriously explains the various puns and the accordion player underlines them with huge winks, raising a couple of polite smiles. Cat gives a franc for the sheet and immediately wonders what on earth he is going to do with it.

He walks on, heading now for the Left Bank, damp all through, his spongy espadrilles making a sucking noise. He crosses the central markets, which he's never seen before, and is amazed by the filth, the stalks and stems in the gutters, the sad, crowded houses with doors opening onto foul-smelling dark intestines. Inside the cafés, lit by sparse flames of gas lamps, indefinite shapes move back and forth behind curtains. He turns at the corner of the Rue Saint-Denis and the Rue de la Grande-Truanderie, moves down an alleyway, and pauses a moment under a café awning to let a gust of heavier rain pass by. There are women standing there, and further along, in front of the walls. He tells himself they must be whores but he isn't sure. It's the first time he's ever seen any, they look like other women. Few men go past, and then hurriedly. He stares at the woman nearest him, who is also waiting under the awning on high cork platform shoes, yellow hair piled very high on her head, a hard, unfriendly air. After a minute she turns and insults him: "Dirty little kid. It's disgusting, at his age, been gaping at me for the last hour. They're all pigs. Little bastard. Standing there getting an eyeful."

The downpour continues, he doesn't know what to do with himself, he doesn't dare answer back, he doesn't dare walk farther down the street in the rain past the other women, who are all starting to join in, from one doorway to the next. He feels himself growing scarlet with shame and is getting colder and colder.

A girl sticks her head through the café door.

"Quit picking on the poor kid. Can't you see he doesn't know what to say?"

Her fair hair is cut short like a helmet, she has a triangular face, a pointed chin, and eyes that are almost green and almond-shaped. She looks very young and is wearing tight pants and thick-soled shoes. Her voice is rusty and warm, a dragging, almost broken voice, like a boy's that has only half changed.

"Well, what are you standing there for?"

"I don't know," Cat stammers. "I'd like to eat."

"Then come on inside."

And as he doesn't move she grabs him firmly by the elbow and pulls him in. The copper bar gleams in the half-light. Men in shirt sleeves sit at the tables at the back.

She looks him over from head to foot.

"Impossible; you've been out in the rain all day."

"I've come from the country," says Cat. "I'm going to Nancy."

"On foot, maybe?" She laughs.

"I don't know. There aren't any trains."

"If you're hungry . . ."

"I've got some money, I can pay."

"Not the prices they charge here. This joint is not for poor people." And she calls out in the direction of an open door behind the bar: "Boss, an order of chitterlings, on my tab. And two glasses of red."

The owner is a wide hairy creature in slippers, short-winded and taciturn. The chitterlings are the fattest, most unctuous things Cat has ever eaten. He tries to fill his whole body with the taste of them so he can describe it to his brother. The wine is bitter and gives him a cramp in his jaw. All of a sudden he feels stronger.

"Don't you know anybody in Paris?"

"My parents . . ." Cat begins. And tells his story once more.

"You can stay here awhile if you want. It's quiet in the afternoons. It's different at night. Nothing dull then. All swing."

"I've got an appointment. With a friend, at Val-de-Grâce. I've got to be going."

He asks how much he owes, and insists, clearly feeling a little as though he's putting on an act.

"It's a present, numbskull. You've got pretty eyes, little brother."

She kisses him.

"What's your name?"

"Luc. They also call me Cat."

"As bashful as you are, I'd sooner have thought of calling you Snail."

He looks cross and she laughs.

"Oh, a pretty snail! Not a slimy snail. A blue-eyed snail. All curled up in his shell."

He shoulders his knapsack and eases cautiously out the door. The big woman with the yellow hair is gone.

"Hey, Snail! If you get back to Paris again, my name is Diane. You can always ask for me at the Petit Roscoff."

She kisses him again, on both cheeks. She's hardly taller than he is.

*"Bon voyage,* little brother."

❖

At the hospital, a bony female with a sharp and penetrating gaze, wearing a khaki skirt and shirt, emphatically bars the way; visitors allowed on Sundays only. The authoritarian voice calling him *vous* is an unpleasant reminder of family respectability, and he is about to beat a prudent retreat when he sees Corporal Bob Bérard, his beret on his head and a large bag slung over one shoulder, heading for the exit.

"Good timing. We're off."

He leads him to the courtyard, shoves him into a canvas-sided American truck, and climbs in after him. Inside, on benches running along the sides of the truck, are five or six soldiers and civilians and one American. The truck starts and rolls through empty streets along the Seine, then jolts over paving stones. Soon they're in the country. Night falls.

"We're going to Meaux," shouts Bob.

Cat lies down on the floor on his stomach, his arms crossed to absorb some of the bumps, and lets himself drift. He shuts his eyes. He's going to the front.

At Meaux they get off outside the station in the unlighted night. They enter a dark building, the inside dim in the light of a single kerosene lamp. A few uncommunicative soldiers are eating a thick soup served by two girls from the Red Cross. They give him a bowl and two chocolate bars. And more wine. Enough to make him sleep for a century. Which is what he does, in a dormitory with double-decker beds; he rolls himself up in a blanket that smells of vomit. It would be even better if the others didn't snore, if there weren't all these snorts and gurgles. And if he weren't permanently steeped in this icy dampness, now mixed with the dampness of the blanket.

In the morning he feels the sun brushing his eyelids. For a second he keeps his eyes shut: he is on the beach. Sound of waves, Ravello's boat. But the porpoise pulls him by the legs, he opens his eyes and sees the room empty and all the beds unmade.

"On your feet, Luc, there's real coffee to drink and I've got news for you."

He sits Cat down at the table.

"Here it is; I'm going to Chaumont. They've already passed the Moselle on the south and are a long way beyond Nancy. From Chaumont to Nancy you should be able to work something out for yourself. I've got brand-new equipment and rations for several days. Seven jackets and three helmets . . . I got a jacket and pants for you, I took the smallest I could find."

The pants drag on the ground over his espadrilles. He tightens the braided elastic belt over the folds around his middle. And the jacket comes almost to his knees. He tries on one of the helmets, the plastic one, it comes down over his eyes. But he is wonderfully dry. Except for his feet.

"You look like a tramp," says Bob. "But not as bad as you did before . . . I'll see if I can find anything else."

He returns with ration kits. Cat inspects them before stuffing them into his knapsack. Tubes of milk, unknown substances, cans of ham and cheese, chocolate bars, a carton of Camels, a creamy pomade with an incomprehensible name; he tastes it.

"Idiot! That's medicine for the clap."

Another tube, marked "Mosquito bites cause malaria." A round tin of solidified alcohol to heat the bacon and beans, some banana-flavored toothpaste. And a long garland of French letters, which one can cross and wrap around one's chest like a Mexican cartridge belt.

"Now for the Red Ball. We stick to her from here on."

Bob is squat and dark, with straight hair growing to a point in the middle of his forehead. Calm and measured, but always sure. He moves with a sort of total certainty, as though he always knows in advance what has to be done, exactly and without asking questions. He talks little and everything he says has a final ring to it. Bob is the perfect antidote to anxiety. When he comes back there is a huge, stocky, placid bear with him, whose small, very pale, very cunning eyes gleam beneath drooping eyelids under a shapeless red cap. Bob tells Cat that his name is Janusz, he's a spahi, they'll be traveling together. And adds that he is also a Polish prince.

"Oh," says Janusz with a deprecating smile, rocking back and forth on his feet exactly like a dancing bear at the fair, "in Poland everybody is a prince, more or less."

"Julius is a friend of mine," says Cat.

"Then you're a prince too." And very delicately, with his great flail of a hand, he gives him a gentle nudge on the shoulder.

Cat feels safe. Things are becoming simple.

Both of them have their travel orders, which they had drawn up by the echelon of the 2nd Armored Division at Meaux. All they have to do is wait at the American post until a truck stops for them, in the endless chain rolling eastward from the sea, the chain Cat saw driving past Chevigny. They put Cat in the cab with them. Nobody asks him any questions. They exchange cigarettes with the driver. He's from Cincinnati. Where on earth can Cincinnati be? They're too crowded on the seat of the Dodge, there is no glass in the windows, the wind they're making, soon followed by gusts of rain, lashes his face, the truck is roaring full speed ahead with its lights on over a straight road full of potholes; it crosses deserted, often devastated villages without slowing down and struggles painfully up slopes in first gear with a deafening roar that puts a stop to any attempt at conversation. They're jolted to pieces because the road is one long rosary of holes, ruts and half-filled trenches, and the driver never slows down for anything. There is almost no traffic in the other direction—the chain returns westward, empty, over a different road—and they see no vehicles in front of them except, on one of the long straight stretches in Champagne, the lights of the truck ahead, over half a mile away. Sometimes, though, they have to pull up suddenly to go around the wagon of some farmer trying to turn at the top of a hill. The driver swears; Bob says, "They really think the war's over," and explains that in theory all civilian traffic is prohibited on the Red Ball road. They also cross a few incongruous automobiles whose occupants appear not to give a hoot about the prohibition. Cat looks at the speedometer, it takes him a while to realize that the figures stand for miles and they're actually doing much more than sixty kilometers an hour, but he doesn't know how to convert. "Five to eight," Bob shouts. After two or three hours they stop at the end of a long line of vehicles among ruins of houses, and wait to cross a river on a pontoon bridge. Each truck moves forward at a snail's pace, setting up a great rattle, over boards laid on top of floating road-bearers. Only one can go at a time; the waiting seems endless. It's raining, the bridge is slippery, it rolls, pitches, and sags. The road surface is nothing but puddles of yellow mud plowed with ruts. A bunch of soldiers move down the line with a fuel tank, filling up the trucks. He tries to understand what they're saying. In his family, everybody always made fun of American accents, of those ducks who talk through their noses, and it makes him happy to hear them actually speaking for the first time. The driver immediately goes to sleep, slumped over the steering wheel; Bob and Janusz smoke in silence, their eyes half shut, motionless, as though they were storing up time.

"I can't just sit like this, doing nothing," Cat murmurs timidly at the end of an hour.

"You've got to learn how to wait," says Janusz, dragging at his cigarette. "You ought to learn. You'll need it. Nothing more useful than silence and patience. I learned in jail. Eighteen months; Spanish bastards. After that, things become precious to you for the rest of your life. A cigarette, for instance. Just that."

Cat jumps down onto the road. Several Americans wave to him. They're eating out of mess tins, standing in the rain, leaning against trucks or sitting on bumpers. They're very dirty. Their faces are young, thin, and tired. They are unshaved, their helmets come down almost to their eyes with the throat strap dangling on one side, their jackets are stained and splattered and wrinkled, without insignia or buttons or belts or leathers or scabbards, the only thing military about them is the khaki color; they are certainly nothing at all like the virile caparisoned warriors he has been watching parade past for the last four years.

He's afraid somebody is going to demand an explanation from him, what is he doing there, why is he wearing those fancy clothes; he feels guilty.

*"Hello, boy, where you from?"*

"From Paris," he replies, dreading the sequel.

But all that comes, instantaneously, is a chorus of exclamations and whacks on the back.

*"Wow, Paris, lucky man! What a great place . . ."*

They tell him they don't know Paris, even though they've been in France for three months, and then they all start asking questions at once, he can't keep up with them and stumbles over his words but he tries to answer anyway because they have such friendly big roars of laughter. The Eiffel Tower? The German occupation? What are the girls like? Rationing? Does he eat frogs and snails? And what about the sewers of Paris, is it true you can walk through the sewers of Paris? They want to know how old he is too, and his name, and whether he has a sister, and where he learned to speak English so well, and where's he's going and why, and what his father does. He says that his father is a teacher, yes, teacher or professor, he can't remember which is right, he really is stammering and stuttering a lot, but they keep encouraging him—professor of what? they want to know. Chinese, he answers, and waits for the usual snorts and sniggers, but not at all. On the contrary, one of them admiringly exclaims, *"Fantastic!"* and another asks how much he earns and whether he has many students and whether he has gone to China himself and doesn't he want to come to the States? He tells them that his parents are prisoners of the Germans, he talks about Antoine, and they all keep saying reassuring things to him, how it won't be long now, they're going to settle Hitler's hash and after the war he will come to see them in the United States, which is the most beautiful country in the world. They give him pink sausages with split peas in a mess tin, the sausages are dripping with fat and have a wonderful taste of smoked bacon, and he eats them so avidly and so fast that they are all impressed and exclaim over him. They call to men further up and down the line to come witness this phenomenon, this *"funny French kid"* who is beating the world's record at eating split peas and sausages. Everybody crowds around him, holding out more sausages.

When he climbs back into the cab, just as the truck is about to start across the bridge, he has a dozen little pieces of paper with addresses in the United States on them, in weirdly slanting, angular writing. They all tell him to come and visit them after the war, they all shout "Good luck!" at him, waving and brandishing sausages.

"You were in Spain?" Cat asks Janusz.

"Eighteen months in jail, starving. A record."

"Don't worry," adds Bob. "There are quite a few of us who have promised ourselves a little trip down that way when the war is over to take care of Franco's boys."

They drive all day long. Cat nods through the bumps and jolts, crammed like a cement block between the cab door and Janusz's shoulders. They're held up again at river crossings or by railroad tracks, where the road turns into a trail weaving between bomb craters and ruins. There are more long waits, often for hours. French women come past with bottles of red wine, he drinks straight out of the bottle like everybody else, the girls kiss him. He's a little drunk. He feels as though he is floating in a thin fog. His anxiety is almost gone, he feels almost comfortable, he tells himself there is no reason why things shouldn't go on the way they are. And yet he is still vaguely worried by the idea that all of a sudden somebody, some officer type, is going to come and ask him what he's doing there; he keeps looking around but nobody challenges him, and every time they realize that he speaks English the soldiers all crowd around with the same curiosity and friendliness. Anyway, how would he know an officer if he saw one?

They reach Chaumont during the night. Bob and Janusz deposit him in another vast dormitory and set off in search of a hypothetical advance unit. They return much later, saying they have to leave the next day for Neufchâteau. The front is not far from there, nobody knows where exactly; they have to keep going east. They've seen a map, Neufchâteau is on the way to Nancy, they were assured that the road is open, they won't have any trouble finding him a truck.

"And where," Cat asks, "is Patton's army?"

"Must be further north, around Metz. Metz hasn't been liberated yet. Why?"

"That's where my brother is," says Cat.

"If you imagine you're going to find your brother in an army of a hundred thousand men on the move! You'd better just sit quiet with your relatives in Nancy. He'll find you there, don't you worry. And you've done enough traveling for a while, shrimp."

At dawn they climb onto the bed of another Dodge truck and find themselves in a company of newly outfitted FFIs from Paris carrying Sten submachine guns, fresh recruits for the division. The men huddle together for warmth, half awake, they've been on the road all night, nobody speaks. Cat crouches on the truck floor, protected by the hulk of the Polish bear. This time it's a whole convoy, with jeeps interspersed among the trucks, creeping forward, wheel touching wheel, over a narrow road as badly torn up as ever. In the villages there are flags at the windows, people along the streets cheer them on, while gendarmes, firemen, and uniformed relief workers direct traffic.

At Neufchâteau they jump down into a square in which pale sunlight is caressing heaps of rubble that used to be houses. An endless convoy of American tanks rolls past.

"I'm going to look around," says Bob. "I'll see if I can find you something for Nancy."

He soon returns. He has seen a column of FFIs from a maquis near Langres who're headed for Nancy. They'll be traveling with the French First Army coming up from the south; the two have joined up. He talked to several of them, they're willing to take Cat along. He leads him to a sort of dilapidated barracks, its walls pitted with shells, or it might simply be a school, across from which a motley assortment of producer-gas-driven trucks stand warming up, their hoods and sides crudely painted with big black Crosses of Lorraine. All around them are men in the bottle-green wool uniforms of the Youth Worker brigades, wearing berets and big hobnailed boots that make an appalling racket. Most have Sten guns slung over their shoulders, some only hunting rifles.

"Here's the little brother," Bob says to a tall thin man wearing little steel-rimmed glasses. "Take care of him."

"Give me your family's address in Nancy," he says to Cat. "Maybe I'll stop by to see you one day."

Cat blushes and stammers, "I don't know the exact address." And gives him the address of the family apartment in Paris. He tells himself he's ridiculous, it's a phantom address, an empty apartment, an abandoned ship.

Bob looks at him with his steady gaze.

"But you really are sure you're going to Nancy?"

"Naturally," answers Cat, shrugging his shoulders. "Naturally."

"Then so long, Luc," says Bob. He gives a little wave of his hand and walks away with his measured tread; he does not look back. Cat feels abandoned again. The beast in his belly starts to gnaw. He bends over.

"Come have a drink," says the tall thin man.

In the courtyard a group of men in green uniforms or civilian clothes with brassards stand around a big cauldron on a wagon, drinking coffee out of pint jars. Along one wall there is a pile of German helmets; along another, a heap of wooden-handled grenades. He squints at them: great items for his collection. The tall thin man follows his gaze.

"No touchee. It seems they're for somebody else. Not that there are so many of us. And we could use them. But that's the way it is. Order, discipline, and damn foolishness. The army."

"I'm taking you back to the truck," he adds after they drink the lukewarm liquid. "I don't want the major getting a peep at you."

He points at a figure gesticulating in the middle of the courtyard. The man makes Cat think of some character escaped from the 1939 or even older copies of *L'Illustration* that he used to look at in Marles. His calves are encased in laced, hooked leggings beneath tan riding breeches, the upper part of his body is sheathed in a long khaki jacket strapped tight by a leather shoulder belt from which hang a pistol and a pair of binoculars that bump against his rear as he moves; broad stripes run all the way around his sleeves and there is a red-white-and-blue band on his right arm; the green beret cutting across his hatchet face makes him look like a poster for the Legion of Veterans: a real ghoul.

"He's a fart," the tall thin man says solemnly.

He and Cat climb into the rear of a canvas-sided truck.

"Aren't you going with them?"

"They make me sick. Screwing around. I piss on the major's cowlick. I didn't come here to play tin soldiers."

From the truck they can see the major giving orders, waving and pointing, at the base of a flagpole in the middle of the courtyard. The men form a square around him and present their miscellaneous arms. The flag is run up. It makes Cat think of school in Toulon in 1941, when all the classes were assembled in the old playground to perform the ceremony known as "saluting the flag," using a salute which was also described as "Olympic" and consisted of a two-beat sweep of the arm and outstretched hand, from heart to heaven; probably it was just an embryonic, self-conscious Fascist salute. Here the style is more traditional, hand to beret. Then the ghoul makes a speech. They can't hear him but they see the jerky gestures that punctuate his words. After that, the men march around the courtyard, bawling out a song which Cat now hears for the first time; he quickly catches the beginning of it because they sing it over and over, like a stuck record: "Friend, do you hear the black flight of ravens above our plains . . ."

"That's the latest invention of that fart. Three days ago he turned up all atwitter with a record fresh from London, he requisitioned a phonograph, he assembled the men, he wound it up, and he played that lugubrious thing over and over for an hour until we knew it by heart. Really deadly. They call it the 'Song of the Partisans.' As if we needed that kind of claptrap. Oh, well, it's so godawful and we're so out of tune that it may make the Krauts run just to get away from it, because everybody knows they're good at music; not like us. I guess that must be our secret weapon. We haven't got any ammunition, so they found us a record. And forbade us to lay a finger on the grenades. Bunch of assholes."

"Then why are you here?" ventures Cat.

"Why?" the tall thin man mutters vaguely. "Why? That is indeed the question, kid. Why? I suppose," he goes on, "there's only one explanation. I'm even dumber than all the other dumb jerks commanding us, and even dumber than that stupid fart there. Yeah, that must be it. And if you can believe it, I'm so dumb, so hopelessly stupid, that when all is said and done I'm almost glad to be here. Nobody was pushing me. And I guess it's the same for the rest of them. They deserve better. I like them. And the worst thing of all is that I'm a two-time loser. When I left in 1943 to get out of the STO all I had to do was lie low and wait. I was in a Secret Army maquis in the Jura. The same type as here. I've always had bad luck. Career officers who wanted to fight 1940 over again, they thought they were still in the regular army; guys homesick for the barracks and all that nonsense that was wiped out by the defeat. I got sick to death of them, so I went to Switzerland. No softies, the Swiss; but it was a long time since I had eaten as well as I did in that jail in Geneva. That time too, I could have worked something, found a way to stay there. But I got even sicker of them, and I gave the Swiss such a hard time that they finally threw me out. Then I looked for another maquis. Out of luck again; all I found was another SA unit. And that stupid fart of a career lieutenant who has promoted himself to major; he'd make us do anything just to give himself an excuse to keep his rank, he's scared to death somebody's going to take it away from him. So here I am now, NCO and all, with this ridiculous uniform from Pétain's work camps—you know, that suit of a becoming shade of green that the old lady had made for Babar the elephant?" (Yes, nods Cat). "Playing the war game. And yet we fought like sons of bitches coming up by Langres and we lost a lot of men. I mostly tried to keep our losses down, that's the one thing I can be proud of. And I tell myself that if I make it to the end without too much damage to my men, maybe I will have won my war too, in a way. When we came away from Langres we felt like gods, invincible, with our two Hotchkiss machine guns, our 1932 mortar and our ten shells. Then we saw the Americans and the First French Army ... You saw that convoy there? That steamroller feeling; there we were by the side of the road, watching the tanks and trucks and that whole gigantic arsenal roll past. They were nice to us; they gave us rations, let us handle their equipment, the way you let children play with grown-ups' things. We felt pretty dingy and small. And you should see how the civilians treat us. That was when I knew I would stick it out to the end. Once the first fighting was over and the *département* was liberated, they said everybody could go home. Not a single one went. We all signed on for the duration of the war. Then we were told that maquis NCOs who had diplomas and seniority could take a course and go into what they call a regular unit; I decided to stay small, with my dingy men. For the last ten days we've been marching flank guard for the 1st Armored Division. We're always short of ammunition. I've got one clip for the Sten: twenty rounds. We do the mopping-up, picking up what slips through the holes in the net, the menial work, the dirty work. I go on protecting my men from the mistakes of that great stupid fart out there. And that's it. Now we're being mustered at Nancy. I promised your pal Bob to take you there and leave you there and all I ask is that you don't move out of the truck and don't get yourself noticed."

The drill in the courtyard has come to an end. Men climb into the truck.

"Hey, chief, I see you're as crazy as ever about the old man's speeches?"

"Somebody had to look after the gas machines."

"He's going to end up believing you've got something against him."

They nudge and poke him.

"We've got a passenger," the tall thin man says. "We let him off at Nancy."

"You've been lucky—an American jacket," exclaims one man. "It's not fair, if they start giving clothes to the kids before us."

He feels the jacket.

"Look at that lining. That really is rainproof."

The trucks move off, creaking and clanking. They drive for an hour, slowly under the gray sky, at the best pace the dying producer-gas engines can muster. The major leads the way in an open-roof Peugeot adorned with a large Cross of Lorraine flag and his martial beret can be seen emerging from time to time like a dizzy periscope. Five miscellaneous vehicles follow him, including one flat garbage truck, a prehistoric animal that squeals and lurches on its solid tires, its cab surmounted by a machine gun mounted on a tripod.

"That's our tank," the chief tells Cat.

They stop at the side of a narrow road in a valley on the edge of a gleaming golden forest. Cat sticks his head out and sees a jeep and three American armored cars in front. The tall thin man goes to find out what's up.

"Change of program," he announces when he gets back. "We're

turning off. It seems we've got to show ourselves in the villages nobody's been to yet. There's a whole district around here. I don't
much like the idea. We don't have enough weapons."

He turns to look at Cat.

"If I'd known ... Whatever happens, don't you budge from
there."

They move forward between hedges of sloe along the sides of a
twisting, caved-in road yellow with mud, following the contours of
little valleys and passing through several villages without stopping.
Long black streaks trickle out from the huge dung heaps in front of
the houses, people emerge and stare at them in amazement, waving
and pointing.

"The silly damn fool," mutters the tall thin man, "the silly
damn fool. Why doesn't he stop? He doesn't know where he's
going."

And then all of a sudden, at the entrance to a village, the truck
brakes hard and skids into the one in front of it. They're thrown
against each other, they hear shots and shouting.

"Down! Get down!"

Somehow or other, he finds himself squatting with the rest behind the wheels of the truck. They hear several bursts of gunfire.
Close to him there is the dry click of the Stens being loaded.

"Don't anybody fire," says the tall thin man. "Not for anything.
The first man who shoots gets a kick up his ass." He stands up and
walks to the head of the column, the rest of the men stay where they
are. Peering over the body of the truck, Cat sees women rushing
about in front of them. There is some shouting, then a short burst of
machine-gun fire.

"The Hotchkiss," somebody says.

Then silence. The tall thin man returns.

"That's all for the moment. There were about ten of them. SS.
Left behind. They must have been taken by surprise and at the last
minute they fired on the first car. We've got seven prisoners."

He laughs.

"Nobody injured, but all four tires on the major's Peugeot are
gone, the car's finished, you should see the look on his face, he's
crazy mad. Serves him right. If he had stopped sooner ..."

Just then the ghoul in person comes striding up, waving his pistol and shouting, "Remount, back in the trucks!"

He stops short in front of Cat, who is just standing up.

"What is that?" he roars.

"Nothing," says the tall thin man. "Nothing at all."

"What do you mean, nothing at all? Where has that kid come from? This is not a nursery. This is a battalion of the French army."

"He's only a passenger, sir. We're giving him a ride for a few miles."

"I don't want to see it again. Get it out of here at once. And where did he get that uniform?"

Fortunately, Cat does not feel obliged to answer questions being exchanged over his head as though he didn't exist. Also fortunately, somebody comes running up just then to ask what to do with the prisoners, who are still waiting at the other end with their hands behind their necks. The ghoul rushes away again after repeating, "Get it out of here at once."

The tall thin man looks at Cat with a mournful little grin.

"Well, *it,* I guess you heard him. I haven't got any choice. Maybe it's better that way, anyway."

"But," he adds, "I'm not going to leave you standing here in the middle of a field. Come on."

Cat picks up his knapsack and, crestfallen, follows the tall thin man, who walks up to a house with shutters over its windows and knocks at the door.

"I'm entrusting this boy to you," he says to the man who opens the door. "Look after him and see that he gets to Nancy as soon as possible. Thank you very much."

And as the man doesn't move, just stands there barring the passageway behind the half-open door, he adds, "That's an order; from Major Bayard of the 1st Battalion of the Langres maquis of the FFI." He shoves Cat into the house and turns away.

Seeing him about to disappear, the man calls out, "Sir, sir . . . What about the Americans, are they coming soon?"

"There aren't any Americans around here. Only French. The country has been liberated. Haven't you heard?"

"Well, yes and no . . . For the last five days we've had no electricity, no radio, no news. Ever since Nancy was liberated we've been waiting for the Americans. It's like we've been forgotten. All we've seen is Germans, they've been coming through the villages here in bands, like locusts, and taken everything away. They're all along the valley."

"We'll take care of them," the tall thin man calls over his shoulder, without turning.

"But listen, sir, sir, they were waiting to surrender to the Americans. Not you. They'll never trust you."

"Guess they'll have to."

And he goes for good, back to the column, which is starting up again. Cat follows the man inside, the door shuts on a dim room.

"That's the end, that really is the end," says the man. "What do they have to come messing around here for? That's all we need. All we wanted was the Americans."

"They'll ruin everything," says a woman sitting at a table.

Cat puts down his knapsack on a big table covered with checkered oilcloth and waits, standing. On the table are bowls and a soup tureen, full. Two women are seated, he can't make out their faces, one is old and the other younger. The room is heated by a wood-burning stove, black and coppery. Warmth, quiet, calm. He wouldn't mind resting here awhile. There is a long silence.

"And what are we supposed to do with him?" the man finally says, turning to look at Cat.

He seems fairly young, he is wearing a dark cap with some sort of silver insignia on it, something like the caps of electricity company employees.

"I don't know," says the older of the two women. "Ask him where he comes from."

"I'm from Paris," Cat informs them amiably; he does not feel that an interpreter is really necessary, and he definitely dislikes being talked about in his presence as though he were a stray dog. "And I'm going to Nancy."

They hear the convoy rolling past, then, almost at once, shots, followed by another burst of machine-gun fire.

"There they go," the man says. "I told you so. Just our luck."

They strain their ears in the silence.

"The soup will get cold," the other woman says. "You'd better eat and keep up your strength. Anyway, there's nothing you can do about it."

"No," says the man. "But it's rotten luck anyway."

He sits. Cat is still standing. He doesn't know what attitude to adopt. Or what words to say. "You've got to learn how to wait," Janusz said; silence and patience. Easy to say.

"We can't keep him here," the man says to himself after three noisy gulps. "A boy alone like that on the road, with things the way they are, looks funny. This is no time for complications. Especially in my position."

Maybe, Cat thinks, suddenly remembering his brother's methods, maybe if I had a Frankish battle-ax I'd make a better impression. No, that's silly.

The old woman says, "You should ring up the gendarmes, the telephone's working. We could find out what's happening."

"You're right," says the man. He goes into another room. Cat hears him cranking up the telephone and talking, but he can't make out the words. The discussion goes on a long time.

"They won't budge," he says when he comes back. "They say they can't come out as long as there's shooting in the village. They asked me to bring the kid down myself."

"But if it's dangerous for them, it is for you too. It's their job."

"Yes. That's what I told them. They're not much help."

"Then," says the old woman, "we'll just have to wait. And after all, as soon as things calm down he can go to the gendarmes by himself."

Cat takes a deep breath, for courage, and the smell of their soup fills his nostrils.

"I think," he finally manages to say, "I think I can go there now."

He walks to the door and opens it. Nobody moves.

"Please, sir," he asks from the door, "what is your position?"

"I am a town councillor," the man says. "But," he adds, looking embarrassed, "you'd better stay here for a while. There's some soup . . ."

"No, thank you, sir," says Cat, walking out to the square.

"The gendarmes are at the other end of the village," the man calls after him. "Follow the road to the left, then straight ahead."

Outside, nobody and nothing. The sky has cleared, weak sunlight plays in the puddles. Old houses, more dung heaps, a muddy square on the right, facing the open country, a fountain, or rather watering trough, water singing under yellow lindens. All the shutters are closed. He walks across the square. There are three black-clad bodies lying in the mud, all pointing in the same direction; they are on their stomachs with their arms flung out in front of them, their helmets lying where they rolled. They have been disarmed, one man's shoes have been taken—did Cat really see holes in his socks? The man had dropped the grenade he must have had in his hand, it rolled a yard away. Cat can't resist the temptation, he bends over to look. The ring hasn't been pulled, it's still quietly hooked to its pin; delicately, he scoops up the grenade and sticks its handle through his belt, under his jacket.

When he straightens up he sees, across the square behind the watering trough, the khaki hoods of American armored cars, covered with their eternal lavender tarpaulin, parked beneath the lindens. He moves closer; there are three half-tracks and a jeep. The men in the half-tracks are sitting silently in their places while three helmeted soldiers lean over a map spread out on the hood of the jeep.

The man behind the machine gun of the nearest half-track calls down to him, *"Hey, Froggy! Where'd you get that snazzy jacket?"*

*"Can I help you?"* Cat inquires politely, trying to reproduce the Oxford accent his family dinned into his ears.

*"Great, you guys!"* cries the American. *"Listen! This guy speaks English."*

The men at the jeep turn and stare at him in astonishment.

*"Really? Fantastic!"* says the oldest one, who wears gold-rimmed glasses and must be an officer. *"Nobody speaks a real language in this fucking country. Can you tell us how to get to w-w-w-w-ville?"* (His pronunciation is so distorted that Cat can't guess, Alsonville, Ersonville, Oursonville?)

*"I don't know the place,"* says Cat. *"But I can ask for you."*

"We've lost our radio contact," explains the officer, pointing to the tall aerial on his jeep which has snapped in two like a hazel switch. "And I think we've gotten ourselves lost too. What's the name of this village?"

"Tennon," says Cat, who saw the name on a sign on the square.

The officer makes him repeat the name several times; he can't say it right.

*"If you like, I can show you on the map,"* Cat offers shyly.

For once in his life it's not just a game, and he's glad he learned how to read maps. They show him an area marked off in pencil and he struggles to locate himself in the maze of roads and valleys hatched in green and brown. It takes a long time, he feels as though this is some very hard test he has to pass. Moving north from Neufchâteau, then out in circles, he finally locates Tennon; then, tracing along the roads with his finger, he comes to Houssonville, at the junction with a major road; that's what they were looking for. They start slapping him on the back:

*"Hurray! Billy, you're a good kid!"*

"I think," Cat adds, *"that there are Germans everywhere."*

*"Okay,"* the officer says, *"that's what we're here for, to pick up the Krauts.* Come down to the village with us."

They get into the jeep, with Cat in the back, and the half-tracks fall in behind. They cross the square, avoiding the corpses. Shutters open, people start emerging on all sides. Some are waving French flags. They stop. From the far end of the street that runs crosswise through the village a little group is trotting toward them, a civilian holding a flag, a fireman, two gendarmes in blue uniforms. The door of the house Cat has just left also opens wide, and the electricity company employee joins the group, firmly settling his cap on his head.

"I am the mayor! I am the mayor!" shouts the man with the flag.

"Lieutenant Schultzberg, U.S. Army," the officer politely replies. *"Do you speak English?"*

"No," shouts the mayor. *"Bienvenue! Willkommen! Heil America!"*

*"Come on, Froggy, translate for me. Ask him if there are any Germans in Houssonville.* And tell him I don't speak German either. Only a bit of Yiddish."

"*What is Yiddish?*" asks Cat.

The officer shrugs. "*Never mind, forget it. Hurry up.*"

"He wants to know," Cat begins, proud and red-faced, in a respectful silence, "he wants to know if . . ."

The mayor says he doesn't really know but he's almost certain there are and they have to hurry, they have to be quick, very quick.

"*I don't understand,*" Lieutenant Schultzberg says musingly, "*why he is in such a hurry to see us get ourselves killed.*"

"He wants to know why they have to hurry," Cat tells the mayor.

"Tell him a column of maquis went through here less than an hour ago, and they'll tear the place apart. So they should go as soon as the others get here and leave us some men for protection."

"*Others? What others?*" asks the lieutenant, looking completely bewildered.

"Why, the others—the other Americans. The main body of troops. The American army!"

"*Oh, fuck! We are the U.S. Army!*" the lieutenant begins, raising his voice.

"What does he say?"

"I don't understand it all," Cat says truthfully, and turns to the lieutenant. "*What is fuck?*"

The lieutenant bursts out laughing, hugs Cat around the neck, and shouts, shaking him, "*Oh, you funny, funny guy!*" and all the other soldiers start to laugh.

Women arrive with white wine and glasses and offer them to the half-tracks. One farmer comes up to the driver of the jeep, who is black and has a nose like an eagle's beak, and yells at him, "Olé, Jimmy! You'm be heap big happy?"

"*What is this old gentleman saying?*" the driver asks, recoiling from the blast but prevented by his seat from moving any further away.

"*He asks if you are happy,*" Cat explains, leaving out the grammatical eccentricities.

"I don't know," mutters the driver, speculatively. "I think I'll wait until I get to Berlin to answer that. Or even better, Washington Square."

"I think I see how it is," Lieutenant Schultzberg says, more soberly. "But I'd be glad if this fellow could tell me, yes or no, whether there are any Germans in Houssonville or on the road between here and there."

"I think," suggests Cat, "the telephone is working."

"Great; let's go!" The lieutenant jumps out of the jeep. "Find me the post office."

"There's a telephone here," says Cat, pointing to the house of the man with the cap.

"You come with me."

The lieutenant pushes him through the open door, back into the warmth and the good smell of soup. The man with the cap follows. Mayor and gendarmes crowd in behind. This is Cat's revenge, but he keeps an eye on the gendarmes even so. They show absolutely no interest in him. They're falling all over themselves with obsequiousness. He goes to the telephone and cranks vigorously.

"I'd like to speak to Houssonville."

"What number at Houssonville?"

"I don't know. This is the American army."

"I'll give you the Houssonville post office."

Another man's voice: "Houssonville postmaster here."

"This," says Cat, "is the American army. We are at Tennon. Are there any Germans at Houssonville?"

"No, miss. They all went an hour ago."

"Are there any other troops?" asks Cat, who is annoyed and tries to make his voice deeper.

"No, miss. Tell them they can come ahead. We're in a hurry to see them."

He translates for the lieutenant, who gives him a big grin, sticks up one thumb and winks at him, tosses him back outside, and shoves him into the jeep. They start out again at full speed, through the village and into open countryside, over the mudholes with the three half-tracks behind them. This time it's real, Cat thinks to himself. It's not a game. I'm really here. If only Antoine could see me now. It makes him homesick to have no one to share his elation with. A quarter of an hour later, at the end of a long descent around hairpin turns bordered by tall trees, they come upon a tall structure with medieval turrets that marks the entrance to Houssonville.

•   •   •

Farther down, by a ditch, at a respectful distance from the first houses, stands a familiar form: a producer-gas-burning truck marked with the Cross of Lorraine and, around it, green shadows, scattered behind the trees. The moment the jeep turns into the last straight stretch another familiar shape emerges. Cat recognizes the tall thin man, who is now waving them to stop with both arms. They pull up short, the half-tracks behind, not more than a hundred yards from the truck. Cat is overjoyed to see somebody he knows again, he hops out of the back of the jeep and dashes toward his friend, who is yelling things at him which, in his headlong rush, he doesn't hear.

"Look!" he says as he comes up to him, pulling open his jacket to show his hand grenade. "Look what I picked up."

"Okay. I can see you mean business. But didn't you hear? I was yelling at you to stay back."

"So what," says Cat.

"Get under cover and don't move. I hope to God your Americans keep their shirts on. We've been waiting forever for the Krauts to come out. They called out not to shoot, they're surrendering. Since then, nothing. It's been going on for hours. I don't like it. They're scared. That makes everybody nervous."

For a moment the scene remains quiet, then suddenly things start to happen very fast. A group of Germans in black uniforms emerge from the dark porch of the tall hewn-stone building with their arms raised; one of them is carrying a white rag. They walk into the square. They're halfway to the truck when a short burst of machine-gun fire is heard. From where? A window in the high wall? One of the trees along the road?

"Don't shoot!" the tall thin man roars.

He goes on roaring, through the fireworks that begin all around the square.

The Germans in black start running toward them; the first one stops a few yards away, his arms hanging at his sides, his legs spread apart, he's shouting. Is it he or the tall thin man who yells again, "Don't shoot, don't shoot!" But who can hear anything with all the firing going on? The man jerks open his jacket, shoves his hand into his belt, and reaches for something but can't pull it out.

"The grenade, the grenade," the tall thin man yells right in Cat's ear.

Cat stands up and pulls his grenade out of his jacket, grabs it in his left hand, it's very easy, he's rehearsed the motions so often in the woods on his way to see the priest at Magny, the rabbits, the heather, the Shepherd's Elm, he pulls the ring and throws it straight ahead of him. His reach is too short, the grenade rolls on the gravel a few yards away, right at the feet of the German, who turns and runs like crazy back toward the building, everybody else starts running too, then they fall down, then an explosion buries everything, the noise knocks Cat off his feet, he thinks his head is bursting, he is lying with his face in the mud, his ears are filled with a strident whine, and he lies there without stirring, hearing nothing but that whine that fills his whole body.

When it finally fades a little and a hand turns him over, he sees heads above him, the head of Lieutenant Schultzberg, white, his glasses gone, his features all awry, he looks like he's crying, and beyond it the head of the tall thin man, and others, and Lieutenant Schultzberg picks him up in his arms and hugs him against his chest, he's talking to him but Cat can't hear anything except that shrill whine that is still banging against the inside of his ears and then ringing away.

He can also hear the far-off voice of the tall thin man, who is talking to him, his mouth right up against Cat's ear: "You're all right, you're all right, it's over. Say something, you can hear. It's over. Shout, you've got to shout. We're all deaf. It's natural."

He keeps shouting, but all Cat hears is a tiny thread of sound, "It's natural."

But his gray face and twisted mouth say the opposite.

Cat doesn't feel like shouting, he feels very far away, very weak, very light, he feels as though if he moves or opens his mouth he's going to fall apart, all that will be left of him will be a thin little cloud that will evaporate, he won't ever be able to catch hold of himself again, so he stays shut around himself and closes his eyes again.

How long is it before he opens them? Now he's leaning against a tree. In front of him, the wheel of the jeep, feet, legs, and on top, very far on top, Lieutenant Schultzberg again. He's got his glasses on now and is grinning at him.

*"Sorry for the trouble,"* Cat tells him.

*"Oh, you Froggy, you funny guy,"* Lieutenant Schultzberg says, bending down and stroking his head. And Cat realizes that he can hear again, only the sounds are a little dulled, flattened. He looks over to the square and sees people moving around, green and khaki uniforms, civilians.

The tall thin man comes over. "That's that. But your grenade, your grenade—I wasn't asking you to throw the thing. I just wanted you to give it to me. I wanted to scare the son of a bitch, that's all. Not throw it."

"Is he dead?"

"Yes. Two Krauts dead and three wounded. And a dozen prisoners. But it wasn't your grenade that killed him. It didn't kill anybody. Either on their side or on ours. Lucky. Lucky."

"Who fired?"

"As far as I can make out, they couldn't agree among themselves, inside. There were about fifteen of them from Alsace and Lorraine, conscripted by force into the SS, you know, and they were definitely going to surrender. But there were also two SS noncommissioned officers, real ones. First, they almost shot each other in there, that was while we were sitting out here like dopes, not understanding, then when they saw the Americans come up, the Alsatians thought they'd get out right away, and out they came, and that's when the other two sons of bitches, who maybe hadn't seen anything at all, started shooting at us. In fact, nobody really knows if it was us they were shooting at."

"So the guy who shouted 'Don't shoot' . . ."

"Was an Alsatian, yes. He wanted to surrender. And when the sniping started he thought he'd been trapped and he panicked, he was trying to get his gun out, I guess."

"But there's some good news too," he adds. "Major Bayard's triumphant march for God and fatherland has been stopped by a bullet from a Mauser in the muscles of his back. He squealed like a stuck pig but he has really and truly been evacuated and dumped on some nursing nuns, who have stuffed him full of gauze, and the battalion is rid of him. And the road is clear all the way to the main highway to Nancy. We're off, I'm taking you with me, and when we get there I am turning you over to your family, delivered to the doorstep."

Then Cat just falls apart.

"I haven't got a family in Nancy. And anyway," he adds with a sob, an unplanned one, it just wells up from the pit of his stomach, "and anyway, I'd like to go back to Paris."

The tall thin man freezes, eyebrows up and mouth gaping.

"Why, you little son of a . . ."

He doesn't finish.

"Oh, blow your nose," he yells, "it'll unplug your ears. I'm the one who's a damn fool. You don't take a kid into a circus like this."

###

Lieutenant Schultzberg gives him his address in Boston; the black driver gives him his in New York. They stuff his knapsack full of chocolate bars and other things. At the rate he's going, with his pockets full of scribbled scraps of paper, Cat will soon become a walking directory for the whole United States of America. What he doesn't know, and will learn as the years go by, is that from now on he has a family in the States. All he has to do is respond. If he wants, years and years later Schultzberg in Boston, Lopez in Denver, O'Connor in Washington, D.C., and all the rest—the survivors, that is—will still be writing him regularly every Christmas to tell him about the marriage of their oldest boy Richard or the birth of their first grandson Simon, to ask him about his own family or whether he can accommodate Cousin Jonathan, who's coming over to discover Europe; if he wants, it will be they who, the day he finally gets his visa, will take him for his first trip around Central Park, the Bronx and Brooklyn, will introduce him to cabins in the Adirondacks, islands off the New England coast at dawn and topless shows in Montreal late at night.

He's back in the producer-gas truck. The men have smiled at him.

"Look, there's our sharpshooter."

"Next time you start throwing grenades, first make sure there's nobody around, will you?"

"Better than the little tailor who killed seven with one blow . . ."

"Seven with one blow, yeah, but those were flies."

He'd like to smile back at them, but his grin won't come straight. He huddles in a corner. He's shivering. He feels ashamed of himself. Partly reassured, though, because nobody seems to be mad at him. The tanks start up and roll away in front, their rear ends loaded down with German prisoners, like clumps of big flies. The truck follows. Cat doesn't try to resist the bumps and jolts. He has stopped resisting anything. He has told his whole story yet again, this time to the tall thin man.

"I'm going to try to get you taken back to Paris," he says.

"Please," says Cat, past all sense of shame, "don't turn me over to the gendarmes."

"Are you crazy? Those stupid farts . . . I won't let you down, don't worry."

At Nancy the tall thin man deposits him in a Red Cross dormitory and tells him he'll be leaving the next day in a van that's going to Paris for medicine. He spends the night curled on a bed with his knees drawn up tight and his arms around his knees, staring into the dark. His formless nightmares are enlivened by the gurgles and snorts habitual to the inmates of these places. In the morning, a boy and girl in gray-blue uniforms come to get him.

"Are you Luc? You're coming to Paris with us."

They all squeeze into the front of the van. The boy and girl talk softly, slowly, together, they keep smiling at him and at each other. They say *vous* to each other.

"They must be in love," Cat decides, fascinated.

It often seems as though they don't really have to speak at all in order to understand each other; sometimes one seems to answer a question the other one didn't ask, and they treat it as perfectly natural. They're living on a cloud and Cat is very happy to share a corner of their cloud. The girl asks him about himself, his family, school, and he tries to find answers that will please her. It's still raining. The windshield wipers don't work. They drive slowly, over narrow, torn-up roads, they get lost, ask their way, and now and then they drive along the main road over which the Red Ball is still unreeling its endless chain in the opposite direction. They often stop, by ditches or under trees. They wait hours for a ferry near the pilings of a ruined bridge, on a bank cluttered with people on bicycles and in oxcarts. They sit on wet grass to eat the big hunks of sawdust bread and sausage they brought with them, and Cat unpacks his chocolate bars, *all* his chocolate bars; they are dazzled, they tell him he must be a prince or a magician in disguise. They take more ferries and drive over more shaky pontoon bridges, always with crowds on both banks. It takes them three days to reach Paris. They spend the first night on the road with relatives of the girl, and he sleeps, unwashed, in real sheets. The next morning she wakes him by stroking his cheek. He wants to cling to her and never move. The next night they sleep in a barn which a farmer opens for them.

They get to Paris late the third night. There they are, in the gloomy street in the seventh *arrondissement,* at the foot of the building. He's still shivering a little.

"Do you want us to go up with you, Luc?"

He tells them no, not to bother, and picks up his knapsack.

"Then so long, Luc. You'll see, everything will turn out all right."

The blond girl kisses him very gently, runs a hand through his hair as though to smooth it down, pulls at his shoulders to straighten his jacket; the boy kisses him too.

He climbs the stairs in darkness and silence, a weird silence that seems strange to him, a silence of death. He rings, his aunt, wearing a dressing gown, half opens the door. She cries out, "Luc!"

She pulls him to her and hugs him until he can't breathe.

"Luc! My baby!"

Then, suddenly, she lets go of him, steps back, and still at the top of her voice: "Where have you been? Where were you?"

And slaps him, very hard, twice, as though in spite of herself, as though she couldn't stop her hand.

"I don't know," says Cat. "I don't know."

His whole body is shaking with sobs, like hiccups, but the tears don't come.

And later, when he has sunk down on his bed without taking his clothes off, she comes in and sits on the foot of the bed. She caresses his forehead, she strokes his arm.

"My poor boy . . ."

Oh, no! thinks Cat, trying to hunch himself up even more, escape into the very bottom of himself, rolled up in a ball. Oh, no, not that.

"My poor boy, my little Luc, you must tell me where you've been."

She says it again, pressing on the arm he would like to withdraw, hide, make vanish, but she keeps stroking it and stroking it.

"Where you've been, where you've been."

What's the matter with them all? Cat whimpers, mute, inside himself. What's the matter with them all that they've always got to be asking questions, why are they always wanting to know?

"We've been waiting and waiting for you," the aunt says. "We've been so frightened."

He squeezes his eyes shut with all his strength, so hard that he starts to see stars, he says nothing, he is spending his last ounce of energy on saying nothing, he knows the tears are coming at last, his body is giving way, he sobs, sniffs, he's about to fall asleep.

But before he drops off for good he says to himself, over and over, "I did it all wrong."

And he hears a friendly, familiar voice, very far off, saying, "Stupid farts!"

# La Petite-Truanderie

I did it all wrong, Luc keeps telling himself. I did everything wrong. I didn't find Antoine. I didn't know how to do it. I behaved like a baby.

The questions multiply and collide, he looks at them from every angle. Why? And how? And could he have done otherwise? And what could he have done to make things different? And how would things have been different?

And first of all, how could he ever have thought he would find Antoine? Bob was right, it was ridiculous to imagine he could find one person in an army of a hundred thousand men. Why make such a fuss? Wouldn't it have been simpler to go on quietly living a "family life," like his aunt said? You have to know how to wait, Janusz said. He should have waited—as he is going to wait now, because now he knows that there's nothing else he *can* do. Suppose he hadn't gone. Suppose the whole trip was just a dream that he made himself dream through to the end, to the moment when the dream turned into a nightmare, the moment when he threw that grenade. He would wake up in his bed in tears, having never left it, never abandoned his family; everything that followed his departure from Chevigny would never have happened—the thousand francs he took from his uncle's drawer (and gave back almost untouched, even that can be erased), the FFIs, the song of the poor Blind Man, Diane and her triangular face, Bob, Janusz, the endless chain belt of trucks, the wobbly bridges and ferries, all his American friends and their addresses in the United States, the tall thin man, the man who worked for the electricity company, the chill of wet ditches, the chitterlings, the smell of vomit in the dormitory blankets, the bursts of fire from the Hotchkiss, the unbearable shrill howl in his dead ears, the protective arms of Lieutenant Schultzberg and the sweetness of those two young lovers from the Red Cross. A dream. What would be the difference? What would have changed? No; he senses, confusedly, that everything would be different. Because if he hadn't gone, he would have spent the rest of his life calling himself names for not going, for sitting there waiting like a good boy, a proper little boy, playing the only part anybody had left for him in the whole production, a part he doesn't want at any price. Then, yes, he would surely have spent the rest of his life reproaching himself for not having attempted anything, trying to imagine what it would have been like if he had had the courage to leave, telling himself feverishly, endlessly, that he might have found Antoine, that he certainly would have found him if he had been less passive, less of a coward. Over and over he recites to himself the imaginary scene of their meeting. He would emerge from the forest, carrying his old knapsack, onto a square where there would be a fountain playing, or rather a watering trough, with companions whose features were less sharply defined than those of Bob and Janusz and the tall thin man, Antoine would come in a jeep, maybe he would be the driver for an indistinct American lieutenant who might look like Lieutenant Schultzberg or anybody else, and Antoine would see him, he would stop and jump out of the jeep, would say, smiling, "Hi, Cat. Now you're not alone anymore."

Today he knows that that, at least, was impossible. He failed, but he did what he could. Everything he could. And it was he who decided to act. Nobody decided for him. When his brother comes back, when he sees him again for real, Luc will be able to tell him that he tried, and it won't be a lie. He didn't follow anybody else's ideas. He bungled it, he always bungles everything. But Antoine knows that very well, that won't surprise him. Maybe he could have done better? But Bob told him it was impossible . . .

Impossible, really? Not so fast. Too easy. Bob is not infallible. The truth is that he did not find Antoine out there, in Patton's army outside Metz, and he might perfectly well have found him. And if he had found him, he would never have let go of him again, he would have attached him, bound him to life. Whereas now, he has the feeling that Antoine is drifting away in a nasty fog. He's already having trouble distinguishing his features; he struggles, he concentrates, but the rest of his face remains blurred around his smile. Antoine is going away. He hasn't stopped going away since that afternoon when he disappeared, standing on his pedals, pumping up the Montainville rise in the play of sunlight and wind and the fresh smell of mown hay. Wait for me, Antoine. Come back. I won't be able to live without you. Not yet. Who will explain to me? Who will tell me things?

Those are the thoughts, often in the form of nightmares, that go round and round in Luc's head during the next few days, while, with the greatest possible detachment—because he has sworn to himself once and for all that hereafter he will speak only about things that have no importance—he resumes his "family life." He knows his aunt is still worried, she was badly frightened, she is showing actual signs of affection, to which he responds by withdrawing even further and shutting himself off more than ever. He pours all his emotion and energy into trading, into labyrinthine negotiations, punctuated by quarrels, tantrums, and profitable reconciliations with his cousins, over the transfer of ownership of the treasures he brought back in his knapsack.

He feels a surge of shame, but a flicker of victory as well, when he hears his aunt say to his uncle, "Really, I don't know what to do with Luc. I am very much afraid that the boy has no heart."

"At his age," says the uncle, "everything can be a game."

"But have you heard the language he has picked up in only a few days!"

When he was seven or eight, his brother told him to write his memoirs. Antoine had stitched together a notebook for him, blank sheets of paper with a purple cardboard cover, and had written on it, in letters opulently adorned with arabesques: "Luc Ponte-Serra, Memoirs, Volume I." Cat had started out in the style of the Comtesse de Ségur: "Dear children, I am going to tell you, when I was little, the furthest back I remember was . . ."

There had been no Volume II. Today he would be incapable of keeping a diary, let alone memoirs, of writing down even two words about himself, about what he is living and thinking. Everything is dammed up inside. All hard and impacted. Nothing can come out. Except maybe some verses, like the ones he wrote last year to celebrate conventional, reassuring things:

> *Do you hear the forest, that all around is weeping?*
> *The great north wind it is, that through the trees is*
> *    sweeping . . .*

The less they say, the more comforting. But he no longer has much desire to play those kinds of games. He finds them a little sickening, he looks down upon them as youthful follies. If he were able to keep a diary, giving form to all the things he feels moving in him, mixing together and mingled inside him, chilling and paralyzing him, he would write something like this:

"I'm over thirteen, people often take me for more, I certainly have not finished growing and yet I feel that inside myself I'm not going to grow anymore. Most people talk to me as though I were a child and I find them ridiculous. A few talk to me as though I were an adult and then I feel that I am fooling them; I can follow what they say (it's so simple, all one has to do is assume an attentive air and nod from time to time) but I can't respond. I shall learn a lot more, no doubt, but I shall never be more intelligent than I am today. I will not understand better than I do now. Especially if Antoine isn't there. Without him I'll never be able to do more than survive, get along somehow. I shall get along, I shall manage. I shall never be a child again, but I shall never be a real adult. I shall do my best to pretend. I shall always be strong enough to look like them. I'll be cheating, that's all; nobody will know the difference, except me."

October 1 is the first day back at school. He's enrolled in the ninth grade at Louis-le-Grand.

"It's absurd," says the aunt. "You did nothing all last year and you'll never be able to keep up; you're too young."

His cousins, the tall one and the fat one, Chicaneau and Le

Frisé, Filochard and Ribouldingue, Laurel and Hardy, Zig and Puce, are one and two years older than he and they are in the ninth and tenth grades.

The huge gloomy building with the deep courtyards, the long galleries of halls opening onto gray classrooms, the dense mass of students, his own class that he identifies by means of a number, these forty-five boys who all know each other and line up outside the door, with him at the end of the line, the roll call by the French teacher. He goes through it all, more passive and alien even than before. He is definitely somewhere else, but he is totally unable to make up his mind where.

Inside the classroom he looks for a seat by himself. He pays scant attention to what's going on at the front of the room. He waits patiently for it to end, drifting far away from the hum of voices that sink into the dampness of the room. Even the writing on the blackboard reaches him as through a dense fog, he has to strain to read it, screw up his eyes and concentrate. The words dance and fall into each other. Most of the time he gives up. Or else, when it really seems important, he tries to ask a neighbor to spell out what he can't manage to read. He gets scolded. He doodles complicated and confused figures or sketches of new imaginary islands. Or sailboats and airplanes. For one moment, the history and geography teacher catches his attention; he's talking about the continental drift. It's only a theory, he says, put forward by somebody called Wegener, a German, it can't be tested and is a little irrational. One can observe, however, looking at a globe, that the continents fit together like the pieces of a jigsaw puzzle; the theory is that they have been slowly slipping apart for billions of years, a thin crust floating on a seething magma around the burning core at the center of the earth. Luc lets himself drift gently away with the continents.

At the end of October the French teacher assigns a composition: "Relate the finest day of your last vacation." A standard topic. Luc has seen it regularly every year since early childhood. He knows all the ins and outs of it. He has always received a good grade on it, sometimes the best in the class. All one has to do is let a series of tried-and-true clichés roll off the tip of the pen, haymaking in the sun, fishing in the pond with water lilies, sitting in the grass, swimming and games in fresh cool water, and, at last, after dark, the crackling campfires and songs soaring cheerfully up to the stars. It all hangs together perfectly, each image hatches dutifully out of his pen and trots off to collect the next one; at no time does he need to make the slightest effort to produce a real, personal emotion of any description. Draping these conventional tinsel festoons reassures him; it makes him feel ordinary, like everybody else. He has not the smallest doubt about the results: he has written a very good composition.

A week later the teacher announces the grades.

"I am happy to observe that you have not missed the mark. Indeed, the vacation period you have just lived through was unique. This summer was the liberation of the homeland, the return of freedom. It will surely remain your finest vacation ever. And you have all realized this, all except one."

A thick mantle of shame settles around Luc. This year, without warning, the clichés and conventions were supposed to come out of a different drawer. His grade is four (out of twenty), the lowest of all.

"In the first place," the teacher tells him, "you made thirty spelling mistakes. That alone shows that this is not the right class for you. But more than that: What planet have you been living on? Did you experience nothing more important this summer than the selfish pleasures of swimming and campfires?"

The whole class snickers.

"You are too immature to remain in the ninth grade," the teacher adds.

And so, at the end of the week, Luc finds himself back in the eighth grade at the Lycée Montaigne.

"You see," his aunt says, satisfied.

But he has had time enough to conclude profitable negotiations with the older boys for disposing of the remainder of his stock of American cigarettes. He makes quite a lot of money on the deal.

Montaigne is a much less gloomy place, on the edge of the Luxembourg gardens, which Cat has to cross in order to get to it. And in the eighth grade he doesn't have to expend much effort to fit into the class. It's first-year Greek, algebra, and geometry, and he did all that at the beginning of the previous year, before going into exile in the country. The history and geography teacher, a small greenish man with a nose like a long twisted finger who purses up his mouth when he talks and sniffs all the time, also teaches at the Colonial School as an expert on North Africa, so he knew Luc's father.

"Aren't you ashamed to be taking the year over again?" he asks when Luc introduces himself at the beginning of the lesson, in front of the whole class, which is attentively sizing up the newcomer. "What if your father could see you now?"

Luc doesn't answer. There is no answer to a question like that. The little green man is stupid. And while Luc stands waiting, staring at the floor, he moralizes to the rest of his audience: "There are many children who have famous names. People ask them to live up to their names but they themselves haven't asked anything, except to be allowed to be ordinary children, to be mediocre if that's what they want. All right, go sit at the back of the class."

Stupid fart, Luc ruminates.

On one point his aunt is right: his vocabulary has become pretty foul of late, and, to tell the truth, rather monotonous. And since he has been living a "family life" again, he has contaminated his cousins; now they, who used to pretend to be so sophisticated and who sneered at the childish naïveté of their younger kinsman, occasionally display a prudish embarrassment when, for example, Luc casually exclaims, if possible within the hearing of grown-up ears, "Bunch of shits, they make my balls ache, the motherfucking cunts."

So this stupid fart of a teacher, who may otherwise be a perfectly nice guy but Luc has no means of finding out, said to him, "What if your father could see you now?"

If my father could see me now, thinks Luc in exasperation, that would mean he would be here, and Antoine and Mother too. And then I wouldn't give a damn about anything else.

Where is his father? They have found out through the Swiss Red Cross. He is in a camp for political prisoners near Buchenwald.

"It's a good camp," Lady Ponte-Serra explains when he goes to see her. "I hear they're well treated there. The only thing is, now it's autumn. He left in mid-August. Has he at least been given some warm clothing? If only I could send him a package . . ."

Meanwhile, she has somehow gotten hold of some wool and is knitting a heavy sweater and socks. She shows Luc a report distributed by the Catholic Relief organization. It states that the Buchenwald camp, near Weimar, is very clean and orderly. That there is sufficient food. That the prisoners have to work, according to their abilities, during the week, and rest on Sunday. That they wear a uniform, "red trousers, blue jacket with black lapels." "They also have an excellent orchestra and organized leisure activities: two films a week and concerts." And that there is a licensed brothel . . .

That report is absolutely trustworthy, his grandmother says. The information has been supplied by a most reliable person, a top figure in the resistance who was interned there. And that is true. He was a man whose wife miraculously managed to get him out, by paying a ransom; she followed the convoy all the way to the end and bargained for his release with the Germans, displaying admirable tenacity, courage, and aplomb. They returned to France via Switzerland. How can Luc explain that he's not happy about it, to him there's something fishy about that story? He feels that it's unfair of him, but he can't help it. (It turns out that the man really did spend a few days—or maybe only one—in Buchenwald.)

Luc can find Weimar on the map. That's some comfort. Weimar is Goethe country, he learned that in German: a tranquil region of forests, a country made for long walks and meditating under great oaks. A place of poetry and philosophy.

And his mother? They say she is in a women's camp much farther east, in Mecklenburg: Ravensbrück. His aunt keeps telling him that the women's camps cannot be too harsh. So . . . As for Antoine, in September he wrote to some cousins living in London. As of the date of the letter the French postal service was still out of order, there was no direct communication between the combat area and the rest of the country, so writing to England was the only solution. The English cousins had sent Antoine's news on to his grandparents.

In October the grandparents come back from the south.

On August 15 part of the Franco-American invasion forces disembarked on the Courdoulières beach. During the night a commando unit scaled the cliff at Battery Point, and at dawn the fleet pounded the coast from the open sea. Buildings collapsed, all the windows of the big house were shattered, the tiles flew off the roof, leaving the timbers open to the sky, the walls were full of cracks. There was one whole day of fighting at La Valerane. The maquisards came down from the Maures. The French massacred an entire detachment of Bulgarians by throwing grenades into the little railroad tunnel where they were hiding. The dead were dumped into graves made from German trenches. The pines burned like torches wherever an incendiary bomb fell, but there was no mistral that day, so the fire did not spread. The big eucalyptus trees were riddled to the core by gunfire. The front swept on very quickly. La Valerane was free and in ruins. Uninhabitable.

The grandparents couldn't bear to go on waiting so far away for news of the others. So they came back to Paris as soon as it was possible, to their big bleak apartment on the Plaine-Monceau. Luc and his cousins go to visit them on Thursday and can hardly recognize their grandfather. The colossus has become an old man. Luc gazes in astonishment at the long frame from which all the flesh has fallen away, the hunched shoulders, the uncoordinated gestures and walk, the absent gaze fixed upon some point that no one can name or reach, not even himself, far within his indecipherable thoughts, and the silences. The aunt says it's the effect of the shock, and his worries about his daughter. At the table he tips his glass over or lets his knife and fork drop from shaking hands. The cousins snicker, and when Luc, cringing, does not imitate them they call him a hypocrite. The grandfather shambles aimlessly, mechanically, from room to room, sometimes sitting down at the grand piano to tap out a few notes. Or else, suddenly gathering his wits together, he takes one of his grandsons into the huge study where piles of abandoned medical reviews lie sleeping alongside the cello with its sagging and broken strings and the stuffed owls losing their last feathers on the shelves, and sits him down to leaf through the sepia-toned reproductions of Renaissance paintings, occasionally uttering a few terse, disembodied comments.

"We must be patient with him," their grandmother says, although they hear her badgering and chivying him all the time, speaking under her breath in the hallway: "My dear, do cheer up, take hold of yourself."

"What an ordeal!" says the cousins.

"We don't have to go," says Cat.

And he contrives not to go. So it soon becomes a family tradition that Luc has absolutely no interest in art. Which may be true.

❖

Winter comes early; the snow starts in November and the weather turns cold and stays cold. Apartment buildings in the seventh *arrondissement* have no more central heating than anywhere else and the aunt's fuel ration can't heat all the rooms. There is only coal enough for the stove in the big room with the upright piano and a large dark painting in a heavy gilt frame, of Susanna and the Elders. In December, when the indoor temperature drops below fifty, she moves the three boys' beds into this room, which opens onto her own bedroom. Luc has to leave the laundry-cupboard at the back of the apartment in which he had made himself a lair. Cold becomes the absolute master of the rest of the apartment. The kitchen, at the end of a long corridor with damp yellowish walls, is a land of mist and fog. At mealtimes it is filled with dense vapor rising up from the pots and pans and from water heating very slowly on the gas ring because there is so little pressure. Dishwashing is an awful chore. There being no soap or hot water to rinse with, the dishes remain permanently sticky, like the walls and furniture, like the frosted glass hood over the cooking stove which is covered with an adhesive film of grime.

Provisions are a real problem. Nobody expected rationing to continue, but in fact it gets worse. Everybody supposed that with the liberation, the departure of the Germans, life would immediately return to what it had been before they came. What actually happened was that, for one day, the bakers made white bread. Then there was a special allowance of "liberation wine," one liter per person. Each of the three boys got his ration, a yellow, muddy wine with shreds of pulp floating in it. Then the bread turned gray again, with bits of sawdust in it and strange greenish agglutinations that smelled of mold. In this family, each person's daily allotment is weighed out and kept in a little bag. Luc and his cousins do not seem very sensitive to the aunt's problems. For her, getting them to do the dishes entails a lengthy and wearisome roundup. In return for the succession of boiled turnips and Jerusalem artichokes interspersed with such rare and sometimes outlandish diversions as buttermilk, calf's pluck, and horse blood in coagulated slabs, which she wears herself out standing in lines to buy, and with such welcome extravagances as a chicken, a rabbit, or a pâté brought from Chevigny by her husband, all she gets is discontented grumbling. Are they totally indifferent to her plight? Before Christmas, the cousins consult at great length about the choice of a present for their mother and, after bitter arguments and expeditions to the shops, they munificently decide to give her a pair of rubber gloves for washing the dishes.

Luc has started drawing maps again. He has invented another island. He's never satisfied, there are always blanks in the tangle of colored spaces. He can lose himself for days in sheets of heavy drawing paper, between the colored pencils and the India ink. He's on his island. But the cold puts an end to this activity. He can't draw in the icy laundry room, and he can't bring his map into the main room, where it is already hard enough for the three of them to do their homework together. Living in a single room with the others, even if he himself is in a different world and doesn't always see them very clearly, makes the presence of those others so intolerably insistent. Why should Luc get along with his cousins, after all, and why should his cousins get along with him? They are older, and they treat him with all the contempt born of their superior experience and knowledge every time he launches into some grandiose explanation of the world and comes unstuck at the first challenge. Is the geography of the far side of the moon known; which is the steepest grade a locomotive can climb, five or fifteen percent; is the range of the guns on a Sherman tank two kilometers or five; how are twins made; do you die if you touch the live rail in the métro (No? Then try it if you dare; but wait, all you have to do is balance on it without touching anything else); which has two humps, the dromedary or the Bactrian camel; can you saddle a zebra and ride it; did slavery exist in the time of Charlemagne; do whales sing and nurse their calves; is it true that there are male and female palm trees (how stupid can you get); are Japanese airplanes made of wood; is there something called an anatomic bomb that destroys everything; do they still have mounted cavalry in the American army; can an airplane fly faster than the speed of sound; is it true that a guillotined head was actually seen to wink as it rolled into the basket . . . It's enough to make them scream, kick, and bite, when the discussion disintegrates into ignorance piled on ignorance and dishonesty on the part of all three combatants, none of whom will budge an inch, as though something were at stake that had nothing to do with the subject of the dispute. Sooner or later, the inevitable conclusion comes: "Nobody could be as stupid as you are."

When the uncle is in Paris, his sons call upon him to arbitrate.

"Dad, Luc says that plane trees lose their leaves in winter."

"No," the uncle affirms, sovereign, sitting at his desk in front of the big green tapestry and holding his reflex hammer in his hand like a scepter, like St. Louis delivering judgment under his oak. "No, plane trees keep their leaves all year."

"But—" objects Luc.

"I simply do not understand," says the uncle, "this constant compulsion of yours to quibble over everything."

Is it because Antoine isn't there that Luc is so helpless? Before, he would ask incongruous questions and it was called curiosity. Now, left to himself, he's all stammers and hesitancy. It isn't a game anymore, it's a series of traps into which he flounders. Things resist him, explanations wriggle out of his reach or get tangled together. He realizes that for some people it is childish, perverse, indecent— and in any case ill-mannered—to keep asking questions about things when it is quite enough to know they are there; if they are there, then there is a reason why they are there, but what is the use of digging and prying at them? Everything has an explanation, right? Fine; then just trust it, because otherwise you make yourself look ridiculous. The truth of the matter is that curiosity is a nasty fault. Especially because he wanders away from the point every time and starts debating idiotic side issues and, after being driven to defend arguments so farfetched they don't even convince himself, he loses the fight.

The uncle is fond of trotting out his collection of riddles. Luc suspects him of using them on his patients to find out whether they are normal or not. They are all variations on the theme of "Which weighs more, a pound of lead or a pound of feathers?" His favorite is: "Can a dog jump higher than the Eiffel Tower?"

"No, of course not," sighs the designated victim.

"Right. But why not?"

And when the victim can't produce an answer, he clobbers him with: "Because the Eiffel Tower can't jump."

Let me just get my hands on Antoine's explosive, thinks Luc in a fury, and you'll see if your stupid old Eiffel Tower can't jump. And a lot higher than all the lousy mutts in the world. And you with it. But that brings no relief.

When you come right down to it, he tells himself, mortified for the hundredth time, when you come right down to it there's only one question that is really important: Does one have to talk to imbeciles? And while he waits for the answer to that he calls himself all the names he can think of, every time he lets himself get caught again and hears ring out the fateful words: "You're quibbling."

The aunt has her own way of putting an end to disputes. When she runs out of patience and arguments—because sometimes Luc is right—she challenges him: "Go ahead and call me a liar!" And he's stuck again. If he holds to his deep conviction, and to the truth, it means a slap for sure. His aunt has a quick temper and a highly efficient left-right stroke, with her ring-laden hand, that leaves her adversary reeling and humiliated. But yielding, groveling, taking back what one has said, that is also humiliating. So . . .

He will not be truly strong, he concludes, until he learns how not to open his mouth at all.

(How could he understand that things are not so simple? After all, his cousins have some justification for fighting back and forming a coalition against the intruder. They're only defending their own turf, geographical and emotional. This twitching, untidy individual— who goes through phases of extreme exaltation and self-confidence when he tries to involve them in disorganized and noisy enterprises and pranks, followed by phases of scowling resentment and silence when one doesn't dare touch him with a feather; who has broken into the space they had carved out for themselves in a distended family unit in which each member had his own private world, one boy with his unrealistic poems and the multicolored pastel drawings that paper the walls of his room and the other with his passion for erecting things, building models, complex assemblages; this little cousin, who quibbles, splits hairs, criticizes, denies everything and anything when, if only by virtue of his youth, he has to know even less than they do—is infuriating. They didn't deserve that.)

✠

And so winter begins. With cold and more rationing. There has never been so much talk about rationing. It's an obsession. The most obvious signs of malnutrition are chilblains on the hands; they turn red and are full of cracks and get infected. If we still don't have white bread, it must be somebody's fault.

"De Gaulle is all very well," explains the aunt at dinner in the kitchen with the streaming walls. "But he is inexperienced. And they say he has poor advisers."

Every day, on the radio, they listen to a reassuring sketch by a comedian who discusses the situation with his straight men, rolling his *r*'s to make himself sound like a jovial peasant. The need for effort, the renaissance of French grandeur, the valor of our fighting men in Alsace, the abnegation of the FFIs holding down the pockets on the Atlantic coast, the restoration of communications owing to the heroic sacrifices made by the railway workers, the arrival in Paris of the first coal barges thanks to the devotion of the miners in the north, the more abundant supplies which are just around the corner, the achievements of the Allies—and the program ends every time with the comedian repeating, "I believe it, oh, I do believe . . ."

Fade, to the sound of someone whistling the "March of Lorraine."

• They also hear, every day without fail, in connection with some news item about the formation of the new French army or the amalgamation of FFIs and regular troops, that "Song of the Partisans" that the tall thin man disliked so intensely.

•  •  •

Early in the winter the Allies on the western front reach the frontiers of Germany and come up against defenses which they are unable to break through. The English are stopped by the flooding of the Dutch polders, the Americans enter Aachen and reach the Rhine north of Strasbourg, and the French First Army is fighting in the Vosges outside Colmar. In the east, the Russians are still somewhere around Warsaw; the uprising was crushed in October but the Allies do not enter the city until December. London and Brussels are being battered by V-2s, rockets launched from Germany which are far more powerful than the V-1s, and it is said that Paris may also become a target. Athens was liberated by the Greek resistance before the English even got there.

On his way to school Luc buys newspapers. There are lots of them now and he can't always tell them apart. *L'Humanité,* he knows what that is, and his aunt gets *Le Figaro* every day. (His grandmother reads *Le Monde* because the headline type is the same size as that of the defunct *Temps.*) *L'Aube,* he has been told, is the clergy. But how can he tell *Combat* from *Libération, Défense de la France,* and *Nouvelles du Matin?* All of them are only two pages, a single sheet printed on both sides, and the paper shortage will shrink them even more before the winter is out. What he's looking for is the one that gives the most detailed news from the fronts, maps, and the sites of bombed cities. Sometimes he buys several. Maybe *Combat* is the one he gets most regularly, because of its subtitle, "From Resistance to Revolution." He doesn't see what revolution it's talking about because for the moment Antoine's predictions are not coming true; but at least the paper has kept the word, like a promise. He spends little time on the editorials, which agonize over general ideas and great principles of no direct concern to him. Each day brings its harvest of fresh discoveries regarding the exactions and atrocities perpetrated by the occupiers, the massacres and hangings all over France, the torture—such as that torture chamber in Issy-les-Moulineaux where naked prisoners were chained standing on a metal bench; the torturers sent an electric current through it and the victims jumped and leaped frantically, the marks made by their hands can be seen at unbelievable heights on the asbestos wall, and so can the traces of bullets in the splintered execution post nearby. There are photos. Each day also brings some new twist in the *Epuration* column, the purges; it's like a serial.

It would never have occurred to him on his own. If he has so much trouble seeing what is written on the blackboard from his seat at the back of the class it is not the result of some sort of predestination or an incomprehensible malediction or a lack of concentration on his part or a mechanism of detachment that removes him from a confused and hostile world by spreading a fog around him. It's simply that he needs glasses. He has become nearsighted, he learns when he goes for his medical examination. His aunt takes him to an oculist. Now he possesses a pair of slender brown-and-yellow-striped frames with round lenses in them and springs at the hinges to hold them tight to his ears. Ghastly. But the moment he puts them on his nose it's extraordinary how everything becomes clear, sharp, precise; colors separate and glow. At a distance, the lines of print on posters form into words. It's almost too much for him, there's something scary about it. And since he doesn't need his glasses all the time and the metallic contraption irritates him, he mostly keeps them in his pocket. So he hasn't had them a week before he is rolling in the dirt of the playground during a piggyback battle and breaks both lenses. His aunt howls and has another pair made. This time he puts them in his soft, worn old satchel and it doesn't take him long to sit on it and break both lenses again. This time he doesn't dare confess. He saves the pieces and squints, blinking, through the biggest one when it's absolutely necessary: in class to see the blackboard, or at the cinema when the film is subtitled. Now and then his aunt asks if he is wearing his glasses at school and he tells her yes, of course, and that he always keeps them in his pocket. He gets through the whole winter that way; the fog has closed in around him again, softening the edges of things, and it actually seems to thicken as the months go by. Not such a bad thing.

He doesn't have much trouble at school. There is little that's new for him to learn. During recreation periods he engages in great piggyback battles again, but he has grown so much that now he is the horse more often than the rider. Even so, he can still clear the field around him. Also during recreation, or the "open air" hour, the class often plays *barrage,* a brutal collective game with alternating moments of action and anticipation that delight him. Sometimes one has to run by oneself, sometimes the whole side is welded together, elbow to elbow, in an unbreakable wall. In French composition he is second: order has been restored. The boy who's first is his friend, a blond boy with a large head, flat nose, and glasses. After four in the afternoon, when school is out, they go together to lean over a balustrade in the deserted Luxembourg gardens and watch with chattering teeth as the sun goes down behind the bare-branched trees and gray roofs; a thrilling moment. He thinks of the Baudelaire line that Antoine used to recite with mock solemnity: *The sun has drowned in its own congealing blood.*

They follow the downward path of the red disk dipping in and out among the clouds.

"Stranger, what are thy dreams?" declaims his large-headed friend. "The clouds, the wondrous clouds . . ."

They tell themselves that they would take notes if they weren't so cold, they would describe the sunset as though they were painting a picture, it would be a very long poem, maybe a whole book, and they would write it together, the two of them. Because his large-headed friend has decided that he will spend his life writing books and has already begun. They discuss the "green ray." "You can only see it in the tropics and even there it's very rare," says Luc, who has read Jules Verne. "Maybe on the Nile, from a boat."

And when the whole world has turned gray they hear the traffic whistles of the park guards beating the corners of the gardens, which are surrounded by a very high iron grille, driving out the last strollers. When it's not too cold they and other classmates have chases with little varnished balls down the gutters of the Rue d'Assas as far as Sèvres-Babylone. The streets are empty. Cars hardly ever pass, now and then there's a Bon Marché delivery van drawn by gray horses with thick tufts of hair above their hooves. At Sèvres-Babylone they sometimes see a bus on the only line as yet in service in the district, a mastodon with an abnormally swollen roof like a dirigible balloon: a producer-gas bus.

He knows plenty of ways to amuse himself on the way home. One he often uses: he is a bomber pilot on a mission and the sidewalk is the enemy territory over which he is flying. Any metal stands for towns; manhole covers are capital cities, and the little rectangular hole in the middle is the main power plant; the water-main plates that have corrugated tops are fortified towns, while the gas connections are lesser subprefectures. Where the asphalt is crazed and cracked he knows there are main railway junctions, or if the cracks are right next to the gutter, rivers and deltas. The trick is to spit accurately without either slowing down or leaning over. Hardest of all is to make an exact hit on the essential target, the power plant of a capital: the saliva has to drop straight through the rectangular hole, and then the whole city is paralyzed. The trouble is that a lot of bombing quickly dries the mouth. The bomb bay is empty, it's time to return to base, circumventing certain strategic points he has identified at intersections, where the enemy flak is particularly deadly.

On Sundays he goes to have lunch with Lady Ponte-Serra.

"Nobody tells me anything," the old lady keeps saying.

She's right. The other side of the family is completely absorbed in the state of his grandfather's health and the orders are to say nothing about anything. No more is said or heard about Antoine or his mother or his father. But even if it were . . .

"He must not be upset," the maternal grandmother keeps repeating.

So in order not to upset the grandfather, silence reigns. Is no news good news? Luc knows that approaches have been made to the Red Cross headquarters in Geneva, which is the central clearinghouse for tens of thousands of names, to find out his parents' exact whereabouts and enter into some form of communication with them, discover how to get packages to them. Lady Ponte-Serra writes to Antoine. But Antoine doesn't answer.

Friends of Antoine's ring her doorbell. Some ask for books or lecture notes they had lent him, or some piece of work they had started together.

"They all tell me they miss him. They all talk about his warm heart, his intensity, his curiosity about everything. They say, 'When is he coming back? His place is here. Classes have started again. We miss him. If the Ecole Normale examination had been held he'd have been at the top of the list.' It makes me happy to hear them talk about him like that. But I also wonder why these big, strong boys don't seem to be asking themselves other questions. Shouldn't they have done something for their country too? They behave as if it was perfectly natural to have sat at home. It's hard for me not to resent them, not to accuse them of selfishness. Is it fair that Antoine should be the only one fighting?"

"Now the really cold weather has come," she also says, "and I can send them nothing. I have written to your father, I sent the card to Geneva, perhaps they will be able to forward it. I told him you were well, only in the eighth grade but I said that was natural, you weren't really taking the year over again because last year didn't count. I've finished the sweater. In Weimar winters are colder than they are here. I wonder if they have decent heating in those camps. I'm told they do and that the food is good. They also tell me that since he speaks German he is probably an interpreter. I write Antoine every week. I don't know if my letters are reaching him. In the first place, he certainly did not enlist under his own name. And he may have changed units too. Or gone back to the French army. I don't know whether my letters are being forwarded. I tell him that I am proud of him. I shouldn't want him to have any doubt on that point. He should be giving us some sign of life now. This waiting has gone on too long."

She has lots of callers. She receives them in her straight-backed armchair, a small shrunken body all in black with extremely sharp green eyes behind a drooping eagle's beak of a nose. There is warmth of sorts in her rooms, because she has a large sawdust-burning stove. The Institut de France has begun felling trees in the forest of Chantilly, which it owns, and is therefore able to heat its academicians and their widows. She often talks about Egypt to her guests. She tells Luc about the long trips up the Nile every autumn to reach the digs, Tentyra, Thebes, Philae, and the Valley of the Kings. In those years they would spend several months on that heavy carved wooden houseboat with the broad sails, the dehabeah they called the *Myriam,* which moved, when there wasn't enough wind for the sails, to the rhythm of the long oars pulled by fellaheen who would sing, softly, for hours. They lived the life of the river, passing fishermen, merchants, pilgrims, feluccas—the small boats with triangular sails that spread like butterflies' wings.

"I remember when your grandfather went down that well in the Valley of the Kings where he discovered some particularly important mummy. He had been looking for it for months. Was it Hornotpu or Thutmose IV? I'm not sure anymore. His guide was a sort of outlaw who had sold him the information, and I didn't want him to go down alone with the man. But he wanted to show that he trusted him. I stayed above waiting for him alone among those barren rocks, looking out all the time for vipers, in the sweltering heat—I had my sunshade, of course—it took forever. And when he came up again all he said to me was 'It's there.' Later, after the sun set, we went back down to the Nile with the fellaheen carrying the mummy by torchlight.

"That was the year your uncle found the blue cat of Deir el-Bahri in a merchant's shop in the souk in Cairo. Your grandfather wanted it for the museum."

The seals have been removed from the front door of the family apartment. The rooms have been cleaned, the shutters are closed, the grandmother has had the big drawing-room rugs rolled and dust-covers put on the armchairs and over the paintings. Emptiness, silence, chill, and death along the corridors. Nothing has been touched in Antoine's room. Luc finds the lump of green explosive gel in his closet again, now dried and hard, almost brittle. He shaves off a sliver with a rusty razor blade, places it on the marble mantelpiece, in front of the ghastly marble fake-antique discobolus whose absurd swollen vine leaf they have often penciled black—a first communion or birthday present from some uncle with the taste of a whale—and cautiously sets it alight with a match. A bright swift flame leaps violently up to the ceiling and goes out immediately, without exploding. This *plastic,* he concludes, is like the black powder in bullets and the macaroni in shells: as long as it is not confined, it can be burned, in small quantities, with no great danger. He shaves off more thin slices, lengthwise, and rams them into empty aspirin tubes, which he affixes to specially built paper airplanes. He opens the window high above the wide expanse of the Avenue Henri-Martin and neighboring streets. He places a table under the window and an inclined board on the table; that gives him a launching ramp. He fires his rockets, one after the other: they streak away with a whoosh and disappear over the rooftops. Soon he has used up the whole green loaf. No more explosive.

He opens a drawer. Inside is a pile of notebooks and sheets of paper covered with notes. He's afraid to look at them. One day, one rainy late afternoon like today, in the darkness of an electricity blackout, Antoine had announced: "I've started a great novel."

"Another one? What's it about?"

"It's the story of the battle between Achilles and Penthesilea, Queen of the Amazons. Nobody could beat her with a bow and arrow. The Amazons lived by themselves in the great forests of the north, always on horseback, always invincible."

"So will there be lots of battles and adventures?"

"I don't think so. That's not what I'm interested in."

"Too bad."

"Achilles was invulnerable."

"Yeah, I know, except for his heel. It wasn't fair. So is he the one who kills her? What a sickening story."

"Why? It was war."

"It could have been avoided."

"It was much too late. Everything had been said, everything had been tried. On the plains of Troy, Penthesilea shoots at Achilles and misses him. She has only one arrow left. So she turns her horse and flees. She flees into a nearby forest because the forest is her ally, that's where she's always lived; she wants to lure Achilles after her so she can kill him with her last arrow. She gallops through the weeds and undergrowth. Achilles comes after her. When she gets to the tall trees she turns, draws her bow, and, without slowing down, shoots and misses him again. Achilles hurls his javelin at her. It goes right through her, she falls from her maddened horse and is dragged through the briars and thorns. When Achilles catches up to her, she is still at last; he looks at her face. Only then does he understand what he has always known, that she was beautiful and he loves her.

Maybe she smiles up at him one last time through her tangled tresses."

"Did you make all that up yourself?"

"No, the Greeks did. It's in Propertius and Quintus of Smyrna. But none of them say she smiles. That bit is my idea."

"It's romantic, that's for sure. Better than *Cyrano de Bergerac.*"

"You'll be disappointed. And I think it will take place in modern times. Achilles will have a nine-millimeter gun and leather jacket and Penthesilea will ride a bike."

"Your story's too sad. If I," Cat said, "wrote a book, I'd rather tell about Ulysses who sets out upon the high seas and Penelope who waits for him, and Telemachus."

And he actually did start a great tragedy entitled *The Return of Ulysses,* in alexandrine verse; he counted the feet on his fingers. In Act I, scene 1, the ringleader of the craven suitors comes to Penelope, who is seated before her tapestry, and demands that she choose which of them is to be Ulysses' successor:

> *Madame, this is too much. These ten eternal years*
> *Your husband has been gone, upon the endless seas,*
> *And sent no word to you. You must now dry your tears.*
> *Ithaca awaits a king, a queen is all it sees.*

In scene 2, Ulysses was supposed to arrive disguised as a beggar, but there never was a scene 2.

"Anyway," his brother told him, "remember that when Ulysses gets back to Ithaca his troubles are not over. He kills the suitors and goes up to the royal bed with Penelope, but he has to leave again. Because the conditions of the prediction made to him in Hades have been fulfilled, all except one. He has to go to the land of the people who do not know the sea. He will know he has reached it when, walking inland with his oar over his shoulder, the inhabitants ask him the purpose of the long shovel he is carrying. Only then can he return to his palace for good. Only then can he live in peace and quiet."

"What does that mean, to live in peace and quiet?"

"It means he will die of old age."

"Does Ithaca really exist?" Cat also asked his brother.

"Of course. It is a primitive island with a little fishing village on it."

"Do you think it's changed much since Ulysses' day?"

"Probably not. There isn't a royal palace anymore. Maybe the palace was just a big farm. Outside, under the olive trees, Eumaeus the swineherd looked after the pigs, like old Andreis at Courdoulières. Dark mountains, vines, reeds. And every night the boats are pulled up on logs to the top of the beach; that's what Ulysses' sailors did too."

"Do they pull up the *bargin?*"

"Sure. When the war is over we'll go there if you like. You'll see."

"We'll go everywhere."

There are three rings at the doorbell. A mad stab of hope: he races to the front door to open it. It's the concierge, who saw a light under the door. When he's gone, Luc stands there in the doorway with the door still open, his arms dangling, shivering with cold, staring blankly into the empty stairwell. Sad beyond words.

❖

The first letter his grandmother wrote to Antoine is returned at the beginning of December. The envelope is unopened. It is covered all over with stamps and handwritten notices in English which she can't decipher. The letter has been to the United States, where all American army mail goes; it has crossed the Atlantic four times.

"It's just as I said," she tells Luc. "He is not using his real name. He must have gone back to the French army. They can't forward it."

His field of vision, the space in which he lives or dreams, has narrowed. The half-fog in which he floats, permanently cut off from even the closest things and people, is not just the result of his broken glasses. His universe has been reduced to certain small, closely defined spaces with frontiers he feels incapable of crossing. There is the apartment in the seventh *arrondissement,* and more specifically, the room where they all live together; even the halls and kitchen are a sort of vaguely hostile no-man's-land; there is the route he follows to school, his classroom, and, the only place where the limits recede a little, the Luxembourg gardens and his games—the pool, the broad paths, the stairs, the merry-go-round of headless wooden horses which the old cripple cranks round with a handle and which he and his friends invade, like conquerors, after school. But even that is circumscribed by the high iron grille and the guards with their whistles; and, farther away, at the end of a métro ride but equally circumscribed, there is his grandparents' apartment, a rambling succession of enormous abandoned rooms on two floors, with massive, crooked furniture, heavy beds covered with thick, tarnished damask, a chaos of crystal chandeliers veiled with dust; and, still farther off, there is Lady Ponte-Serra's apartment where the blue cat watches eternally. It, at least, is proof that other worlds exist, other realities, other histories, other dreams, a past and a future. Perhaps its eyes are looking into the land of the people who do not know the sea. Or that of the Button Molder.

Even his body has stopped speaking, has become strange to him. While his daily life glides around him like an ice floe, smooth and regular and uneventful, he often feels as though he is somehow absent from his body, a detached, even critical witness to its agitation; he has withdrawn that far into himself, somewhere into his depths, some very secret place. One curious thing, for instance, is that he never has any stomach pains anymore. The beast has fallen silent, has stopped gnawing and biting as though it had been discouraged by so much emptiness and indifference; and Luc actually misses the familiar presence inside himself. One time, he deliberately hurt himself. He held a lighted cigarette against the back of his hand for over two minutes. The purulent blister he raised leaves a scar for life; it's as though the pain reassured him.

"You see," trumpets his aunt. "That stomach trouble of yours is over and done with. No more playacting. I knew that all you needed was some regular habits, a little order and authority."

But he also heard what she said to the uncle: "If Luc keeps on like this, we'll have to send him to boarding school next year. He is quite ungovernable. He needs discipline."

His body has changed and he is no longer quite sure he recognizes it as his own. He has grown much taller. He isn't so well coordinated as before. He used to be compact and supple, now he's turning into a bean pole and occasionally trips over his own feet. Only a short time ago he felt far more certain of his movements. When he used to run along the eaves troughs of the old house at Marles, for instance, forty feet above the paved courtyard, he made a point of not slowing down at the corners; would he dare do it today? Everything in him, limbs and muscles, used to function in unison; when he worked in the chain of people feeding the thresher and would pass on the sheaves of wheat at the end of his pitchfork, what he liked most was keeping in time, remaining just within the limits of his strength without the work ever becoming really effortful. It was like the great swimming races he used to have with Antoine; and sometimes they would both float on their backs with their legs twined together, forming a single body with a head at each end. Then, when they straightened up without separating their legs, they would plummet down a moment together, front to front, skin against skin, into the roar of green water, and only then let go of each other and heave their way up with huge frog kicks. In moments like that everything in him spun and sang. Today . . . For instance, he doesn't like these bony knees sticking out of the wrinkled short pants (luckily, he can wear his cousins' old golf trousers). Everything in this stretched, angular structure seems peculiar, out of control. And all these hairs, now . . . it's so silly.

But he really would like to do something about those sermons on order and authority which his aunt keeps preaching at him. He tries his old métro excursions again, but they don't give him the thrill they used to. The métro is no longer an incentive to explore unknown worlds; he has already traveled it to its outermost limits. And that winter the métro is sad and seedy. Half the stations are shut down and dead, the windowpanes have been replaced with plywood boards, the trains are few and far between and have only three cars, or, in the case of the Nord-Sud, are reduced to a heap of jolting, heaving scrap iron that makes an infernal racket, as of dying machinery, with one light bulb out of three lit and the feeble glow of the yellow filaments barely relieving the darkness. They have never been so crowded, and never have so many people been so sad and silent. During the rush hour one has to wait and wait and wait, the doors roll shut on leaning lines of people, it's suffocating inside.

Maybe the idea of cutting school is less tempting than last year too. He's not too miserable there; his grades are at least average, his teachers leave him alone, and he gets along well with his classmates. He's the heart and soul of the action. He has great ideas, such as the paper airplane competition. For more than a month he has the whole class behind him, feverishly fingering sheets of paper in search of novel bends and folds; and in the school playground and the Luxembourg gardens the air is striped with white arrows pursued by packs of screaming schoolboys, Luc always in the lead. It's astonishing how many different techniques and rival factions can spring up in connection with the manufacture of a paper airplane; opposing factions develop even on the issue of the manner of blowing down the nose of one's aircraft before it is launched.

The quarrel that has separated Lady Ponte-Serra from his aunt and the rest of the family has become permanent, and he continues to take advantage of it for his own ends; it is always he who tells his aunt at what time and on what day he is to pay a visit to his grandmother, and who likewise tells his grandmother when he is supposed to go home to his aunt.

He returns to the markets several times, always in the afternoon and always with the same sense of melancholy. But he is drawn there as though by a magnet. He prowls around the Petit Roscoff but doesn't dare go inside, he tries to walk past the windows and peer through them without slowing down, until he turns the corner of the Rue de la Petite-Truanderie. Then he walks around the block, back to the Rue Saint-Denis, and repeats the performance all over again. He's afraid of being noticed and is very careful not to stare at the few women standing there. He walks, his eyes doggedly fixed on the ground, through a stench of rot, the remains of cabbages and turnips, and horse manure, navigating through the piles of garbage by guesswork. Every time he passes, he looks for Diane's face. He can't see clearly and the lighting is bad; but there are never many people inside, always a few men sitting quietly at tables and one or two girls; even from the back he knows that none of them is Diane.

One afternoon in December he puts on his American jacket. ("I forbid you to wear that jacket," his aunt says every time. "I don't want you walking around outdoors in that secondhand military outfit. You look like I don't know what. And people might think you stole it.") He goes to the stamp market with his cousins and leaves them there, engaged in some delicate negotiations involving stamps from Monte Carlo and American cigarettes. He walks toward the Rue Saint-Denis. This time he has made up his mind, come what may. When he gets to the Petit Roscoff he resists the temptation to keep going past the door and begin his round all over again. He takes a deep breath, pushes the door, and goes in. He is staggered by the heat in the café and pauses, holding the door open onto the icy street.

The fat hairy owner behind the bar raises his eyebrows and bellows, "The door, for Chrissake!"

"I'm looking for Diane," he mumbles. And he sees her, sitting alone at the same table as two months ago, on the left at the back. The first thing he notices about her is an improbable sweater she's got on, shiny orange-pink wool with white stripes. He shuts the door and walks over. She looks up from the cards spread out on the red wooden table.

"Well, well, if it isn't the Snail. You've come just in time, I'm looking for somebody to play poker with."

"I don't know how," says Luc.

"It's easy with dice. I'll teach you. So, still wet, I see. Where are you going today? Marseilles?"

"No, I've come back to Paris. That's all."

"Too bad. You could have taken me with you. Didn't you find your brother?"

"No. I didn't find anybody. I didn't find anything."

"Sit down, silly."

He sits on the edge of the bench. She looks at him with her green eyes the shape of slightly wrinkled almonds, eyes like a spring with golden algae in it, and smiles, stretching her thin lips and showing, for a fraction of a second when one side of her mouth lifts, a very white pointed canine.

"Hello, Cat."

That's good; nobody has called him that for months.

"So you remember me?"

"Idiot. Alley cat, tabby cat, blue-eyed cat, mangy cat, cat that arches its back and likes chitterlings. Are you cold?"

"Yes."

"Boss, a glass of hot wine."

Hot wine, even when there's no lemon in it and it's sweetened with saccharin, gives one a pleasant burning sensation; it lights a fire in one's whole body; it blurs the scenery a little, goes straight to one's head, especially when it's the first time one has ever drunk it.

A full house of aces and queens, four kings, straight flush; he learns, he loses continually, in a state of euphoria, he hardly complains. Diane is a noisy winner. Later on, he wins too.

"You don't look any happier when you win than when you lose. You look as though you don't like to win."

"Could be. I don't like to lose either."

"Well, you'll have to get used to it. Either you win or you lose. You're never halfway between. It always ends up one way or the other."

"I just don't want the game to stop, that's all. I don't care about the rest."

"Then you're even worse than a cheat. And more dangerous. At least with a cheat you know where you stand, he'll do anything to win. Games are serious. If you don't take them seriously you throw everything off and you're the biggest cheat of all."

"It's who I'm playing with that counts."

Around five, when night falls, the café starts to fill. The movement around the cardplayers' table has been growing noisier for some time, and the talk louder. Shadows have come in, dragging their feet, and are sprawled at the bar demanding brandy or white wine. The owner comes to life, chairs are pulled squealing over the tile floor. A few light bulbs are lit. Then some girls come in, overweight and weirdly dressed, with bare white legs that give him goose pimples, heavy jackets, neck scarves, and big shoulder bags. Their talk is all about nurses and milk teeth and layettes, they compare balls of yarn bought on the black market. The atmosphere is still muted, almost like in a family. Everybody seems to know everybody else. Some of the women wave to Diane, who scarcely looks up. A little later, the glass door is flung open, there are exclamations, heavy boots thump on the tiles. Cat looks around. A group of very young men tumble into the café.

"Right. Here's the 24-4," Diane says, unruffled. " 'Tenshun! Eyes front."

She snatches up the dice and cards and tosses them into her bag. Several of the boys head for her table. They are dressed in what look like military clothes, but all unmatching. Two of them sit on Cat's bench, shoving him roughly down to the end. A tall blond who needs a shave, with a few scattered hairs on his tanned cheeks and a thick lock curling over his forehead and partly hiding a sharp, precise, almost inquisitorial gaze, sits down on the other side next to Diane, pulls her to him, and gives her a long kiss on the mouth.

"What's this, Diane, have I got competition? Are you cradle-robbing now?"

"No, no," says Diane with a shrug, unsmiling. "No, Max. It's nothing. Meet the Snail."

Cat sits frozen, scarlet-faced, on his end of the bench, with one half of his behind resting on nothing.

"This is more like it," the one next to him says, unbuckling a hefty brand-new yellow leather sword belt that was holding in the waist of his long khaki overcoat, which now hangs shapeless down to his feet like a heavy skirt. "This is more like it. I've had enough of goddamned barracks."

"Don't talk about rope in a hanged man's house," Max says, tight-jawed, with a grimace. He stretches his long arms, cracks his knuckles, and makes the table dance with his feet.

"You're right, this is more like it. It's almost human here."

Cat decides to break out of his trance and stand up. He edges across the room, now full of smoke and expansive men in berets and wrinkled khaki coats. He's almost relieved when he opens the door and is back in the cold air of the street and the complex smell of discarded bits of vegetables. It's night. Behind him, a hand tugs gently at his hair. He turns.

"Give me a kiss, little Cat," says Diane. "And come back again. It's better in the afternoon, like today. I'm almost always free at that time of day."

Behind Diane, through the open door, he catches a glimpse of Max, who has stood up and is on his way to the old yellow-toothed black piano next to the toilet by the bar. Cat's ears are struck by two or three dissonant chords crashing together, then the door shuts. Diane is gone, he is standing in the dark on the Rue de la Petite-Truanderie, and damp, scattered snowflakes are falling and melting on the greasy pavement.

∷

December is the big German counteroffensive. Patton's army is almost smashed in the Ardennes. In Alsace, Leclerc's division is going to have to hold out alone for several crucial days, Strasbourg and the plains around it have only just been recaptured and are already threatened again. On the seacoast, the scattered pockets from Lorient to the Pointe de Grave are still resisting; the FFIs, who have now become regular troops but are no better equipped than before, are managing to keep them from breaking out but cannot destroy them. It all seems so far away from Paris. The war is treading water again, but at school the singing teacher is getting ready for V-Day anyway, just in case, by teaching the students to sing the Allied anthems in chorus, with French words as obscure as they are grandiloquent:

> Dans la nuit obscure, ô bannière étoilée
> C'est toi qui nous guidais sous tes plis glo-ri-eux
> Puis le jour est venu dans son albe lumière . . .
> ("The Star-Spangled Banner")

> Puissante indivise est l'Union soviéti-que
> Par la volonté de ses peuples bâtis
> . . . Drâ-â-peau soviéti-que
> Drâ-â-peau populai-re
> Conduit le pays de victoire en victoire.
> (Anthem of the U.S.S.R.)

(Luc learns on this occasion that the "Internationale" is not the Soviet national anthem. He suspects the singing teacher of a reactionary trick.)

Before Christmas, the French teacher reads out a circular letter requesting all prisoners' children to identify themselves so they can be invited to a great party with a real Christmas tree. Luc raises a finger. The teacher hesitates.

"I don't know if you qualify. Your father isn't exactly a prisoner of war."

At home, the aunt is offended. "As if you didn't have a family. As if we weren't enough for you."

The party takes place in a local cinema, into which file two thousand kids of all ages to watch cartoons and clowns and hear patriotic speeches about their beloved daddies for whom the whole of France is waiting with bated breath, who will soon be back to take part in the magnificent task of rebuilding the country for which they are suffering so greatly. The audience is made to sing "Mon Beau Sapin" and the "March of Lorraine" and, of course, the "Song of the Partisans." The tall thin man was right, that song is an abomination.

> *Oh, you killers*
> *With bullet and knife,*
> *Hurry and kill!*

Easy to say. The whole audience, clowns and speechmakers included, the two thousand children and the ladies who came with the littlest ones, all intone in unison:

> *You see us here?*
> *We march, we kill,*
> *We die.*

He goes home with a coupon for a pair of new shoes.

On Christmas Eve his aunt drags the three boys into the throngs in the department stores so they can choose their presents. Luc's feet hurt and he doesn't like anything he sees. Nothing appeals to him, nothing interests him. That evening his aunt gives him a piece of paper on which she has written: "Good for one present." The next day they go to high mass at Sainte-Cécile: a jostling fairground, a sermon, and three collections.

The whole family has been invited to the grandparents' for dinner, prewar tradition restored. The grandfather creeps about, a fumbling shadow held together by his straight-backed and energetic wife, who doesn't let go of him for a second; he hardly ever emerges from his daze. The entire clan is gathered, great-uncles and great-aunts, remote aunts and uncles, first and second cousins, and old spinster friends of the family.

One uncle who is a film producer talks about the film he is making; one cannot conceive, he says, what an attentive, obliging person Jean Marais is. But the studios, so deadly cold! And where is he ever going to find one hundred and fifty Empire costumes for the ball scene?

"Business has not picked up," says Uncle François. "This government has no authority. De Gaulle is a pawn of the Communists. He's giving in to their blackmail. All this social welfare in a bankrupt country is pure demagogy.

"And the purges. They keep going on and on. As if the atrocities of the liberation weren't enough. Mind you, I can understand them wanting to set a few examples. It's just too bad about poor Sacha Guitry; that doesn't do anybody any harm. And even Brasillach, after all; all he had to do was keep quiet. But this business of economic collaboration, it's got management all on edge. How many men are quaking now who acted within the limits of the laws and in perfect good faith? You can't put an economy back on its feet in that kind of atmosphere."

There is the naval uncle too, the one who commanded the cruiser. He's wearing his fancy-dress uniform again, with the five gold stripes.

"He put it on to please his mother, who is dying," says the aunt. "It is quite brave of him, because he doesn't have the right to wear it. He has to go before a purge commission."

You put your bravery where you can, thinks Luc; why not in a uniform? (A month later the uncle is cleared.)

Luc endures the embraces of a few weepy-eyed old ladies wearing pestilential perfumes, who press him to their squashy bosoms: "Oh, you poor little fellow!"

He sneers loftily, drinking fizzy wine with his cousins. They stick together.

One youth is making the rounds with a glass in his hand. He is wearing the khaki outfit Luc has seen before, half gunnysack, half uniform: the outfit worn by FFIs after being incorporated into the army and by the 24-4. He has also seen that reddish pelt and those pink eyes and heard that goat's laugh before, that cordial, self-satisfied voice and those sweeping gestures that accompany all his words. No doubt about it, it's his cousin Bernard Maury, the one who was at the surprise party.

"I'm at the Quiberon pocket," he explains. "What a mess! We have no heavy artillery, they've forgotten us, the Krauts are in there tight as bugs in a rug and receiving supplies by submarine and aircraft, they can hold out forever. Without big guns, the Atlantic wall is invulnerable. And for me it means another year lost. For nothing, nothing at all. Classes have started again at the school of engineering. And you should see the men I have to command, no discipline, a bunch of tramps."

"Well!" mutters Luc. "He ought to be proud, the stupid fart; after all, he was the one who built the Atlantic wall."

Cousin Maury recognizes Luc and bears down on him wearing his damp boy-scout, head-salesman smile. He looks pleased with himself and everybody else, pleased with everything, in spite of his lamentations.

"That's a good-looking uniform," says Luc.

"Hideous ... I hear your brother is in the American army. At least some people are lucky."

"Yeah," says Luc, "he's lucky. Very lucky."

And that is how the year ends. Christmas definitely is a dead loss.

It wasn't always like that. In 1938, at La Valerane, the whole family took the little train after high mass and went down to the foot of the village of Cogolin. They climbed among the bare vineyards and chestnut groves, walking through thick, moist winter grass; they crossed the silent village dressed in its Sunday best; they heard the mules stamping in the stables opening onto the narrow alleyways, they could see their rumps as they passed. They walked along a stony path and stopped to picnic on the flat rocks by the Paillasse mills, the ruined remnants of their great wings thrust up toward the winter sun. He has a snapshot of that: his father, seated on a ruined wall, is waving a bottle in one hand and a glass in the other, and singing. That was a real Christmas.

✠

Something is starting to worry him. He's afraid he is losing his memory of absent faces. It's mostly at night, of course, that it bothers him. He tries to recall his mother's features exactly. He knows from experience that that is the worst possible method; the harder you try, the more the recollection blurs. Exact memories rise up when you're not trying for them: for instance, the sugary smell of marzipan and dried flowers on his grandfather's desk at La Valerane (he doesn't know exactly what marzipan is but he's certain it's the only word that defines the smell of that room), certain inflections of Antoine's voice ("Of course I love you, stupid"), the taste of his wet skin when they would roll in the sand together after a long swim, the smell of both of them when they came back from a race over the hilltops, the pearly sound of the waves from his window on mornings when the sea was calm, the scratch of his father's moustache against his cheek at bedtime. The faces you clutch at desperately slip away; it's when you're not thinking about them that their features flash past. It can happen on a street corner, at the turn of a staircase, because somebody said a word, because some image, any image, has passed. Then the face is there for a split second, very fragile. One mustn't grasp at it, or it whisks away. One might as well try to catch a cloud. It was a cloud.

But how can one be satisfied with a cloud? How can one be sure, each time it takes one by surprise that way, that this won't be the last time? So he insists, he clutches, fiercely. But nothing comes, except the fear of having lost the image for good.

When he was little, his mother used to tell him Japanese tales at bedtime. There was the story of Urashima-Taro, the poor fisherman who found a little golden fish in his nets one evening when the moon was full, and it turned out to be no less than the son of the king of the fishes. Luc is too old for fairy tales now, but some evenings he shuts his eyes and imagines his mother coming to sit on the side of his bed and telling that story to him. He can almost hear her voice.

Clouds, phantoms: one can't help being constantly on the look-out, ready to snatch them as they pass by, stop them from escaping, growing even dimmer; one has to be very careful not to make a false move, a rash gesture that will cloud the reflection. Even photographs, which ought to be indestructible signposts, life buoys, are not completely trustworthy; if one stares at them too long the features dissolve and all one is left with is a scatter of isolated details that it's hopeless to try to stick together again.

So the best thing is to keep whatever is left of the shadows very carefully shut up inside oneself. Not take risks, like talking too much or too mechanically about people who aren't there; because that can also be a way of letting their substance escape, and is therefore dangerous.

He hears his aunt talking about him again: "Have you noticed," she asks the uncle, "have you noticed that Luc almost never speaks of his parents? I wonder if he even thinks about them."

That winter is so long and sad. And so cold. A tunnel.

In February 1945, nobody believes the end of the war could come soon. The forces Germany has mustered to withstand the siege of her natural frontiers are formidable. Her propaganda still talks about secret weapons that could turn the tables overnight. There is still the Rhine to cross, and the Alps, and the Oder . . . London has become the target of a hail of increasingly deadly V-2s. People are looking for hints, signs; some optimistic remarks of Churchill's are much commented upon: it seems he expects a final victory in Europe sometime in the autumn of 1945, but he has also said that it would definitely take another eighteen months after that to finish off Japan. In the last few months the fighting around Aachen has transformed the whole area into what the reporters call "an apocalyptic landscape." Waves of bombers are pounding the German cities daily; as many as five thousand planes have been counted in a single night, carrying tens of thousands of tons of bombs. But the big problem in the west now is crossing the Rhine.

．．．

How long, Luc wonders, will this silence last? For the moment, the newspapers are saying almost nothing about deportees and camps. The first survivors of Auschwitz are starting to come back, via Odessa, along with prisoners liberated by the Russians, but people are only beginning to hear about the Struthof camp, which the French troops discovered, empty, when they entered Alsace. From now on, in addition to the daily-growing stockpile of commentaries on and eyewitness reports of atrocities committed by the Nazis, the Gestapo tortures, the SS massacres and shootings that took place in France during the occupation, both press and radio begin broadcasting descriptions of the Struthof. When it isn't some new horror story about Oradour in *Le Figaro* it's Jean Nocher on the radio, narrating, night after night, abominable tales of Germanic barbarity in a grandiloquent voice backed by hideous sound effects, sounds of boots, bursts of machine-gun fire, choruses of *Raus* and *Schnell*.

The high point of Hitler's bloodthirsty insanity, according to the press, was reached at the Struthof, for in this camp, a complex of green sheds built exactly to Red Cross specifications—this camp which, the journalists say, seemed exactly like all the rest—are discovered not only the crematorium, which was in operation until the very last moment before the evacuation, but also, connected to it by a hoist, the gas chamber. Luc reads and learns those words "gas chamber" for the first time this snowy morning, March 3, 1945, at noon, when he gets home from school and opens *Le Figaro* with his chapped fingers; it is four pages long that day because it contains de Gaulle's program speech. The paraphernalia used for experimentation on living prisoners in the laboratory directed by Professor Hagen is also described, with a special mention of the experiments in cerebral localization; the huge pile of hair and scalps found in one room of the laboratory is supposed to have something to do with these experiments. According to the camp archives, twenty thousand prisoners died in two years at the Struthof. Fifty-nine women from Ravensbrück went through the gas chamber and crematorium in three days. *Ravensbrück,* Luc reads, looking unsuccessfully for further details in other papers. Ravensbrück.

．．．

Maybe it is then that death, at certain moments and without warning, starts to inhabit him. He's thinking about it more and more often. That's exactly it: the death of Antoine, the death of his mother, the death of his father are becoming possibilities. Truths. Capable of assuming shape and color. Clothed in increasingly discernible images. Yet death should long since have ceased to be a stranger to him. Exactly when does death become something one is no longer looking at from the outside?

When he was little, he used to ask questions about death. Later, he was reassured. People were forever telling him about the gigantic strides being made by science: it seemed obvious that death would be eliminated by the year 2000. Wasn't that the purpose of progress? His parents would smile and let him talk. There had been painfully intense discussions with Antoine about the soul and eternal life. Antoine wavered, depending on the day, between icy negation and a somewhat less categorical skepticism. Less cut-and-dried. As a rule, he claimed that all that kind of talk was just fairy tales and in any event the affirmations of religions were not to be taken literally. (He discoursed at length on the relativity of religions in general and the avatars of Christianity in particular—did Cat know that there had been many other prophets, many other Messiahs tramping the roads of Palestine in the time of Jesus? As usual, Cat didn't follow very clearly.) But quite often his conclusion was that however unreal these notions were, they should not be systematically ridiculed. They must be taken into account. Too many questions were still unanswered about the nature of life itself. One could not just shrug away several thousand years of beliefs which had made human beings what they were today. It would take time, patience, and a great deal of work.

Luc, like everybody else, has challenged life, of course, tried to test its limits. He has stared at the sun without blinking, even after the green fire started pulsing in his head, until he was blind for many minutes afterward. He has held his breath until he spun into unconsciousness. He has dived so deep that the surface of the water looked like a far-off silver leaf he would never be able to reach. He has crept out to the edge of the cliffs, at the extreme limit of his balance, and stared down at the waves sweeping the litter of boulders below. But testing the limits of life does not teach one anything about death, does not really have to do with death.

The images are fleeting but stubborn: a mass of women prisoners in striped uniforms—who told him they had striped uniforms?—are marching toward the open door of a gas chamber, the gaping maw of a crematorium.

His aunt would rather he did not spend so much time listening to the radio. And especially Jean Nocher.

"I don't want Luc to hear that," she says when he is in bed listening, through the door, to the voice reeling out its usual rosary of horrors, torture, waiting lines of people condemned to die, raucous barks. "I don't want Luc to hear that. He's too young."

But she doesn't turn it off.

Then, against the onslaught of the images, he fights back, telling himself he's making things up, he's imagining things, nothing is tragic, he's being ridiculous. His father is in a good camp. The women's camps are supervised by the Red Cross. And Antoine ... He has to turn to more reassuring images. Antoine pedaling uphill on his bicycle. His mother's voice. Walking through the sodden woods with his father. But the images won't go away. He is alone.

But that doesn't stop him from being as highly strung and moody as ever, or quarreling with his cousins, or having absurd tantrums and flying at anybody who crosses him with feet and fists flailing, or making up new rules for the chases with the varnished balls, or leading raids on the merry-go-round with the headless horses. He goes to the movies too: he sees his first Western, *Ghost Riders in the Sky*, in three episodes; his first American comedy, *Mr. Deeds Goes to Town*; *The Devil's Envoy, Deuxième Bureau contre Kommandantur*, and a whole series of dubbed Laurel and Hardys.

The only thing that has any real attraction for him, though, is the markets and the Rue de la Petite-Truanderie. He keeps going back. He enters the Petit Roscoff whenever he sees Diane alone through the curtains. On several occasions she was not alone, and he turned around and left. She always greets him with that mixture of mocking brusquerie and sweetness that leaves him speechless and incapable of reacting. She barely raises her head; it's as though he had left her only five minutes before, his presence seems natural to her. And always, her smile . . .

With her, he feels good. Maybe it's because she is the only person who calls him Cat, in her cracked voice, or "little brother," and also the only person who doesn't talk to him as though he were a baby. When he is not with her his thoughts are explicit. He puts his arms around her, he kisses her, the way Max does. He runs his hand over her body, under her pink-orange sweater, under her skirt, over her skin, her belly . . . Why not? But after that, the images get mixed up and unclear. The one thing he's sure of is that they are leisurely and romantic, nothing like what Lucien used to talk about on the farm. But will he ever be capable of performing actions like that, with that assurance, like Max, like all those men in whose eyes he doesn't count, who seem so tranquilly impervious to doubt? When he is with her, the images disappear.

Max left with his battalion early in December, heading east.

"Those guys were really tough," Diane says nostalgically. "Kings of the scam, the trick, the traffic, the market, black, gray, and red . . . Red, that's for sure, red. Max was always talking about Communism and the revolution. He used to say, 'We're getting ready for the Big Night, but that's no reason why we have to stand around and bore our asses off doing nothing in the meantime.' And he certainly wasn't bored doing nothing, that's for sure. Talk about a circus: what with the supplies the Americans have stockpiled at the Porte d'Orléans, and the rations, the cigarettes, the jackets, the gasoline, jerry cans every day, and Teepol—that's great stuff, you use one drop and it cleans everything—and tools, all kinds of tools for doing everything, like in a dream. And whiskey. No, of course, you don't know what that is. And weapons. Sure, weapons.

"So you can imagine," she concludes, "when the Americans asked for reinforcements in the Ardennes, it was the 24-4 from Romainville that got sent first. It must have been a relief to some people. And now, it feels weird and empty here without them."

Diane talks about Max a lot. Cat has a hard time relating what she says to the tall boy with the possessive gestures whom he once caught a glimpse of.

"He's always telling stories that are so complicated I can't figure out what he's talking about. For instance, he's telling you—at least you think that's what he's telling you but you've already forgotten why he's talking to you about *that*—how when mountain climbers fall into a crevasse it takes the glacier a hundred years to bring their bodies back, it drags them frozen in its stomach, two or three yards a year, and when they reappear it's their great-grandchildren who come to collect them, and they haven't changed, they're still young, their clothes are new, the same colors, the sandwiches in their packs are still fresh, all they've got is a little growth of beard and their hair's a little longer. Right, so you're trying to follow what he's saying, to think about all that, imagine the scene, and then all of a sudden before you've had time to realize how it happened the scene changes and he's telling you about islands in the middle of the Atlantic where people live on volcanoes that spit fire, and when they want to cook something all they have to do is dig a little hole outside their front door and they've got a crater just for them, the fire hops out, just enough to cook their soup. He also says that cats . . ."

"What about cats?" ventures Cat, who is beginning to find Max even more of a nuisance when he isn't there than when he is.

"Cats are much more intelligent than people but they don't let on. They've been living in our houses for three thousand years. They wait and watch us and say nothing. One day when they know everything there is to know about us they'll take over, just like that. And then . . ."

"Then what?"

"I forget."

"He didn't make up that story," Cat says, "I've heard it before." He hadn't, but somehow it didn't sound original.

He doesn't dare ask Diane what she's doing in that café, as though she is riveted to the red table for the rest of her life. He tries to guess, putting together snatches he hears now and then, but that whole universe is beyond him.

One time she said to him, "I work at night. Ah, you should see me at night . . . You wouldn't know me."

Another time she snapped at a stout man who was signaling to her from the bar, "I'm no whore."

The owner, who is not a talkative type, treats her as though she had always been in his café. He serves what she asks for without comment and never brings her a bill. The women on the street, the real whores, often come in and sit down beside her. They always talk about the same things, nurses, presents for baptisms and birthdays, and, in the spring, preparations for the first communions of little sisters or brothers. They also utter strings of morose considerations on the state of the world: "This government doesn't know how to handle things. Business is still dead."

It's all pretty much the same as what he heard at his grandparents' at Christmas. Only now and then, by chance, one of them makes a professional remark: "I work American blacks. They're not real Negroes."

They display their cartons of cigarettes and nylon stockings, and go back out into the cold, their wooden heels clacking on the floor.

"You'll have to come in the evening one time," Diane says to Cat. "But not just any evening. It's too bad Max isn't around anymore to play the piano. Sometimes we get some terrific Americans on the trumpet . . ."

Lady Ponte-Serra has not given up writing to Antoine, even though other envelopes have been returned bearing the same inscriptions as the first one, which she still can't decipher, and she has kept them all. His maternal grandparents have also had their letters returned. So?

"I don't understand," the old lady says. "I do not understand. Of course, since he is not getting our letters he doesn't know we are writing to him. And hearing nothing from us, he must think we are angry with him; that's what your aunt and grandparents think, anyway. But he must know that I, at least, am not angry with him. He must know that that is impossible. But how to get in touch with him, how to let him know we are proud of him? I know your aunt and your grandparents are doing things. But nobody tells me anything. Nobody ever tells me anything."

What else can she say?

She writes:

My child, perhaps this letter will have better luck
than the previous ones. Where are you? What are you
doing? Do not leave your grandmother, who loves you,
and Luc, who needs you, without news any longer. I
know it isn't your fault, but so much worry ... I am very
much alone this winter and it is too hard. If I only knew
the name of your generals, your army, I could follow you
by listening to the communiqués. I do listen to them all,
day and night, except when the electricity is cut off. Your
parents are in good camps, we have had confirmation
from Geneva and I am sure that they, like myself, are
proud of you. You have done your duty. This week I took
the advice you gave me last year, I reread your Sophocles.
How right you were, and what an attractive person Anti-
gone is. I am not cold because I have been able to get in
two steres of firewood. I am sending this letter to the
same address as before. I tried to approach the American
Red Cross and have them look for you, or at least tell you
we were all right, but they told me they could not give
out any addresses because they were military secrets, and
they were not taking any messages from France. My dear
boy, shall we have to wait until you all reach Berlin before
we hear from you?

At the end of March the weather turns. The boys go back to their
own rooms and life begins moving through the corridors again.

The Allies cross the Rhine. The Russians have been fighting at
the Oder for a month. Luc scrutinizes every change on the maps
printed in the newspapers. It is he who moves the pins, often twice a
day, on the big map of Germany. Is this the final offensive? He also
sticks pins in a map cut out of a newspaper on which two arrows indicate the gap between the eastern and western fronts. In the north,
the English and Russians are 290 miles apart; in the south there are
230 miles between Patton's army and the tip of the Russian offensive. But what he sees most is that the arrow in the north goes
through Mecklenburg. He still doesn't know where Ravensbrück is

but it's clear the Russians can't be far from it; and in the south the arrow passes close to Weimar, the Americans are advancing on Nuremberg. Luc is magnetized from then on. Everything he reads and hears he relates to the distance between the liberation forces and his parents' camps. When Frankfurt is conquered the Allies will advance on Eisenach, then Erfurt, and once Erfurt is taken Weimar is only thirty miles away. Then . . . Then he has to try to remain deaf to the other things he is hearing, the self-congratulatory recital of the awesome havoc being wreaked by the steamroller in action, the hammerings of heavy artillery, the carpet bombing that leaves the conquered towns without a wall standing, the civilians fleeing along the roads, whole towns of dead buried in ruins: 80,000 tons of bombs in one week, 555 tons an hour, the communiqués triumphantly announce. Can the concentration camps escape this universal flattening?

Probably they can; because the concentration camps are now being protected by the Red Cross. That is the great event which has monopolized his grandmother's attention throughout the whole month of March. Luc followed the developments day by day, his heart leaping with hope. For the first time a distinction is actually being made between prisoners of war and what are known as "political internees." The first piece of good news is announced in the papers on March 1:

> Political prisoners' conditions of internment have improved. Approaches to the German authorities undertaken by the government through the Red Cross have now produced substantial improvements, both physical and in terms of morale. The sending, to all camps, of personal parcels containing food, underwear, shoes, and pharmaceutical products will be permitted in the future as well as the dispatch of collective parcels. . . .
>
> As regards the humanitarian aspect, the Germans have now accepted visits to the camps by the confidential agent, who will act as a go-between for the German authorities and the Red Cross. This is a significant guarantee, although the Red Cross delegates themselves have still not been authorized to enter the internees' camps.

Lady Ponte-Serra is packing parcels. She cannot decide which should have priority: clothing or food? She sends her aged maid out on complicated missions to the shops, she pulls every string she can find. Corned beef, chocolate . . . On March 7 it is announced that the first Red Cross convoy, carrying one hundred and twenty tons of parcels on twenty trucks painted white, has left Geneva for Germany and that the German authorities have promised to give it free passage on the roads. And, best of all, on March 20:

> Terms of agreement will soon be reached in regard to the
> civilian deportees, old people, women, and children. One
> question remains to be determined: the designation of a
> "Geneva" or neutral zone.

On April 2 the Germans hand over three hundred women from Ravensbrück to the Red Cross.

(This needs amplification. On March 30—Good Friday—the day the Red Cross mission reached the entrance to the camp, about three hundred and fifty women were sent to the gas chamber. Some tried to escape the SS, who hunted them through the camp. Several times, the truck carrying the naked women to the gas chamber drove past the Ford of the Swiss doctor leading the mission.)

"Sixty thousand deported women will soon be home," the press announces.

"Mom's coming home," Luc tells his aunt when they are all eating lunch in the kitchen. "They're letting all the women go."

He makes plans. What will she be like?

"I hope they haven't cut off her hair."

"You'd better prepare yourself for one thing," the aunt says peremptorily. "Cut or not, your mother's hair will be gray."

Luc shrugs. Ridiculous. How can his aunt know ahead of time what color his mother's hair is going to be? That's just malice.

With the crossing of the Rhine and the cave-in of the German defenses, more prisoners are being released all the time. There were one million two hundred thousand French prisoners in Germany. Also seven hundred thousand STO workers. But how many civilian deportees, political or racial? One hundred sixty thousand, maybe (if

they are all alive). They're lost in the crowd. That's why it has been
so hard, all this time, to identify what applies specifically to them in
the news about the "repatriates," and this is still true. Like other
people, Luc has trouble sorting things out. In the first days of April,
the repatriates are pouring in by the tens of thousands. The Allies are
anxious to get these wandering hordes away from the combat areas.
Clearing centers are opened at the borders, railway stations are requisitioned, even two movie houses in Paris, the Rex and the Gaumont.

The first measures taken for the reception of the deportees coin-
cide with the Americans' entrance into Weimar. On April 15 newspapers and radio announce the liberation of Buchenwald. In his
aunt's *Figaro* Luc reads a paragraph confirming the news and, on the
same page, an announcement of the arrival of 197 women from Ravensbrück; de Gaulle himself went to welcome them at the Gare de
Lyon, where the train from Switzerland came in.

"MONSIEUR JULIEN CAIN LIBERATED FROM THE BUCHENWALD
CAMP," says the headline.

> Weimar, April 14. The Third Army has liberated 21,000
> prisoners from the Buchenwald camp near Weimar.
> Among them is M. Julien Cain, who, before becoming
> Deputy Secretary General in charge of information in the
> Paul Reynaud government, was Director General of the
> National Library.

That's all. Succinct. But enough. It means that along with Julien
Cain and twenty-one thousand others, his father has been liberated
too.

His mother is not among the first women repatriated from Ravensbrück. But for her too it can't be long. When? How can he find
out exactly?

The Hôtel Lutétia is requisitioned as a clearing and accommoda-
tion center for the deportees; because it is only now that people have
begun to realize that they need special treatment. The hotel is on his
way to school, Luc goes past it four times a day. As soon as the center is open, little groups form on the sidewalk outside, waiting and
debating.

Among them are a few men with shaved heads, wearing what

look like the rags of blue-striped pajamas and haranguing the crowd. Why are they still in those peculiar clothes? Haven't they been given anything else to wear? The first one Luc listens to, a man of indeterminate age, dirty, with a drawn, wrinkled, unshaven face, in the center of an attentive circle of listeners, is relating horrible and unlikely privations. What makes his tale even more doubtful is that at regular intervals he turns to the people closest to him to ask for cigarettes and money, like some down-and-out actor.

Just a tramp, thinks Luc.

The very first day he musters all his courage and goes inside, accompanied by his large-headed friend. He asks a girl behind a desk if Mr. or Mrs. Ponte-Serra is there or if any information about them can be obtained.

"We do not give out information," she answers, sounding overworked, her mind on other things. "We notify families directly."

"But," Luc begins, "I ..." Then he stops, because he doesn't know what else to say; she has already looked down and is busily writing away on more important papers.

It is very warm, the sky is clear, the sun hot. Now the people waiting outside are holding photographs. The man in the striped pajamas is still talking. People ask him questions, give him names. Luc decides to do the same.

"You didn't happen to know Mr. Ponte-Serra?"

The man shrugs. He utters a sort of moist snicker that shows the stumps of his teeth.

"If you think we had nothing better to do than remember everybody's name ..."

He coughs, sniffs, starts to blow his nose through his fingers, thinks better of it, and looks around.

"Anybody here got a handkerchief?"

❖

When the first American soldiers reached the outskirts of Buchenwald they saw a few ghosts in striped tatters moving toward them, and those ghosts were armed. The deportees had revolted, they had liberated the camp themselves and liquidated their SS guards. The

Americans got their next surprise before they were inside the barbed-wire fence. A convoy of freight cars was parked alongside the camp, abandoned, and inside it were thousands of corpses. They were the bodies of prisoners from Dachau who had been sent to Buchenwald by the SS. There were no survivors; every one of them had died behind the padlocked doors.

Then the Americans entered the camp, and the next day the whole world was introduced to the concentration-camp universe. When the other camps were liberated—Dachau, Mathausen, Dora, Bergen-Belsen—and when people finally started paying attention to the tales told by the survivors of Auschwitz who had come back via Odessa, the horror unfurled until it covered the entire planet.

It could have been known long before. It was known, and had been for a long time, by some. The fact is that those who might have told the world about it were silent.

In a few days, thus, Luc learns the truth about concentration camps. He will have the rest of his life to think about it, to try to understand, and it won't be too long.

Buchenwald was not a "good camp"—although, as objective specialists will point out, it was not, unlike Auschwitz, for instance, actually designed as an extermination camp. There was no gas chamber at Buchenwald—yet; it was still being built. The thing is, there were no good camps. All the camps were death camps; anything beyond that is a matter of degree or percentage of horror.

From now on, he can fill his days and his nights with these stories and these images that are displayed everywhere and assail him everywhere; he can go over them again and again. These are not nightmares. They are precise images, true images. One cannot negotiate with them. One cannot arrange them. One has to take them as they come. Some people will be able to make poems out of them. Not him.

He hurts, badly. He doesn't call it fear, it's just a dreadful blank; he feels like a stone falling through endless emptiness.

Here are the first photographs of the mountains of fleshless corpses flung into contorted, grotesque postures. Here, in *Actualités,* are the survivors, skeletal, naked or in rags, who can hardly be propped on their legs, hideous creatures with shaven skulls, a thousand times more hideous than real skeletons, their obscene sex hanging between the stilts of their thighbones. Their faces are almost completely gone, nothing left but huge, staring eyes, expressionless, and hands like talons, some of them still gripping their only possession on earth—because losing it, having it stolen, means sure death by starvation—the tin pan that holds their soup but also the diarrhea of their dysentery. Here come the articles of the first war correspondents on the scene, the eyewitness stories; the convoys trundling their cargoes of the dying, demented, and dead, the cullings and discardings, the barefoot roll calls in the snow, the hard labor in the stone quarries that kills in days, the unprovoked floggings, the dogs that tear people to shreds on command, the synthetic fiber clothing at twenty below zero, the famine, the clear soup and the white soup, the dysentery, the lice and the typhus, the killings, by a bullet from a revolver, by machine gun, by hanging, by battering, by an injection to the heart, by the gas chamber, and sometimes, on busy days when there's no time to bother with details, by immediate dispatch to the crematorium. But one has to be fair: there was an orchestra at Buchenwald, its musicians were got up in outlandish costumes. And Goethe's oak was on the camp premises.

Next come the sadistic side stories. From the very beginning the newspapers specialize in them, collect them. They positively adore them. It's a contest to see who can be the most gruesome. There is the discovery of warehouses full of goods manufactured from cadavers, the heaps of hair to make fabrics, the gold teeth and crowns gouged out with hooks, the medical experiments and the bitch of Buchenwald who collected tattoos, the lampshades made of prisoners' skins. And that is only a start. The field is inexhaustible. A gold mine. Later, in a religious boarding school, the boy next to Luc in the dormitory wakes him one night, in the dark. "Is it true that in the camps the SS . . . ?" And Luc will hear him masturbating and wheezing in the next bed.

(Luckily, he runs away from that school the next morning. That will be his only experience of a religious educational institution.)

For every story, every prisoner, every victim mentioned, Luc has a name: that of his father, his mother. When he sees the photographs, he puts their faces on every anonymous mask, every shaven skull, every dead gaze, every gaping rictus. On every stumbling silhouette or shape lying on the crematorium stretcher, on every head sticking out of the tangle of bodies and limbs in the burial pits, he puts their features. He will never stop.

And these days, when he finally falls asleep and everything gets mixed up together, sometimes he sees flames leaping out of the crematorium, then a bony head with a death-mask grin: his father. He tries to argue himself out of it, he tells himself he is wallowing in tasteless, self-indulgent melodrama. He turns on the light. His aunt sees it through a crack in the door, comes in, and scolds him for reading in bed after hours. She turns it out again.

Three days later he learns that his father is dead. It is lunchtime. A beautiful day. The chestnut trees are in full bloom. As always, he has been hanging around outside the Lutétia. Everybody else must already be sitting down to eat. He comes in expecting a scolding. In the doorway, in the shadow of the hall, his aunt tells him to follow her to his uncle's study. She sits down on the consultation couch. He stands in front of her. She takes hold of his wrists and squeezes very hard. She looks up at him and says, "Luc, your father . . ."

She breaks into sobs and he stands there in front of her, between her open knees. Congealed, hard and heavy as a stone. He might like to comfort her but there is too much going on inside himself. Sobs rise, but are blocked in his throat. He sees the big map of Germany on the wall, the pins he moved day after day, the joy he felt in performing that trivial gesture with every advance, every morsel of ground gained. The pins have moved beyond Weimar. It's over.

He looks at the map of Germany again.

"What about Mother?"

"You know the Germans are going to release all the prisoners from Ravensbrück. They are going to send them to Sweden. She will soon be back."

It was Julien Cain, she tells him, the first to be repatriated by airplane, who came to tell his grandparents. It has not been possible to keep it from his grandfather, although he ought not to have been told, he is so unwell just now, it would have been better to wait until he is stronger. But it's already in the papers.

His father died in March, the aunt adds. He did not suffer.

That's a useless sentence, thinks Luc. Another one of those ready-made sentences. Like in books. Why does she say that? For whom is she saying it? For me? For herself? I don't believe it. For seven months he suffered his death every day. He starved to death.

"How did he die?" Luc asks.

"We don't know the details. But there were friends caring for him until the end. He slipped away gradually, he did not suffer."

❖

She doesn't tell Luc, he doesn't learn until much later. They do know the details. But why tell him about them? And there will be many more. Was it Julien Cain who brought back his father's diary, saved by somebody in the next bunk? A single sheet of cheap paper folded into sixteenths, a camp administration circular on the blank back of which he drew three columns in pencil and, in microscopic writing, wrote a calendar for the months of August 1944 to April 1945. Space for one line a day, filled in as the days passed. The last day for which he wrote a date is Saturday, April 23, and opposite it he wrote: "Spring." The capital S of that "Spring," is very peculiar, a kind of writing he didn't ordinarily use—his swift chicken scratches were always very simple, unfussy, without twiddles; but this S is so elaborate, it has sweeping curves almost with little tails on them, a very painstaking S, the kind people were taught in primary school, the kind they called "embellished script." After March 5, the column is blank. And for March 5 there is only one letter, D. D for diarrhea, a letter that recurs often in the preceding days. He died before spring.

He fought to the end. He fought with his own weapons, as he had done when he was in solitary confinement at Fresnes in 1941. The underground Communist organization inside the camp functioned efficiently when he was sent to the quarries, it got him out of there and assigned to easier work. Another two or three days in the quarries and he would already have been dead. Because the organization was selective too; at another level, it too had powers of life and death. Cat's father got all the help it could give. The orders were to preserve, if possible, anyone who represented a value for the country's heritage and future, and since Cat's father represented a very definite intellectual value the underground organization tried to preserve him. If it didn't manage to save his life, it was because the struggle against the opposing system was too unequal.

He joined a sort of clandestine university in the camp, a university for starvelings. At some lectures he had as many as fifteen students. There was the cold and the hunger, the forced labor, the roll calls day and night, the delousing sessions; and there were these men who somehow found one another and somehow managed to meet. Each one talked about his research, his subject, his special field of knowledge, his travels: the discontinuity of matter, the atom, the art of cathedrals, the introduction of spices into Western cookery at the time of the Crusades, old Norman customs. Luc's father talked, among other things, about his pilgrimages to Buddhist monasteries in Japan, where he had lived, his visit to the sorcerer king on the Tonkinese high plateaus. Until the very last days, a few of them continued that superhuman effort, from pallet to pallet, in the stench of the *Revier*. He tried to write to his wife at Ravensbrück, through the camp administration; he never got any answer. Until the end, he talked about Antoine, saying he approved of what he had done; and he worried about Luc at school.

Luc was right, he spent a very long time dying. The last month: open wounds, bedsores, and vitamin-deficiency phlegmons in the foul odor of his soiled pallet. A few days before he died, he managed to wash his underpants. He put them somewhere to dry, and they were stolen while he slept.

Professor Ponte-Serra died at the Buchenwald camp.

To the long list of crimes against culture and civilization perpetrated systematically by Nazi barbarism it will now be necessary to add the name of one of Europe's foremost sinologists, Victor Ponte-Serra. Professor at the Collège de France, author *inter alia* of a monumental history of the introduction of Buddhism in the Far East,

> Victor Ponte-Serra personified the very ideal of those
> French scholars who . . .

That is what he reads in the afternoon newspapers, in tiny print at
the bottom of page two. He wants to go to school anyway. At the
beginning of the lesson the French teacher utters a few ceremonial
words with much emotion but Luc only half hears them, nailed to
his seat, blushing fiercely in the silence of the classroom, staring at
the wooden top of his desk. In the next class the history teacher, the
green monkey, comes up to shake his hand and commiserate.

"I hope he didn't suffer too much." Then "How old was he?"
he adds in a sort of technical voice.

"Around fifty," Cat says evasively (because one seldom knows
one's parents' exact ages).

"Oh, well, of course, at that age . . ." says the green monkey—
who's at least as old—nodding wisely.

The sun still shining, and the air so warm. On the Boulevard
Raspail, people are still waiting in little clumps outside the Lutétia,
their photos in their hands, for men in striped pajamas to emerge.

The next day is Thursday and he goes to see Lady Ponte-Serra. When
he gets there the little old lady is in the entrance hall, trying to stand
very straight as she ushers out a man with broad, hunched shoulders
and drawn features under gray hair cut very short, whose gaunt body
floats in a beautifully tailored gray suit.

Luc leans over to kiss his grandmother. (In Cat's family when
people kiss they barely brush the other person's cheek with the lips,
once, almost never twice. None of those repeated smacking noises.
That would be common. Nothing, no exceptional circumstance, not
even death, can disrupt this ritual.)

"Grandmother, I . . ." He is mute. He has nothing to say.

His grandmother is crying. Julien Cain gives Luc an affectionate, absentminded wave, and goes out. He will never see him
again. He is startled to discover that he resents the man. He is about
to learn that he cannot easily feel affection for survivors. That he
cannot easily accept the fact that they have survived. It's a primitive
reflex, he knows. It is unfair. He can't help it. Too often, in the sur-

vivors' tales, the dead appear as shadows who happened to be un-lucky. Shadows who simply highlight the calvary of the narrators themselves. And then there are all those people who put words in the mouths of the dead. The commemorations: martyrs and heroes. One day he will read a book by one survivor who says the dead do not need flags, only a pure and fraternal gaze. He'll like that one. And a few more like him. A few.

His grandmother is already installed in her grief. She lost one son, the first Antoine, in 1915, in the last war. Now she is losing her other son. When she weeps, she makes faces and contortions that frighten Luc. But she also knows the gestures and motions that pre-vent her from losing control altogether. She is saved, as always, by the power of ritual.

"My poor child, I cannot understand how your aunt could allow you to go out in that state. I must say, some people are quite irresponsible."

There they are, she and her maid, digging through drawers, pulling out scraps of black crepe of every size and description: the remnants of all the bereavements of her whole life.

They sew a thick band around one sleeve of his jacket.

"There. That's more appropriate. Now you are in mourning."

Friends come and go in the drawing room.

"If only little Antoine were here."

⚏

At night there are those images that keep coming back, as he stares open-eyed into the dark. And in the day he needs to shout, to run away.

Is it only the next day? It's a Thursday, anyway, he's at home with his cousins. He makes paper planes, the most sophisticated ones he has ever designed; they sweep up to the ceiling, soar and bump into the walls, chandelier, furniture, like great blind butterflies. He runs after them, jumping, shouting. His cousins manufacture water bombs in paper bags and all three post themselves on the balcony, looking out for pedestrians. Luc wants a faster game. He goes to the medicine chest, fetches his old friend the enema bulb, and, hiding behind a shutter, squirts long, well-aimed jets at the people in the street. He is detected. Somebody comes upstairs and rings. The aunt receives the first blast of indignation from a dripping gentleman.

"I'm going to call the police."

"It was Luc," say the cousins, who have had time to get rid of their bombs. The aunt, perforce, passes on the sound and fury, further amplified. She lectures him: "Aren't you ashamed of yourself? Two days after your father's death."

Is he ashamed? It's extraordinary, Luc thinks: he can know that something in him has broken that cannot be repaired, that nothing is like it was before or ever will be again. And yet nothing is changed. There isn't really any before or after. Everything is the same color. Things and times weigh the same. Other people's faces, motions, words are the same. He can live with this definitive emptiness inside himself, feel himself sinking as though pulled by leaden weights and, at the same time, he can let himself float above it, very far, very high, quite naturally, with every appearance of having forgotten. And not only appearance. Sometimes he plunges into instant, blinding flashes of joy, a fleeting stroke of lightning. And if, at that very same instant, he hears in himself a soft voice—his own—whispering that it is all trivial and meaningless, then he plunges even harder than before, laughs even louder. He sings, shouts, fights, and hears them saying, "That child decidedly has no feelings."

What they think about him does not matter. Let them think what they like. He can't bother about that. He will not try to oppose it. It's not worth the trouble. Few things are really worth the trouble of fighting over and certainly not what other people say about him. He knows that the things that really deserve to be fought for exist, he will spend his whole life finding them and defending them if he has to. He is sure Antoine would agree.

# Snow in May

On the morning of May 1, 1945, Luc looks out the window of the old laundry room where he has his lair and sees, in amazement, that the top branches of the flowering chestnut trees are weighted down by a thick blanket of snow, already being stroked by the sun.

His mother is alive. She was liberated in February by the Russians. She was not at Ravensbrück but in a *Kommando* much farther east. She is in a hospital in Poland. She weighed sixty-six pounds when she was released. She has a bad abscess on one leg. She can't walk. She is being well cared for. She is getting better.

It was a woman repatriated via Odessa who brought the news. She came to dinner at the house. The aunt managed to get a pork roast and some potatoes from Chevigny. In the entrance hall the guest hung up her grayish synthetic-cloth coat with a big yellow X sewn across the back and a number and a red triangle on one sleeve. She took second helpings of everything.

"I was so hungry for two years," she says.

"Oh," says the aunt, "we suffered here too. Why, we went all last winter without a drop of oil."

Between mouthfuls, the woman talked volubly about her life in the camp and the great battle during which they were liberated by the Red Army. Luc did not speak, except to ask one or two questions at the end. Had his mother's head been shaved? The woman said yes, but that her hair would grow again quickly and she would undoubtedly wear it *à l'aiglon,* which is said to be most becoming. He asked if she had enough to eat in Poland. The woman explained that in the first days of liberation the fighting was still going on all around them, but the Russians had shot a cow for them with a submachine gun and afterward they had been able to take what they wanted from the SS barracks storerooms. One woman had flung herself on a bucket of jam and eaten it all up at once. It had killed her. Then they had helped themselves in the houses abandoned by German civilians, all along their truck trip through Pomerania to the east, behind the Russian lines. They hadn't felt any pangs of conscience about that because the Russians were burning everything anyway. They had been helped by French prisoners of war who had taken charge of them. And in the Polish hospital where she had seen his mother for the last time, his mother had everything she needed, the Polish nuns were most considerate.

But why hadn't she gotten in touch with them? Why hadn't she written? The woman explained that in the Soviet army there is no mail, the soldiers themselves can't write to their own families. First they were caught in the battle of the Oder and then it was a very long time before they managed to establish contact with the French embassy in Warsaw; they had no way of making their existence known. And when it was decided to repatriate the able-bodied women in their group, it all happened in a few minutes one beautiful day. The Russian trucks were there waiting; his mother hadn't time to write so much as a note.

"But she can't walk," Luc repeated, suspicious.

Because if his mother comes back with short hair—gray hair—she might just as easily come back with a leg cut off, a wooden leg; he can already see the black stump sticking out under her dress, like the one of the moustachioed grandfather in the family of refugees at Marles. After all, at this point, what difference does it make? And if that's the way it is they would do better to tell him so right away. The main thing, for God's sake, is that she should come home and not stay out there in some hospital in a town with an unpronounceable Polish name that he can't find on the map; it's somewhere near Poznan, they tell him, but you have to look under Posen, that's the German for it. A good hospital, of course; he's heard that song before.

The evil spirit must be conjured. These days, in the playground at school, in the Luxembourg gardens, on the sidewalks, he will roar out his new war song at the top of his lungs:

*A wooden leg had she,*
*But so people wouldn't see,*
*She ran rubber rings around it*
*From her toes up to her knee.*

❖

When the women in the convoy that set out from Paris on August 15 were removed from their cattle cars at Ravensbrück on August 22 they passed columns of lugubrious women prisoners marching and singing German songs. Then, going through the fortified gates of the camp, they saw the wagon that transported the dead bodies to the crematorium. Stripped, numbered, showered, issued shapeless old rags to dress themselves in, they were assigned three to a bed in the quarantine ward.

Two weeks later Luc's mother and most of the other French women from the same convoy left for a camp in Brandenburg, a *Kommando,* where they were supposed to work in a munitions factory. Locked in their cattle cars, they spent the night abandoned in Berlin-Tempelhof station during a bombardment. Upon reaching this other camp the French women said they would not manufacture munitions, and most of those who did go on the job sabotaged their work efficiently. The "rebels" were sent back to Ravensbrück. Luc's mother was one of them; she was assigned to the earthworks and sand quarries. This time the coat she was issued was too big and during roll calls she shared it with one of the little English parachutists—who was later shot. Then she was sent to a new women's *Kommando* on the right bank of the Oder, where she was to work on the construction of an airfield. There they found abandoned black shacks in the middle of a muddy field, triple-decker bunks and blankets alive with lice. Nine hundred women were shoved in there together, two or more to a bunk. Luc's mother worked, to the lashes of the *Meister*'s belt, laying rails. Until December the women kept their "summer" rags, without coats or socks, working barefoot in their galoshes. At the beginning of December they were issued additional clothing, made of rayon. They were given two soups a day; the noonday soup, eaten on the work site, was always cold. The *Oberauf-*

*seherin* punished them several times by depriving them of food for twenty-four hours while they worked. They dragged out the job so successfully that the airfield was never completed. What with the cold and hunger and the vitamin-deficiency phlegmons, dysentery and typhoid decimated them. At the *Revier,* which was finally opened, there were neither bandages nor medicines; they made compresses out of paper and lice got into the pus. The absence of basins or any other receptacles was an additional nightmare for the dysenterics. Luc's mother, immobilized by her suppurating knee, suffering from dysentery and delirious with fever, was able to get herself admitted to the *Revier.* For a while she shared her pallet and blanket with a little Greek girl, the only survivor of her family, which had been picked up in a raid at Salonika. She soon died. On February 1, when the Russian army was approaching, the Germans herded together all the able-bodied women left, a hundred or so, and drove them on foot to Ravensbrück. Many died on the frozen roads, finished off by the guards where they fell. The next morning, the women who had been left behind in the *Revier* heard shooting in the camp. German troops entered the shacks, tipped over the stoves to set fire to them, and then left. The wind dropped and the *Revier* didn't burn. Later, other soldiers came past; they shot down some women who had gone outside; their corpses lay in the snow. For three days the survivors were caught in an artillery battle beneath the screams of the Russian rocket guns. They heard the rumble of tanks; then three Russian soldiers rode in on bicycles. They had an Asiatic look, they were wearing fur hats and boots. The women had to stay in the camp another week or more because they were still in the front line of combat. The Russians gave them what food they found—the German supplies, the machine-gunned cow. Women kept on dying, from exhaustion or indigestion. One went crazy and started out one night walking straight ahead through the snow, saying she was going home. She was not found. At last they were evacuated, in open trucks. It was ten degrees below zero, maybe more. There were thirty French women left. They camped in ruined towns. They were bombed by the German air force. They were caught in the vast throng behind the Russian lines, troop convoys going up to the front in American-made trucks followed by vehicles of every description, motor- or horse-drawn, packed with women and children. And in the other direction were columns of German prisoners on foot, trucks loaded with German equipment, wheat, straw, flocks of livestock driven eastward by the fighting, and, along the roads, requisitioned German women working with shovels.

When Luc's mother was finally hospitalized by the Russians in Poland, when she was finally able, weeks later, to make contact with the French embassy in Warsaw and ask for news of her family, she was told that everybody was well. Professor Ponte-Serra was liberated. Luc and Antoine were waiting for her in Paris.

⚏

On this first of·May Luc learns that Antoine is dead. For some time he had been talking about his brother incessantly. As though he sensed that Antoine was escaping and he had to try to hold on to him any way he could; and the only way left now was to catch his shadow in a net of words, to weave a web of words and images and imprison him within it. So for weeks, several times a day, he would say,

"When Antoine comes back . . ."

"I'm sure that at this very moment Antoine . . ."

"Antoine will certainly think . . ."

Lately, he had even started making up stories about him. One morning when he got to school, he told the boy next to him that his brother had just been awarded the Military Cross. He liked the sound of it, the impression it gave; most of all, it kept him alive. Anyway, Antoine deserved it, so all he was doing was affirming a reality a little prematurely. At bottom, he knows that he is indulging in a shabby subterfuge.

One time, at the table—always the same setting: lunch, the assembled family, the kitchen misted with steam—he was gabbling away about his brother's return when all of a sudden his aunt reacted violently. He must have been saying that his grandmother had just sent the aged maid down to clean and straighten Antoine's room and that they had put clean sheets on the bed.

"In my opinion," she snapped, "in my opinion, your grandmother is out of her mind. It is insane, after all these months, to act as though nothing happened. To dream about Antoine coming back. It is insane."

At the time, it hadn't really worried him; his aunt is always short-tempered wherever Lady Ponte-Serra is concerned. That kind of pronouncement, sharp as a slap in the face, is habitual with her.

Early in the afternoon of that first of May—a holiday, the first Labor Day of liberated France—while the radio is retransmitting the elation of the workers parading through the melting snow, his maternal grandmother rings the doorbell. He opens. His cousins have gone to some stamp sales. Her face is shut, her mouth twisted. She seems not to see him. She walks straight in and almost pushes him aside with her hand. She shuts herself up in a room with his aunt. Luc goes back to his own room. He crouches on his bed. He waits. He hears outbursts from the two women's voices, sobs. Later, his aunt comes to find him. His grandmother has disappeared. She has gone home again. Maybe she didn't have the courage. She has gone back to her husband. He had to be told too. Since the news of his daughter's liberation, he has seemed better. His gaze not so staring. His speech less wandering. It would have been better to wait a little longer, until he could take it. "This time he won't rally," she said to the aunt.

The aunt is brave; it certainly must take a lot of courage to tell Luc. But is there really any need to say anything? She has sat down on the edge of the bed. He has thrust himself back into the corner with all his strength, one shoulder pressing against the brass rails, his knees against his chest. No, it doesn't take many words. Is it true or is it a nightmare? Does she really say, "You see, I told you so?"

It must be just another nightmare. She cannot have uttered those words. She is as unhappy as he is. She strokes his arm. He pulls it as far away as he can. He bites his fists. A low unbroken cry is rising and getting stuck in his throat, he doesn't let it out, maybe it's only a murmur, but all of him is in that cry. She leaves him alone.

Alone, hunched up on his bed in the empty bedroom. The fog of tears that do not flow.

It doesn't take many words, not many seconds, to tell. One instant, a few seconds to hear. A whole lifetime to understand.

When they played together before the war, Antoine used to say, "Today I am the king and you must follow me everywhere, like my shadow. I shall make you a knight. I'll draw your coat of arms, with an eagle in them. You must call me Padishah, Your Highness, Caliph, Sheik el Islam, Commander of the Faithful, Emir, Mikado, Maharaja, Dalai Lama, Great Mogul, Supreme Inca, Emperor of all the Indies, and Pope of Bonzes."

There. Antoine is dead.

Beneath the numerous stamps of the French and American postal services (two of which, with different dates, indicated a passage, once on the way out and once on the way back, through Fort Campbell in Kentucky), the envelopes of the letters to Antoine which came back one after the other all bore, front and back, purple prints made by repeated applications of a large stamp sloppily placed and poorly inked: a hand emerging from a buttoned cuff with the index finger pointing nowhere (it was probably meant to indicate the sender's address) and, under the folded fingers, the words *"Return to sender."* Beneath were various words that were hard to read because there was either too much or not enough ink: *"Reason checked: Unclaimed / Refused / Unknown / For better address / Moved / Left no address / No such office in state."*

The relevant words were supposed to be underlined or crossed out, but none were. In one corner there was a hasty scribble, almost illegible, in a slanting, run-together hand: *"Deceased, 9-44."* A signature followed, or rather initials, and then "Capt. inf." and another date. Just that, so little, so compact, so lost among the other notices, the blots, the fuzziness and worn folds of the cheap paper. The word *"deceased"* and the signature forming an insignificant series of signs, they might easily be taken for a record of passage through one more unimportant departmental office.

To each returned envelope the French post office had conscientiously added one final stamp, further muddling the overall effect:

A RETURNED
ENVELOPE CAN
BE USED AGAIN.

Antoine died in September. He was in Patton's army, Luc had been right about that. He died more than two weeks before Luc set out to look for him. In one month he had crossed France from west to east, always at the bulge of the big loop made by the American Third Army from Alençon to Le Mans, then the Loire, and from Orléans to Reims and then on to Verdun. One month, long enough to be adopted by the battalion, to make friends in it. His appetite was legendary. The soldiers crowded round to watch him bolt down several days' rations at one sitting, exactly like Cat on the Red Ball road. He had given only his first name. He had not talked about the past, except to say that he had fought before and that he had a special account to settle with the Krauts. He was always trying to be in the front lines, he was known for that too. And as he was near-sighted and had broken his glasses during his escape and was a menace with a gun, the others tactfully tried to moderate his ferocity. Sometimes, in conversations, he would refer to events and people and periods in American history, with which he seemed much more familiar than the people he was talking to, and as he was completely unassuming about it, that surprised them and made them like him. (When, at the end of 1945, Sergeant Peter McLore is demobilized and returns home to Bangor, Maine, one of the first things he does is rush to the bookshelves to see whether it was really true, as that crazy Frenchman said, that General Pershing, the victor of the war of 1918, had been given a trouncing shortly before by Pancho Villa on the Mexican border.) After Verdun was taken and the Meuse crossed, his division headed toward Metz. The advance was slowing down. A summons came from Metz telling them to hurry, the Germans were in complete disarray and mustn't be given time to reorganize the town's defense; in a few hours the Americans could seize control of the strongest fortified bridge in the Lorraine lowlands.

But, somewhere between Verdun and Metz, they bogged down. The incident staff headquarters had been dreading since the disembarkation finally occurred. The supply lines were overloaded, the thread that now stretched over four hundred miles from the cramped Atlantic ports to the very tip of the offensive was too tenuous, and it broke. They ran out of fuel. Those hours were decisive. By the time the armored columns could move again the forts had been able to reorganize. After becoming the key to the whole German defense system on the near side of the Rhine, Metz was to hold out another two months. When Antoine's battalion reached the banks of the Moselle it was caught almost immediately in heavy artillery fire from the forest above Metz. The first units, which had started across the river, had to fall back in disorder. The village they were in became a hell. The battalion, which had had eight hundred men in it, lost four hundred of them in one day. Antoine's body lay in the no-man's-land of the ruined village. The captain had his billfold recovered by a night patrol. He gave his men special orders to get it, and hoped they would also bring back the notebook in which Antoine used to write every day, but a German patrol had already searched the body on the side where he kept the notebook. In the billfold, the captain found an unfinished letter to his grandmother giving Antoine's full name and the grandmother's address. The captain had liked Antoine a lot.

When, some time later, the regiment was sent to rest and the captain was able to get to Washington on furlough, he put the bill-fold in a heavy envelope, enclosed a long letter with it, and sent the parcel to Mme. Ponte-Serra, Paris. *"Why it had to be Antoine instead of me or the man next to me or a man up the street, I don't know,"* the captain wrote. He talked about the will of God. In January the envelope and its contents were back in Washington: the round of *"return to sender"* was still not over. The envelope was marked: *"Return to sender. Reason for return: Weight of letters addressed to France limited to 1 ounce."* Bad luck? All that was left of Antoine still weighed more than one ounce. The captain was already back at the front.

It was not until April that the inquiries made by Luc's family produced any results. The American Red Cross finally managed to trace Antoine, and the captain, once they had located him in his new posting, confirmed his death.

In Antoine's billfold, along with snapshots of the family, there were still a few bread stamps marked, amateurishly and almost illegibly: *"Etat français. Mairie de Choisel."*

There had been Uncle Antoine, the one who died in 1915 at the age of twenty-six, the one who had already published his thick, learned tomes about Ptolemaean Egypt, the one who left his poems, his drawings, his painting, the one who was eternally Cat's father's little brother. Cat's brother Antoine had been given the same name, as though to make him live on or bring him back to life. To distinguish between the two, his grandmother called him little Antoine. But she sometimes mixed them up and her confusion was not entirely involuntary. Now they were together again. The grief of Luc's grandmother is, to use the conventional word, unendurable, which means on the contrary that, having been hit much harder than any person can endure, she is still there enduring, and Luc with her, watching her cry. Within a few days, her son and her grandson, both. She has been making arrangements for her own death, down to the smallest details, for almost thirty years. She has talked to her family about it as though it were the most natural thing on earth. She has spent those years writing, on every object she was specially attached to, some lengthy message intended for whoever was to inherit it: "For my son Victor, these bracelets which his father brought back from Montevideo at the age of twenty. They were given to him by Mr. Gonzalez Fernandez in recognition of his assistance with his research into the semantics of the Aymara language ..." "For my grandson, this telegram from Lord Carnarvon informing me of the discovery of the tomb of Tutankhamen; may he always remember his grandfather ..." "Fragments of terra-cotta pipes found when clearing the Sphinx of Giza, abandoned by soldiers from the Egyptian expedition. If Antoine does not wish to keep them, I request that he present them to the La Sabretache society, which collects memorabilia of the Emperor." By this means, meticulously organizing everything that was supposed to take place among the members of her family after her death, she was in a sense preparing her own survival, through those objects—the inanimate witnesses which had marked her life—among which she had lived. While she was lavishing such care upon her preparations for their transmission, she could never have imagined she would be leaving them to the dead. She does not understand why she is still alive, and it is this injustice that, lost in her tears, she keeps explaining to Luc. As for him, what can he do but sit there before her, mute, and endure his own agony of the unendurable. Lady Ponte-Serra has always labored to instill in him, more and better than anyone else, the fundamental principle of a good upbringing: there is nothing more inappropriate, more out of place, than to express one's emotions in unregulated gestures. Whatever happens, to kiss his grandmother suddenly or put his arms around her is utterly unimaginable; that is not the behavior of a dutiful child. So he sits, speechless and unmoving, as her grief washes over him. He accompanies her in her soliloquies. Sometimes she refuses, she doubts; maybe it is a mistake. Antoine had not given his real name, maybe he has been confused with somebody else. It isn't Antoine who is dead, it is some other person, somebody unknown. That letter he wrote to England had no date on it; it reached London over a month after he was supposed to have been killed.

"It is not possible," she says again. "We must wait. Wait a little longer. Just a little longer."

But the next minute:

"We must do something, write. We must find out where they put him. We must find his body."

No, thinks Luc in horror. No, anything but that. Not the body. No.

<hr />

May 8, late morning, sun shining into the classroom through tall open windows. The sirens, the sirens on the school roof, all the sirens in the district, send out one long wail in unison. The alert is over. The war is over. Everybody pours into the playground. The principal makes a speech. The singing teacher's great moment has come; the whole school sings, in parts, the anthems they have been rehearsing all winter. For good measure she also taught them, to the tune of the chorus of Handel's *Judas Maccabaeus,* these words which may be her own invention:

> *Our hearts uplift*
> *In victory chant;*
> *To our conquering soldiers*
> *All glory grant.*

> *The homeland hails*
> *To honor's height*
> *The heart-strong hero:*
> *Victorious his right.*

(During rehearsals she patiently explained that "hails" means summons and not pellets that fall from the sky, and "honor's height" is not a specific measurement but a summit or acme. It's de Gaulle's problem now, to keep his balance up there. Anyway, nobody ever listens to that kind of lyric. And besides, that verse is a solo, sung by his large-headed friend with glasses, who manages, with great effort, to reproduce the angelic soprano of his infancy despite his recent voice change. So all the chorus has to do is let him worry through it and then chime in with "Our hearts uplift" again.)

"Children," the principal must have said, "may this be the finest day of our lives." Or if he didn't say it, it was only because he's a little peculiar. But he did talk about building the peace, all of us together, and about friendship between peoples and democracy; he did say, "Never again."

"Now, children, on this day of celebration, go home to your parents."

That afternoon Luc sets out with his aunt and cousins, as part of a huge and delirious crowd, to walk to the Champs-Elysées. What happens that day, the awesome tidal wave of joy that engulfs everything in its path, he will never see again. Millions of people are laughing, singing, embracing. Rockets fired by antiaircraft batteries shoot up on all sides and burst into bouquets. A huge flag floats under the Arc de Triomphe. Luc walks a long way. His feet hurt. He doesn't see what's so great about it. He grumbles.

"Luc," his aunt says to him kindly, when they are being buffeted by the waves of the happy throng at the top of the Champs-Elysées, "Luc, if you're tired, you can go back to the house by yourself."

He goes. He has a hard time forcing his way through. People are dancing on the Place de la Concorde. He struggles around dense human masses and zigzags through side streets to reach the Boulevard Saint-Germain.

There he is, at twilight, crouched on his bed again, as he seems always to be since last winter. He is hungry but he doesn't want to move. The darkness thickens. The bursting rockets make the whole neighborhood vibrate, the flares and plumes of fireworks light up his window, huge searchlights sweep the sky, their beams flickering through the branches of the chestnut trees.

He's not thinking of anything in particular. He doesn't want to think about anybody. Just stay like this in the darkness, fog, vague. Maybe, from time to time, he tells himself: "The stupid farts."

Or, for variety: "Bunch of turds."

The French teacher assigns the theme for the last term's composition: "A boy your age makes his first visit to Paris this May. Describe his impressions."

They're not going to get him this time. He has understood, he's an old hand now. He gives it the works: This month of May is the month of joy, Paris bubbling in the effervescence of peace restored, the spring sun, the Eiffel Tower illuminated and the Arc de Triomphe beribboned, airplanes zipping through the skies and, on the street corners flush with fresh green foliage, accordion players . . . Paris is the City of Light again, which, as everybody knows, is to be taken figuratively as well: the city of spiritual, intellectual radiance. Oh, yes, what a lucky boy he is, to see Paris for the first time in this period of rejoicing and elation. There must be no pearl missing from the necklace that Luc strings conscientiously for two hours and six pages, no pearl, and above all not that final touch, his apotheosis, when the heart of his boy, who is a good boy, soars aloft to higher sentiments, and he quotes from the poem by Victor Hugo which the teacher appositely had them learn a few weeks before:

> Glory to France, she ever shall abide,
> Glory to those who for her sake have died:
> The martyrs, the valiant, the strong . . .

Sure enough it pays off: when the teacher hands back the papers he announces, with a shade of vibrato in his voice, that Luc Ponte-Serra gets the highest grade in the class, 16 out of 20.

Now that the warm weather has come, he spends a lot of time hanging around the Luxembourg gardens. He and his large-headed friend channel the leaks that fizz out of the watering hoses along the pathways. They build canals, lakes, waterfalls, working the sandy mud. They raid shipwrecks in the pond, around the fountain. Between noon and two in the afternoon the guards are off duty, disappearing into their green huts to heat up their lunches. That's the most opportune moment to shed one's sandals and plunge up to the knees in the cold, clouded water. Spreading their fingers to make dragnets, they rake the bottom for ships that have gone down with all hands on board during the great storms on windy days, battered by the spray of the fountain gone wild or stove in by collision. Sailboats of every description, Jep 2s and Jep 3s, enameled tin motorboats sky blue and white with snub noses, that haven't even had time to rust yet. They also find, groping through the slime and rubbish on the bottom, a few coins with holes in them. The guards accuse them of trying to catch the fish in the pond; but the boys are not in the least attracted by those red or bleached gray goldfish, albino carp with mossy scales; in fact, they are revolted by the slimy feel of them. No chance of discovering the enchanted fairy-tale fish here. One day the guards attack from all four sides at once, surround the pond, and trap the boys. Luc escapes and unheroically abandons his friend to their clutches. The friend's father is notified. He has to come and claim his son, who is being held under stern surveillance in one of the green huts. Written report, humiliation, sermon. The father is a Protestant minister.

The Musée du Jeu de Paume reopens, and they discover Van Gogh and Gauguin. Luc has a few books in the Braun series but all the illustrations are in black and white; he has seen some color reproductions of the Impressionists. All he had noticed before about Van Gogh's painting was the violence of those thick masses crowding each other as though in some great battle, trying to storm a steeple or bridge, haystacks or sky. Maybe it was the painter's legend that impressed him most. Van Gogh with his ear cut off, Van Gogh in an asylum that could be Chevigny, the three suns and suicide. And Gauguin ... That winter his friend read *Le Grand Meaulnes* and is showing an increasing tendency to take himself for Augustin Meaulnes; Luc is supposed to be his admiring shadow. All he has to do now is find the mysterious park and unknown girl, but those are minor details. The main thing is to leave. Like Gauguin. The wondrous clouds ... (That winter they both set off on the trail of Jack London too; they were Smoke Bellew and Shorty struggling along on their snowshoes, tramping over the endless expanses of hard, squeaky snow behind the dogsleds drawn by their faithful huskies. The Great North was inspiring. But it was also very demanding. When spring came they gave it up without too much regret.)

"But Gauguin; look," Luc objects, with his little book in his hand. "You can see that the last thing he painted out there in the tropics was this village under the snow; so what's the point of going all that way if on the day you die ... And Meaulnes himself, when he tried to come back, what a disaster ..."

"You've got to go," his friend affirms, settling his steel-rimmed glasses more firmly on his flat nose. "You've got to go."

When the museum is almost empty, lighted only by the weary rays coming through the dirty skylight; when, walking between the paintings, they feel great waves of shapes and colors ebbing out of the frames and into them, slowly at first, and then, little by little, rising and rising until they almost drown; when, at last, they stop, paralyzed, in front of Gauguin's "White Horse," they no longer speak. They stand there frozen, their fists crammed into their pants pockets. Each one shuts himself into a resentful, almost hostile silence, he's so afraid the other will disturb what he's feeling, because nobody else, not even one's best friend, should have the right to feel it too. Looking at Gauguin's "White Horse," Luc realizes that his friend is right: you've got to go. He tells himself that it's worth risking and losing everything, life included, to achieve what he sees *there*. A great whirl of images spins in his head.

But there is nothing fanciful about what he continues to see at night, with his eyes wide open, or about the thoughts he thinks, shifts around in his head, watches parade past; those same images which have now grown so familiar as to seem ordinary. Of these images, of course, he is not the master—but is he any more the master of the ones he sees in broad daylight, those among which it is natural to live, those that are called normal? They visit him, envelop, assail him, but he does not try to chase them off. These images are not inventions. They are not nightmares that can be dissipated by shaking one's head; the nightmare exists. The nightmare is true. These are the images of reality. Maybe his imagination is not even strong enough for them.

His father, over and over, and that rictus of the fleshless head, and the crematorium. And Antoine? Antoine's body. In the mud on the bank of the Moselle. Was it raining that day in September? He thinks it was. What was he doing himself that day? He remembers perfectly. That was the evening he went to throw his supply of gunpowder down the unused well and lit that giant flare. At that hour, Antoine had probably already been killed. Antoine's body—a shapeless mass, a stained khaki rag, torn to pieces. How did he die? They were on low ground, at the riverbank, in this village, under heavy artillery fire. Picked off like sitting ducks. The houses must have collapsed, one by one. Trapped under the rubble, their backs broken by the crash of some big tree, trying to drag themselves along, clutching at earth and stones. Or maybe, the head smashed in. Twitching for minutes in spasmodic jerks. Or even longer. Like a rabbit under the blows of a bludgeon in the farmyard. If he didn't die at once, he cried out. Called. Called whom? His mates, the other men? His last words in English? Screamed.

Luc wasn't with his father. He wasn't with Antoine. They died alone. He would like to have been there. Talked to them. Touched them. What difference would that have made? He doesn't know. He *is* dreaming, no doubt about it. But that loneliness, their loneliness, death ... It isn't human. But what does that mean, human? Even Jesus Christ was less alone. He ought to talk to somebody about that. He has nobody to talk to. The priest at Magny, maybe.

And now? Now he ought to be with his mother. That's obvious. He doesn't like this "good hospital" story. And that tale of an infected leg that is going to get better: bullshit. They can't fool him anymore. Of course, he couldn't do much. He'd sit on the edge of

her bed, without moving. He would be there. He would try to catch
her eye, her gaze; he absolutely must see her eyes again; it's got to
stop, these foggy wisps of memory that are raveling away. He is sure
that if he were with her she would feel calm, quiet, secure. A child
who watches at the foot of one's bed without saying anything: all
the quiet and peace in the world. She would sleep. She would get
better. He would bring her big glasses of scalding black tea. He has
made inquiries, that's what people drink in Poland—with vodka, of
course. He even knows the word: *herbata.* Do they have samovars
there? Turn the brass handle. Black tea with no sugar; there's no
sugar there, apparently, even less than here. And the tea is probably
made of carrot greens. But black and scalding.

This whole business has gone on long enough. His mother has
got to come home.

They tell him it's impossible for the time being. There is no way
to cross Germany, there are no railroads, the ordinary roads have
been torn to bits and are clogged with troops, liberated prisoners,
homeless hordes, all the bridges are out. They tell him he must wait
until his mother is able to walk. They tell him . . .

No; definitely, this whole business has gone on long enough.

One afternoon when he has just bawled his great tune, "A
wooden leg had she," down the corridors of the apartment for the
thousandth time, he hears his aunt explaining to some visitor, in her
sweetest voice, as though to excuse him: "You know, Luc is still a
child. Life goes on."

✠

The merry month of May comes to an end. One Thursday his aunt
lets him go to Marles by himself. He has spent weeks patching up his
father's old bike—its name was Pegasus—which had been rusting
away in the cellar in town. He and the bicycle board the train at
Denfert on the Sceaux line. His aunt has asked him to bring back
some potatoes. If nothing else, potatoes. The Massy-Palaiseau section
has been reconnected and the train goes through the marshaling
yard, which is full of bomb craters. He goes to the old house, where
the refugees are still living. There's nothing left of their home in
Boulogne-sur-Mer and they have decided to stay on in Marles until

the prefabricated huts that are supposed to come from America can be put up in what used to be their neighborhood. Luc is welcomed with a flood of tears and hugs, he renews his acquaintance with the grandmother's sticky apron. Her son the prisoner is back. He shakes Luc's hand vigorously, looking him straight in the eyes, with a manly, responsible air.

"Tough, eh, old man!"

"Yeah," says Luc. "Tough."

"What the hell, that's the way it goes. Nothing anybody can do about it. Nobody had it easy, believe me. Now, why it was your dad and not me, you figure it out. I remember at the end of '43, an English bombardment on the farm where I was working. I can tell you . . ."

"What the hell," he says again. "Your brother . . ."

Luc doesn't say he wants anybody to do anything about it. Except leave him alone. He asks about his animals. He wasn't cherishing many illusions about the fate of Patachou and Timoshenko. But what about the guinea pigs?

"Oh, my poor boy, the guinea pigs . . . Didn't you know? When the last Germans—because we had to take in more Germans—well, they ate all the guinea pigs. We were afraid it would upset you. Kraut bastards," says the former prisoner with conviction.

"Kraut bastards," repeats Luc.

He observes that the refugees' hens and rabbits are all fat and flourishing, and that their numbers have multiplied, survivors of the Massacre of the Holy Guinea Pig Innocents. Everybody knows that guinea pig is the favorite dish of retreating barbarians.

He leaves, loaded with blessings and potatoes. He doesn't have the courage to stop at the next farm. Being unhappy alone isn't all that much fun, but what's even tougher is playing one's part without forgetting one's lines, coping with other people's compassion, their comments, being there with the right line when they give the cue. Other people always look as though they know their parts a lot better than he does. He dreads these scenes. Even when he's fond of the people.

He rides his bike through the sun toward the Montainville rise. This is where he saw Antoine for the last time. Almost a year ago now. It's too early for haymaking but there's already a smell of hay in the light air. He stops on the small, silent square of Magny, across from the church and cemetery. He leans his bike against a shutter of the priest's window. He knocks at the solid wooden door. The priest who opens it is a young man, fair-haired, slightly stoop-shouldered in his neatly buttoned cassock.

"I'd like to see the priest," says Luc.

"I am the priest, young man. Please come in."

He steps back from the open door to let him in, smiling broadly.

"No," said Luc, who stands there and doesn't move. "No; I mean, you're not the one I was looking for."

"Heavens, my poor child, you were wanting Father Malbry." He's still smiling.

"Yes, Father Malbry, that's it."

"My poor child. Father Malbry left us last winter. God ... That is, he died last winter. I am his successor. But do come in. I like to see young people. I haven't ever seen you before."

Why doesn't he stop smiling?

"No," says Luc. He mounts his bike.

The young priest moves forward with his hand outstretched, a friendly gesture, wanting to take hold of his arm, hold him back.

"No," Luc says again, louder.

He pushes down hard on the pedal and rides off. He's already in the middle of the street. Behind him he hears the voice calling: "My child, if you want to see his grave ..."

And then, fainter: "Come again. Come again anytime you like."

Luc pedals with all his might across the plateau, into the wind, his jaws clenched. He growls, "The stupid fart."

The priest of Magny never spoke about anything directly related to the practice of religion. On that point he left Cat blissfully in peace. "Faith," he said, "is something you have to decide about alone, alone with the good Lord. It's between you and him. Everything else ..." He would shrug.

"For most of the people around here, religion is like insurance. It's just one more contract they have to sign. Afterward, they make what they can out of the clauses. They cheat, they fib. This is a hard, tight-fisted region. And as I am not an insurance salesman, they often resent me."

"I don't exactly understand," Cat ventured to say one time. "God became man, then Christ went up to heaven. And after that he came down to earth again in the form of the Holy Spirit . . ."

The priest banged on the table.

"You don't understand, you don't understand. Of course you don't understand. 'He went up . . . he came down . . .' What is this, some kind of shuttle? Do you take God for an elevator? If that's the way you think, you'll never make any sense out of the Gospels. And what is this mania everybody has, always wanting to explain everything? Don't you feel that God is precisely something that cannot be explained because otherwise he wouldn't be God?"

What would the priest of Magny have been able to say to him today? What did Luc want him to say? He hasn't the foggiest idea. He would just like to have talked to him. Listened to him. Anyway, there is nobody else with whom he *can* talk. But what a crazy idea too; why want to talk to somebody? There is nothing but walls all around, and that's the way it is. He must be nuts, to try to change the way it is.

He has one more thing to do. He rides back to the Dampierre road. The "seventeen turns" among the trees. It is already past midday and very warm. He has trouble locating the house, having caught only a glimpse of it in the early dawn. Finally, he identifies it, at the Chevreuse end of the village, low, the little windows, the overhanging roof. He knocks and the old man opens, in slippers and a brown wool vest. He peers inquiringly through the circles of his glasses.

"Hello, sir," says Luc, still holding his bike with one hand. "You don't recognize me."

"No," says the man uncertainly, holding the door half open.

"We stopped by last year, about the same time of year, my brother and I. It was at night."

"Oh, yes. Of course, I remember. Oh, yes. Well, what about that . . ."

"My brother said we should come back and thank you, after the liberation. So."

"Don't just stand there. Come in. Come on in."

He winks.

"You've come from your uncle's at Cernay, eh?"

In the darkness of the workshop, everything is exactly as it was before. The table with the oilcloth cover, the garden chairs, the workbench and vise, the tools neatly lined along the wall. The plants. And garlands of newly harvested onions.

"We've got a visitor!" the man calls out.

She appears in the inner doorway, looks him over, and laughs.

"I knew you'd be back. We talked about you often."

"You bet," says the man. "You should have seen the look on the faces of the gendarmes coming back from Choisel, the day after you were here."

"Are you alone? What about your brother?"

"He's not here," says Luc. "He ... Well, he's dead. He was killed. You know."

"Sit down," the woman says.

"Give him some of your grenadine. He must be thirsty. He's come on his bike."

"You poor children," says the woman.

She serves him pink grenadine in a tall glass with water in it, slices some bran bread she must have baked herself, and sets a half jar of jam in front of him.

"I darn near chucked you out, you know," the man says. "In those days, youngsters on the roads after curfew most often meant something fishy. Because the resistance, around here ... But your brother was so well spoken; we really couldn't refuse."

"That's right," says the woman. "We could see you were decent boys."

"Except when your brother started lecturing me, when he started talking about politics, really, you know, I had to laugh."

"You poor boys," the woman says again.

"What about your son?" asks Luc.

Then the woman starts to cry, she sits down with her head in her hands and her shoulders shake. And looking at her, Luc feels all of a sudden that he wants to cry too, the knots in his throat loosen, he bursts out sobbing and the tears run into his jam. He feels as though a huge weight has lifted off him; he almost feels good.

It is only then that he sees, on a shelf near the workbench, the photograph with the decorations in the left-hand corner of the frame.

"When the army came," the man says, "in August, by the Cernay road, and we saw that they were French, everybody was out on the road shouting. We stayed here, by the door. We looked at every tank that went past, at the men on it. Every chance we got, we called out our boy's name. They were in a hurry, they were having trouble clearing away the people who were blocking the road, you understand, and then with all the shouting, and the noise of the motors . . . We fetched his photograph and showed it to the ones we could catch hold of. They all told us no, they didn't know him. And then the days went by, the weeks went by . . . All the boys his age who came to call on us were going back to work, back to their families, and they said to us, a little embarrassed, you know, 'He shouldn't stay away so long, so far away, without letting you know.' And then one day that winter they told us he had fallen in Provence on August 18. At Draguignan. He was going through the forest and his submachine-gun jammed. That's all anybody knows. He wasn't found. It was the gendarmes who came to tell us. Can you imagine? The gendarmes. Afterward, there were decorations. And official letters."

He gets up and ruffles through a drawer. He tosses a sheaf of papers down in front of Cat.

"Here."

Cat reads: "Sir, I have the honor to enclose the text of the decree of posthumous award of the Military Cross, with bar, to your son Fernand D.: After escaping in 1941, he went to North Africa . . ." Luc skips to the end: ". . . all those who knew him remember him as a brave man. In my capacity as Captain *chargé de mission* in the French First Army attached to the Ministry of Defense, I salute the remains of a glorious soldier of the French Army. With deepest respect, Sir, I remain, Yours faithfully."

"The dumb cluck," says the man, sitting down again. "What a dumb cluck. You read it? He salutes the remains. His body was never found, you understand."

"At least," says his wife, "if I had him here, in the cemetery, I don't know, I think that would be something. . . . Nobody can understand," she adds. "Nobody can understand how it feels."

"No," Cat answers. "Nobody."

It is after six o'clock. Time to catch the train back from Saint-Remy.

"Come again," the old people say, watching him from the doorway, between the windows splashed with big red geraniums. "Come see us again."

"Yes," says Cat. "I'll come again."

A disaster. Definitely a disaster.

He gets home to his aunt's late.

"Did you have a good day?" she asks while he is in the kitchen wolfing down the noodles she warmed up for him.

"No," says Luc.

"I wonder if you'll ever be satisfied with anything . . ." She sighs. The cousins snigger and poke each other with their elbows.

"Is it because of the guinea pigs?" the aunt asks. "I didn't want to tell you."

"Yes," says Cat. "It's because of the guinea pigs."

Another Thursday afternoon, on the Rue de la Petite-Truanderie.

"Max is back," Diane announces, without looking up from the cards in front of her. "Sit down and don't move. The cards are very black. *Sehr schwarz.*"

The atmosphere in the Petit Roscoff is grim. At the next table, surrounded by empty benches and chairs, a thin girl is sitting up very straight. She's young, almost as young as Diane. But taller. A serious face, delicate features, like a little boy's. Short blond hair sticking straight up in stiff clumps; that's probably what they mean by *à l'aiglon.* Beneath the table he sees very long, bare, smooth legs. The skirt is extremely short and shows thin, golden thighs emerging from white underpants he doesn't dare look at for more than a second. With her forearms flat on the table and her narrow chest thrown out, she stares straight ahead of her, at nothing. Huge gray-green eyes ringed with black pencil, lashes stuck together with mascara. Her gaze lost, drowned in tears. She is sniffing quietly, the wings of her narrow nose twitch and flare. Now and then a sob shakes her shoulders. She shuts her eyes, then opens them very wide with a jerk, her eyes stare again and the tears roll down. What Cat sees in those wide staring eyes is the utter misery of a beaten child. And more: fear.

Behind his back he hears thick throaty laughter. He turns. In the far corner of the room he sees the usual group of card players, a little larger maybe, and noisier. Just as he looks around, one of them points at the girl; they roar with laughter. He can't make out all they are saying but one word sticks out, repeated several times, and comes home to him: "Slut."

The one who was pointing, a chubby little man in a dark suit with slicked-back oily hair, gets up and walks over to the girl. He grabs her by the arm. He's still laughing.

"You come with me."

The girl sits still, straight, stiff, not moving. The man grabs her arm with both hands, squeezes hard, and forces her to her feet. In her cork-soled shoes, with her long legs and knobby knees, she is taller than the man. He keeps one hand around her arm while the other reaches out for a buttock barely covered by the skirt, grabs hold of it at the fold above the thigh, and pushes her toward the door. She walks like a machine, her head still straight, her eyes still staring and lost. She is still sniffing quietly. He laughs again.

"You'll see, I'll cheer you up. You'll see."

The street door shuts behind them to yells of laughter. The men shout louder, slap their thighs, even the owner behind the bar is writhing as though he has just witnessed the funniest scene in his life, he calls out: "A round on the house."

Diane hasn't looked up. She shuffles the cards and growls: "Bastards. Bastards."

"What's the matter?" asks Cat.

"Forget it."

But she says it again, through her teeth: "Bastards."

The owner brings glasses, clinking together on a tray. The men count up the score of the game and yell some more. Cat feels something hard, dangerous, in that group of men. Something deadly.

Men alone together. A welded, inhuman block. You don't have to be in the SS, wear a uniform, boots, carry weapons. What radiates from those men is the same brutal complacency, the same contempt, that turns his blood to ice. They are absolutely ordinary and they reek of death.

"I can't stand any more of this," says Diane. "Let's go."

She pushes the cards together.

"But easy does it. No point in making a spectacle."

They walk across the room. Diane opens the door. Calls ring out.

"Hey, Diane, you can't leave us."

"Don't tell me you're going with that kid."

"Hey, Diane, if you're hunting, I'm here."

"Don't you want my pencil? It's more reliable."

Diane is already outside, Cat hard on her heels, hunching his back. Among the sniggers and bursts of laughter he hears it again: "Slut."

They are in the street. He feels like throwing up, he's trembling a little. Diane turns her face to him, closed tight, her little triangular chin stuck out.

"We're going to my place."

They walk a little; a narrow door, dark staircase, scaly brownish fake-marble paint, uneven plaster, yellow light bulbs, even dimmer than in the métro; at every floor, hallways, or rather intestines, plunge away toward rows of doors, only the nearest ones visible. On the landings Turkish toilets gape, reeking. Diane pushes open a door. A tiny room, also dark. Cat goes to the dirty window and gazes down into the depths of a narrow courtyard between black walls. It is full of old paper, garbage, torn towels, broken bottles, as though all the people around it threw their rubbish out the window. The sky is invisible.

"Sit there on the bed," says Diane, "while I change."

The bed is narrow, covered with a spread printed in blazing yellow flowers, its freshness startling in that dreary room. The metal springs sag and squeak.

"I'm sick of it," says Diane. "I'm fed up and I want to leave. I've got to go. Otherwise . . ."

He watches her change. She does the same as boys do when there are more than one in a room: she turns her back and organizes her movements so he can't see her body at all. He's disappointed. First she puts on a light, pleated flower-print skirt that was rolled up in a ball on the only chair in the room. Only afterward, under the skirt, does she drop her slacks down over her bare calves. For an instant, because her timing wasn't quite perfect, Cat sees the top of her white Petit Bateau ribbed cotton underpants, not very different from his own. She pulls her T-shirt over her head. He looks at her back, her bare shoulders. White, smooth skin, scattered with freckles. The little chain of spine rolling under skin when she leans over. A girl's back, almost a child's, absolutely without mystery, but he cannot take his eyes off it.

"I can feel you behind me," says Diane. "I don't like people looking at me like that."

She whips around suddenly to face him. He sees very small breasts, wide apart, and more freckles. No mystery there either. A clean simple body. He would like to spend more time looking at the breasts but she's staring at him and he has no choice but to move his gaze up toward her green eyes. She puts on a white shirt.

He stammers, "But . . ."

"No." She smiles at him, wrinkling her almond-shaped eyelids. "And not you. Especially not you."

She sits down next to him, the bed squeaks again, she relaces her canvas shoes. Cat feels a shiver run over his body as though his skin were bristling. He is unhappy.

"Don't count on me for that," she says.

They go out into the sun that is warming the old crowded black houses and walk through the filth in the Rue Saint-Denis, now much more animated than in the winter. Crates of vegetables are being stacked, wheelbarrows piled high with teetering pyramids rumble noisily toward dark green bungalows at the far ends of the maze of narrow alleyways.

"I've got a date with Max," says Diane. "You can come too."

On the far side of the Boulevard Sébastopol they enter a region unknown to Cat. Narrow, quiet streets where children are playing, the houses still black and crowded above rows of old-fashioned, decent-looking shops with half-closed folding wooden panels over the windows. Some have wide, deep portals with half-ruined stone carvings over them, leading to tumbledown courtyards littered with shacks and lean-tos, in which there is a great bustle and noisy activity. They can hear the sounds of tools, hammering, the screech of hacksaws. Men go past pushing trolleys and barrows or carrying heavy bales of clothes on their shoulders. A whole district, sufficient unto itself, intensely, calmly busy.

They cross a huge empty space, a sort of vacant lot covered with paving stones and earth heaps between the tall blind walls of houses propped up by heavy timbers, and on the walls they can see the marks of chimney stacks, bedroom wallpaper, brown or blue rectangles showing the faded traces of old flower prints, kitchen wall tiles, all hanging over the void. A few trucks are parked among the stones. Some ageless cataclysm seems to have occurred here.

"This is the Beaubourg plateau," says Diane. "I don't know why it's like this. I thought it was German bombardments but it seems it's older than that. I like those walls, the marks of all those apartments, all that life that has vanished. Like a sunken city. Can you imagine, old people come by and point to some spot way up there at the top of the wall and say, 'Look, that's our bedroom. You can see where the bed used to be.'"

They come out onto a square in which there is a garden and heavy-leaved trees surrounded by a high rusty iron fence. All around it stand tall houses built over arcades, their black roofs climbing all over each other, with every imaginable sort of chimney stack: stone chimneys, periscope chimneys, black chimneys as long as the ones on the old steam tugs on the Seine. Their peeling walls are a mixture of every shade of pink and gray, and gaunt shutters hang from high blind windows. They walk under the archways, which look and smell like a huge urinal.

"You don't know the Place des Vosges?" asks Diane. "That's funny. Parisians never know the Place des Vosges. Max says he'd like to live here for a hundred years. I know he's looking for an apartment here. They're easy to find and don't cost much. But they almost never have running water, just a faucet on the landing. It's rotten with damp and cockroaches. Worse than the Rue Saint-Denis."

They sit on a garden bench near a pedestal on which, the inscription says, there used to be an equestrian statue of Louis XIII (for years there have been nothing but empty pedestals in Paris, hundreds of empty pedestals), surrounded by yelling kids. It's Thursday, so the kids are out in the streets. A bunch of boys are playing on the bars. Some of them are the same age as Cat.

"I don't know what's going to become of me," says Cat.

"Yeah," says Diane. "It's bad, what happened to you. It's lousy. Really shitty."

They sit for a while in silence. Cat feels sorry for himself.

"But you know," Diane resumes, drawing vague outlines in the sand with the soles of her shoes, "you know, you can't go overboard about it either. Okay, so you're miserable, and that's something you can't do anything about. Nobody will ever be able to do anything about it. That's something you'll have to get into your dumb, thick, wooden, grouchy camel of a cat-snail head. You're going to have to learn to live with that. Or else."

What Cat is drawing, leaning over and tracing with a finger between his feet, is a boat. A child's boat, just one mast and a boom, two curving triangles for sails bellying in the wind. And around it, little wavelets.

"It's funny, you know. Things really get put together backwards. There are so many people your age, and lots older too, mostly older ones, if you knew everything I hear, they're complaining all the time about their parents, their family. They moan and groan, you'd think they'd do anything to get rid of them. If you could hear them. 'My dad is a swine, my mother gets on my nerves, they don't understand, they're filthy bourgeois, they won't let me live my life, oh, if they would just leave me the hell alone.' And you ... The sons of bitches!"

"I know," says Cat.

It's true. Even his classmates; it makes him feel strange to hear them griping about the tyranny of their families. Even his large-headed friend, the one with the father who's a Protestant minister. Whenever he wants to ask something important he doesn't dare actually talk to him; he waits and worries for days and in the end writes a letter and leaves it on his father's desk at night. And dreams of going away.

"And what about me?" Diane goes on. "How do you think I wound up at the Petit Roscoff? My parents live in Versailles. I was in a convent school. Keep your eyes lowered modestly at all times. I left last year, just before graduation. Do you know what a convent school is like? We took a bath once a week and we had a special sort of shirt for the bath, a wide canvas shirt tied around the neck, without sleeves, that covered the whole bathtub. Shit. One day I said shit. Just like that. My dad was a collabo. A real one. Tough and pure. He believed it all. He had a beautiful blue militia uniform that my mother ironed every Saturday. He said everything had been spoiled by the Jews. He'd let me marry a Negro sooner than a Jew. And if you knew what he thought about Negroes . . . That's why he couldn't stand the Americans, because they were rotten with Negroes and Jews both. No matter how much I told him that America was no Garden of Eden for the Negroes, the Ku Klux Klan and all that . . . No; it didn't matter. As far as the Jews were concerned, it's funny but I think he had a complex or something because our family name ends in 'mann,' you know, and he couldn't stand to be asked questions about the origin of his name. Alsatian, he said it was, so he must have gone too far the other way to try to convince people. He went too far all right. He said we were too good to the Jews, they were all the same, French or not. They ought to send all of them out there to colonize Poland, and even that was too good for them. 'Give them to the real patriots,' he said, 'give them to the real French, you'll see what we'll do to them.' Now that we know what they did to the Jews I think in one way he ought to feel better. He disappeared at the liberation, my father. He had to. I read in a paper last winter that he was sentenced to death in absentia. Vanished into thin air. Lying low somewhere. Spain, maybe."

"Spanish bastards," Luc says with conviction.

"He wasn't really bad, my father. I'm sure there are millions like him. The Rue Saint-Denis is a good place to find out. When he talked to people in the neighborhood, they used to listen. He was respected. He could have spent the rest of his life like that, talking rubbish, giving his thirty employees a hard time—he was head of something or other in his factory. Only there was Pétain, Darnand, his idol, and all that bunch. That's what went to his head. He just had to get out and parade around with his buddies. His buddies, that was sacred. And then there was my mother. He did all that to dazzle her. To show her that he was a man, a real he-man. But otherwise, he was nice, my dad. What he liked most of all was Christmas trees. Christmas trees made him cry."

"They make me sick."

"What do you think they do to me! After seventeen years of *Tannenbaum* with candles, talk about sick! And my mother swallowed it all, admiring him and sewing on his little insignia. When I went I left a note, I said I didn't want to live with collabos anymore, bye-bye. That was political, it looked better, but I'm not so sure that's really what it was. Collabo or not . . . I tried to see my mother once. She gave me a load of nonsense about how she cursed me, how I was no longer her daughter, and at the same time she was crying, she gave me some money. And my brothers called me a whore. Later, I learned that they gave it to my mother. They shaved her head, they dragged her through the streets naked, they sprayed her with a fire hose. The men who did it claimed they were in the resistance. My eye, men from the neighborhood they were, the same ones who used to listen to my father, decent self-respecting folks like him, the ones you used to see out walking their lousy mutts, the café owner, the grocer, men like the ones in the Petit Roscoff. I know them. Poor suckers, always trying to play Tarzan.

"I got odd jobs around the market. Not easy. I was under age, no parental authorization. The owner of the Petit Roscoff kind of adopted me. At first, sure, he was after my ass. I didn't let him. Then he left me alone. It's been like that for a year. He says I'm his niece, so I haven't had any trouble with the police. I do him favors at night. I help out at the bar, get people to drink, I talk to the customers, I dance with them when there's music, even though dancing is illegal. I'm pals with the girls. I know all the stories about all the streets in the neighborhood. I write their letters for them. I am the chronicler of the brothels. That would make a good topic for a theme paper for my old convent. One day I'm sure I'll write books.

The girls are worried, there's talk about closing down their houses. In the end their pimps have adopted me too. It must flatter their manly instincts somewhere, to be protecting a minor for real. Maybe some of them think it's a good investment. If I'm being bothered by some guy who hasn't understood, who's starting to hover around too close, it never lasts long, they soon change his mind for him, they put him in his place all right. I can't complain. They're straight with me. They know all about order. Men of order. In the underworld that's all there is. So when you say, 'What's going to become of me?' you understand . . . I mean there's a difference. You're going to stay at school. You'll go to a university. You've got a family. Your mother will come home and you'll look after her."

"It's easy for you to talk," growls Cat. "In the first place, I'm not going to a university. I don't want to. I'm sick to death of all that crap. And then, I'll never know for sure. If I were four years older . . ."

"You'll know. You're clever as a monkey. You'll pretend. You'll make believe. Nobody'll know the difference. Except you. And you'll screw them all. And what would you do if you were four years older? I'm exactly four years older than you. I've got a right to ask, 'What's going to become of me?' I can't stay here forever. I don't want to. In the end I'd turn into a whore for real. Max is back; he's changed. He's tough, hard. Sweet and affectionate, but hard on the inside. You break your teeth on him. He's still telling his crazy stories. He says he wants to spend his whole life on the Place des Vosges. He wants to set up a radio transmitter with an aerial on the fountain in the middle of the garden, and transmit surrealist poetry all over France and the world. He also says that one day there'll be television everywhere, like radios now. It's a thing that lets you see pictures in your own home, your own home cinema. He says it's already like that in America. He's the first to know and he'll be the first to do it. And then he says he's going to cross Tibet on a camel, go over the Andes on a llama, or maybe it's the other way around, I can't keep them straight. But one thing I can see for sure in all his stories is that there isn't any room for me."

"If I were four years older," ventures Cat, "I'd take you with me."

"Dope," says Diane. She gives him a very soft, very gentle kiss on the corner of his eye.

"Remember," she says. "You're not a one-eyed snail, so don't pull in your horns. That's what I like about you, you don't say much, but you're not blind. For your age you already know lots of things that the rest of them will spend their lives learning. Even when you shut up inside yourself it's as if you've got antennae that let you feel things. Don't pull them in. Keep them."

"What things?"

"How should I know? Things. Important things. I've got a feeling about stuff like that."

A shadow above them. Max, a tall silhouette with the sun behind him. He takes two rusty yellow chairs, sits in one and stretches his feet out on the other. It's true he's not the same. Hair cut short, no more blond spit curls, his face bony and smooth, clean, his features somehow rubbed bare. But still the pale, gold-glinting, shadowless, utterly clear eyes. He's in civilian dress. A wrinkled pair of pants, grayish, and a worn blue jacket with its buttons hanging loose, like the one Antoine wore.

"Hi," he says with a vague wave of the hand. He adds, almost without opening his mouth: "The bastards. Now they want to send us to fight the Japanese. Reconquer Indochina. They asked me to re-enlist."

He speaks as though he doesn't want to let go of the words, with a thin half-smile that makes it hard to understand what he's saying.

"I'm going to be free."

"Cat says he doesn't know what's going to become of him."

"Diane has told me a lot about you. I don't know what's going to become of me either. You've got to to stay free. That's all."

"Free?"

"Today, all I know is that being free is being here. Here, Place des Vosges, at six o'clock in the evening in the sun. Did Diane tell you? I feel as though I could stay in this place forever. What I like about it is that the bourgeois didn't know enough to stay here. Maybe it was too beautiful for them. Here, it's all ordinary people and it's all beautiful—for anybody who knows enough to take the time.

"It's strange. It seems to me that I never really knew what freedom was until it was taken away from us and we had to fight. It was a dream. Today it's as though it's already slipping through our fingers. Maybe it's because we didn't have the revolution. At all. And then there are all those people settling back as though they were putting on their old slippers. There, we've got our freedom back; an old habit. We mustn't let it become a habit. I'm sure of that, anyway. What I'd like is to be discovering new things my whole life long; learning things, finding out how to use them. Doing things, and doing them right. Not necessarily important things. And I'd always need to be able to get out, whenever I didn't feel free anymore. Get out without hurting anybody. That's the big thing. They call you Cat: that's something a cat has to know; anytime, whenever it wants to, it has to be able to go."

"My brother," says Cat, "used to talk a lot about freedom. And the revolution. Lot of good it's doing him now."

"Listen," says Max. "You haven't finished growing up, you're going to get older. You're going to live your whole life. Your own life. Your brother will be beside you forever but he'll never grow older. You'll die holding his hand. Maybe you'll be very old, but he will always be nineteen. His friends are going to turn into big men, some of them will be important, presidents of this and that, and some of them will be failures too, poor slobs, they'll have liver diseases, they'll grow bald and obese. Not your brother. His friends will have their careers and if they want to succeed they'll have to forget your brother as much as they can. Not because they're bad people, it's just that remembering would keep them from getting ahead. Not you. That's why you'll never go quite the same way as they do. Whatever you do, even if it's completely crazy and wrong, you'll always be a little bit different. That's your good fortune too."

"No," says Cat, trying to resist the rapid bursts of words. "No. That's just hot air. I want Antoine to be alive, that's all."

"You're right," says Max. "You're the one who's right."

❖

Julius Kleinberg telephones one evening.

"Luc, it's for you," says the aunt. "I think it's somebody from school."

"Do you remember me?" asks Julius. "And Bob? The 2nd Armored Division."

Julius is in Paris for only a few days. He wants to come around.

"No," says Cat. "Meet me instead tomorrow night at seven." He gives him the address of the Petit Roscoff.

"That's funny," says Julius. "That's a funny sort of place."

"It sure is," says Cat. "You'll see."

The next day Luc goes to a social event. He and his cousins attend an engagement party in the seventeenth *arrondissement,* for one of the innumerable horde of relations on his mother's side. He can never keep them straight. He wears a jacket and plus fours belonging to one of his cousins, with a strip of black on the lapel; he has pasted his hair down with water so he could make a side part. The fiancé is in an officer's uniform; he's been to the Ecole Polytechnique, they say. The girl is wearing a pink dress. More old ladies clasp him to their scented bosoms. He wards them off as best he can. He is bedewed with tears.

"Ah, when I see that poor miserable child . . ."

To tell the truth, it isn't all that hard to keep himself under control. All the weeping and lamentations aren't really addressed to him, he's just a dress extra. All he has to do is stiffen up and wait for the embraces, the sobs and bedewing to stop.

"Over there," his cousins tell him with a jab of the elbow, "there're some great things called petits fours, with a sort of whitish cream that squishes out when you squeeze them."

"Sounds awful."

"Yeah, but it's good."

Many people are talking very loudly in the string of drawing rooms. Coming from a long way away, in gusts, he hears a piano. Luc wades through the groups toward the source. The pianist is alone in a sunny corner room. He can see him from the back, sight-reading a piece of music with his nose almost on the page. It's a kind of quick waltz, strongly accented, with all of a sudden peculiar dissonant chords. The player stops abruptly and utters an assortment of oaths, in which Luc vaguely makes out the words "balls" and "goddamned piano," and suddenly spins around on the stool.

"Beethoven, Sonata No. 29, also known as *The Cuckoo*. It's five years since I last played a piano that was in tune. You're Cat, aren't you?"

"Yes," says Luc. "And you?"

"I'm Gabriel. Have you forgotten me too?"

"No. Of course not. I didn't know you were back."

"I'm not back. Not at all. I'm a mirage. A mistake. I'm just passing through. I am Lieutenant Gabriel Delage, in the service of the glorious Red Army, at present quartered in Berlin, Unter den Linden, yes, I mean it, and about to depart for Kiev, Nizhni Novgorod, and maybe even Arkhangelsk, the wide-open spaces and the steppes, and here in Paris for two days. Secretly. Almost a deserter. I may find myself in the guardhouse when I get back. And I'm glad to be going back. I'm off tomorrow morning. I've got nothing to do here. I'm a Martian. I come from a different planet. In transit.

"Of course," he goes on, "of course you didn't recognize me. You were nine years old last time we saw each other."

"There was a piano then too."

"Yeah. In those days I knew how to play."

He stands up. He's not much taller than Cat. No longer the lean quick boy who climbed trees at La Valerane. He's filled out; there's a horseshoe-shaped bare patch on his forehead. He's wearing a dark striped suit, a badly ironed double-breasted jacket, a tie knotted like a piece of string, and Cat smells mothballs.

"What the hell am I doing here?" Gabriel asks, raising his voice above the waves of conversation eddying in from the other rooms. "I heard Antoine was dead. That's all I can think about. I see the way people are living here, and I think of him. Did you get my letters?"

"Yes. But you know, Antoine . . ."

"I know. They were full of nonsense, my letters. And dangerous too. But out there, you see, how were we supposed to know, how were we supposed to guess what was going on here? If I stayed here, how long would it take for me not to feel like a stranger anymore, the way I do now? And when I come back for good . . ."

Just then Cousin Bernard Maury appears in the doorway. He

is dressed in an elegant officer's uniform, a khaki tunic of some soft material that fits closely about his waist, a white shirt and matching tie.

"Gabriel, what a surprise. Have you got your discharge? Five years in camps, must have been tough, no?"

"No," says Gabriel. "On the contrary. I'm going back to Berlin tomorrow."

"My poor Luc," says Bernard Maury. "Antoine wasn't lucky."

"No. He wasn't lucky. What about you? What's that thing on your arm?"

Cousin Bernard Maury is sporting a wide woven red stripe.

"I'm a cadet. Things are working out. There's a special session in the *grandes écoles* for students who were in the army; I'm certain to come out of the engineering school with a good rating. In the end my year won't have been a complete waste. And I'm going on vacation at Vaufoin."

"You're right," says Cat. "Things are working out."

He turns his back on Cousin Bernard Maury. He rests his forehead on the windowpane and stares at the sunny, empty street. He hears Gabriel striking a few chords on the piano.

"The cousin has gone. What have you got against him?"

"Nothing," says Cat. "Nothing. He likes uniforms. Well, here's what I've got against him: he's a fart."

"I certainly am out of things. But you know, I've got a snazzy disguise too. Yesterday morning when I rang the door at home and my mother saw me in a Russian army uniform, she screamed, 'Good God! How awful!' That first, *then* she kissed me. I think she'd almost rather see me dead than dressed up like a Bolshevik. Funny homecoming."

"You should have worn it here."

"Five years out of civilian clothes. You can't imagine. I wanted to know if I would feel really free if I changed my clothes."

"And?"

"And, I don't know. I'm floating."

"I didn't know there were any French in the Russian army."

"You're not the only one. That's all I've been hearing since yesterday. At the War Ministry they dragged me around from one office to another. They were all saying the same thing. I was a sideshow freak. They even went to fetch the minister so he could see my act."

Gabriel tells how, in January, the Germans evacuated his *Oflag* and sent the prisoners out in columns on the roads of East Prussia in eighteen-below-zero weather. He finally managed to escape, with some friends. They survived, hiding, living like animals, moving only by night, until the Russians came. Never, says Gabriel, could he have dreamed it was possible to live through cold like that. They offered to form a unit of liberated French prisoners for the Russians. What made the Russians agree, in the end, was that the highest-ranking man among them, a captain, was Foch's grandson. Zhukov liked the idea of having a Foch as an officer in the Soviet army. So they were off to war again, a battalion of almost a thousand men with arms and equipment, fur hats and Terechnikovs, from the Oder to Berlin. From battle to battle they advanced through the cold, alongside the Russian tanks.

"One time, during the big breakthrough, we drove over whole columns of dead German soldiers. They'd been machine-gunned; they were crushed under the tanks."

"What was it like?" Cat asks, curious.

"Like a sort of frozen gray felt carpet on the road.

"When we got to Berlin," Gabriel goes on, "they thought the end of the war meant the end of their enlistment. They went on camping there on Unter den Linden, a field of ruins as far as the eye could see. The camp is a real gypsy caravan. On the way they picked up all kinds of lost French, drifters, STO women who didn't dare turn themselves over to the Russians, an eighteen-year-old militiaman who didn't know where the hell he was . . ."

"A militiaman? But didn't you know . . ."

"No. I didn't know. Try to understand; we had been cut off from France for five years. We'd have had to live through the collaboration to know what it was about. All we got was nonstop propaganda. The Scapini mission really looked after us, and in the beginning Pétain was pretty popular with the officers. But what also kept us completely out of touch was the fact that everything came to us via the Germans. In one sense we were protected. Sure, there was routine cowardice, we thought, the quitters, the lazy, the profiteers. It wasn't as though we believed in Santa Claus. No war is different from any other war; the rot was already pretty far advanced in the winter of '39. And the more Vichy talked about the new order and redemption, the more I felt the rot gaining on us. But not to that point: the French Gestapo, the militia, the deportation of the Jews ... The real blow fell when we started coming across the deportees who had been abandoned on the road. We got there too late. Skeletons. They kept on dying in front of our eyes. They were already on the other side, there was no way to get them back. They couldn't even hear us. Until then, hatred was something we had experienced secondhand, through the hatred of the others. We had seen the Russians, Ukrainians, Poles. They knew, they really knew: the total Nazi terror, extermination, degradation. Until then, we had enemies, but we didn't really hate them. Today I think I know what it means to hate; and it isn't the Germans I hate, it's something that's bigger even than them. Something that can survive this war. Unless everything is changed. I mean really, completely changed. I think I'm only beginning to understand Antoine now. And here I am in this drawing room with these clowns. They're exactly the same as before. A nightmare. I'm going back to wake up in Berlin in my gypsy caravan of screwballs disguised as Russkies, that's the only thing left for me to do."

"But you'll be repatriated."

"Believe it or not, that's what I'm here to find out. We've got a feeling they aren't in any hurry to let go of us. They're talking about taking us back to Russia with the division, to be discharged there. But how far is back, for the Russians? I've come to explain our situation to the French authorities. In a French airplane with a French mission order issued in Berlin by de Lattre's staff officers, without consulting the Russians, of course. That's why I'm going back tomorrow. But none of this tells me why Cousin Bernard Maury, who has a snotty boy scout's mug, I grant you, and a ridiculous uniform, and pink eyes, is ... well, what you called him."

"It's nothing serious." (During the winter, Cat has had time to supplement his information and digest it.) "Just a sort of idea. Engineer in the Todt organization: brown uniform. Resistant in September '44, enlisted FFI: khaki uniform. And now ... I tell you, he collects uniforms. Like he says, everything is working out."

"I think I'd like some fresh air. It stinks here. How about if we went outdoors?"

"Okay. I even know where."

"Way back in 1939, when I was quartered in Charleville, I couldn't stand the social gatherings in town. Anyway, we home-grown officers were not popular; we were not received. In the end, the only place where I felt comfortable was the brothels. It was quiet there."

"Well, that's okay," says Cat, "because that's where we're going."

"One thing that hasn't changed," Gabriel says in the métro, "is the smell of citronella. I really like that."

"For five years," he also says, "I dreamed about drinking a *café au lait* on the boulevards."

"I know—with croissants. And about a piano looking out to the islands across the sea."

"Yesterday I ordered a coffee. Sickening. Maybe I've lost the taste. There weren't any croissants."

"At La Valerane, you know, the piano is about the only thing that's left. Nothing around it."

"Even so, there's the sea. But maybe it'll be like the coffee. Bitter."

"What will you do when you get back for good?"

"I don't know. I think I'd like to keep very quiet. Listen to other people and try to undestand them. Underneath it all, what I really need is to pray. Of course, that raises the problem of God. If you want to pray, it helps if you believe in God. But at the point I'm at now, that's got to be easier than everything else."

"That's not a job."

"Funny the way you say that, a job ... What about you?" Gabriel asks. "The last time I saw you, you were at the age when people talk about becoming a fireman or a general or a train engineer when they grow up ..."

"No. Back then I wanted to be a sailor. I remember exactly: to serve on a warship. I've changed my mind."

"Why?"

"A stupid story. Today what I'd really like is to go very far away. I hear you can make a fortune in the Congo growing tomatoes on a plantation. They ripen in the winter and you send them to Europe, you get two crops a year. Between the harvests I'll paint pictures."

"And you'll drive your Negroes with whips and clubs. Bravo."

"No. You're right. Well, then, I'll go to Cambodia. If I were able to, I'd study archaeology and complete the restoration of Angkor Wat."

The shade of Bahadur Shah tries to edge into the métro car, but there are too many people and they won't make room for him. In 1945 the métro is not made for elephants to trot in; he gives up and gets out at Solférino.

"But you are able. Is there something wrong with your grades at school?"

"That's not the problem. I'm just not able, that's all."

"Why not? You're smart. And history, in your family . . ."

"No. It makes me barf. All that makes me want to barf."

Cat grins a little.

"They make my ass ache, all of them."

"Did you see all those guys with little bits of barbed wire in their buttonholes?" Gabriel asks as they come up the métro steps.

"Sure. They're ex-prisoners."

"I'll be damned."

They're outside the Petit Roscoff. It's evening, the street is already full of action. Tons of crates, carts, and trolleys; the girls are out, men calling to each other.

"I must say," Gabriel muses as Luc pushes the glass door, "I must say, this Cat is a weird one."

The room inside is still quiet. Julius is seated alone at a red table, reading *Combat*. He is in civilian clothes. Cat wouldn't necessarily know him again, all he can remember are glasses and a moustache beneath a naval beret, by night, in the glow of a cigarette lighter. But in that empty corner of the café there is a man alone with glasses and a moustache. So Cat walks over to him.

"Julius?"

The man looks up.

"Like I said, this is a funny sort of place."

"I've got my cousin Gabriel with me. He's in Paris for a couple of days. He's come from Berlin."

"Me too, I'm only here for a couple of days."

"Have you got your discharge?"

"Not so fast. We've only just been brought back to France. It'll come through in a while—unless we volunteer for Indochina."

"I've still got your lighter, you know. But it's out of fuel."

"I thought about you a lot last winter," says Julius. "Bob was worried. He kept saying, 'That kid told me a lot of fairy stories. I'm sure he didn't have any family in Nancy. And I didn't know the Germans were only fifteen miles away. I was a fool.' A little while ago, just by accident, I read about your father's death in an old newspaper. I always remembered that liberation night in Paris when I didn't feel like partying even though everybody had been dreaming about it for so long. Whenever I ran into Americans I gave them your brother's name. Nothing, naturally. It would have been a miracle. When I got to Paris I called your place. I got your grandmother's maid, I think. She told me, about your brother too."

"And Bob," Cat asks. "How is Bob?"

"Bob's dead. Last winter. In Alsace."

(How to tell Bob's death? That icy night of snow and frozen mud when, caught in an ambush in the middle of a village, hit dead center by a mortar shell, he leaped out of his burning tank with one arm torn off and rolled, screaming, into a hole, a hole that was actually a deep manure pit. He died shouting the name of a girl nobody had ever heard him pronounce before, died after shouting the name for an eternity in the strident voice of a dog at bay. It took them several attempts to get his body out of the pit, the stench around him was so suffocating. It was almost dawn by then. He had stopped shouting long before. There, it's told.)

"What about Janusz?"

"Oh, I've heard from Janusz. He's resting. It seems he turned peculiar. More and more distant, more and more absent. He would stand in places without moving, just waiting. He said he was waiting. Nobody could get him to say what for. He would rock back and forth from one foot to the other, smiling sweetly, doing his Polish bear dance. Just one time, he said they were waiting for him in Spain . . . I think he's in a psychiatric hospital."

"Barman!" Cat calls out with authority. "Barman, three glasses of red!"

"You're not going to drink red wine?" Gabriel asks anxiously.

"Lay off it," says Cat. "Don't bother me."

Julius talks about his return to the Rue Vieille-du-Temple. His parents are back in their apartment. But he doesn't know a single one of the other tenants. The old ones, swept away in roundup after roundup—everybody knows they'll never come back.

"When I left this part of town I was seventeen years old. It's not my neighborhood anymore. All that's left are the buildings and walls. I went down the Rue des Rosiers and the Rue des Ecouffes, I felt cold as hell. I went as far as the Ecole Normale de Musique but I didn't dare go inside. Every day the concierge brings the mail up to my parents, just the same as before. 'Good morning, Mr. Kleinberg, lovely weather this morning.' I couldn't look him in the face. No, that's not what I fought for. I don't know if I'll stay in Paris. I'm not going to Indochina. I guess maybe I'll take a look at Palestine."

Julius talks about Berchtesgaden and Gabriel about Berlin, about Stens and Terechnikovs, the thickness of armor plating and Katyushas.

Cat hears a familiar voice at his back, choppy and sarcastic: "Old home week for the veterans?"

It's Max. He sits down, hardly even smiles. Cat stammers introductions.

Max sneers. "The aristocrats of the 2nd Armored Division, the Pretorian Guard. De Gaulle's SS. I didn't realize there were French in the Red army. Back here, we've been taken in hand again by the reactionaries, the Colonel Blinkers, the Vichy boys. You'll see. Pétain won't even get a death sentence. Oh, to be in the Soviet army, where the officers are democratically elected by their men—what an experience!"

"I don't know who you've been talking to," says Gabriel. "The Russians are openhearted and brotherly, the Russians are crazy as coots, but I never saw them electing their officers, democratically or otherwise."

"Then you must have seen wrong."

"No doubt." Gabriel sighs politely. "No doubt. I must have seen wrong."

"I don't understand," Max goes on. "All I meet are people talking about getting out. Life here isn't possible, they say; they're disappointed. But it's here that things have got to be changed. Getting out . . . Petit bourgeois fantasies."

Cat giggles into his wineglass. Max, looking nasty and tight-jawed, asks him what's so funny.

"I'm thinking about your radio, your poetry."

"You can snigger, you lousy upper-class brat. For you, of course, poetry is so natural it's ridiculous. It's full of books where you live . . . At your school they stuff the classics down your throats. You can't imagine that there are millions of people who don't get any of it. Culture is just like everything else. I don't know if I'll have a radio or a newspaper or write books or make films or even television, assuming it actually does exist someday. But I know there are words and pictures that can make the world move. It's all going to have to be shaken up."

"Good luck," says Gabriel. And he laughs.

"You, who're in the Red Army . . ."

"Sure." Gabriel thoughtfully rubs his pale face. "Sure. Anyway, I'd rather listen to that."

Suddenly Gabriel stands up. He holds out his wineglass with a steady hand. He cries, *"Za Stalina!"*

They look at him, a little startled.

"No," says Max, "to the Soviet people!"

"It's the same thing. *Da zdrastvuyet tovarishch Stalin!"*

"Oh, okay," says Max. "In that case . . ." They drink.

The café has filled up. Men come over and thump Max on the back. The noise of exclamations and arguments rises, the smoke thickens. The owner is working at top speed.

"Where's Diane?" Cat asks Max.

"Diane disappeared two days ago."

Max gets up and goes over to the yellow-toothed piano. He plays jazz. Gabriel gets up, goes over, takes his place for a while. He plays jazz too. On the red table, Julius, pensive, keeps time with his fingers and drums imaginary chords. Then a man in a dirty American jacket comes up, with a clarinet, and stands next to Max; later, another one comes with a guitar. Cat hears "Basin Street Blues" for the first time in his life. Suddenly, nothing exists in the whole world except that rising clarinet and the fusion in the final chorus; he enters a new universe. Everything is still possible, hope is there, life will be different.

Later, they all sit around the table and the owner brings chitterlings. They drink vast quantities of red wine, including Cat, they talk and gesticulate. Cat feels good. But why isn't Diane there? "Not a one-eyed snail . . ." He stops talking. His eyes are half shut. Later still, they're out in the street, talking loudly. Cat has never seen the stir and bustle of the markets at night. He's dazzled. They separate, swearing great oaths of eternal friendship. Cat is reeling. Gabriel is a little worried and walks him home, but he's not very steady on his feet either. He leaves him at the door to the building. Cat hoists himself laboriously up the stairs, sneaks into his room, and collapses. He has no bad dreams. No image of death visits him. It's his first drunk. On red wine. A mild one.

❖

The following Thursday Luc goes back to the Petit Roscoff. The owner is basking in the sun in the doorway, his furry chest wide open to the air.

"Oh, there you are. Diane's gone."

"Gone where?"

"I don't know. She didn't say anything. Just goodbye. That's all. Not even thank you."

He looks straight at Cat with his little pig's eyes, suddenly alive, almost human.

"She didn't say anything. And you know, when you think about it, I guess it's better that way."

At the beginning of July the great question for debate is vacation. Classes are drawing to a close, in a state of torpor. More and more desks are empty, the teachers become chummy, the green monkey tells the boys dirty stories. The weather is magnificently hot, short pants and broken-down espadrilles reappear. In the Luxembourg gardens the leaves scorch in the sun. Even the paper airplane club has gone limp; despite Luc's vigorous haranguing, his troops are scattering. His large-headed friend is still there, but his dreams of escape have momentarily condensed into preparations for the family departure to some beach on the west coast, Protestant and apparently still full of mines.

At home Luc's aunt is also talking about vacation; will they go back to Chevigny one more time and be coddled by the loonies?

He often tries to imagine La Valerane. It's hard to shut his eyes and think of it without seeing images of a ruined house, fire-blackened walls, blind windows, and tall leafless trees mortally wounded by shrapnel. Will he walk again down the road with the glittering white quartz pebbles? Will he send flat stones skipping four times over the smooth surface of the sea on dead-calm days? Is the *bargin* still being pulled up on the big beach? He can no longer hear the cries of the children when they see the first glint of fish. He has heard that the fishermen are using dynamite now—one dull explosion underwater, the surface boils and thousands of the most beautiful fish come floating to the surface, belly up, there for the taking. Sometimes he takes out the brown-coated garnets he got from his brother's cupboard and rolls them between his fingers; the charm doesn't work too well, three garnet pebbles like rabbit pellets with golden glints in them are not enough to revive the missing landscape; he feels the past dying within him.

One afternoon he comes home from school and his cousins tell him his mother has arrived. She's at the Lutétia. His aunt has already gone.

At a dead run, the apartment is ten minutes from the Lutétia. He didn't know it was possible to be happy with that much force and violence. He gets there breathless, his shirt and hair sticky with sweat, his ears buzzing. He asks for his mother at the desk. Lists are consulted, he is made to wait, the waiting hurts his stomach. At last, through a fog, he hears somebody tell him that his mother is already gone, she has been called for. He asks who came for her.

"Why, her family, of course."

He goes back to his aunt's. His cousins tell him that she called to say his mother is at his grandparents'. He takes the métro. It's a long way.

He enters the big dark apartment. His grandmother opens the door. His grandfather hasn't been there for weeks, he's being treated in a clinic. She tells him, in a low voice, that his mother is lying down, that she is very tired and he won't be able to stay long. It has taken her two weeks to get through Poland and Germany in trucks and trains and it was only last night, crossing the frontier, that she learned her husband and son were dead. He follows his grandmother down the halls to what used to be his mother's childhood room. He walks into a dimness; the light filters through dusty drapes. He just says hello. Maybe he kisses her cheek lightly. He sits down at the foot of her bed. Does he dare to take her hand? He looks at her. It's true, her hair is gray, and short. And her features are drawn and accented as though carved by a knife; there are curious blotches on her skin, bigger than freckles. And her blue eyes. She looks at him, smiles, and says, "Hello, Cat. How you've grown."

Then he tries to grin back. It's a little difficult.

# FOR THE BEST IN PAPERBACKS, LOOK FOR THE

In every corner of the world, on every subject under the sun, Penguin represents quality and variety – the very best in publishing today.

For complete information about books available from Penguin – including Pelicans, Puffins, Peregrines and Penguin Classics – and how to order them, write to us at the appropriate address below. Please note that for copyright reasons the selection of books varies from country to country.

**In the United Kingdom:** For a complete list of books available from Penguin in the U.K., please write to *Dept E.P., Penguin Books Ltd, Harmondsworth, Middlesex, UB7 0DA*

**In the United States:** For a complete list of books available from Penguin in the U.S., please write to *Dept BA, Penguin, 299 Murray Hill Parkway, East Rutherford, New Jersey 07073*

**In Canada:** For a complete list of books available from Penguin in Canada, please write to *Penguin Books Canada Ltd, 2801 John Street, Markham, Ontario L3R 1B4*

**In Australia:** For a complete list of books available from Penguin in Australia, please write to the *Marketing Department, Penguin Books Australia Ltd, P.O. Box 257, Ringwood, Victoria 3134*

**In New Zealand:** For a complete list of books available from Penguin in New Zealand, please write to the *Marketing Department, Penguin Books (NZ) Ltd, Private Bag, Takapuna, Auckland 9*

**In India:** For a complete list of books available from Penguin, please write to *Penguin Overseas Ltd, 706 Eros Apartments, 56 Nehru Place, New Delhi, 110019*

**In Holland:** For a complete list of books available from Penguin in Holland, please write to *Penguin Books Nederland B.V., Postbus 195, NL–1380AD Weesp, Netherlands*

**In Germany:** For a complete list of books available from Penguin, please write to *Penguin Books Ltd, Friedrichstrasse 10 – 12, D–6000 Frankfurt Main 1, Federal Republic of Germany*

**In Spain:** For a complete list of books available from Penguin in Spain, please write to *Longman Penguin España, Calle San Nicolas 15, E–28013 Madrid, Spain*